Mark of the Beast

I0662764

T.J. McKenna

Grace Creek Press

Mark of the Beast: Puzzle Master Saga Book Four

Mark of the Beast/T.J. McKenna. -1st ed.

Summary: Eighteen years have passed since Cephas Paulson survived his brutal ordeal inside the mountain. Faith has returned to the world, but the "Mark of the Beast" vaccine has inflicted unforeseen genetic damage. With the Four network disbanded, Cephas and Martha stand as the only remaining hope for the Christian world - until they too disappear.

Their children, Jocie and Austin, are left alone with nowhere to go and no one to trust. Born with her father's talent for puzzles, Jocie realizes that Cephas has scattered the clues for finding her parents not only throughout her life but through time itself.

ISBN: 0-9821932-9-7
ISBN-13: 978-0-9821932-9-7

1. Religious Fiction, 2. Mystery, 3. Speculative Fiction

DEDICATION

This book is being published in late 2020. Between the pandemic and politics it seems like we'd all like this year to be in the rearview mirror. I would urge all who have enjoyed the first three books in the Puzzle Master Saga to look at it differently. This was a year in which many people decided to make changes in their lives. Some found their way to the Lord, some found their way back, and others just smiled - knowing all along that He was in control. I dedicate this book in general to them all.

I also dedicate it more specifically to our three children. Some of the characters in this book might bear a physical resemblance to our kids, but virtually all of the characters are inspired by them in one way or another. If you find that the characters make you laugh, fill you with pride, or just plain frustrate the heck out of you … that's our kids!

ACKNOWLEDGEMENTS

Special thanks again go to the ever-patient and meticulous Diane, for all her work in copy editing. Any grammatical, punctuation, or formatting errors you may find are likely a result of my failure to follow her advice.

Mark of the Beast

Puzzle Master Saga Book Four

PROLOGUE

Colorado Springs, Colorado 2208 A.D.

When I was four years old, I visited an old military base with my parents and all of my relatives. There was a camera crew that followed Daddy everywhere he went, which was strange because he wasn't anyone special. He was Daddy. The entire base was inside a mountain, which I thought was cool, even though Daddy's face told me that he didn't want to be there.

First, we all visited an old room, empty the exception of an old clock and a screen, and everyone got really quiet - especially Daddy. I didn't understand why everyone cared about it; so I decided to watch them and see if I could figure it out. I've always liked figuring things out, especially the things that grown-ups care about.

Next we all went into a big room with a stage in it. Daddy came in through a door at the back of the stage, followed by the camera crew. He walked slowly, like his feet were feeling heavy, but he made it to the front of the stage, where two wooden posts were bolted to the floor.

The posts weren't any more interesting than the room with the clock, but everyone got really quiet again while Daddy touched the posts, which seemed to make him both happy and sad at the same time. When they put the light behind him, I realized that this must be the place that was pictured in my puzzle of Daddy. He wouldn't talk about it, but Mom had told me that this place was where Daddy had once solved a big puzzle. That made me even more confused. Why would solving a puzzle make Daddy sad?

"What are you remembering, Cephas?" Mommy asked Daddy. "Pain? Fear?"

"Both; but they're not the strongest memories. The strongest memory is still love. Jesus did what He did out of His endless love. He loaned some to me, to help me through what He asked me to do."

I was standing in the front row and, as I looked back at all of the grown-ups, I decided that maybe I didn't want to understand grown-up puzzles, if they were going to make everyone sad. Then I realized that my baby brother Austin was fussing and Mommy wasn't holding my hand anymore. I didn't like seeing Daddy sad, so I thought I should go cheer him up. Maybe I could remind Daddy that puzzles are supposed to be fun.

I ran onto the stage.

"Daddy? Is this where you solved the big puzzle?" I asked.

My question made him look even more sad; so I did my best to brighten my smile and my eyes.

"I didn't solve the puzzle, sweetheart," Daddy said, slowly. "It's a secret only the puzzle maker knows."

I was still thinking about that, when Mommy took my hand and led me out of the big room. She wasn't mad, but she also wasn't going to let me help cheer Daddy up anymore, either.

After that, it seemed like Daddy was always surrounded by family and friends. I could have asked him more questions with everyone around, but I'd always thought that Daddy's answers were more interesting when it was just the two of us, so I waited.

In the afternoon, Austin and my little cousin Cam Jr. were put down for naps and Mom said I should have a nap too, after such a busy morning. I didn't want to nap, so we agreed that I could play quietly in my room. That's when Daddy came to see me. It turned out that he'd been waiting to talk to me alone, too. First, he gave me a big hug and kissed me on the head.

"Of all the questions that reporters and family and friends asked me all day, your question was the best," he said.

"Really? All I asked was if that was the place where you solved the big puzzle."

"I know…" he said, "…but it wasn't the question. It was the way you asked it, and the look in your eyes. You see, the first time I was inside that mountain, there were a lot of bad men there with me; so when I got there today, I made the mistake of thinking about them. Then, when you asked your question, I stopped thinking about the bad men, and instead I thought about all the puzzles that can be solved, and how much fun it is to solve them. You reminded me that the whole point of a puzzle is that it's meant to be solved."

"But Daddy, you said the puzzle is a secret that only the puzzle maker knows. That means God, right?" I asked.

"Yes, sweetheart. I was talking about God."

"Daddy … you're the best puzzle solver in the whole world, ever. Why did God create a puzzle that even you can't solve?"

Daddy smiled.

"Jocie, you reminded me today that God created puzzles we can't solve so that we'll always have something greater than ourselves to keep reaching for … because if we're always reaching for puzzles, we'll always be reaching for Him. Besides, maybe I'm not the best puzzle solver ever. Maybe there's someone else who will be even better … once she's a little older."

He gently touched his pointer finger to the end of my nose, which made me giggle.

"Do you think Daddy, that we could solve some puzzles together someday?"

Daddy smiled again.

"I know we will, sweetheart. I know we will."

******

One of the friends who stayed the whole day was Mom and Dad's old friend, Albert. Albert knew how to make his own fireworks and had brought some with him, saying that we'd light them off after dinner to celebrate the anniversary of Daddy being inside the mountain. It had been dark for an hour, and I was looking for him, to ask him to start the show. I heard his voice in Daddy's office; so I waited outside and listened.

"Cephas, there's something I need to tell you," Mr. Albert said.

"I've been waiting for over five years to hear this secret, Albert."

"Five years? Are you saying you've known since …"

"… since the day Bethany House was destroyed," Daddy replied.

"Wow. Do you also know that Martha is …"

"… planning a surprise party for my birthday? Don't change the subject. I assume you're telling me now because of the memo?"

"Yes. I should have told you on the day Austin was christened. When you said his full name …"

"Austin? What does Austin have to do with it?" Daddy asked.

"His initials are on it, Cephas. See for yourself."

I heard the sound of something made of metal being set down on Daddy's desk, and then they were silent for a long time.

"Will you do me a favor, Albert? Take it to Ogallala and ask Cindi to hide it. Then give this message to Cameron for me: 'Buried Treasure.'"

CHAPTER ONE

Colorado Springs, Colorado 2223 A.D.

Start with the eyes.

I've been playing the "mirror game" my entire life. I don't even remember how or why it started, but every day I look at myself in the mirror to remind myself that we are made in God's image.

Icy blue eyes like grandma, but with extra sparkles - just like Mom's.

Designed by God, so I can see the wonder of His creation.

Slender hands and fingers.

Used to do the Lord's work.

Thin, pink lips.

To speak the truth.

Bouncy red ponytail.

Just to make one man smile.

Thinking of him makes me lose my place. I miss him. I place my com in my ear and do what has typically become the last part of the daily ritual.

"Computer, search all worldwide networks and locate Cephas Paulson."

"You're so smart … find him yourself," the com replies.

"Austin," I sigh under my breath.

My kid brother has reprogrammed my com again. However he did it, the code is so deeply embedded that it pops up randomly no matter how many times I attempt to purge it. I attempt yet another purge, and continue with my morning routine while I wait.

First on is the make-up. Using it, I put a large purple blotch on the right side of my face and another on my right hand. Next up are the "living scars," which I created by genetically recombining plant cell walls with a bacteria engineered to produce a sticky polymer. They stick to my skin nicely, but the oozing polymer is pretty gross. Austin says that having scars that ooze and grow over the course of a day makes them more realistic.

When I'm done, I look over my handiwork. Nobody would question whether I'm truly one of "The Marked." Before I was born, a man named Henry tried to kill me, and everyone like me, by releasing a deadly toxin into the water and the air. To make sure only his enemies died, he also made a "vaccine" containing some extra DNA that spelled out his great-grandfather's name.

Henry thought it was a great joke, but that extra DNA turned out to be a true "mark of the beast." Within a few years, everyone who had taken the vaccine was showing signs of its effect. Some died from scars on their internal organs; many will have their lives shortened by decades; all have permanent bruises and scars that never quite heal, like the ones I've replicated.

My parents received a different vaccine long before I was born, a vaccine created by the Christian group "Four." The Four vaccine didn't contain the extra bit of DNA. That makes me one of "The Washed." It also makes me a target every time I go onto the street.

When the long-term effects of the mark of the beast vaccine first became apparent, washed Christians proudly displayed their new status. They could walk down the street without wearing a hat and could go sleeveless because their skin was free of unhealed bruises. Unfortunately, they didn't always treat "The Marked" in the way Christ taught us to treat everyone - with love.

Then came the babies. It was no surprise that both The Marked and The Washed passed those genes on to their children. What no one foresaw was that washed genes are dominant. My children will be "washed," whether their father is marked or not; but like any recessive gene, it could show up in later generations, if I were to marry a marked man. For that reason alone, most of The Washed started to date and marry only those who are also washed.

Scientists worked for years on gene therapies to reverse the mark of the beast, but failed. That's when Christian men and women started donating eggs and semen. I was young, but I remember how wonderful it seemed at first. The spirit of giving a gift of life was all around, with donation centers springing up in every city. Then came the realization that demand exceeded supply by many millions of times. Bidding wars erupted among the rich, as they clambered to obtain 'washed' samples. Rape and kidnapping followed. People would do anything to have a washed child. We were no longer people. We were a commodity.

And so we hide.

My com indicates that it has reset; so I repeat my previous question.

"Cephas Paulson is not visible on any worldwide networks," it responds.

"How about Martha Paulson?"

"Martha Paulson is also not visible."

"Cindi Stone? James Stone? Geoff Stone?"

I list them and a half dozen others.

"None of the listed individuals are visible," the computer says.

"Cephas Paulson - where are you?" I yell.

My brother Austin walks into the room and puts his arm around my shoulder. At just sixteen, he's nearly a foot taller than me. I put my head onto his shoulder and he puts his head down on top of mine.

"It's time to face it, Jocie. We're on our own," he says.

But I still need you, Daddy...

******

I knew something was wrong before Austin and I even left on our trip to visit Aunt Cindi and Uncle Cameron in Nebraska. As always, it was Mom's behavior that tipped me off, and it wasn't any one thing. It was more like a hundred little things that didn't go together just right. It wasn't a single thing she did; her routine was as normal as ever. It was her voice, and the way she watched me and Austin. It made me feel like we were going away forever, rather than just a week. Then Dad started inviting me with him, everywhere he went. He knew what I was seeing, because he could see it too, and he didn't want me observing Mom's behavior and putting pieces together. Like so many other times, I decided to just enjoy spending the time with him, trusting that whatever was happening, it was playing out according to some plan.

The night Austin and I returned from Nebraska, it was clear that something was wrong when neither Mom nor Dad were at the tube station waiting for us. Austin's hand was halfway to placing a com into his ear to contact them, when I grabbed it and told him not to do anything that could be traced.

We walked home and snuck up on the house through the neighbor's bushes. The front door was wide open, but there were no signs that anyone was home. After an hour, a Corps team showed up, but they seemed as mystified as we were. We heard them report that the house had been ransacked and that there were signs of a struggle inside.

After that, we came here, to an abandoned house where Dad told us to go if we ever needed a safe place to hide. The water and electricity are on, and we found a small supply of dried food that got us through the first day until we could get something better at the local food center.

Like every day since, we leave our hiding place and walk towards the house where we grew up, waiting for an opportunity to go inside and see for ourselves how Mom and Dad could have disappeared.

As the children of Cephas and Martha Paulson, you'd think it would be impossible for Austin and I to walk down the street without being recognized. Mom and Dad had made too many public appearances to hide the fact that Mom was pregnant with us, but we were both born at home and our DNA was never added to the national database. Of course, enhancements were also out of the question.

Mom and Dad worked hard our entire lives to ensure our anonymity in the secular community, but things are different within the Christian community. Among Christians, Austin is something of a rock star and the heir apparent to the Paulson family legacy. It's a role he sometimes relishes a little too much for my taste.

Our daily walking route takes us near the campus district, and we walk past a for-profit genetic testing and donation center. The amount you get paid varies with the quality of your genes.

"Do you have any idea how much a sample from me is worth?" Austin whispers.

"Not enough to risk getting kidnapped and used as a stud horse for the rest of your life."

"Hey! Just because nobody would want your rotten eggs …"

He shuts his mouth when someone abruptly opens a door close enough to overhear what he might say next. I'm used to this from Austin. From the time he could speak, our relatives have been telling him how special he is and how he'll one day do important things. Next to him, I'm treated like a disappointment. I can handle the second-class treatment from the rest of the family, but it's painful when it comes from Dad. There are times when I catch him looking at me and his face can only be described as a bottomless well of sadness.

It's as if Dad is the only person in the world who knows a terrible secret about me.

I've mentioned it to Mom and Austin, but neither of them can see it. I've tried to point out that sometimes, even when he's laughing, you can still see the sadness. Sometimes it's just a millimeter movement of his eyebrow that tips me off. Mom and Austin say I'm imagining it.

As we turn onto our old street, Austin takes my hand. To anyone else, we probably look like a young couple who are out for a walk. They'd probably also think that Austin is nervous about holding a girl's hand, because his fingers are moving non-stop. In fact, he's talking to me using a complex code of finger movements that we developed after Mom and Dad disappeared.

Yes, I see the man on the right, I signal back with my fingers. *He's ex-Corps. Give him a wide berth and look the other direction as we pass him.*

The members of The Corps were the first to receive the "mark of the beast" vaccine, but unlike the general population, their dose was injected, rather than given in pill form. They all have dark lines that radiate out from the injection site on their upper arms. In most cases, the lines extend across their shoulders and necks, and onto their faces. The lines will continue to grow for the rest of their lives. Skin-altering enhancements help some, but the lines can never be completely erased.

They're not all evil, Austin replies.

Tell that to the scars on Dad's back, I say, and he drops the subject.

In truth, a large percentage of The Corps converted to Christianity after what happened to Dad because they were given the new task of protecting the faithful. Daniel, one of the guards who beat and whipped Dad, even leads a large church in Iowa that we once visited when I was young. He had two of the lines across his face. I couldn't believe it when Dad hugged him. I wanted to run and never look at him or those black lines again, but I pretended to like him - for Daddy's sake.

It's the members of The Corps who left government service that have always worried Mom and Dad more. They call themselves "The Temple Guard" and claim to be a peaceful group, dedicated to informing the public about the dangers of religion. The black lines tell us everyone who served in The Corps, but they can't tell us who they serve now.

There's another, Austin says with his fingers, as we turn the corner onto our old street. The woman smiles pleasantly as she passes us on the sidewalk. The black line from her injection only reaches up to just under her ear and is covered with heavy makeup, but it's easy to see when you're looking for it.

As always, there's a car with a man in it parked in front of our house. He's younger than the others, so he doesn't have the black marks, but he has scars and blotches that mark his inheritance.

One hand, Austin says. *You'd need both hands, plus a foot.*

Austin is referring to how little effort it would take for him to disable the young man in the car - and teasing me at the same time. As part of hiding us, Mom and Dad regularly sent us to "summer camp" to train with our Aunt Cindi, her husband, Cameron, and our many cousins. They live on a big property on Lake McConaughy in Nebraska that's equipped with all sorts of training facilities. After the government insisted that all Four houses be disbanded, it was the only place left to send us.

Austin gets a full combat training regimen whenever we're there, while the best I can ask for is intense physical training, including hours of running, weight lifting, and obstacle courses. Aunt Cindi says that I have the highest strength-to-weight ratio she's ever seen, but what good is muscle if I'm never trained how to fight my way out of a rape or kidnapping?

Why don't I just take them all out while you go search the house? Austin asks. *You know Mom or Dad must have left something inside that will help us to find them.*

Because we're washed. Staying hidden is our best weapon.

Dad didn't stay hidden, Austin replies, but I don't respond. Mom has always said that one of my jobs is to protect Austin - including from himself.

As we turn the corner at the end of the street, Austin drops my hand and we return to speaking aloud.

"We can't just walk past the house every day, waiting for something to happen," Austin says. "We need to do something, Jocie. We need a plan."

"You're the favorite child. You come up with a plan."

"You're the one who inherited Dad's talent with puzzles. Shouldn't you have it all figured out by now?"

Like I said, Daddy … I need you…

CHAPTER TWO

My parents' house was very old compared to the houses around it, with real hardwood floors instead of carbon fiber and actual staircases instead of hover lifts. We all had rooms on the second floor, with mine being the smallest. I never thought that was fair, since I'm older than Austin, but that's the way it was. My room was also the coldest, which must be why someone had cut a hole in the floor to allow heat to rise up from the first floor. It was covered by an ancient metal grate, with metal louvers that I could rotate using a lever to block the heat from rising into my room in the summer.

The best part was that my room was over Dad's office, and if the louvers were open, we could talk to each other. When I was very young, he'd sometimes sing lullabies to me through the grate at bedtime. It wasn't until I was about six-years-old that it occurred to me that I could also use the opening to eavesdrop. The metal grates would squeak if I opened them quickly; so the only way to eavesdrop without Daddy hearing me was to open the louvers over a full two minutes of constant pressure. By the time I was ten, I could open the louvers without making the slightest sound.

Uncle Cameron was visiting all by himself, which was unusual, but he and Aunt Cindi had four kids now, so I suppose travelling had become more difficult. Uncle Cameron had a very clear "mad voice," and I was surprised to hear him using it when speaking with Mom and Dad.

"You ordered 'Buried Treasure' for a reason, Cephas!" Uncle Cameron said. "You've seen the reports. You know how many Washed children have been kidnapped this year. What makes you think it can't be one of your kids next?"

"I ordered 'Buried Treasure' to get the intelligence gathering operations up and running, not to make our children into an army. Let them have a normal childhood."

"Martha? Would you talk to him?"

"Cephas …" Mom said, "… you've made it clear to everyone that we're at war again. Children have been growing up during wars for millennia. They'll be fine."

"Four was officially disbanded," Daddy said. "I signed the treaty. As adults, we can make the decision to break the law, but they can't."

"Nobody is saying they'll be operatives," Cameron replied. "They just need to be able to defend themselves."

Daddy was silent for a while; then sighing, said: "Train Austin."

I wanted to yell about how unfair it was, and I think I may have let out a tiny squeak of surprise and anger; but it wasn't worth revealing my eavesdropping spot, so I stayed silent.

"They should both be on a full training schedule," Uncle Cameron replied.

"I agree," Mom said. "Girls her age are being kidnapped."

"She can do it, Cephas," Uncle Cameron added. "She's as tough as Martha, and she's a fast learner. She could be great."

"Give her extra conditioning - especially running - but no combat training."

"Why are you being so stubborn about this, Cephas?" Mom asked.

"Do you remember how I learned to fight?" Dad replied.

"You pretty much figured it out on your own."

"Then let her figure out fighting on her own, just like I did."

My first "summer camp" with Uncle Cameron came just a few weeks later. While Austin was learning combat with my cousins, I was sent for kilometers' worth of running in the woods. The thing is, they had no idea just how fast I could complete the course; so I spent hours in the trees that week, watching everyone else train, then practicing the moves I'd seen.

******

Austin and I finish our walk and return to the abandoned house. The house has a high fence and the backyard is surrounded by ancient cottonwood trees that grow along Monument Creek, so it lends itself well to the next part of our daily routine: Austin giving me combat training. Since there's little chance we'll be seen as we spar, we remove the living scars and leave them in the sunshine to grow and ooze without us.

This is Austin's favorite part of the day - beating me. Copying and practicing the moves I saw helps, but it didn't really prepare me for actual fighting. Even so, I've learned that my hands and feet are a little faster than his, but it's going to take more than that to overcome the fact that he's bigger, stronger, and more aggressive. He also talks more.

"Joice, hold your hands higher! Turn more sideways! Kick with your left foot more!"

His constant talking usually throws me off, rather than help, and his advice works well for him, but not for me.

We don't have a scoring computer like Uncle Cameron, but at the end of each session, Austin always announces the informal score he's kept in his head.

"I'd score that as eighty-six to twelve," he says, but I'm not listening. I'm thinking about Mom and Dad.

"There's no way Dad was taken by surprise and ambushed at the house," I say. "He spent hours every day gathering information and putting together the pieces of what's happening in the world."

"Could they have faked the ransacking of the house as a cover?" Austin asks.

"It makes the most sense," I say. "Even if they were attacked, I've seen Mom and Dad fighting side-by-side. It would take a small army."

"When did you see Mom and Dad fight together? You've never been interested in combat. You'd always go off running instead."

He doesn't know.

"Austin, I didn't *go* off running. I was *sent* off to run. Dad decided years ago to train only you, but I'd sneak back and watch from the trees as everyone else trained."

He lets that information sink in for a moment.

"You may have seen a lot from the trees, but you missed the biggest family match ever," he says. "Dad and Uncle Cameron had *the* rematch!"

Years ago, Uncle Cameron was the only person in all of Four who ever fought Dad to a draw in hand-to-hand combat. Mom says she could beat them both, but they both claim that they let her win. They talked for years about having a rematch, but Mom forbade it.

"How did they talk Mom into that?"

"She doesn't know. They did it four months ago, when you and Mom were visiting Great Aunt Kimberley."

"What happened? Did they let you watch the match?" I ask. "How could Dad even stand a chance? Uncle Cameron is huge!"

"Actually, it was Uncle Cameron who didn't stand a chance! Dad went ahead on points in hand-to-hand and never looked back."

"How could Dad beat that kind of power?" I ask.

"It was weird. It was like Dad knew every move before it happened, and was ready. Sometimes he even used Uncle Cameron's power against him. What I remember most though was Dad's face. He had the same look on his face that he gets when he's solving a puzzle. You get it too, you know."

"I do not … do I?"

"Yeah, it's kind of like this," he says, and makes a face that looks like he's been hit in the head with a stun gun.

I smack him on the arm, which is as good as ringing a bell, signaling that the next sparring session has begun.

Austin is much more powerful than I am … I wonder…

I don't attempt any counter attacks. I just watch him carefully and block.

Combination attacks almost always start with his right hand.

He gets a curious look on his face when I block.

His eyes are tricky, but his head tilts just a centimeter in the direction he's going next.

I can see him getting frustrated.

"Hold your left hand higher, Jocie," he says.

No way. You use that against me. I wonder what other advice he's given that doesn't work for me.

I drop my left hand even lower, and instead of turning sideways like he does, I square my body up towards him.

"You're making yourself a bigger target," he says

But I'm a tiny person. I'm always a small target and this feels much more natural.

Once I'm squared, I stop favoring my right arm and leg.

Now I'm balanced.

He's getting ready for a major assault on this new style I'm developing, when I hold my hands up to signal for him to stop.

"There's someone inside the house," I say.

"There can't be," Austin replies. "All the silent door and window alarms are tied to our coms."

"I saw a shadow move in the kitchen."

"Should we bug out?"

"No," I reply, "but let's get the scars back on. We can pretend to be just a couple of marked kids hanging out in an abandoned house."

Once the scars are in place again, we creep into the house. Austin is correct that the security system is functioning, and we both get a signal in our coms when we open the door. Austin motions for me to check the rooms on the left, while he goes into the kitchen on the right. The first room is empty, with the curtains drawn, but through the door I can see that the second room is lit with a bright sunbeam. I approach the doorway, but don't enter.

The house hasn't had automatic cleaning robots for years, and in the sunbeam I can see sparkles of dust. Dad loved dusty sunbeams, and when I was little, I enjoyed sitting on his lap and watching them with him. As I watch this one, I can see that the movement of sparkles isn't random. Someone moved silently through this room, but they couldn't prevent the dust from taking on a lazy spiral as it settles back to the floor.

"Austin," I whisper over my shoulder.

I hear the hand move to grab the door frame before I see it, and somehow know that a foot is about fly around the corner; so I lunge to the left and land a kick on the person's side as they come through the door. If it hurt him, he shows no signs of it. He's just a couple of inches taller than I am, but has a larger frame. Still, he'll be no match for Austin, who I can hear rushing back this way.

My attacker is wearing a black leather coat and a hat. If the coat is restricting his movement, he shows no signs of it, as he attempts a karate move that Aunt Cindi likes to use, which I block. My counter-attack is blocked just as easily.

He's not from The Corps. Whoever he is, he fights like a Christian.

He switches to a martial art form I've never seen before. The first punch lands hard on my stomach and the first kick on my thigh, but I somehow see that the next kick will be to my head and deflect it; then land a kick that glances off his hip. He is thrown off balance, and when I move to the right, I can see that Austin is standing in the doorway, watching.

"I could use a little help," I say.

"From him?" my attacker says, and I realize that I'm not fighting a man. It's a girl.

She attacks again, using yet another martial art form. Again, her first attack is successful and I compensate, making her follow-up strikes useless.

"I'd have him on the floor by now," she says. "Why didn't you use everything you've got against him when you were in the backyard?"

She turns her back on me and faces Austin; then in two steps, launches herself into the air in some sort of flying kick.

He should spin to the right.

Austin spins to the left, which avoids the kick but allows her to land a loud slap across his face. She could have hit him with a fist. She backs away, staring at her hand.

"Cool! Can I have some of this?" she asks.

When she slapped Austin, one of his artificial scars was transferred to her hand. I get my first good look at her face and see that she has bruises made with makeup.

Austin's face is red, both from the slap and because he's mad. He crouches into an attack pose, but I put myself between the two of them.

"Break it in half. They double in size every few days anyway," I say. "If you ever grow too much, rubbing alcohol will kill the extra."

"It's alive? Even cooler!" she says.

"We're friends now?" Austin asks.

"She's obviously washed, Austin."

"We can keep going - if you want…," she says, as she sticks half of the living scar to her face and throws the other half back to Austin. "…though I am disappointed. I expected a little more from the great Austin Paulson."

"I'll show you more, right now," Austin says, and tries to push me out of the way. I give him my best 'big sister' look, and he backs off.

"Who are you?" I ask.

"I'm Zera."

"Why did you say it like I should know who you are?"

"How could you not? Your mom and dad are my Godparents!"

CHAPTER THREE

When I was about twelve years old, Dad and I were rock climbing, when he asked me an unexpected question. Maybe I could even call it an unwelcome question, because rock climbing was always my special time with Dad and I just wanted to enjoy being outdoors with him.

"Jocie? What does it mean to you to be a Christian?" he asked.

I'd never really thought about it before. I had always been a Christian. It was just who I was.

"It means that Jesus died for my sins," I said.

I stretched for a hand hold that was nearly out of my reach, and ended up hanging by one hand for a moment, until I found places for my feet. There were much easier holds available, but I knew that such a simple answer to Dad's question wouldn't end the discussion; so I might as well try to delay him by climbing hard, and give myself more time to think.

"That's what it means for all of us," he said. "What does it mean to YOU?"

This time I didn't reply right away. I knew he wouldn't mind waiting, so long as I was thinking about the answer.

"It's both happy and sad," I said. "The happy part is obvious. I have a Savoir who loves me."

I paused, as I switched my hand holds.

"What's the sad part?"

"That's pretty obvious too. I feel hated. There are men and women out there with black lines on their faces, who would gladly snatch me and sell me just because of my genes."

"Is being a Christian genetic now?" he asked.

"You know what I mean, Dad."

We each hauled ourselves over the last bit and sat on the very top of the rock formation.

"That was a great climb," Dad said. "You really stretched your abilities, but are you sure you took the right route to get here?"

"There is no right way to get here. You choose a path and it takes you to the top."

Dad smiled, and it became clear that there was a lesson in his questions.

"I'm so glad to hear you say that," he said. "I'll tell you why while we eat, but first, let's pray."

It was something Dad and I did at the top of every climb. We'd sit on the rock, look out over creation, and say thanks. For Dad, giving thanks always began with the same three words, spoken directly to Jesus: "My dear friend."

Dad handed me an apple.

"Today is the anniversary of the death of a man who chose a very difficult path on earth," he said. "Even now, most people refer to him as 'Michael the Assassin', but that's not how I remember him. I remember the gentle man who loved his neighbor as he did himself - so much so that he sacrificed himself to save the life of another. The woman he saved was named 'Zip' and she then nearly sacrificed herself while saving a whole town. They had very different routes to faith, neither of which is better or worse than mine or yours. I'm just happy that we've all arrived at the same place."

A large drop of rain hit the top of my head; then another hit my shoulder. Sudden afternoon rains are a common occurrence for Colorado summers, but are not good news for rock climbers. We descended quickly but by the time we reached the bottom and were packing our gear, we were in a steady shower.

"I hate rain," I said.

"Really?" Dad asked. "I've always enjoyed it."

He raised his chin so the rain could pour directly onto his face, until the drops were running from his jaw and down his neck. After a while, he looked at me with a big smile on his face that did nothing to hide the sadness I knew was just under the surface. It occurred to me that when it rains, nobody can see you cry.

******

Austin and I share a bewildered look after Zera's announcement.

"In a way, your dad named me. My full name is 'Zerahiah,' which means 'brightness of the Lord.' My mom thought it was the perfect name, as she watched the map of the earth light up behind your dad."

"Who's your mom?" Austin asks.

"Zipporah, though most everyone calls her 'Zip'."

Zera gets a sad and confused look on her face.

"They really never mentioned me? Not once?"

"Sorry," I say.

"Your dad has always had a strange relationship with our family. Mom always said that he keeps too many secrets for his own good. I just never thought that I was one of them."

Her face returns to smiling and happy, as if she's completely shrugged off her earlier disappointment and moved on.

"If you know Mom and Dad so well, where are they?" I ask.

"Let's talk more downstairs," she says.

"This house doesn't have a basement," Austin replies.

Zera studies our faces to see if we're serious.

"Mom's right," she says. "Your dad sheltered you too much."

She leads us to the front room and walks straight to the fireplace. When the house was built, it was probably a real fireplace, because the house has a brick chimney. It now has an electric fireplace that's been inserted into the opening. She slides her hand along the side of the insert and presumably pulls on a hidden release, because she's able to swing the entire insert out of place, revealing a hole with a ladder leading down.

"Welcome to Mount Sinai House," she says, when we all reach the bottom.

"It can't be," I say. "Four was disbanded ages ago. It was part of the agreement to restore the First Amendment to its original wording and guarantee religious freedom."

"Four may have been disbanded, but some of the houses are still out there. Mom gave me the location of this one, but it took me a long time to find the buried escape tunnel."

"That's how you got into the house without opening any doors or windows," Austin says.

"Are you just now figuring that out?" she replies.

People have fussed over Austin his entire life. Neither of us is used to the way Zera speaks to him.

"Well, do you know where our parents are?" I ask.

Zera takes off her hat, releasing her long, dark hair with a shake. I see Austin's pupils expand slightly.

He finds her attractive.

Next off is her black leather jacket. Her shirt is sleeveless, and on her upper right arm is a tattoo of a cross with black lines snaking away from it, much like the lines that begin at the point where Corps members were injected.

"No, I don't. I also can't tell you where to find any of your aunts and uncles or any former member of Four. I can't even find my own mother."

"Then what do you know?" Austin asks.

"I know that something big is happening and the planning has been in the works for a long time. Mom has always kept herself in shape, but a year ago she started a physical training program so hard it was like she was getting ready to fight a war all by herself."

"Did you notice Aunt Cindi when we were there last month?" Austin asks me. "She looked like she had gained a lot of muscle. I thought she was just fighting the fact that she's pushing forty-years-old, but ..."

"... and Dad never stopped training," I say. "Whatever is happening, he's known for decades."

I think about the sadness in Dad's eyes.

He's borne so many burdens ... why has another been thrown onto his back?

"What else can you tell us?" I ask.

"Two things: I overheard Mom mention 'Five-X.' Given that Mom and all the old members of Four took their game up a notch, I figure that's what they're calling themselves now. The other is this ..."

She reaches into her pants pocket and brings out a piece of paper.

"Mom left this for me the day she disappeared. The front has the coordinates of this house … but there's a drawing on the back that might mean something," Zera says.

Austin holds out his hand, naturally assuming he should see the paper first, but Zera hands it to me. I look at the drawing:

Austin looks over my shoulder.

"Did Mom and Dad leave on a spaceship?" he asks.

"I thought it was the sun," Zera adds.

"It's from Dad." I say. "It's a puzzle."

"What does it mean?" Zera asks.

Austin and I exchange a look.

"No clue," I say.

******

For the next hour, we debate different theories about what the strange shape could mean, but get no closer to understanding what Dad is trying to tell us.

"My mom always said your Dad has a messed up mind, but that God made him that way for a reason," Zera says. "Didn't you two get any of it from him?"

"Austin is the gifted one," I say.

32

"So I've heard," Zera replies. "He's a real 'boy wonder' all right."

"When it comes to puzzles, Jocie is the Paulson you're looking for," Austin replies. "Dad was always giving her puzzles to solve when we were little. She even solved 'The Impossible Puzzle' all by herself when she was thirteen."

"Dad did it when he was eight," I say.

I remember how disappointed he looked when it took me so much longer than him.

"Are either of you hungry?" Austin asks. "I'm going upstairs to make some sandwiches."

"There are some blackberries growing near the creek, just outside the end of the escape tunnel. I'll go pick some," Zera says.

"Blackberries?" I say. "Dad loves blackberries. Sometimes when he eats them, he looks like he's having a spiritual experience. It takes a while though, because he crushes them against the roof of his mouth, one at a time."

"I suppose he was bound to either love them, or hate them," Zera replies.

"What do you mean?" I ask.

"Blackberries were part of Henry's torture. The crown was made of blackberry canes."

33

"Oh," I say. "We've never seen the video of what happened inside the mountain. Mom wouldn't allow it in our house. She said seeing it live was enough for her."

"My mom always says that closing your eyes won't make evil go away," Zera replies.

My mind shifts into a different gear.

It can't be a coincidence.

"She has that look," Austin says. "Expect a solved puzzle ... right ... about ... now."

"The dashed line," I say. "When I was little, Dad would create three-dimensional paper puzzles for me to solve. You always cut or folded along a dashed line. Look at what happens if you cut Dad's drawing along the dashed line."

I carefully rip the piece of paper.

"One is a sunrise and the other is a sunset?" Austin says.

I flip one of them over:

ㅠㅠ ㅠㅠ

"Closed eyes," I say.

"So?" Austin asks.

"Dad would send a puzzle that's also a personal message; something that only we would know about him, so only we would know what it means. Haven't you ever watched Dad when there's a pretty sunset? He scans the colors from north to south as far as Pike's Peak, but he closes his eyes before they reach Cheyenne Mountain - as if closing his eyes will make what happened there go away. We live in the shadow of the mountain where he was tortured, but he won't look at. It's also the last place anyone would expect him to hide."

******

"Your mother invented the hacked com. Why are we running to the mountain instead of taking a bus?" Zera asks.

"It's what our family does," I reply. "It's good exercise, and there's no way we can accidentally show up on the grid this way."

"Besides, no public buses go there," Austin adds.

"This is easy," I say. "Dad taught me to rock climb in North Cheyenne Canyon. Try doing the run with climbing gear on your back."

"Rock climbing?" Zera asks.

"Yeah. It's great for building finger and arm strength. And when you get to the top, first you get to enjoy the view and then you get to rappel down."

"And it was her special thing to do with Dad," Austin says.

"You got to cycle with him," I reply. "That was just as many hours."

"Aren't you a little old for playing on hover bikes?" Zera asks Austin.

"We didn't use hover bikes. We used old-style bikes with wheels."

"Did you rob a museum?" Zera asks.

"No, we made them ourselves. We even created our own lightweight composite material for both the frame and the wheels. We had to learn a lot of chemistry, but when we were done, the bikes were both lighter and stronger than most titanium or aluminum composites."

We reach the end of the old dirt path, which is an overlook giving us a view out onto the plains. It also allows us to see the old road that leads to the underground base where Dad was tortured, but not the entrance itself.

"Zera?" I say. "What happened to Dad in there?"

"You don't know?"

"I know he was beaten and whipped, and that he almost died. I know that he asked the world if they wanted God in their lives and they lit up a map to say 'yes' … but …"

"Nobody could go through that sort of torture and come through it unaffected, Jocie. My Dad once said it took my Mom years to recover from her role in the whole thing. She still stockpiles water."

I tilt my head when Austin nods his head a miniscule amount in understanding, while I don't understand the reference. He knows that he's been "caught," but doesn't explain. He doesn't want my brain to treat his reaction as a puzzle, so he changes the subject.

"Can you see the road well enough through binoculars to tell if there's been traffic?" he asks.

I take binoculars out of my pack and scan the road. The integrated electronics allow me to zoom to the point where the road appears to be about one hundred meters away, rather than several kilometers.

"There's no dust on the hover plates; so someone has been there."

"Your parents would have come on foot, like us," Zera says. "What about footprints?"

I hand the binoculars to Austin and look Zera in the eye.

"Mom and Dad don't leave footprints."

When we reach the tree line along the hover plates, we have a view to the giant tunnel entrance. There are no signs that anyone is around; so we sprint the two hundred meters, then stop to rest once we're inside. There are dim lights above us, many of which are flickering.

"How do you plan to get through the blast doors?" Zera asks.

"I don't. If Mom and Dad are here, they've already taken care of that for us."

"I bet they had Albert do it with explosives," Austin says.

I give him a practiced 'big sister' look.

"If you tried it, you'd create a multi-ton obstruction. Big doors like that are perfectly balanced and aligned. If you throw it off with explosives, it might never open again. The control systems here are old; so the easier route would be to hack into them."

We reach the massive door, we find it closed.

"Now what?" Zera asks.

I find a flashlight in my pack and shine it along the walls. Ten meters from the door, I find a spot where a conduit has been cut and an ancient computer pad patched into the system.

"This is Mom's handiwork," Austin says, as he taps at the pad. "It looks like she used an old transmitter wire to gain access. It's protected with both voice recognition and a password."

"Voice print recognized. Hello, Austin," the pad says - in Mom's voice - followed by "Password, please."

Austin looks at me and I shrug.

"How should I know?" he says.

"Incorrect password, error code E Four-Ten, access denied," the pad responds.

Austin turns to me.

"It could be anything," he says.

"She just gave you the password," I say. "E Four-Ten isn't an error code. It's a Bible verse."

Austin gives me a blank stare as I approach the pad.

"Computer," I say.

"Voice print recognized. Hello, Jocie. Password, please."

"If either of them falls down, one can help the other up. But pity anyone who falls and has no one to help them up," I say.

We hear a series of clunking sounds inside the door. Austin and Zera don't move, as I pass between them and to the door. There's a handle, which I pull on, and the giant door begins to swing outward. I was correct that the door is very well balanced, but Austin lends a hand and we swing it open just enough to pass through. I search the inside for another computer pad, but don't find one.

"We'd better leave it open," I say.

"I still don't know how we got it open in the first place," Austin says. "What was that password all about?"

"It's Ecclesiastes 4:10. It's so ingrained into the way Mom and Dad approach life together, they should have used it as a wedding vow. I think it was also a message to us … to watch each other's backs."

"Why is there no pad on the inside to let us back out?" Zera asks.

"Because they didn't stay here, and neither should we," I reply. "There must be something in here that we're supposed to find. You've watched the footage of Dad's time here, Zera. Any idea where we should go?"

"He only spent time in two rooms: the one where they held him, and the stage.

I expect the complex to be a maze of corridors, but it looks more like they hollowed out a giant cave and then built a small town inside of it, complete with roads and street lights. Despite the size of the complex and the number of buildings, Zera takes us straight to the room where Dad was held. There's a large screen on the wall, and an old-fashioned clock with arms, which is on the floor and smashed to pieces.

Time's up?

There's nothing else that might be a clue to finding Mom and Dad; so we move on.

We find the stage even faster, thanks to signs reading "Auditorium." A single spotlight is shining on two wooden posts that are bolted to the stage. I can see the lighting controls and conclude that Mom rigged that light to come on when either Austin or I said the password.

I remember this place. I was here when I was four years old.

Austin and Zera stay back, as if they're afraid to walk on hallowed ground, but I jump onto the stage and approach the posts, just as I did when I was little; so they follow me.

I turn around, and see that Austin looks as white as a sheet.

"That black stuff on the floor …" he says. "…it's Dad's blood. Why would someone write that in Dad's blood?"

I look down at the black stains on the floor. Someone has recently scratched the words: "God's Judgement."

CHAPTER FOUR

When I was nine years old, the Christian world celebrated the tenth anniversary of Dad's time inside the mountain - without the Paulson family. We gathered in Nebraska and celebrated privately - without Dad. He mostly spent the time alone, running in the woods or on the obstacle course at Aunt Cindi's property. Mom and I were sitting together on the big back porch, sipping iced tea, but I could see that Dad was now on the stun gun range, shooting tiny drones.

"Mom? What happened to Daddy inside the mountain?" I asked.

"You know the answer. Some bad people hurt him."

"Is that why Daddy doesn't want to think about it?"

"I suppose it is."

I was quiet for a minute while I thought.

"Why does everyone else celebrate Daddy getting hurt?"

It was a bad question to ask just as Mom was swallowing some iced tea and she had to spit a little back into her glass to keep from choking.

"I guess it's because Daddy didn't allow being hurt to change who he is or what he believes," she said. "He was faithful, even when it was possible that he would die for those beliefs."

"Uncle Cameron told me that you and the rest of the family fought off the bad people and saved him," I replied.

"We were all there at the end…" Mom said "… but we didn't save him. God did that."

Later that day, I watched as Dad set off for another run in the woods. I waited a few minutes and set off after him. I knew he'd hear me following. He wouldn't even need to look over his shoulder to know that it was me. He left the trail almost immediately, signaling that he knew I was behind him, and the chase was on. It was only a matter of time before he'd try to jump out from behind a rock or a tree and scare me. It had been a while since he'd been successful, so I knew he'd be determined.

He broke into a sprint which I couldn't possibly match, but it made him easier to track. When the tracks showed me that his pace had slowed, I knew he must be hiding nearby, so I decided to throw him off by doing something random. I stopped looking for tracks, and sprinted away in a wide arc, hoping to catch a glimpse of him from an angle he couldn't anticipate. I searched for the next half hour, without any luck, and then returned to the spot where I first lost him and sat against a large fir tree to think.

A soft fir cone hit me on the leg. A second one would have hit me on the head, had I not rolled out of the way.

"Was that some sort of lesson? To look up to find my father?" I asked Dad, who was sitting on a branch fifteen meters above me.

"Well, maybe to find your earthly father, but I certainly hope you wouldn't limit yourself to looking to the sky for your Heavenly Father," he replied.

I climbed the tree and sat beside him.

"Slice of apple?" Dad asked and produced a bag from his pocket.

I took a slice and waited while Dad gave thanks, beginning as usual with "My Dear Friend." We had a good view of the forest from our perch, and Dad smiled as he looked out.

"Dad? I've never heard anyone else in the family begin a prayer with 'My Dear Friend.' Where did you learn to begin a prayer that way?"

"Jerusalem … in the Temple."

"Did you learn it from Jesus?"

"You could say that. I got to look Jesus in the eyes several times, but I only spoke to Him once. When He healed my vocal cords, He told me to return to my people and use my gifts, and I said 'I'll use my gifts for you, Lord.' The sadness in His eyes was unmistakable."

"Sadness?" I asked. "Why would that make Jesus sad?"

"Because of the formality; because I didn't treat Him like my dear friend."

"But Jesus is God," I replied. "We have to treat Him with reverence."

Dad smiled.

"Yes," Dad said. "I revere Him like a trusted friend, but I'm careful not to let revering Him get in the way of loving Him. Constantly using all of the 'Thees' and 'Thous' can sometimes make us overlook the humanity of Jesus, which was the whole point of Him becoming flesh in the first place."

It was a lot to take in, so I didn't respond.

"Let me put it another way, Jocie," Dad said. "I believe that kind of false reverence is like stitching the veil back together, after God went to such pains to rip it in two in the first place."

******

We all stare at the message scratched into the dried blood.

"We should leave," Zera says.

"Wait," Austin says. "I need to do something."

He stands between the posts; then reaches out to the two cuffs that they used to restrain Dad as they whipped him. Austin's arms aren't long enough to reach both cuffs at the same time, so he shifts to the left to grab just one.

"Don't touch it," Zera says. "It just feels wrong."

"Sometimes it seems like I've never really understood Dad," Austin replies. "I just thought…"

He grabs the cuff on the left and lets his hand close around it, but gasps as he does it. His hand comes away quickly, and he looks at his palm before clenching his fist.

"We need to go … NOW," he whispers.

We're only halfway to the main entrance when we hear voices. Zera motions for us to follow her. We move to the shadows at the back of the stage and are standing silently when three men enter the room. Each has black lines on his neck and face.

Are they Corps? Or Temple Guard?

"I told you they'd come here someday," one of them says. "It looks like my motion sensors weren't a waste of time after all."

"You can gloat later. They turned on a light over the stage, so let's see what they've been doing."

The three walk to the posts.

"God's Judgment," the tallest one reads and snorts. "It looks like 'Five-X' has been here alright. We'd better report it."

"They'll lock us in," Austin whispers.

Zera takes my hand and I take Austin's, as she slowly leads us farther into the dark at the back of the stage. My foot knocks something over with a clatter.

"Don't move," one of the men yells, as flashlights come on and light us up.

They've all drawn stun guns.

"It's just some kids," he says, and relaxes a bit.

"We're sorry," Zera says. "Sometimes we go into the old tunnel to mess around. The big door has always been closed before, but this time it was open. We came in to look for a bedroom, but we got lost."

She's good at lying.

"I don't care how you got in here. Get your hands up!"

Zera releases my hand and puts both of her hands up into the air, so Austin and I follow suit.

"Since we were up here to mess around …" Zera says, "… maybe we could make a deal … to help you forget that we were here."

She takes a step forward, swinging her hips from side to side. The men are clearly interested in the deal. Zera removes her jacket, revealing to me a stun gun holstered in the small of her back.

If I play along, maybe I can get to the gun - but I've never shot one before.

I try to take a step forward the way Zera did, and find it unnatural to play the part of a seductress. It seems as if the men will laugh at how awkward I look, but they don't. I drop my arm to Zera's shoulder and she does the same.

"We're a great team," Zera says. "But three is an odd number and my friend here has a lot of firepower."

She drops her hand down to my hip, and I do the same.

"Do you have some more guys outside who'd like to join?"

I look at the black lines on their faces. The thought of any of these men touching me is revolting.

"Just one," the tallest man says.

"That's all I wanted to know," Zera replies.

She turns her body so that my hand slides from her hip and onto the grip of the pistol. I've never held a pistol before, but it feels like a natural extension of my arm. As Zera rolls to the ground in front of me, I click the safety off and shoot first the tallest man, then the man to his left. The third man is so surprised that he shoots the floor, and then tries to run, but Zera has already regained her feet and kicks him in the back. He shoots the floor again on his way down, then loses his grip on his gun as he's sent sprawling.

He crawls to recover his gun, but Zera easily beats him to it and kicks it across the floor to Austin, who picks it up. The man sits up and stares at each of us.

"I didn't know The Corps was carrying unregistered stun guns now," Austin says, as he examines it.

"All the better to leave no trace that they've been there…" Zera says, "…but these guys aren't Corps. They're Temple Guard."

"And you three aren't from Five-X," the man says. "You're all marked, and to Five-X, this is holy ground. They'd never scratch graffiti in his blood."

So Five-X must be where ex-members of Four went when they were disbanded.

"So I take it you kids are marked Christians?" he continues. "Pray until you're blue in the face. It won't change that your parents took the vaccine, and it won't remove those bruises and wounds."

"You seem to know a lot about Five-X," I say. "How do you find them?"

"For you three, finding them would be a waste of time. Five-X doesn't care how devout you are. They only accept The Washed. For that matter, they only accept people who are smart, and you three don't qualify for that either."

Zera and Austin jump back with surprise when I shoot him with the stun gun.

"Why'd you do that?" Austin asks.

"He was stalling us. Run!"

Zera leads us to a door at the back of the stage, then through a maze of half-lit corridors until we emerge from the building and onto the "street." She pulls us into a small building, just in time to avoid a patrol of four heavily-armed men. Three more groups pass, spreading in different directions as they form a search pattern.

"The blast doors where we came in are just around the next corner," Zera says. "If there's less than a dozen, maybe we can shoot our way out."

"The doors where we came in? Are you saying there's another way out?"

"There's a second set of blast doors at the south end of the complex," she replies.

I look at Austin.

"Mom always has a backup plan," he says.

Another group of four armed men passes our hiding place, and we fall in line behind them, working our way deeper into the complex. We somehow manage to stay between groups, until Zera motions for us to turn to the left while the men go straight.

I take Austin's hand and talk to him using our finger code.

Something isn't right, I say. How does she know the layout of the complex?

Beats me… he replies. *…but I don't see much choice except to follow her.*

He's right; so I release his hand.

The street we're on dead-ends onto a larger street that runs along the cavern wall. Zera motions for us to stop as she peeks around the corner of the last building.

"There's nobody in sight," she says. "We cross this road and take the one just to the right. If there's anyone guarding the doors, they might get the first shot as we round the corner. When I give the signal, go hard and fast."

Austin and I again have little choice but to follow her lead.

We cross the road quickly, and then flatten ourselves against the cavern wall. Zera raises her hand to tell us that she's about to go, when we hear a shout from two hundred meters behind us. When I look, men are firing at us. I can feel a slight tingle as the shots pass and even hit us, but the stun waves are too dispersed at this distance to have any real effect.

Zera forgets the hand signals and says "Go!"

I go first, and find that there are two young men standing in front of the door. They don't have the black lines on their faces, like the older men, but do have unusually large numbers of bruises and wounds compared to most of The Marked. I shoot them both before they can raise their weapons.

Good. Maybe getting stunned will cause more wounds to open up on them.

I realize that Austin and Zera aren't behind me. They're standing at the tunnel entrance and preparing to return fire, buying me time to get the door open.

The area is well lit and there's no sign of where Mom may have cut into the old systems. My eyes follow the various conduits, until I see a small box embedded into the wall like an electrical panel. I open it and relax when I see a small computer pad.

The men must have closed the distance, because Austin and Zera begin firing.

I activate the pad and use the same password as before to gain access. This time, I can control a lot more than just the door. I can control virtually every system. I open the blast door behind me, then close and lock the one we used earlier, to ensure we can't get cut off. Then I turn out all the lights, before disconnecting the pad.

I turn on my flashlight and yell "Let's go!" to Zera and Austin, but they're already on their way. When we get through the blast door, we push it shut behind us.

"They'll just push it open," Zera says. "We need to wedge it shut somehow."

There's another control panel on this side of the door; so I open it and smile when I find more of Mom's handiwork. I plug the pad back in and lock the door.

I could do more than lock the door. I could shut down the ventilation and turn on the generators to use up all the air. I could make sure they never hurt another Christian. The world would be better off without them.

"Jocie? What are you doing?" Austin asks.

"I'm programming the door to open in an hour," I say.

I could kill them, but I shouldn't. I shouldn't even be thinking about it. Why am I enjoying thinking about it?

******

We run for several kilometers, walking only as needed for Zera to catch her breath. She's in great shape, but she isn't accustomed to the thin air at this altitude; or the steep terrain. When we start seeing hikers along the trails, we finally relax into a stiff walking pace. Dad once told me that when he was a kid, nobody hiked or did any exercise at all, but that there's been renewed interest since …

He never finished the sentence. Renewed interest in exercise began when people started reading the Bible, but he never connected the dots back to being tortured. He'd never take credit for what he did. Dad viewed it as God's work, rather than his own.

"It's been over an hour," Zera says. "There have been no drones in the skies searching for us. The men we trapped should be out by now, and the one we talked to should have given a description."

"It was pretty dark in there …" I say, "… and he was pretty scared. He may not be able to give a good description."

"Even so, you'd expect drones to be tracking everyone within ten kilometers, given what we just did," Zera says.

Austin has barely said a word since we left the mountain. Now that we're walking, his right hand barely leaves his pants pocket. Even when we were running, he kept tapping his pocket, as if he was checking to be sure something was safely in it.

"Then maybe they did something foolish," I say. "… like trying to blast the doors open. Maybe they trapped themselves inside."

Austin stops and turns to face me.

"Spill it, Jocie," he says. "What do you know? More to the point, what did you do?"

I say nothing.

"C'mon, Jocie. Whenever you start presenting alternative theories; it's because you already know the real answer and you're trying to hide it."

"Fine," I say. "I didn't set the door to open in an hour. It will open in two days. They have plenty of air and water. Besides, there's probably already another bus full of their buddies trying to get them out. I'm sure it's mild compared to what they would have done to us, and it must be mild compared to what they did to …"

I don't want to finish the sentence. I start to turn away from him and Zera, but Austin grabs my shoulder and spins me back.

"Dad," he finishes the sentence for me. "Don't tell me you did that for Dad, because it's the last thing he would have wanted. He never would have asked for anyone else to suffer in that place. He'd rather … he'd rather …"

His hand slides back into his pants pocket, while his chin lowers to his chest. Austin is usually happy and carefree, but right now he looks like the weight of the world has been placed on his shoulders.

"Austin?" Zera says, and places her hand on his arm.

His right hand is balled into a fist inside his pocket.

"I'm not ready," he says. "Albert has been telling me for years that someday I'd do something special, but I'm not ready. I don't want it to be my turn."

Zera withdraws her hand.

"What's the deal with your family?" Zera asks. "Why is everything secrets and riddles? You just accused Jocie of knowing more than she's telling, and now you're doing it."

"Dad always said that knowledge can be painful," Austin says.

A tear rolls down his cheek and his fist tightens even more in his pocket.

"Austin. What's in your right hand," I ask.

"Something I don't want," he says. "But now it's mine, whether I want it or not."

He brings his hand out of his pocket and opens it - to reveal Dad's gold wedding band.

Zera gasps.

"Where'd you get that?" she asks.

"It was on the cuff, inside the mountain. He must have left it for me … to pass the torch to me."

"No," Zera says. "It's not real."

Austin hands the ring to me. On the inside I see the words "Not Today" engraved.

"It's real," I say.

Now tears start to run down her cheeks as well.

"It's just his ring," I say. "He must have left it there for a reason. We'll give it back to him when we find him."

Zera looks at me with disbelief.

"It's his ring, Jocie! It's the ring that wouldn't come off no matter how much they beat him, or whipped him, or starved him. The only way that ring came off his finger is if he's …"

"…creating a puzzle," I say. "The ring is a piece in a puzzle!"

"…dead," she says. "I was going to say the ring is only off … if he's dead."

"Zera? How did you know the layout of the complex?"

"Your Dad thought I should know it, so he asked me to memorize it. He said I might visit someday and …"

Zera stands with her mouth open.

"…he said it was easy to get lost in there."

"Austin?" I say. "The film of Dad's time inside the mountain wasn't allowed in our house. What made you stand between the posts and reach out for the cuffs?"

"Dad showed me the film last year," he says.

"But he didn't let me watch it," I say. "Maybe it was so I wouldn't jump to any conclusions about the ring being off his finger, like you and anyone else who might find it would. Everything we've seen so far has been personal. It's a puzzle only we can solve."

"What does that mean?" Zera asks. "Are you saying we have to get inside your father's head to figure this whole thing out? How can anyone possibly do that?"

"Not 'we'," Austin says. "The only one who has a chance at getting inside Dad's head is Jocie. Her mind works just like his."

"Then what does the ring mean?" Zera asks.

I realize that I have no clue, which is when it hits me...

To help Austin do whatever it is that he needs to do, I have to solve a puzzle created by Cephas Paulson! What if I can't do it?

"For the record," I say, "... getting inside a Paulson brain isn't difficult. The hard part is finding your way back out again."

CHAPTER FIVE

"Mom…" I asked, as she passed my room one day, "…do you and Daddy love Austin more than you love me?"

I was twelve years old and I felt like a little kid for asking such a dumb question, but Austin and I had just gotten back from a training camp at Aunt Cindi's, and I was feeling glum. Waiting for Mom to pass my room was no accident. Dad was in his office downstairs and I had opened the floor vent. Eavesdropping could work both ways.

"Why on earth would you ever think that?"

She dropped what she was doing and crossed the room to hug me, then backed off.

"Well, everyone treats Austin like he's special; so I thought maybe you think that too."

Mom sighed.

"You're right that our family …"

"It's not just our family," I cut her off. "Everyone who was part of Four treats him that way, likes he's a crown prince or something."

"I won't speak to how other people act, Jocie, but your father and I …"

"Are the worst of all!" I cut her off again. "You send me to Nebraska for training, and I have to spend the entire week running and conditioning, while everyone else is learning to fight - including all of my girl cousins, who are all younger than I am."

Mom closed her eyes.

"That wasn't my decision," she said, as she opened her eyes.

We stared at each other in silence.

"Why, Mom? All I want to know is why Dad is doing this."

"I don't know, Jocie. I asked him and all he said is something I've heard too many times, but I've learned to accept. He said 'knowledge is dangerous.'"

******

We walk until we reach the base of the rocks where Dad and I used to climb.

"Dad used to treat rock climbing like just another puzzle," I say to Zera, as I sit back and stare at the rocks for inspiration.

"He never brought me here," Austin says. "I was always strong enough, but I could never see the routes up the rock the way you and Dad see them. He knew I wasn't up to the puzzle."

Austin leaves to find a better spot to watch for drones, but I assume he really just wants to be alone with his thoughts for a few minutes.

"I like him," Zera says, when he's gone. "But he's not at all what I expected."

"Really? What did you expect?"

"I always pictured him as the perfect blending of your parents. My Mom says that Martha Paulson is the toughest and bravest person ever to join Four. Of course, she also says anyone would have to be brave and tough to marry your Dad. And your Dad is … well … your Dad. He's a living legend."

"It's like you're talking about people I've never met, rather than my parents. To me, they're just my mom and dad. I know what you mean about everyone having high expectations of Austin though. It's been like that his whole life. It's as if everyone is waiting for something to happen, where Austin will have to ride in and save the day."

"They are. The rumors say your Dad figured it out and has been preparing him his whole life. But now that I've met you both, I'd say you're the one that's the perfect blending of your parents. You look more like your mom, but your red hair is like a blending of her blonde and his brown. You solve puzzles like your dad, but - deep down - you're as tough as your mom. You have less experience, but you're also a better fighter than your brother.

"I wish. I've never beaten Austin in hand-to-hand combat, and before today, I'd never handled a stun gun."

"Then the problem is in your head," Zera says. "When we sparred back at the house, you adjusted to every fighting style I threw at you within seconds. You have the same gift as your father. You can see the attack before it comes. As for stun guns, the safety was on when you took mine from the small of my back. If you've never touched one, how did you know to use your thumb to disengage it?"

"I don't know. I didn't really think about it. I just did it," I say.

We hear Austin running back to us.

"There are dozens of high-level drones to our south, and one coming in low and fast straight at us!"

"We can't outrun it," I say.

"Can we shoot it down?" Austin asks.

"If we do, the rest will be here in minutes," I say. "They're looking for three kids. Let's split up. You two try to look like a couple hiking towards town and I'll hike back the way we came, by myself."

I put on my hat and sunglasses, and move my fake scar from my forehead to my cheek. I'm only one hundred meters back up the trail, when I hear the buzzing change from full-speed to a hover somewhere above me. If I can distract it for another minute, Austin and Zera should reach a small grove of trees, where they'll be harder to track. I don't look up at it. If it sees my face, it will take a scan and most likely move on to scan Austin and Zera when it can't find me in the Federal database.

It follows my movements as I continue up the trail, then plunges straight down and blocks my path ten meters in front of me. I move to go around it, but it blocks my path again; so we just watch each other for a minute, before it circles me and moves away down the path, back the way I came. I want it to think I'm a hiker; so I continue the way I was going. After three steps, it zips in front of me to block the path again; then repeats the pattern of moving down the path towards Austin.

The next time, I only take one step before it zips in front and blocks the trail again. I watch it closely. There's a slight side-to-side motion as it hovers, and when it changes direction, its movements are somewhat hesitant. A computer would have smoother motion.

It's not autonomous. Someone is controlling it.

"Do you want me to follow you?" I ask.

I follow it back down the path towards Austin and Zera. As I do, it gradually gains speed until I have to run to keep up. A half kilometer later, I'm at a full sprint, when I see Austin and Zera lying along the side of the path - and I don't like where their hands are on each other. I slide to a stop, but the drone accelerates and is quickly out of sight.

"I thought it was chasing us … not the other way around," Zera says.

"I thought you two were a couple out for a hike - not a honeymoon," I pant, as they withdraw their hands.

"We heard it coming and thought acting like a marked couple might fool it," Austin says. "I wouldn't be the first in this family to fool cameras in that way, you know."

Actually … I don't know. What other things did Mom and Dad do when they were young that I've never heard about?

"Get up, and run," I say. "It would seem that someone is watching over us, and whoever is controlling that drone just let us know that it wants us out of here - fast."

******

We get back to Mount Sinai House without any further trouble, though once or twice I thought I spotted a high level drone that could have been watching us.

We decide it would be best to remove all traces that Austin and I lived in the house above; so I gather our clothes and supplies, and bring them down the ladder. When I'm done, I find that Austin and Zera have been busy testing the old equipment. They have to write some software patches to get our coms to interact with the system, but soon all the screens are coming to life.

"How did our parents beat The Corps using this old junk?" Zera asks.

"It's a case of divine intervention, if I've ever seen one," Austin replies.

He's flirting with her!

I choose a screen and ask for the national news. Dad generally skipped the news, because he'd rather dig for the stories that weren't being reported, but in this case, I made the better choice.

The screen is showing footage of Dad exiting a large government building.

"Dad!" I yell, and Austin and Zera join me.

My enthusiasm ends when the announcer begins to speak and I realize I'm seeing old footage.

"Government officials confirmed today what others have suspected for a week: Cephas Paulson, his wife Martha, and children, Jocie and Austin are all missing, as are virtually all of his family and close associates."

The screen switches to a shot of our house, which now has even more security around it, including a police line of laser eye beams and identity scanning drones. The announcer continues:

"Just prior to his disappearance, Paulson was scheduled to appear before a joint session of Congress to deliver a speech supporting a bill to make it a federal crime to trade in reproductive samples obtained from washed Christians without their consent. In Paulson's absence, the speech will now be delivered by Mr. Tyrone Bauer, the multi-billionaire businessman and well-known advocate for the reproductive rights of The Washed."

The screen switches to a shot of the outside of the Cheyenne Mountain facility.

"In related news, Federal officials believe as many as a dozen marked intruders are responsible for breaking into and defacing the historic site where Cephas Paulson was held and tortured live before a worldwide audience."

The shot switches to a scene of the men I trapped inside the mountain being led away in handcuffs.

"At least we're not mentioned," Austin says.

I don't respond. The shot has shifted to the "defacing" inside the mountain and the words "God's Judgment" scratched into the dried blood on the floor.

"The ring isn't the next piece in Dad's puzzle," I say. "It's the scratching. 'God's Judgment' is the rough translation for the name 'Daniel.' We need to find Daniel."

******

When Four was disbanded, there were many secrets that were deliberately left untold, such as how a hacked com works and how Four had long used cargo cars on the tube line to get around unseen. In retrospect, these weren't oversights on Dad's part. He somehow knew that those technological advantages would be needed again someday.

We arrive in Ottumwa, Iowa on a Sunday morning, and head straight from the tube station to Daniel's church on Gateway Drive. It's been set up in some sort of an old warehouse or manufacturing facility. I see why Daniel chose it for his church. It has easy access to the Des Moines River for summer baptisms, but I wonder why they haven't done anything about the smell. The place has a slightly sweet odor that I swear is embedded in the walls.

We arrive thirty minutes before the first service is set to begin; so we slip into the last pews and join a dozen or so others who have arrived early to pray. There is a boy of about twelve setting up the altar. He has many more bruises and wounds than you'd expect of a marked child of his age.

The boy looks confused about something and calls out, "Dad? Where's the bread?"

"Right here, Danny. I left it exactly where I said I would."

Daniel enters through a side door, carrying three small baskets of bread.

There are now three black lines on his face, and the two lines he had when I was a child look darker than I remember. I make a sound that reflects my disgust.

"Is there a problem?" Zera asks.

"Not with me," I reply.

Daniel looks up and approaches us. He hasn't seen me or Austin in a decade, so there's no way he should recognize us. Austin takes my hand.

Dad sent us. We might as well tell him who we are, he signals with his fingers.

I still don't trust him, I signal back.

"Hello, I'm Daniel. It's always nice to see new young faces," he says, and extends his hand to Austin first, and then to me. I don't want to touch it any longer than necessary, but Zera takes his hand and gives it a long and vigorous shake.

"We know who you are," I say. "You beat and whipped Cephas Paulson ... nearly to death."

His eyes narrow as he scrutinizes each of us, but he's not mad. He spends an uncomfortably long time assessing my eyes, but I don't break the contact.

"Impressive," he says, then smiles. "If you're here to speak to me privately, go with Danny after the service."

CHAPTER SIX

Two months after I asked Mom if she and Dad loved Austin more than me, she announced that we were all going to visit Aunt Cindi. When we got there, Dad assigned me a ten kilometer run, but Mom joined me as I stretched, and spoke softly to me.

"That big ash is a nice tree, don't you think?" she asked. "Little birds must love it. They get a nice view of the training area, but would be hard to spot once they're back in the branches."

"Little birds that don't have ten kilometers' worth of electronic checkpoints set up to make sure they visit every one," I replied.

Mom discreetly handed me a small electronic device of her own making.

"It's pre-programmed," she said. "Link it in at the first checkpoint, push the red button, and it will do the rest."

The first checkpoint was only half a kilometer away. I reached it in record time and was back into the ash tree before everyone else was finished with warm-ups. I got comfortable on the branch and took out a pair of binoculars, which virtually gave me a ringside seat. It even had a sound collector, so I could hear what was being said. To my surprise, the training group was much more than just my Aunt Cindi and her family. Uncle

James and Uncle Geoff were there, as was Albert, a big man named Hank, and five other men and women I'd never seen before.

"I feel like I'm at a Bethany House reunion," Aunt Cindi said.

"There are three houses represented," Uncle Cameron replied. "We'll see which one still has its old moves. Back in the day, I would have put Gethsemane House up against any house in the network."

"Does 'the day' include having Cephas as part of Bethany?" Mom asked.

Uncle Cameron got a sour look on his face.

Dad put his hand on Uncle Cameron's shoulder.

"Martha says there will be no rematch today, Cam," Dad said. "Her heart wouldn't be able to handle it again, after last time."

The yard had room for three different fighting areas, and the matches began immediately. Although Four had been disbanded for a decade, none in the group seemed to be in the least bit rusty.

Within a couple of minutes, I saw half a dozen new fighting styles and countless new moves. More importantly, I was seeing self-defense in a whole new way. It was like a complex puzzle, where an opponent's moves could be anticipated, countered, and even influenced.

Mom was assigned to a match against Hank in the third round. He was at least double her weight, yet he was the one who looked scared and hesitant. I soon found out why. Mom's attacks were lightning fast and unending. Hank kept trying to back off and reset, but that just made him an easier target. Her match ended when the points total became so lopsided that the computer automatically called it off.

Dad came up in the fourth round against Aunt Cindi. Watching Dad fight was hypnotizing. No matter what Aunt Cindi tried, he seemed to know it was coming, and was ready. Her pattern was random. How could he possibly predict her attacks? Eventually, I broke off staring at him, and focused on Aunt Cindi.

I could see it. Everything about her was telegraphing her future moves: her eyes; the tilt of her head; the way she held her hands.

I started to whisper her moves aloud before she made them.

"Right kick, left punch, left punch, right punch."

I felt as if Dad and I were saying the moves aloud together.

When the match ended, Dad and Aunt Cindi first shook hands, and then hugged. Dad turned around and stared directly at me, then at Aunt Cindi and Uncle Cameron. When he didn't find what he was seeking in their faces, he looked at Mom. Her expression said it all. We'd been caught.

We never spoke of it.

******

I enjoy the service, partly because Daniel teaches the lesson directly from the Bible, the way Dad would, and partly because I feel safe here. Everyone in the congregation appears to be marked, but all appear to be sincere in their faith in Christ.

Not quite everyone is marked. There are some fake bruises made with makeup.

When the service is over, Danny clears the altar, and then smiles at us, motioning for us to follow. He leads us through three offices and into a small meeting space with a kitchen, a dining area, and some couches.

"Dad should be here in a minute," Danny says. "Are you hungry? The Washed are usually hungry when they come here to hide."

"Do we look washed?" I ask.

"No, but Dad says you are, and he's usually right."

Over Danny's shoulder, I see a picture of Daniel and Dad; so I walk over and pick it up. It looks like they're cutting a ribbon together to open this church.

"That day was the last time I saw you," Daniel says, as he enters the room. "You were about five-years-old. These lines on my face scared you. You pretended to be brave and I pretended that it didn't break my heart. Of course, your father saw right through both of us."

"I remember," I say.

"It wasn't the first time I'd met you. Your parents visited me many times when I was in prison. When you were a toddler, you made a game of tracing the lines with your fingers. You'd start laughing, then I'd start laughing, and for a few minutes I could forget where I was … and what I'd done to land there."

"I called you 'dot-to-dot'," I whisper, and look at the floor. "I would say 'dot, dot, dot,' as I traced along, and pretend that the lines were going to make a picture."

"Don't be sad, Jocie. For me it's one of the happiest memories I have from that time in my life. Besides, maybe someday they will form a picture. In the meantime, I have some instructions from your father."

"Do you know where he is?" Austin asks.

"No, I didn't even know he had disappeared until I saw it on the news. Then, when you showed up in my pews, everything he said when I last saw him suddenly made sense. Classic Cephas."

"What did he say?" I ask.

"He said he'd be sending you to see me, and that he wanted us to watch something together. I refused, and he smiled. He knew when the time came, I'd have no choice."

"What is it?" I ask.

"My shame."

Daniel sits on one of the couches and activates a file on a screen. It shows Dad on an old medical gurney in a dim room.

He was just a kid.

"It's when Dad was inside the mountain," I say. "I don't want to watch this."

"Neither do I. I've never seen it either," Daniel replies.

When we reach the part where Daniel and the other guard beat Dad, I'm angry, but Daniel starts to sniffle and eventually moves to outright sobbing beside me.

"Computer, stop the film," Daniel says, and places his face in his hands. "I can't watch anymore."

71

Zera has been silent during the film, but she kneels in front of Daniel.

"You have to Daniel. Cephas wanted you and Jocie to watch this for the first time together. He had a reason."

Daniel rolls up his sleeve, revealing more black lines that have snaked out from the injection point down to his forearm.

"Every cult hunter was injected in their upper arm. Only one has lines that go down his arm - me! They're going down to my knuckles. They won't stop until they reach the first knuckles that punched Cephas Paulson. The knuckles that punched him so many times that they bled."

"We know," Zera says.

"How could you?"

"Don't you remember what happened the next day?" she asks him.

"Of course I remember. I whipped him. I whipped him until my arm was tired, and then I kept on whipping him, because I enjoyed it."

"Before that. Do you remember what Cephas said to you as you walked him down the hall the next morning?"

Daniel sighs.

"Computer, skip to Daniel and Cephas in the hallway the next morning," Zera says.

Dad's face is covered with one large bandage with holes for his eyes, mouth and nose. He's holding his ribs as he walks.

"I wish I could heal those for you," Dad said to Daniel, and their eyes met.

"What?"

"Your hands," Dad said. "They got nicked and bloody from beating me. If I had the power, I would heal them for you. I've already forgiven you."

"No talking," Daniel grunted.

"Perhaps your hands aren't the highest priority. I'll pray for the healing of your soul," Dad replied.

Daniel shot Dad an angry look, and Zera stops the film again.

"How did I ever reach that point?" Daniel asks. "Why was I so full of hate?"

"You already know the answer. Tell us," I say.

"Small steps," he says. "Did you know that virtually every member of The Corps started out as a guard for Christian prisoners? Cephas was a rare exception."

"Why prison guards?" I ask, but Daniel doesn't hear me. He's lost in his memories.

"I always thought that the process of dehumanizing prisoners was solely to break them," he says. "I never realized that the process was also carefully designed to dehumanize the guards too. It started off with words, like calling Christians "fish heads." Then they'd give you a real rotten fish head, covered with maggots, and tell you to put it onto a food tray. The next thing you knew, you were making one of them eat it and laughing when they puked."

He takes a deep breath.

"It wasn't just prison guards and Christians though. They dehumanized an entire planet, one small step at a time. They pushed swearing and violence into videos, then nudity and drugs, and eventually all sex. They redefined the 'mainstream,' one small step at a time, and called anyone who wasn't on board 'out of touch.' After the Final Holy War, the Christians were the only ones left to fight back; so they were the first to be dehumanized."

He finally removes his face from his hands and looks up. There are streaks of tears on the sides of his nose and on each cheek.

"It's happening again, isn't it, Jocie?" he asks.

He's right. Anyone with black lines on their faces somehow seem less human to me.

I reach out and start tracing the lines the tears made down his face

"Dot, dot, dot," I say. "I think I like these lines better than the black ones. I think they're making a prettier picture: a picture of remorse ... and repentance ... and forgiveness."

He gently takes my wrist and holds my hand against his cheek, with his eyes closed.

"Dad was a cult hunter too," I say. "All he'll say about that time in his life is that nobody can become who they are, without first being who they were."

******

We continue watching the video of Dad's torture. We cry a little, and we cheer a little, but I see nothing that leads me to where we should go next. The video ends with Dad collapsing into Mom's arms, then being carried from the stage.

"Powerful stuff," Zera says. "I think I sat with the same look Jocie has now for a full day, just thinking about what Cephas did."

Austin sits down next to me, takes my hand, and starts sending messages.

You found something, he says.

Yes, but I don't know what it means.

Try me, he says.

Why would Henry Portman tap his com and say "Showtime" and then nod to the guards to bring the pills to Dad? Who was he talking to? And what does "Showtime" mean?

"Now for the last of your Dad's instructions," Daniel says. "He insisted that teenagers are always hungry, and that I had to feed you."

"That's it?" I ask. "He just told you to feed us? There were no other messages for us?"

"Nope. Just watch the video and eat a meal together."

"I don't understand. Why did Dad send us here if it isn't part of a puzzle to find him?" I say.

"Your Dad would never send you on a journey to find him … but a journey to find yourself? Well, … that's another matter," Daniel replies.

"Danny? Will you set the table?" Daniel asks. "That reminds me. Cephas asked that if you did eat with us, that we set the table Paulson style."

Danny puts out an extra place setting, to remind us that someone is missing from our table, but not from our hearts.

Austin and I look at each other.

Great Aunt Kimberley…

******

"So, you two are saying that your Dad somehow planted the idea of setting an extra plate into Daniel's head so even he wouldn't know he was giving us a clue on where to go next?" Zera asks.

"That's the theory," Austin replies.

"Then why not just leave an empty plate in Colorado Springs? Why send us into Cheyenne mountain, then to Daniel, and then to your Aunt? Why waste all this time?"

Time … maybe Dad needs more time …

Austin takes my hand and signals two letters: "TG."

I scan the scene in front of us and see that Temple Guards have been positioned outside every door into the Ottumwa tube station.

I grab Zera's hand and turn her to look at dresses in a shop window. I laugh, because the clothes displayed in the front window are outrageously revealing, but there's a big sign in the back that says "Christian" and displays a more modest look.

"What are we going to do?" Zera asks.

"We're going to go shopping," I reply. "Look in the glass instead of at the dresses. There's a man across the street watching us. He was in church this morning, and in the tube station when we arrived yesterday.

"Do you think he's from the Temple Guard?"

"No, I think he's washed. He sat two rows in front of us in church and the bruise on his face looked like makeup."

As we enter the shop, I look through the window and see that the man is crossing the street. He's about to enter, when two Temple Guards grab him. By the time we get back outside, two more Guards have arrived and pushed him into an alley. We stop to listen.

"Just as I thought," one of the Guards says. "Washed. You all got that stupid tattoo on your hands - so now you all wear makeup in the same place to cover it up."

"What's your plan, line face? Beat me up then sell me to the donor market? Didn't you learn anything from Cephas? Torturing me will only make us stronger."

I hear the first hit on the washed man, and all I can think about is the video of Dad being beaten. When I turn the corner into the alley, the man is down on the ground and the Guards are kicking him.

I don't know why, but I forget about using the stunner that's in my pack. I launch myself into the air so high that I kick the first guard in the back of the head, and then ride his back to the ground. The next one gets a spinning back fist, while another gets a kick to the knee that sends him to the ground. Both are stunned, but not out of the fight. The last one attempts to draw his gun, but it's snapped into its concealed holster, giving me time to kick him in the chest.

For the first time in my life, I truly understand why Dad called fighting a puzzle. The pieces are clear to me now. I kick and punch them each in turn, never allowing any of them to draw a gun. I don't know how long it goes on before three of them run out of the alley, opposite the way we came in, leaving the first one I hit by himself, moaning on the ground.

Austin and Zera are standing in the mouth of the alley, guns drawn. The Washed man crawled to one side.

"Why were you laughing?" Austin asks me.

"I was laughing?"

"Like a hyena," Austin says. "Explain later. I hear drones inbound."

"Don't worry; they're ours," the washed man says. "I called them."

"How many?" Zera asks.

"They usually send two."

"I hear three," she replies.

Two small surveillance drones hover above the alley at roof level. The third drone is much larger.

"Go back into the store," the man says. "Our drones will cover us."

We're just about to clear the alley, when I hear the familiar buzz of a large stun gun and the two small drones fall to the street in front us. I hear the large drone fly away. We enter the store and a female clerk motions for us to follow her to the back. She opens a hatch in the floor and we all climb down a ladder, before she closes it again.

There are a few dim bulbs lighting the way, as the man leads us through a maze of damp tunnels. They weren't carved out by Four though. They're much older, and lined with concrete. He doesn't say a word until we pass through a rusty old door that's secured with a modern electronic lock that's keyed to his voice.

"We're safe now," he says, and leads us into a large room, where dozens of people - young and old - are reading and playing games.

None of them are wearing makeup. They're all Washed.

CHAPTER SEVEN

If you were there, watching the map of the world lit up behind Dad as he stood with his arms out, you might have thought that the world was united and would stay united - if not in fellowship, at least in agreement that there was no place in the world for extremism or torture. In truth, the divisions began almost immediately. Those who had been in power wanted to stay in power, while those who had been oppressed ... saw opportunity.

Dad was not a natural politician. He spoke too frankly for that. But he did know how to get things done and how to ride a wave of popular support; so in just months after he was released from the hospital, the First Amendment to the U.S. Constitution had been restored to its original language. Unfortunately, there were those who wanted more. When the effects of the Mark of the Beast vaccine became apparent and Christians became the target of violence, rape, and kidnapping, all sides started making plans ... including Dad.

I was eight years old when a man visited our house. He came after my bedtime, but I was still awake, reading. I didn't need to open the grate to eavesdrop, because the man's voice was naturally loud and Daddy's voice got louder the more they talked.

"Everything I predicted three years ago when I wrote the memo has come to pass, Cephas," the man said. "The effects of The Mark of the Beast vaccine cannot be reversed and, once again, it's Christians who are bearing the burden. It's our children who are made to fear for their lives and hide their faces from the world."

"I know ..." Dad said, "... but what you're proposing goes against everything that I stand for. Aislin made me the same offer..."

"Don't you dare compare me to that woman! She was a heretic the moment she took the vaccine."

The man was yelling now.

"I think it's a perfect comparison," Dad said. "You're proposing the same thing that she did. You dress it up in political speak, but you want to take control of the government and create a Theocracy. In fact, you're worse than Aislin; you want The Washed to be the new ruling class, and The Marked as a permanent underclass."

"Who told you that?" he asked. "I've never said that in a public speech."

"It doesn't matter how I know. What matters is that you're not denying it."

"Why shouldn't we rule? We are the faithful; we are pure ..."

"We are done!" Dad yelled.

There was a long pause, as I think they stared at each other.

"We are just beginning, Cephas. I'd hoped you would see reason and join us, but we don't need you anymore. While you were working with the government, and foolishly disbanding the Four network, we were building our own organization. Our path is clear."

"I already know exactly what path you're walking on…" Dad replied, "… when you get there, say hello to Garai for me."

The man let out a hateful sounding hiss, then stomped out of the house.

******

"What is this place?" I ask.

"This is a Five-X safe house, and I'm in charge. My name is Seth."

"How did you know that we're washed?"

He looks at my hand.

"The Marked punch hard, but not so hard that their scars come off."

I look down, and see that the scar is hanging like a ribbon.

"May I?" he asks.

I nod, so he takes the scar and holds it up.

"It's alive. How remarkable."

"Take a piece. It grows quickly," I say.

People are starting to notice us and come over to watch.

Half of them have tattoos on their hands, like The Guard mentioned.

The tattoos are all about three centimeters long. It's a cross with an X on each point and another in the middle, for a total of five.

The people start to ask questions, but the man we saved turns to me.

"We should speak privately," Seth says, and leads us into some sort of command center, where a half-dozen people are working at computers.

"Levi, these three will be joining us. Find them quarters," Seth says to one of the men, then turns to another. "Pedro, the Temple Guard now has armed drones that shot down two of ours. Figure out how they did it and see if you can replicate it."

He turns to us.

"Arming unmanned drones was outlawed over a hundred years ago. The Guard has no respect for tradition, or the rule of law."

"Or the right to walk down the street without being beaten to death," I say.

"Yes. I'd hoped to talk about that, young lady. You just beat four armed members of the Temple Guard with nothing but your fists and feet. Forgive me for being blunt, but - who are you?"

I get as far as "I'm Joc-," when his eyes light up.

"You're Jocie Paulson!" Seth says and all heads around the room come up.

"I should have seen it! The fighting skills, your technical abilities with that scar material, and ..."

He turns to Austin.

"... you're Austin Paulson!" he says, as he grabs Austin's hand and shakes it. "I knew it was only a matter of time before you'd end up with Five-X."

"Are you in contact with our father?" I ask.

"No. His disappearance was a surprise to us," Seth says, addressing his answer to Austin even though I asked the question; then gets a concerned look. "If you don't know where Cephas is, then perhaps our worst fears are true. He may be in the hands of the Temple Guard."

"It's not just Dad," I say. "Everyone we can think of who was a member of Four is missing. That's our entire family."

"That is a very unwelcome development," Seth says to Austin. "Please excuse me. I must report this to Tyrone."

"Tyrone? Do you mean Tyrone Bauer, the man who is giving a speech to Congress in Dad's place in a few days?" I ask.

"Yes. He is our leader," Seth says, and disappears into a private room.

******

For the next two days, Austin is treated like a visiting king, while Zera and I are largely ignored. We find a large, unused room, and spend time sparring.

"I told you that losing to Austin is just in your head," Zera says, as I knock her down for the sixth time. "You fight like a combination of your Mom and your Dad - and they're both deadly."

"I don't like hurting him," I say. "I'm supposed to protect him."

Zera puts her hands down.

"What about the Temple Guards? Did you like hurting them? I didn't want to say anything, but the way you laughed was kind of creepy."

I drop my hands, and then throw Zera a towel to wipe the sweat off her face.

"I don't know that I liked hurting them …" I say, "… but I know that I felt … free. We've been hiding from men with black lines on their faces for so long - it just felt good to show them that I'm tired of hiding."

"You have a real problem with former Corps members," she says. "It's just lines on their faces, Jocie. It doesn't tell you anything about their hearts."

We're interrupted by two girls, each about ten years old, entering the room.

"Were you fighting?" the taller girl asks. "We heard that you fight like a Four."

"You say that like it's a bad thing," I say, and smile.

"Daddy told me that Four was bad," the girl says. "He said it was good that they went away, because they fought too much."

"If you don't learn to fight, how do you keep men like the Temple Guard from taking you away?" Zera asks.

"We don't need to fight," the other girl says. "Daddy says all the fighting is going to end soon and then we'll live outside again."

"Why is the fighting going to end?" I ask.

"All the bad people are going to go away."

******

When Zera and I try to find Austin, we're told that he's in the command center and we can't disturb him. We go to the common area, where everyone hangs out. There are three people close to our age, just sitting at a table and talking, so we ask to join them.

"You're Jocie," a red-haired boy says. "What's it like to be Austin's sister?"

"It takes patience, but I'm surviving," I reply.

"Who are your parents?" he asks Zera.

"My mother is named Zipporah," she replies.

The boy's eyebrows went up a millimeter - he knows who Zipporah is.

"Who's your father?" he asks Zera.

"My father wasn't in Four," she says. "They met after the war was over. He's dead now."

"Did the Guard get him?"

"You could say that."

"What about all of you?" I interrupt. "Were your parents in Four?"

"Certainly not!" the girl sitting to his left says. "Our parents were all among the truly faithful. They were all registered, but refused to take the government vaccine when it was offered to them. They knew they were chosen by God to be saved."

"God, and the Four vaccine," I reply.

"They didn't know they had taken the vaccine," the boy says. "That's the mark of true faith."

"If your parents weren't part of Four, how did Five-X come to be?" I ask.

"How do you not know any of this?" the girl on the right asks.

"I've led a sheltered life."

"Five-X started when our parents left their false leader and refused the mark of the beast vaccine," the boy says.

"False leader?" I ask.

"We don't say his name, but you know who he is. He died at your father's feet, thinking he was taking vaccine."

Garai? Five-X was born out of Garai's organization?

87

******

I find Austin at lunchtime, surrounded by all of his new friends; so I sit by myself. The boys ask him endless questions, while the girls mostly bat their eyelashes. One look at his face tells me that he's loving every second of the attention. I'm studying his face, when his attention shifts to the doorway.

His pupils dilated and he's blushing slightly.

I follow his gaze, and see that Zera has entered the room.

He likes Zera! I'm going to tease him forever…

Zera grabs a sandwich, walks straight to the table where Austin is sitting, and uses her hip to move the girl who was sitting across from him. I watch the faces of Austin's fan club. Word has spread that Zera is Zip's daughter, and they fear her. One by one, they drop out of the conversation and leave, until Zera is alone with Austin.

They talk for some time before Austin notices me and waves me over.

"Why didn't you sit with us?" he asks.

"When I came in, there wasn't room; so I let you enjoy your new fan club."

"You sat and watched me, like Dad. Well, if you're trying to piece together secrets, don't bother. I'll just tell you what I've been doing. We started talking about the fact that the Temple Guard has armed drones and I thought we could arm our drones more easily if they were lighter. I told them about the composite material that Dad and I created to make bicycle frames, and they were interested; so I've been teaching them how to make it."

"You invented something lighter than graphene composites?" Zera asks.

"Just a little lighter, but it has other properties that we could find useful. It has virtually no electrical or heat conductance, so it should provide better shielding against stunner hits."

"Did your new friends tell you that Five-X wasn't created by old members of Four?" I ask.

"Of course. That's why Dad is so special to them. He rejected Garai, too."

I lower my voice even farther

"Don't you find everyone here a bit odd?" I ask.

"They all seem nice to me."

Our conversation is interrupted by a tall woman asking for everyone's attention.

"The speech by Mr. Bauer is going to start soon and I have exciting news. As you all know, Cephas was supposed to give this speech; so instead of giving it inside Congress, Mr. Bauer will now deliver the speech on the steps of the Department of Energy, just like Cephas did after the Traveler's Initiative."

A huge screen lights up on the wall and I see a scene that's quite familiar to me: the marble columns and steps where Dad stood so many years ago. This time, instead of the tens of thousands of people that showed up to hear Dad, there are at most a few hundred.

Two men exit the building and descend the steps together. One is a man that Dad used to meet with often, the Secretary for Religious Affairs. He is a former member of the Corps, complete with a black line that cuts diagonally across his face. Dad said that his name is Anderson, and that he is both a kind and a fair man.

I presume the other man is Tyrone Bauer, because some of the younger people here in the room can be heard saying "there he is." He is a good looking man in his late thirties or early forties, with the clear skin of The Washed. The pair of them reminds me of the contrast between Dad and Henry Portman when they were both on these stairs.

But which of them is Henry, and which is Dad?

Mr. Anderson makes the introduction. He talks about the rule of law and the fundamental rights of The Washed guaranteed in the Constitution. He promises that his department is doing all it can to crack down on the trafficking of human reproductive specimens.

Mr. Bauer steps up to the podium and takes a long, dramatic pause. He inhales deeply to say the first word of his speech - when his head jerks back violently and he collapses.

Members of the audience, both here and in Washington scream.

The cameras show that he's still alive, but has been knocked senseless. Armed security guards come out of nowhere, but there's no sign that anyone in the audience had anything to do with his collapse.

The room erupts into accusations and curses, as it's presumed that The Marked must have somehow attacked Bauer to stop him from delivering his speech.

I find a screen with public access and start replaying the scene. I watch it from every camera angle, including from drones that were above the area.

"He wasn't shot with a stunner by anyone in the crowd," I say. "Nobody raised a weapon."

"The Feds reached the same conclusion," Austin says. "They did a medical exam, and all of his muscles were functioning after he collapsed. If he was shot by a stunner, his muscles would show it."

I lean back and contemplate the evidence.

"What is it?" Zera asks.

"Computer, show a recreation of the scene from the vantage of the speaker podium," I say.

From his vantage point, there were two buildings directly in front of him.

"Have you two ever heard of ENB's?" I ask.

"Extreme narrow beam stunners?" Austin replies.

"Are you thinking there was a sniper?" Zera asks.

"It would fit the evidence," I say. "The pulse from that sort of stunner doesn't disperse like most stunners and hits in such a small area that it wouldn't affect large muscle groups. If it hit him on the forehead, it would knock him down, without leaving a trace."

"Look at the buildings in front of him," Austin says, and points to the re-creation on the screen. "There were armed Feds on both rooftops. They'd have to be in on it."

"Computer, magnify the space between the buildings," I say, and point to the rooftop of another building. "There was a clear shot from that roof."

"Jocie, that building is over a kilometer away," Zera says. "The reason the government gave up on narrow band stunners is that they're only accurate out to about two hundred meters, under good conditions. The pulse is affected by every tiny bit of electromagnetic interference. Those buildings were pumping out tons of interference. Every com signal, every computer, every light puts out a small field that would throw off the shot. The shooter would even need to account for miniscule fields given off by the trees in the courtyard."

"I'm aware of all of that," I say.

"You think someone made a precise shot to the forehead through all of that random, invisible interference? Jocie, a computer couldn't do it. Nobody could make that shot."

You're wrong, Zera. There's one person on earth who could make that shot ... Dad.

CHAPTER EIGHT

By the time I was fifteen, I gave up on arguing with Dad about combat training. I was more interested in understanding the bigger picture that led to his decision. Dad never kept computer files because he knew any system could be hacked; so I would sit in his office every morning and watch what he was reading, trying to put together a puzzle from the same pieces he was seeing. Much of what he read was about the medical challenges faced by The Marked, and the resulting hostility that The Washed faced around the world.

I also committed to observing everything Dad did, in an effort to understand why Austin was treated differently than I was, and how that treatment might reveal to me the bigger picture Dad was seeing. That included poking my nose in when Austin and Dad were having time together.

"Jocie, you're not even interested in cycling. Why don't you go read a book?" Austin said.

"You're not cycling yet; you're still making the bicycles. Besides, maybe this new material you're working on will be useful in rock climbing."

"You don't even understand the chemistry," Austin replied.

Dad and Austin had already made dozens of attempts at creating the perfect material for a bicycle frame. Austin may have understood the chemistry better than I did, but what I really wanted to understand was what was left to accomplish. On the fifth try, they had gotten a material that was lighter than graphene and stronger than most titanium alloys. It would have made a fine bicycle frame, and yet, Dad kept on refining the process.

"Do you really think low heat and rapid cooling will make a difference, Dad?" Austin asked.

"We're about to find out," Dad said, as he removed a thin plate of their latest attempt from the freezer.

"You see, Jocie," Austin began, with an air of superiority, "on our first run with this formula, we heated to two hundred and fifty degrees Celsius for one cycle. That's when we knew we were onto something; but when we tested it for heat resistance, it was only good up to about one thousand degrees Celsius. I'm sure we can do better."

"That's five cycles at one hundred and fifty degrees Celsius, followed by cooling to zero," Dad said, and Austin dutifully marked the data in his notebook.

Dad attached a thermometer to one side of the plate. It read zero degrees. He then turned on something I'd never seen before - a blowtorch - and blasted the other side with flame.

They both studied the computer screen.

"Wow!" Austin said. "It worked! Its thermal signature is seven times better than the last attempt."

"We're definitely onto something ..." Dad said, "...but I think we can do even better than that."

The two of them started making plans to adjust the annealing temperature by five degree increments and try additional heating and cooling cycles until they found the perfect balance. Austin was infatuated by the science and the challenge, but only one thought was on my mind...

Why would anyone need a heat-shielded bicycle frame?

******

When the news comes that Tyrone Bauer is expected to make a full recovery, the people of the safe house calm down a bit, but continue with cursing anyone who is marked.

Austin disappears into the command center for the afternoon. This time, dinner is taken in to him, so I don't see him again until he comes out to sleep. I meet him at his door.

"We're leaving," I say.

"You heard the news then?"

"No. What news?"

"Mr. Bauer wants to meet me. I'm leaving for North Carolina in two days."

"You're leaving for Aunt Kimberley's house tomorrow. Have you forgotten that we're trying to find Dad?"

"Five-X needs me, Jocie."

I take his hand and start sending him code. I don't want to even whisper what's on my mind.

Dad could have made the stunner shot that hit Bauer. After we'd rock climb, he would practice in the woods. He had me set up random sources of electrical interference and studied how it affected the shots.

I watch his eyes carefully. He knew something was wrong with Five-X, but didn't want to admit it to himself.

I need to finish teaching them how to make the composite, he says. I promised.

"I'll help speed things up," I say aloud. "I know you hate writing. You dictate the process, and I'll write the whole procedure out on paper for them.

We work until the middle of the night, with Austin dictating how to create the material. No detail is too small or insignificant for him, which reminds me of Dad.

"If I remember correctly, all that leaves is the heating and cooling," I say.

"I didn't think you were paying attention as Dad and I experimented. I'm impressed," he replies. "The combination that works the best is to heat the material to exactly one hundred and seventy-six degrees Celsius and as soon as it gets there, rapidly cool it back down to zero. You need to do it at least ten times to get maximum heat resistance."

"That never seemed hot enough," I say.

"I thought the same thing," Austin says. "But Dad and I tried higher temperatures and the heat profile would get all weird. It would have great heat resistance until about one thousand degrees, but at temperatures higher than that it would become brittle and just fall apart. We think there's some sort of slow crystallization that happens at lower temperatures that makes it all work."

He puts his hands out to take the stack of paper from me.

"I should double-check all the details," he says.

I pull the papers back to my chest.

"Paulson's are known for details. I'm sure you got it all right. Get your things packed. We're leaving."

I take the stack of papers with me and slip into the room that Zera and I share. She sleeps on her back with her arms at her side, like she's a soldier standing at attention. She's awake before I can touch her shoulder.

"What's going on?" she asks.

"We're leaving."

"It's about time."

As we finish packing our few possessions, we happen to face each other as we both conceal stun guns in the small of our backs.

"I hope we won't need these," I say.

"But you already know we will," she replies.

******

Austin is ready, when Zera and I return to his room. I place the stack of papers on the small desk and watch Austin's face as he looks somewhat longingly at it. I shift to block his view.

"This could get ugly," I say.

"Why?" Austin asks. "These people are our friends."

We'll see…

There are two sets of doors that are password protected from the outside to keep out intruders. When we arrive at the first door, we find that it now has a guard and there are some wires hanging out of the wall where new electronics are in the process of being installed.

"Can I help you?" the guard says.

"No. We're just not used to being underground for so long," I say. "We thought we'd go for a walk before the sun comes up and there are people on the street."

"You two can go, but Austin needs to stay here."

Austin steps forward.

"I need some fresh air to think so I can complete the project. Stand aside!" he says.

The guard doesn't move.

His eyes shifted slightly to something over my shoulder. I bet they installed a camera.

I will my face and eyes to light up in a friendly way.

"Sorry, Austin," I say, like I'm teasing him. "It looks like this is a girls' night out."

He grumbles and turns, then stops short when he sees the camera.

"Time to go!" I say, and give Zera a gentle nudge in the back.

She's too close to draw her weapon, so she kicks the guard's knee and punches him twice as he staggers. I draw my stunner and spin just in time to catch three armed men rounding a corner. I fire dangerously close to Austin's head before he drops and gives me a clear shot. I hit the first two in the chest, but only get the third man in the leg, as he dives back around the corner.

The first door opens easily, but the outer door has an internal punch pad, requiring a code to get out. I set to work hacking into it.

"We're not your enemy," we hear Seth's voice say from around the corner. "It would be a mistake to make us one."

"Our family has an aversion to being held underground against our will," Austin replies.

"That's why you should join us," Seth says. "Together we can ensure none of The Washed ever has to experience what your father had to endure."

"Maybe ..." Austin says. "... but not today ... and never as a prisoner."

I override the lock and the door clicks open. There's nobody waiting to ambush us in the ancient tunnel, so we slip away. A minute later, we hear stunner rounds hitting the door and wall as they begin their chase, but we're already long gone.

"They never would have made it in Four," Zera says. "They're all lousy shots."

"Maybe so …" I reply. "… but they certainly seem ready to learn."

******

The old tunnel ends at a hidden hatch near the river, which suits us. Ottumwa has a separate cargo station on the other side of the river, and we slip into a random car that takes us to Kansas City. From there, we find passenger cars to take us first to Lincoln and then to Ogallala, where Aunt Kimberley lives.

Her house is surrounded by ancient trees. She always said it was to provide homes for the birds, but I wonder if the real reason they're here is to create a canopy that drones can't see through during the day.

"Getting to the house is easy, but how will we get inside undetected?" Austin asks. "For all we know, The Guard has been here and hacked the palm scanner."

"I'm working on the assumption that Aunt Kimberley is still inside," I say. "Dad is pretty persuasive, but I bet even he couldn't get her to abandon her house. If he was his usual five steps ahead, it was an anticipated part of the puzzle."

"Then we need her to come to us," Zera says. "How do we do that?"

I look at the house. The curtains are drawn in every room except for one, an upstairs window with a rocking chair in front of it. There's a small table, where I can see something shiny reflecting in the sunlight. It's a pair of binoculars.

"The birds," I say. "Aunt Kimberley sits in that chair in the morning and the afternoon, and watches the birds on her feeders."

"There's only one feeder that's still full," Austin says. "The drone that fills them must be broken. All we need to do is leave a message on that feeder."

Why would a broken drone still fill one of the feeders and not the rest of them?

"What kind of message?" Zera asks.

"A familiar one," I say, and begin to rummage through my pack. "She'll know this locket. It's ancient."

I take out a gold locket that Mom gave to me the last time I saw her. It's the one Dad bought in Alexandria when they travelled through time together. There's plenty of cover over the feeder; so I hang the locket over one of the perches that the birds land on. We all sit under a giant willow tree to see what happens.

In the late afternoon, when the shadows are deep enough that someone could sit in the rocking chair without being seen, I hear a scratching sound above me in the tree. I look up, expecting to see a squirrel, but instead I find myself looking into the familiar eyes of my great-aunt, Kimberley.

I gasp, which makes Austin look up, then Zera. Aunt Kimberley motions for us to be quiet and to climb the tree to join her; then her head disappears.

Austin and Zera climb first, and also disappear. When I get there, I see how. Like many old willows, this one has a hollow

101

trunk where someone cleverly hid a small hatch. It's quite a squeeze, but we all manage to wriggle around and climb down until we reach a ladder that takes us into a small tunnel and then through a hidden door into the basement of the house.

I barely get to stand before Aunt Kimberley releases Austin from a bear hug and crushes me with one.

"I cursed your Uncle James for years for digging that darned tunnel. It took me ages to clean up all the dirt, but if it brings family home again - I'll dig another one myself!"

She switches back to hugging Austin, then to me again. She even crushes Zera once, before she asks her who she is.

"Come upstairs," Aunt Kimberley says. "I refuse to be driven into the dark like a rat."

She leads us through the dining room, where I see the massive table has been set as if it's waiting for everyone to gather. She sees me looking at it.

"They'll all be back one day," she says.

"Do you know where they've all gone?" I ask.

"Back to Four, I should think. They didn't tell me, and I didn't ask. The Corps can't get information out of me, if I don't know any."

"So the Four network has been reactivated?" Zera asks.

Aunt Kimberley stops and cocks her head to one side, which she does when she wants to drive a point home.

"When you were still in diapers, my dear. It happened when Jocie was about four years old. Cephas left the entire network hidden, like buried treasure just waiting to be dug up when it was needed again."

Buried treasure - Four was reactivated on the fifth anniversary of Dad's time in the mountain, the day Albert brought Dad something made of metal with Austin's initials on it. Whatever it was, it told Dad to bring Four back to life.

"Four has been active for thirteen years?" Zera asks. "What have they been doing all of that time? And what happened to make them all disappear now?"

"You'll find no answers with me," Aunt Kimberley replies. "But you will find hot food and comfortable beds, which is what your father told me to provide."

"When did you last see Dad?" I ask.

"He and your mother stayed here for a night, the last time he briefed congress on religious freedom."

That was two months ago.

"Tell me everything you talked about," I say. "Every detail you can remember."

We all sit at the kitchen table.

"He came because he wanted to see something that he'd given me many years ago - an old data storage device," she says. "It was the same one that held the information about your grandparents' headstone."

"Did he take it with him when he left?" Austin asks.

"No, but he asked me to put it into the hiding place I always used for hiding my Bible in the old days. I'll go get it for you."

Aunt Kimberley leaves the room for a minute, then returns with what looks like a fifty-year-old storage device. It has some wires hanging off of it that look like modifications to make it accessible to modern computers.

"We can't access it with a com," Zera says. "If we access it here, your house will make an electronic footprint and give you away."

"Not to worry, dear," Aunt Kimberley replies. "Cindi hacked me into every house on the block with some sort of scrambler gizmo that can't be traced back to here."

I slip a com into my ear.

"Computer, access the information on the storage device that's on the table and display all files."

There are hundreds. Many of them are from when Dad was a child, but many more were added by Grandpa James the year I was born, including a list of everyone who received the Four vaccine as he and Grandma traveled around the world.

"This will take forever to sort through," Austin says.

"Computer display only the files that were looked at the last time the device was accessed," I say.

Only one file comes up, in the folder marked "family." It's a genealogy chart that goes back nearly a dozen generations.

"That file is the reason he gave me the device in the first place," Aunt Kimberley says. "See, there I am, and there's your grandmother, and your father, and he even added you and Austin."

Dad, grandma, and I are in a slightly different font from everyone else. Dad knew I'd notice. He's trying to tell me something.

"Computer, move back two generations," I say.

My great-grandmother is in the different font, as is her father, but none of their siblings.

"Keep moving back," I say.

"What are we looking for?" Austin asks.

"I don't know."

There it is again, but only in a straight line of inheritance.

The trail of the different font ends eight generations back, at a woman named Atarah, whose parents aren't listed. She emigrated from Israel to the United States when she was adopted as a baby by a family named Winters. She died young in 2037 in Baltimore, Maryland.

During the Final Holy War.

She had one child out of wedlock, a son named Jordan, my grandfather with six "greats" in front of it. I look at his information and see that he lived to be quite old. There are several pictures of him. In one, he's a boy of about eight or nine years old, and is quite handsome. The rest of the pictures, though, beginning with one of him in his early twenties, show that he spent the rest of his life covered with many disfiguring scars and even lost part of a tooth. What's funny is that in the picture when he was handsome, he's sneering at the camera; whereas in those where he's covered in scars, he's smiling.

"It's fun to see your roots, isn't it?" Aunt Kimberley asks, ending my thoughts.

"But why is any of it important?" Zera asks. "What was your Dad doing?"

Once again, I have no clue.

CHAPTER NINE

Five years ago, on the day before my thirteenth birthday, Dad presented me with a pile of wooden blocks. It wasn't a birthday present. It was the same pile of blocks that he'd pulled out each year since my tenth birthday. It was known as "The Impossible Puzzle," over nine thousand unique laser-cut pieces that would fit together only one way, and in one order of assembly, to create a perfect sphere. It was designed by a computer, and only one person had ever solved it without the use of a computer - Dad.

"Will you give it a go again this year?" he asked.

"Austin turned ten this year. Shouldn't it be his turn?"

"I gave Austin a different puzzle," he replied.

"Are you talking about that thing you made him do with sounds? That made no sense."

"Are you sure?" Dad asked. "You solved it in no time."

"No, I didn't. I couldn't hear the difference between half of the sounds, and I certainly couldn't remember them."

"Neither could I; so I had the computer assign each sound a number and gave it to you a week later."

"That was the same puzzle?

Dad smiled.

I looked at the wooden pieces. I told myself that I hated that puzzle; yet they were drawing me in, begging me to solve the mystery that had eluded me on my three previous attempts.

"I guess I have nothing better to do today," I said.

I worked steadily all day, building on the progress I remembered from earlier birthdays. I was easily halfway done that afternoon, when I walked downstairs with an overnight bag and a pillow. Tonight would be my reward for the efforts.

"I'm going to the sleepover at Jenny's now," I said. "I'll see you tomorrow."

"I just spoke with Jenny's mom," Dad said. "Your plans have been canceled."

"Dad! I'm only going to be a block away. I've had lots of sleepovers at Jenny's house. Why are you cancelling it?"

"It's cancelled to save you embarrassment in front of your friends."

He knows. How could he possibly know?

"You were going to start at Jenny's house, but you were planning to sneak out by ten o'clock to go to a party in Black Forest … party where there would be a lot of drugs - some of them legal, but most of them not."

"I wasn't going to try any!"

"It's still no place for a thirteen-year-old girl. Especially a girl from a Christian family."

"You mean especially a girl from *this* family!" I yelled.

I found no sympathy when I looked to Mom, so I took a deep breath.

He was right and I knew it.

"I was so careful," I said. "How did you know?"

"Solve that puzzle, and maybe you'll be more successful next time," Dad said, and left the room.

"Why does he always have to figure everything out?" I asked Mom.

"Because he's Cephas Paulson. He can't stop putting puzzles together any more than he can stop breathing."

"We can all choose to hold our breath, once in a while."

Mom smiled.

"I know it seems like your father has everything figured out, and believe me, I've seen him put together puzzle pieces that I couldn't even see existed, much less how they fit together … but one of the things I've always found most endearing about him is all of the puzzles he messes up."

"Messes up? What puzzle has Dad ever messed up?"

She smiled again.

"The one I'm looking at right now. He first held you when you were just a minute old and I've never seen him stare at anyone or anything so intently. You stared right back at him, then he put his little finger out and you wrapped your entire hand around it."

Her voice trailed off and she got a curious look on her face.

"What is it?" I asked.

"I just remembered the next thing he said to you. He asked 'Which piece will you place, Jocie? The first ... or the last?'"

She reflected on the question for a moment, then shook it off and looked at me.

"Since then, your father has said that you're the greatest puzzle in his life because you're always in motion and the pieces change before he can fit them into place."

I went back to my room. I wanted to smash my progress on The Impossible Puzzle to pieces, but instead I calmed myself, and prayed for the next thirty minutes. When I finished, I looked at the puzzle, which was sitting in front of a mirror, allowing me to see two sides of the puzzle at once. I rotated it, while watching it in the mirror.

"Puzzles are always in motion," I said aloud.

I thought about the moving puzzle of my life that allowed Dad to figure out the sleepover plan. The signs of my deception had been everywhere for Dad to see. I had washed my favorite dress; I had bought new makeup, Jenny and I had stopped giggling when Dad walked past my room; those and dozens of other moving pieces were all there, waiting for Dad to assemble into a picture.

I moved the Impossible Puzzle to the middle of the room and started picking up puzzle pieces as I walked around it. Piece after piece revealed its secret to me as I circled, until, at just after midnight, I slid the last one into place.

There were still lights on downstairs; so I picked it up and carried it down with me. When I saw Dad, I tossed it at him. He caught it, and for a moment he looked proud, before his face shifted completely.

"Go to bed, Jocie," he said.

I heard him leave the house. He didn't return until after breakfast the next morning.

"I'm sorry I missed your birthday breakfast," he said.

He tried to hug me, but I pulled away. I was still mad at him about the party and the puzzle, and now he'd even missed my breakfast. He let me go, ate a quick breakfast, and left again. Mom came into my room a while later.

"Jocie?"

She stopped when she saw the completed puzzle.

"Wow. Did you do that in just a day?" she asked.

"It's nice of someone to notice."

"If you're referring to your father, he noticed. Something came up last night. Something I need to talk with you about. Dad chose not to warn the other parents about the true purpose of the sleepover. Your friends all went to Black Forest, but someone had heard that there were Washed girls coming to the party and they laced the food with drugs. They were all attacked. Dad has been with their families all night."

******

Aunt Kimberley fulfills Dad's request: she feeds us a massive dinner and offers us comfortable beds for the night. I'm up early the next morning and Aunt Kimberley catches me at the basement door, where I'm looking at growth marks on the wall. Every Easter, Austin and I, along with all of our cousins, would get lined up and measured.

"I guess I'm officially the shortest now," I say. "Even little cousin Alice passed me this year."

"Your father started that tradition the first Easter that you could walk," Aunt Kimberley says.

"When I was little, I loved being measured," I say. "It became a lot less fun as everyone caught up and eventually passed me. Do you remember how Austin acted the first year that he was taller than me?"

"He was even worse the year after that," she replies, and we both smile.

"Mom said that God made me the perfect height to be me …" I say, "… but I remember Dad's look more than anything. It was like I'd added to the list of ways he could be disappointed in me."

"Jocie? Why on earth would you think you've ever been a disappointment to your father?"

I can't help it. My face turns to sadness as I think about it.

"Aunt Kimberley, would you say that my Dad is a happy person?" I ask.

"I've never known anyone happier," she says. "They say that when he was The Cult Hunter, he could part a crowd just by looking at it, but after he met Christ, all of that was lifted from him. I've only watched what happened to him inside the mountain once, but even as he was being whipped, you could see in his eyes that he was unburdened. Live or die, he knew in his heart that the Lord was with him."

My eyes start to tear up as she speaks.

"Why then …" I start, but can't finish the sentence.

"My dear, whatever is the matter?" she asks.

"Why does he …"

I start to cry.

"Let it out, Jocie," she says, and holds me gently.

It comes out in spurts, as I sob.

"Why does … he always get so … so sad when he … when he looks at me?"

"I don't know, Jocie."

"There are so many moments of my life that should be happy memories, but all I remember instead is Dad's face. I was so proud when I solved 'The Impossible Puzzle,' but he looked disappointed; I was proud when I finally free-climbed a rock with a big overhang, and he was proud for just half a second, like he'd forgotten to be disappointed and then remembered, and there was that face again."

"Jocie, you listen to me!" she says. "Your father has never been disappointed in you."

"Then why ..."

"He knows something, Jocie. He's pieced together a thousand little things that nobody else could hope to understand, just like he did when he was your age. Whatever it is, he's not disappointed in you. He's scared for you. He's scared because he loves you, and ..."

"And what?" I ask.

"He knows, Jocie. He never told anyone, of course. Not even your mother, until recently."

"What does he know?"

"He knows that you received the same gift that he has."

"The whole family knows that I'm good at puzzles."

She smiles and shakes her head.

"Then he even kept it a secret from you," she says. "The way your minds work is beyond being good at puzzles. You see things most people can't see, and put together the pieces."

"If I'm so gifted, why wouldn't he be trying to develop it?"

"A gift like yours doesn't need to be developed. It's just who you are. For some reason, Cephas wanted to keep your gift out of the spotlight ... to keep it a secret until the gift is needed."

"It's a nice theory, Aunt Kimberley."

"Jocie, I wasn't going to tell you this, but I eavesdropped when your parents were last here. They quarreled, and I'd never heard either of them raise a voice or say an unkind word to each other; so I listened as he explained it her. You didn't solve 'The Impossible Puzzle' when you were thirteen."

Yet another disappointment.

"You solved a version that your Dad had altered to make it ten times harder."

What?

"Why did that cause a fight?"

"They were fighting because he said the burden is now yours to bear. Jocie, he knows the burden his gift has brought him. He would never have wished it onto you. He loves you too much. Every time you did something incredible, it just reinforced what he already knew, and it made him sad."

"Anything else?" I ask.

"The fight also had something to do with a woman named 'Amelia.' After that, your Mom stormed out of the house for an hour, and your Dad spent some time staring at those growth marks on the wall, just like I found you this morning. I heard him say 'just small enough.' When your Mom came back, they spoke quietly for a while; then left, hand-in-hand."

******

Austin and Zera wake up and join us for breakfast an hour later.

"Where do we go from here?" Austin asks.

"Don't say it out loud!" Aunt Kimberley says. "We're all better off if I don't know."

"I have one idea," I say.

"Austin, before you go, will you see if you can fix the drone that fills my bird feeders?" Aunt Kimberley says. "It broke when your parents were here, but they left so quickly that your Mom forgot to fix it for me."

When the breakfast dishes are all washed, we use the exit through the willow tree; then find the drone parked in the garden shed. Austin looks at it, while Zera and I sit in the tree and enjoy the fresh air.

"There's nothing wrong with the drone," Austin says. "It looks like a programming issue."

He inputs some new code via his com.

"That should do it," he says, but the drone zips to the same feeder, fills it, and parks in the shed.

"Good job, boy wonder," Zera says.

Austin looks at the software again.

"Somebody put a self-regenerating override code in it," he says. "This is weird. All we need to do is take down that one feeder, and it should reset."

He walks to the full feeder, which is hanging on an odd shepherd's hook. He takes the feeder down, but the drone stays put.

"Move the hook, too," I say.

When he pulls it out of the ground, the drone activates and begins filling feeders around the yard.

"Thank you, Austin!" Aunt Kimberley says from the tree.

"Aunt Kimberley, where did you get this hook?" he asks.

"Your Aunt Cindi gave it to me ages ago."

"How long, exactly?" he asks.

"At least a ten years. Why?"

"It's very interesting. May I keep it?"

"Since it's messing up the drone, go ahead."

An hour later, we've said our goodbyes and been crushed by Aunt Kimberley's hugs many times over. Our backpacks are full of all the food she gave us, but as we exit the tree, Austin grabs the old hook and finds a way to stuff it in as well.

"What's the story with the hook?" I ask.

"Not here," he replies.

By the time we're just two blocks away, Austin can't contain his excitement anymore. He stops under a tree and takes out the hook.

"I know where I'm going! I know the special thing I've been called upon to do!"

He holds up the hook.

"You're going to be a shepherd?" Zera asks.

"I know this material," he says. "It's the same composite that Dad and I created five years ago to make into bike frames."

"How? Aunt Kimberley says its ten years old," I say.

"I know, but look at this."

He points to some letters engraved in the material.

"Those are my initials, written exactly the way I write," he says.

Zera looks confused, but I already know where this is going.

"No," I say.

"Yes, Jocie. This is part of a time machine arena. I'm going to build a time machine!"

CHAPTER TEN

"Daddy, tell me the story about how I named myself," I said one night, when he came to tuck me into bed.

At six years old, I'd heard the story many times, but it always seemed like telling the story made Daddy happy; so I asked often.

"You named yourself when you were nothing more than a tiny speck of cells growing inside Mommy," he said. "Mommy and I were in a time machine, and we …"

"… could hear each other's thoughts!" I jumped in.

"That's right. We could hear each other's thoughts, but only Mommy could hear you, because you were inside of her, and …"

"…and I told her my name."

"Who's telling this story?" he asked, and we both smiled.

I paused for a while; then asked a question I'd never asked before.

"How did I know my name?" I asked.

"You knew your name because it's the name that God gave to you. He knew every hair on your head before you were even a speck of cells. He already knew that you'd name yourself after a friend of mine."

"The lady from the videos?"

"That's right. Her name was Jocie. I time travelled with her, and heard her thoughts, too."

"Was she nice?" I asked.

"When I first met her, she wasn't very nice at all. Later, when she knew more about Jesus, she was nicer."

Daddy looked at me with a very serious face.

"I have something that belonged to Jocie that I've been planning to give to you when I was sure you could be responsible with it. If you can promise that you'll always keep it safe, I'll give it to you now."

"I promise."

He left the room and I heard him go into his office. When he came back, he had a small pouch.

"Hold out your hands," he said.

He dumped the contents of the pouch into my hands. It looked like a pirate treasure of rubies, emeralds, and diamonds. There were also a lot of smoky, greenish crystals that seemed ugly compared to the rest.

"What are the ugly ones?" I asked.

"Those are the most important ones of all," he said. "Those are our secret family crystals. You can never show them to anyone or tell anyone about them. Not even your brother."

I placed all of the stones onto my bed and looked at them.

"I promise to keep the secret, Daddy, but I don't want the family crystals. What if I lose them?"

Daddy picked up the crystals and put them into his pocket; then put all the pretty stones into the pouch.

"Okay. Then you keep the stones that belonged to Jocie, and I'll keep the family crystals," he said.

Two weeks before he disappeared, I noticed that the pouch of gemstones I'd protected since I was six years old had been moved on the shelf in my bedroom. It was only moved a few millimeters, just enough so I'd notice. When I opened it, the family crystals were inside.

******

For the next hour, all we hear is Austin asking things like "Where do you think I'll build it?" and "Do you think I'll be meeting Christ, too?"

When Zera can't take anymore, she speaks up.

"Have you forgotten that there are no more large native crystals of tellurium 120? Your Dad blew them all up before we were born."

I reach back and touch my pack to be sure a small, outer pocket is zipped.

121

"We must find some," Austin replies. "The bar of composite didn't jump back in time all by itself."

"Well, I don't know where. The world's minable supply was used sending your parents back and forth. There were barely enough left to even send the small package with vaccine."

The little pouch of gems I've carried for most of my life ...

"We can argue about it later," I say. "Right now, the only idea I have of where to go next is to find someone named Amelia."

"Doctor Amelia Lake?" Zera asks.

"I don't know," I say. "Who is she?"

"Her last name wasn't 'Lake' at the time, but she was the member of Four who got her hands on the sample of the Mark of the Beast vaccine that she and your Aunt Cindi used to make The Washed vaccine that was sent back in time. She later became an expert on it and was named head of the Center for World Health. I met her once when she came to speak with my parents."

"She spoke with your parents? Any idea why?" I ask.

"It was a family matter," Zera replies. "My Mom also said Amelia had a thing for your Dad and your Mom was jealous."

That might explain the fight between Mom and Dad ... could it also explain Dad taking off his wedding ring? It can't be. Dad would rather chew his own arm off than betray Mom.

We've entered the Ogallala tube station, and I go to a public computer terminal.

"Computer, please locate Amelia Lake, head of the CWH," I say.

"Former head of the CWH, Doctor Amelia Lake, lives in Post Falls, Idaho," the pleasant voice responds.

After an hour in a tube car, we find ourselves standing at her front door.

"May I help you?" she asks over the intercom.

"Doctor Lake? We need your help," I say, and hear a sigh in response.

A few moments later the door opens. Amelia is a tall woman, with dark black hair, speckled by just a few that are gray. There are dark circles under her eyes that look like they were imprinted there through years of hard work and worry. She looks over our faces.

"You kids need to read your history books. I tried to help you. I failed."

I reach up to my face and peel off the sticky, living scar.

"We have read the history books. We need to hear the things that were never written down."

Her eyes widen - first with surprise, and then with curiosity.

"I think you'd better come inside," she says.

We walk down a hallway and into a large living room, though it doesn't appear that she's doing any "living" here. The room is filled with tables, each covered with stacks of papers; and three of the walls contain ancient chalk boards. My eye is drawn to the fourth wall, which contains a projection of a world map with spots marked in various colors and dates.

"I'd love to know why three washed children need my help, but first: who do you work for?" Amelia asks.

We look at each other, then back at Amelia.

"Four," I say.

"Shouldn't you be out blowing things up?" she asks.

"That's Albert's job," I say.

That got her attention.

"You do know your history …" she says, "… but you're too young to be members of Four unless, someone went back on their word and started recruiting a new generation."

"We're not actually members," Zera says. "Our parents were, and they've disappeared."

"Your parents? Anyone I would know?"

"My mother is Zip, and this is Austin and Jocie Paulson."

Amelia looks at each of us.

"It figures," Amelia says, and looks at Austin. "If anyone's children would be mixed up in current events, it would be all of their kids. I should have known when you showed me that scar material. Is that your Aunt Cindi's work?"

"No, it's mine," I say. "What current events are you speaking about?"

"Current events, old events; what difference does it make? Nothing has really changed since I was with your parents in Four, except this time there might actually be a winner in the war," she replies.

"What is it with people who were in Four?" Zera says. "My Mom barely told me anything; their father only works in puzzles; and now you! Why can't any of you just spit it out?"

Amelia walks over to the fireplace and looks at a picture on the mantle. She's wearing a wedding dress. The man in the picture is sporting a tuxedo - and a black line across his face.

"They say Cindi and I saved the Christian world," Amelia says. "This room is testament to the fact that whatever we saved, it wasn't worth saving. You want a lesson on unwritten history? Why don't you go ahead and walk around this room? Let's see if you can work a little of the Paulson family magic and put all of the pieces together."

She leaves the room.

"I think everyone who was in Four went nuts," Zera says.

I walk to the mantle and look at the wedding picture.

"She married a guy from The Corps," I say. "Why would she do that?"

Zera says nothing, but rolls her eyes.

"Do you suppose they're still together?" Austin asks.

I look over the other pictures on the mantle.

"He died," I say. "In these pictures, it looks like he's getting sicker as time goes on, and in one he's in a hospital bed."

She saved all of The Washed, but she couldn't save the man she loved.

"This table is covered with her research on how to counteract the Mark of the Beast vaccine," Zera says.

I walk to the wall with the world map projected on it. The points are marked in three different colors: there are black points that are concentrated around the equator in Asia and Africa; there are white points that are concentrated in the far northern and southern hemispheres; and there are red points that are mostly in North America and Western Europe. The oldest dates are the black marks, some of which are from when I was about six years old. The most recent date is in red. It's from last month.

Austin walks over.

"What is this all about?" he asks.

"I'd say she traveled around the world looking for a cure. The question is: what was she looking for? Any clues over there, Zera?"

"I'm no biochemist, but it looks like she was obsessed with finding a sample of the toxin used in the Final Holy War."

"Wasn't it the same toxin that Henry Portman put into the water?" Austin asks.

"Apparently not," Zera says. "After the war, all samples - and all information on how to make it - were destroyed by international agreement. The toxin Henry had was a best guess, but apparently not quite the same thing, especially when they took off the part used to target certain genes."

"The black markers on the map are where the bombs fell," I say. "She visited every site, looking for residue."

"Then what are the white markers?" Austin asks.

"They're all in cold places," I say. "There are mountain tops and both poles. Maybe she was taking ice cores?"

"Neither the old toxin nor the new one could be made to be very heat stable," Amelia says, from the doorway. "They break down in a couple of decades at room temperature. Ice cores were my best hope for finding a preserved sample."

She crosses the room.

"The Mark of the Beast vaccine is like a slow-acting poison," Amelia continues. "Those extra amino acids that Henry added to spell out his grandfather's name aren't merely unnatural. They're toxic."

"I never understood why the added part can't be edited out of everyone," Austin says.

"It was designed to be irreversible." Amelia says. "We've tried everything we can think of to remove it, but it can't be done without inactivating the vaccine part too."

"Who cares?" Zera says. "The Corps no longer controls any toxin; so why not just use genetic engineering to un-vaccinate everyone?"

"Show time!" I say.

Amelia turns to me.

"You are definitely your father's daughter," she says.

"What does 'show time' mean?" Austin asks.

"When Dad was being tortured, just before Henry had the guards bring out the choice of toxin or vaccine, he touched his com and said 'show time.' He didn't need a com to talk to the guards; so he must have been sending a coded message to someone else."

Zera and Austin both give me expectant looks.

"Dad was there to delay the release of airborne toxin. For a moment, Henry thought Dad was broken and that he'd won; so 'show time' must have been the order to go airborne. By the time Dad was rescued, it must have been too late to call them back. If the toxin persists in the environment for decades, altering the DNA of The Marked again will kill them all."

"They dropped hundreds of metric tons of the stuff," Amelia says. "Test any surface on earth you like, and you'll probably find trace amounts. Every exposure causes a little more damage to The Marked, especially former Cult Hunters who received injections."

"That doesn't explain the ice cores." Zera says. "How would a sample of the old toxin help find a cure for people marked by the new toxin?"

"Antivenin," I say. "Some antivenins are cross-reactive, so you were hoping the old toxin could be used to cure the new toxin."

Amelia looks at me.

"Paulson family magic," she says. "I even broke Federal and international law and tried to make my own toxin to produce an antivenin, but they either killed the test animals too quickly or weren't cross-reactive. That's how I lost my job as head of the Center for World Health. I worked on it with a private company for a while, but I gave up when my husband, Ted, died."

My head snaps to a picture on the mantle, which I pick up and ask the computer to transfer to the screen. Amelia's husband is pictured in a hospital bed.

"Computer, zoom in on the logo on Mr. Lake's hospital gown," I say.

Under the logo read the words "Bauer Corporation."

"Did you work for Tyrone Bauer?" I ask.

"Yes. After the CWH let me go, he was very accommodating of my research ideas and arranged for Ted to be cared for in the building where I worked. Ted died there, just a few days after that picture was taken."

Austin gives me his best 'I told you so' look. He still thinks Bauer is one of the good guys.

That's not how I see this puzzle.

******

"Where to now?" Austin asks, once we're alone in a tube car heading east.

"I need one more history lesson," I say. "Did you notice that Amelia said nothing about the places on the map marked with red dots?"

"Why didn't you ask?" Zera says.

"It's something Dad taught me: when you're solving a puzzle, always find the pieces yourself."

I slip a com into my ear.

"Computer, check the news for the past eighteen years and tell me if the following locations all have something in common …"

I list off the locations of the red dots, which range from Everett, Washington to Marietta, Georgia and many points in between in North America, as well as points in France, Germany, Spain, Russia and China.

"Each location was the site of an attack by the environmental group 'Nature's Way'," the pleasant voice replies.

"Show me an example," I say.

The computer produces a video account of an attack, which shows a number of large airplanes that are on fire. The next two videos are of massive buildings burning, followed by 'aftermath' shots showing the charred remains of more airplanes.

"Why does 'Nature's Way' destroy airplanes," I ask.

"The stated goal of 'Nature's Way' is to allow forest fires to burn naturally. The destroyed planes are all air tankers used in aerial firefighting."

Air tankers?

"How many planes have they destroyed?" I ask.

"Over one thousand planes have been destroyed or disabled worldwide, most of them through sabotage of the engines."

"How else do they hinder firefighting?" I ask. "Do they attack firefighters or spot-fire drones? Do they destroy chainsaw or bulldozing drones?"

"There are no recorded attacks of those types by 'Nature's Way'," the computer says.

I remove the com from my ear.

"Okay, so Amelia follows the news on environmental activism," Zera says. "How does that tell us where to go next?"

"It doesn't," I say.

How can neither Zera nor Austin see the connection?

CHAPTER ELEVEN

"I don't understand. Why is a hole in the ground, with some burned junk in the bottom, so important?" I asked.

That was four years ago, while we were visiting the Bethany House National Historic Monument. I'd also been here when I was nine, but all I remembered from that trip was that Daddy gave a speech, and I was bored. This time, we'd come unannounced, and Dad was wearing a hat and sunglasses so he wouldn't be recognized.

"You're right…" Dad said, "… this is just a hole in the ground."

Mom shot him a look.

"We make monuments and memorials to help us remember things," Mom said. "The hole itself isn't important. What's important is that we remember what the hole represents. Bethany House meant a lot to this family; so I'd like you to show a little more respect."

An automated tour kiosk rolled up to us.

"Do you have any questions?" it asked.

"How deep is the hole?" Austin asked.

"The crater is fifty-seven meters deep, at its deepest point," it replied. "There is evidence that there were deeper explosions that attempted to collapse the hole all the way to the underlying coal mine, but they failed to achieve that result. Instead, the crater collapsed only as far as an equipment storage area above the main mine."

"Is this where the Paulson's fell in love?" I asked.

"The first recorded kiss between Cephas and Martha Paulson occurred in Colorado Springs, Colorado. Their first recorded copulation occurred…"

"That's quite enough," Mom said. "No more questions."

The machine rolled away.

"Bethany House represents hope," Dad said from behind me. "Before it was a hole in the ground, Bethany House was a place where people lived, trained, prayed, and yes, even fell in love. It's also where the gene therapy used to save millions of Christians was developed and then sent back in time."

"And then you blew it up," Austin said.

Dad smiled.

"No matter how much I loved that place, it was an easy decision to make. If the dirt walls could have spoken, I believe they would have insisted on their own destruction for the sake of what was achieved."

His eyes drifted off into the distance for a moment, and then down to me. That look of bottomless sadness covered his face.

"Bethany House was like a person," he said. "Sometimes, one person, with faith, can make all the difference."

******

The computer announces that our tube will arrive in Sheridan, Illinois momentarily.

"Why are we here?" Austin asks.

"We're testing a hunch," I say.

"Mom says that Dad doesn't have hunches. I'm suspecting that you don't either."

The car glides to a stop and Austin stands.

"We're not getting off," I say.

I stare out the window and watch the comings and goings of the station, until the car speeds away.

"What was that all about?" Zera asks.

"I saw four Temple Guards and two members of Five-X watching the station," I say. "I bet they're watching everywhere Dad traveled and every stop near an old Four safe house."

"The Guards are easy to spot …" Zera says, "…but how did you pick out the members of Five-X?"

"They were both wearing the scar material I created. They must have distributed it to all of their facilities. If one of them gets caught, our disguises will be blown."

"Do you think they were watching for us?" Austin asks.

"Definitely. Older people walked past The Corps and The Guard without receiving a second look, but every young person in the station was being scrutinized."

"So where do we go?" Austin asks.

"You're the one who's going to make a time machine, Austin. Where would *you* put it?"

"Well, I'll need access to a primary power line, so that limits the choices."

"He'll need the raw materials to build the arena, plus computers," Zera says.

"And the arena that gets sent back will need to stay hidden until …" Austin stops, mid-sentence.

"…until the piece in your backpack is found," I say.

Austin makes a face.

"Jocie, I hate when you and Dad do that. If you already knew the answer, why didn't you just tell us?"

Because it's more fun this way.

"Mr. Albert brought something made of metal to our house when I was five. I never saw what it was, but Dad asked him to give it to Aunt Cindi. It must have been your shepherd's hook, and she hid it in plain sight, holding up a bird feeder."

"But where did Albert find it?" Zera asks.

"When Albert gave it to Dad, Dad said he'd been waiting since the day Bethany House was destroyed."

"You can't be serious," Zera says. "That hole is a national historic monument, filled with pilgrims day and night. You can't just attach a rope to the handrail, rappel down, and build a time machine."

Why else would Dad teach me to rock climb, if not to climb down into that hole?

"How about a small drone?" I ask.

Austin taps his com.

"Computer, display an aerial view of Bethany House National Monument," he says, and the picture comes up on a screen.

"I can see four cameras positioned around the edge of the hole," he says.

There are at least twelve.

"Those antenna's on top of the light posts are probably jammers," Zera adds. "Even a small drone would be seen and knocked out of the sky."

"This is all irrelevant," Austin says. "Federal drones have explored every inch of it. If there was another arena cage at Bethany House, they would have found it."

"Doesn't it seem strange that the hole would be shaped like a giant teardrop?" I ask. "Anyone who knows Albert might think he created a directional explosion to ensure all of Bethany House was destroyed. But what if the real reason was that he was trying to protect something from the blast?"

I look more closely at the picture on the screen.

"Finding a secret way in?" Austin asks.

"I'm definitely finding a secret."

How in the world did Dad ever pull that off?

******

The tube stations in Winchester and Strasburg figured prominently in Mom and Dad's escape from The Corps; so instead we get off in Chicago. I do see some members of the Temple Guard, but the station is so busy that we walk right by them individually, without being given a second glance. They must be focused on finding a group of three. Although I see several washed people in the station, none of them are wearing my scar material, which I hope means Five-X doesn't have the manpower to be everywhere.

Cargo areas are so automated that we generally just walk around without worrying about being seen. Unfortunately, the Chicago cargo area is larger than most, so as we wander to find the correct loading area, we walk right past the office of the cargo station master. He looks up as we pass.

"Keep walking," I say to Austin and Zera.

"What are you kids doing here?" the man asks our backs.

"Couriers," I say, and we keep walking.

"Well, *couriers* … this is *my* station … and my station, you log in," he says.

"Don't hurt him any more than necessary," I whisper.

We turn.

"Two cameras," I whisper. "Ten meters on the left and fifty meters on the right. Don't look directly at them."

"Will this take long?" I ask the station master. "We missed our passenger car. Now we have to catch a cargo car to get to our next pick-up."

"Not long. Just come into my office."

His office is barren of virtually anything you'd expect to find in an office. There are no personal items, and none of the creature comforts you'd expect someone who sits all day to have around. It's just a table with a screen on it, and a chair that squeaks when he sits in it. The one exception is a large electronic picture frame that could have been placed on any of the bare walls, but instead is hanging over the office window that looks out over the loading area.

"Take one step forward," I say to Austin and Zera, so that we're all nearly standing against his desk.

"You've been here before then?" the man asks.

"No, but the only reason to hang the picture frame in front of the window is to block the view of the nearest camera."

I look up at him for the first time. Nearly his entire face is covered with bruises that have dried into a cakey mess. It apparently flakes off regularly, since a large accumulation is lying on the desk and floor.

"It's not a pretty sight, is it?" he asks. "Believe me … nobody wants to hang out in my office for any longer than necessary."

"I imagine it's the only way someone who's washed can hold a public job like this," I say, and he smiles.

"You are a very clever young lady. What direction are you going?"

"In whatever direction the Lord guides our steps," I reply.

"Then he's guiding you to my house in Parkersburg. I was done for the day anyway and I have a small private car."

He stands and heads for the door, and we follow.

When we get into the car, he starts to pick at the flakes on his face.

"You would not believe how much this stuff itches when it dries," he says.

"You're welcome to try gooey," I say and peel up the scar on my hand.

His eyes go wide.

"You're washed?" he asks. "We've been getting high priority messages from The Corps to watch for three marked Christians about your age. I figured you might be them, but nobody knows that you kids are actually washed."

"The Corps is looking for us?" Zera says.

"The Corps, the Guard, Five-X ... they've all stopped by my office," he says. "Even ..."

We all give him an expectant look.

"Even what?" Austin asks.

"I have no proof ..." he says. "... but I think a woman I met years ago snuck into my office yesterday and fiddled with the system. A drone on the loading floor went kind of crazy and when I got back from repairing it, I saw her slip out of my office. I tried to follow her, but she disappeared like a ghost. She looked just like a woman who was part of Four back in the day. I remember her because of her amazing eyes."

He looks pointedly at my eyes.

Aunt Cindi! He's talking about Aunt Cindi ... and she was here just yesterday!

"Everyone knows that Four was disbanded long ago," I say.

"Maybe so," he says. "And yet, my cargo cars have had a lot of couriers in them lately."

*****

When we reach the man's house in Parkersburg, West Virginia, a woman meets him at the door with a wet towel.

"I just cleaned the floor and I don't want you flaking your face off all over the place again ..." she says, and then looks at us.

"Hal, who are our guests?" she asks.

"Just get them inside, Chelsey," he says, as he starts to rub his face vigorously with the towel.

She bids us to sit at the kitchen table, but doesn't say anything until Hal comes in. She's clearly angry about our arrival.

Hal's face is mostly clean of the thick flakes, but you can see some in his hairline and along his jaw.

"Let me help," Chelsey says. "You've got some stuck in your ear again."

By the time Chelsey looks back at us, Zera has removed a scar from her hand and has stuck it so that it's dangling from the end of her nose.

"How about me? Did I miss some too?" she asks.

I break one of mine in half and stick the pieces to each ear.

"These gooey earrings are all the rage in Paris and Milan," I say.

Austin uses one of his to make a smiley face on his cheek.

"Is this what Dad meant when he said to turn the other cheek?" he asks.

Chelsey takes a deep breath, as if she's going to fly into a rage. Her lips start to quiver a bit and you can see her chest shaking a little. I'm about to suggest that we leave, when she first snorts, and then breaks into one of the largest and most sincere fits of laughter that I've ever seen.

"Washed kids, playing with fake scars … it's so sad and yet so ridiculous …" she says through the laughter. Her laugh is infectious and soon we're all laughing along with her.

"You don't know how long I've needed that," she says. "I haven't felt so joyful since the day…"

Her voice trails off when she looks at me.

"Those eyes," she says. "I know those eyes … and that pony tail … it reminds me of … Hal? Who did you bring home?"

"They didn't say; and I didn't ask. My heart just told me that they needed me."

"We last saw Cindi Stone and her kids about five years ago," Chelsea says. "You're not little Alice, are you?"

"Little Alice is taller than I am now. I'm Jocie."

She looks at Austin.

"Yes," is all he says.

"And I'm Zip's daughter. My name is Zera."

"I was so sorry to hear about your father," Chelsea says to Zera. "He was a dear man."

Chelsey turns to Austin.

"Where are your parents? We've been praying for their safe return nightly. Are they okay? Did they send you here?"

"We don't know where they are. We're trying to find them," Austin says.

I stand and part the blinds of the kitchen window just a hair.

"We wouldn't have come if we'd known you were old friends of the family. They're watching everyone with a connection to Mom and Dad, and every tube station where they traveled eighteen years ago," I say.

Too late.

"Tell me about your neighbor across the street," I say.

"The elderly couple? They're devout atheists from the old days. They stopped speaking to us years ago."

"Maybe, but they're not ignoring you. There's an armed man in the upstairs window watching this house and I can see tracking drones."

"Get back to the station," Hal says. "There's an old passenger car, number P732-6, parked in the maintenance area. You can drive it manually, but it's going to be dangerous."

"It can't be that dangerous," Austin says. "When Mom and Dad escaped from The Corps, that car was driven manually."

"This is different," Hal says. "In that case, the tube was cleared of traffic by The Corps and its beacons were operational. I disabled all of the security lockouts and beacons on car P732-6. It can be driven manually, but it will be invisible in the system."

"Isn't being invisible a good thing?" Austin asks.

"Not with tube cars," Hal says. "If you're invisible, the system isn't planning for you. Other cars won't know you're there until they're within ten meters. You'll also have to regulate speed and open the switches to branch lines manually."

"That's crazy," Zera says. "The timing would need to be down to the fraction of a second. Nobody can do that without crashing."

"Only one person has ever wanted to travel invisibly enough to attempt it," Hal says, and nods towards me and Austin. "Their father."

CHAPTER TWELVE

When I was fourteen, Mom called another special training session at Aunt Cindi's house and again gave me the device that would tell the system I had done all of my assigned running. There were more former members of the Four network in attendance than I had ever seen in one place. Even during warm-ups, it was obvious that they'd all been doing intensive combat training, as there wasn't an extra pound of fat to split among them.

The participants divided themselves up by their former Four houses. This was clearly going to be a competition. I frowned when I saw Mom and Dad standing, just the two of them, to represent Bethany House, while the other six houses participating had many more people. Gethsemane house had Uncle Cameron, his brother Andrew, and six others, all of whom were in top shape. They seemed to be the clear favorite.

There were three rounds of competition: The first was the average time of each team through the obstacle course; the second was the score on the stun gun range; and the last was combat using fighting sticks. The children of the participants were allowed to watch, and I could see Austin seated with many of the other children around him - like he was holding court. My cousins were all there, too, while I was stuck watching from a tree through binoculars.

Friendly bets on the outcome were tossed around, but Mom and Dad still stood off to the side, speaking quietly, despite some teasing from Uncle Cameron. The teasing got worse when Mom lined up for the obstacle course with a full-length fighting stick.

"You're not allowed to trip other teams," Uncle Cameron said.

"I know," Mom replied.

"Then why carry something that will slow you down?"

"You designed the course, Cameron. You figure it out."

I watched as the other teams travelled the course. There were mud pits to swing over, monkey bars over water and the like. They had all seen the course ahead of time and they all attacked it as individuals, until they reached the final obstacle: a wall four meters tall. The fastest member of each team would reach it, and then stand there, waiting for a teammate to catch up. Each team would then build a human pyramid to get one member atop the wall. Once one member was on top, the rest would be boosted up as helping hands reached down to haul them over. When a team was down to just one person on the ground, a team member would be dangled from above by the wrists and used as a human rope for the last person to climb.

When it was time for Mom and Dad, they attacked the course the same way they do everything: as a team. Mom was slowed down by carrying a stick, until she used it to vault over the mud pits, saving Dad the time it would take for the rope to stop swinging. She threw it like a javelin to the other side of the monkey bars, while she and Dad quickly swung across.

I expected them to be stopped for good at the wall. At four meters high, there was no way for just two people to get over it. There was some chuckling from the other teams, until Dad held the pole for Mom to shimmy up. When she reached the top, she did something I wouldn't have thought possible. Using the wall for support, she somehow got on top of the pole. Then, standing on just one foot, she hopped off and grabbed the top of the wall. Dad threw the pole up to her and climbed it like a rope, while she held it from above.

The shooting gallery was another lesson in teamwork. The targets were mini-drones and the entire team was allowed to shoot at once. All the other teams shot as individuals, with the drones swerving to avoid the shots. Dad told Mom to call out which drone she was targeting. When her shot missed, the drone would swerve directly into Dad's shot, fired a split second later, as he predicted which direction it would go as it tried to dodge.

Firmly in first place, Mom and Dad didn't have to fight in the first round, nor did Gethsemane House, which was in second place. I watched each team intently as the other four teams squared off, making mental notes. Matches of three-on-three or four-on-four weren't nearly as easy to predict and call out the moves in advance as they were in single combat. There was a randomness to the action that made me worry that Dad's abilities wouldn't be as effective as usual.

Soon it was down to just Bethany House versus Uncle Cameron and Gethsemane. Mom and Dad walked to the center of the ring.

"I assume you read all of the rules," Uncle Cameron said.

"We did," Mom replied. "Which rule, in particular?"

"The one that says this is a team competition, house against house. The fact that you only have two members isn't our problem."

Aunt Cindi had fought with Mount Carmel House. She stood up.

"Cameron, I know you're mad that Bethany has won every time, but you can't be serious. Eight against two?" she said.

Mom and Dad switched positions so that they were back-to-back.

"Okay, Gethsemane. Bring the house," Dad replied.

Uncle Cameron positioned his team so there would be four members attacking, with four in reserve. They looked like a pack of wolves, surrounding a deer, so what happened next surprised everyone. Mom attacked first, and kept on attacking. She hit the man in front of her, and the woman to his right, and even two of the people standing in reserve. As fierce as she was, it was Dad who was more amazing. Without ever turning around, he kept his back to hers. He moved, and ducked, and rolled without ever looking at her, all while keeping the wolves off her back.

At first, the action looked like another example of teamwork, but the strategy actually centered on allowing Mom to fight as an individual, while Dad read her moves just like he was reading the moves of their opponents. As I continued to watch, I realized there was even more going on, and that even Mom didn't know it was happening. Dad wasn't just reading Mom's moves … he was secretly directing them by manipulating the position of everyone in the ring. The randomness of the earlier fights disappeared before my eyes, and I watched Dad form the fight into a pattern that he controlled.

What struck me the most was that Mom never took a single hit. Dad purposely took them all. Whether this was to free Mom up for counterstrikes, or if he simply wanted to protect her, I don't know. What was clear to me was that self-sacrifice was just another part of Dad's game plan.

*****

Hal proposes that he create a diversion in the front yard while we leave through the back. Both doors are surely being watched, but he hopes that enough eyes will be drawn to him to give us a chance.

"I don't like this," I say.

"Me either," Zera says. "A washed man is walking straight into armed Temple Guard."

"That, too," I say, "but what I mean is that I think the main group is waiting for us in the back. I can't explain it. There's just something about the way that tracking drone is flying. It's just a hunch."

"That's good enough for me," Austin says.

"My family has always favored direct assaults," Zera adds.

We watch Hal walk down the front steps and towards the street.

"If we were going out the back, they'd be expecting us in about thirty seconds," I say.

"Then I'll open the back door," Chelsea says.

She doesn't even get the screen door open, before stun gun hits start pelting the back of the house. From the sound of it, every window is broken.

Hal turns at the sound, but takes only two steps towards the house before he's stunned in the back.

"Give them ten seconds to wonder if they've messed up," I say.

We burst through the door. One of the Guards must have thought they had the wrong house, because he steps out from behind a tree and gets shot in the chest by Zera. Austin shoots another as he comes from behind the neighbor's house. I shoot at the tracking drone that has descended to within twenty meters of us, but it dodges the shot.

I tell Austin and Zera to follow me, as I run straight across the street and into the house of the elderly atheists, then straight out their back door, but the drone finds us again a just half block later. I shoot at it twice more.

"Don't bother. They're too fast," Zera says.

"You try," I say.

She takes three shots, all of which miss by a meter.

When they see they're being targeted, their rotors turn more slowly on the side they plan to go. I can hear the difference. It must speed up the turn.

"See?" she says.

"One more," I say.

Zera takes a bead on the drone and I hear the rotors on the left slow down. I shoot a split second after her, and the drone twists straight into my shot, then crashes.

She looks at me with her jaw open.

"Don't question it … just run," Austin says.

Without a tracking drone on us, our human pursuers quickly lose our trail. We don't have time to be evasive. We run straight for the tube station and locate the maintenance bays.

"Once they've covered the passenger terminals, they'll look here next," I say. "Who's driving?"

"You are!" Austin and Zera say together.

"There are only two relevant controls," I say. "The speed control stick in my left hand and the switches to open branch lines in my right hand."

I pull up a display of the cars in the area.

"The tubes are full," Austin says. "There's a car every twenty meters, riding the slip steams."

"How long is this car?" I ask.

"Ten meters."

"That gives me five meters on each side."

"Jocie, for all we know, Dad attempted this in the middle of the night when there were only a few cars in the area," Austin says.

"How will you synchronize to their speed?" Zera asks.

"I don't know," I say, and hit the loading sequence to put the car into position.

We hear the docking clamps unlock with a clunk, then the whole section of tube moves to align us with the branch line door behind us.

"You might want to hold onto something," I say, as I hit the button to open the doors and place us in the branch line stream. The acceleration is immediate.

"We're not going to make it!" Zera says. "We're going to hit a car in the mainline when we reach the junction.

If I open the switch early, it will kick them forward a couple of meters.

"Where's the door?" Austin yells.

It looks like we're heading straight into a dead end. I force my eyes back to the display. Watching the tunnel ahead is useless. The cars moving on the display are like a swarm of gnats circling over a pond near sunset. All seems random, but there's actually an elegant design to how they move.

I hit the switch and we enter the mainline tube just two meters behind a large passenger car. A proximity alarm starts screaming.

Hal rigged an audible proximity alarm. How thoughtful.

The passenger car speeds up and I slow down.

"Behind us!" Zera yells.

There's a cargo car bearing down on us, so I adjust our speed until I'm equidistant between the two cars. The passenger car in front abruptly disappears down a branch line and the door closes behind it, leaving a nice gap in front of me, so I speed up.

"Two cars are entering at the next junction to fill this gap," Austin says.

My only chance is the small space between them.

I accelerate.

A large private car appears out of nowhere into the line in front of us, then another behind us. The one behind starts to close the distance, to ride the slip stream.

"We're going to get crushed between them," Austin says.

At the last moment, I open a switch that sends us down a different line.

"Where are we?" Ausin asks.

"Halfway to Pennsylvania," Zera says.

I widen the field of view on the display.

Wrong way. We need to turn around.

I see a large loop that will take us all the way across New York State, then down into Ohio. For the next twenty minutes, I continue the dance, slipping in between cars, in and out of various branch lines, with Austin and Zera yelling out dangers well after I've seen them and adjusted. When we're halfway across Ohio, I see the branches I need.

"Just ten more switches," I say.

"Good," Zera says. "Even you can't keep this up forever."

"Jocie, where are we going?" Austin asks.

"West Virginia."

"The only way to get to the proper line from here would require a double switch," he says.

"What does that mean?" Zera asks.

Austin points to the map.

"See this point that looks like an intersection? It isn't. The only way to cross is to open the first switch, then the second almost simultaneously. It's like riding a hover bike through an intersection packed with buses going in the other direction - blindfolded."

Now Zera points to the map.

"All we need to do is make a wider loop here and here, and come around," Zera says.

"That will miss the stop we want. Don't distract me," I say.

When I open the first switch, we're looking at the side of a large cargo car. Zera and Austin scream.

If I open the second switch even a fraction too early, it will slow that car down and we'll collide. Don't panic…

I close my eyes.

Now.

We miss the cargo car by less than a meter, but the proximity alarm does little more than chirp, because we're only behind it for a fraction of a second before exiting through the second switch.

"There now," I say. "This line carries very little traffic and we should be at our station in just a minute."

I look at the reflection in the window and see that Austin and Zera are holding each other, but let go awkwardly, as I speak.

"Why?" Austin asks.

"Because I knew I could," I say. "It's just a puzzle, after all."

Have I always known I could do things like that? Have I been holding it back? Why?

"You almost broke us into a billion puzzle pieces!" Zera says.

"Shall we go around and do it again?" I ask.

"No!" they say together.

"Suit yourselves. We're here anyway. Welcome to the cargo station in Romney, West Virginia."

"Why here?" Zera asks.

"Because Mom and Dad never came here, and the cargo station is unmanned because it only gets one car per week."

We spend some time learning how Hal disconnected the safety features, then reconnect them and send the car back to Parkersburg.

"Let's never do that again," Austin says when the car is gone.

"I'm glad to hear you say that. Mom and Dad used the hover line between Gore and Wardensville a lot when they were at Bethany House, so we should avoid it. We'll need to catch a bus to Rio and walk over the mountains from there."

"Over the mountains?" Zera asks. "Where are we going?"

"We need to talk to an old friend of the family," I say.

"Capon Springs?" Austin asks, and I smile.

CHAPTER THIRTEEN

Dad wouldn't always leave me in a tree to watch, as others trained for combat. He still loved to run and would sometimes suggest that we run together. He could have easily talked and run at the same time, but mostly he enjoyed using a run as an opportunity to think. I didn't always give him the chance.

"Dad? Can I ask you something?" I began.

He didn't reply, but he slowed his pace as an indication that he was listening.

"When you were back in time, why didn't you ask Jesus questions? From what you and Mom have said, you could have spoken to him in English. Nobody would have understood; so it wouldn't have posed a risk of changing the Bible, or history."

"What do you think I should have asked?" he replied.

I didn't have an answer, so we ran for nearly another kilometer in silence before he spoke again.

"Do you remember the first three-dimensional hologram puzzle set we to gave you?" Dad asked.

"Of course. It had one thousand different puzzles programmed into it."

"That's right. The first puzzle was easy, but they got harder as you went along. Do you remember puzzle nine hundred and twenty-eight?"

"No."

"It's the one you got stuck on," he said.

"Oh … right."

"You never asked me for the solution, and if you had, I wouldn't have told you. Puzzles are created for just one purpose: to be solved. Being given the answer would have ruined the puzzle for you. I could have asked Jesus for the secrets of the universe, but I assume that He would have felt the same way. Why ruin such a magnificent puzzle?

******

We run in the forest for hours after getting off the bus in Rio. We're running out of both energy and daylight, when I see our destination: an ancient house shaped like an octagon. There's a light glowing in a second floor window.

Being an octagon, the house has many doors, all of which are left unlocked; so I pick the one with the welcome mat and walk inside.

"Brill? You home?" I call.

"Upstairs," we hear from above.

We find him in bed.

"Are you my grandchildren?" he asks. "Wait, you're too young for that. Are you my great-grandchildren?"

"No, Brill. We're friends. You were friends with our parents, Cephas and Martha Paulson, remember?"

"They were a pair, those two. I thought they'd never admit they were in love with each other."

"We're trying to find them, Brill, but first we need to find the location of Bethany House. You built it. Can you tell us how to find it?"

"Bethany House?" he says. "How hard could it be to find? It's a national monument."

We lock eyes and it's clear to me that despite being over a century old, his mind is as sharp as ever. Sharp enough that he's only going to give me the information he chooses.

I use my com to display the aerial shot of the national monument on a large screen; then I split the screen and request a very old newscast.

"That's the footage of when Bethany House was destroyed," Austin says.

"Compare the shots," I say. "What do you see?"

"Two smoking holes in the ground," Zera says.

"Look at the original footage," I say. "It's like a bomb crater - the slopes are slightly angled. Then look at the monument site."

"The sides are nearly vertical," Austin says. "Like it was precision - cut by digging drones."

"They can't do that!" Zera says. "Bethany House is like holy ground."

"They didn't touch Bethany House …" I say, "… because that's not the real Bethany House."

"The entire national monument is a fake?" Zera asks.

I turn to Brill. He wants to smile, but he won't allow himself.

"Mom said they'd sometimes run from Capon Springs to Bethany House. The National Monument is fifty kilometers from here. That's a pretty long run."

His face returns to the pretense of senility, like he's forgotten my statement.

"I have something here for your father," Brill says. "I found a whole box of the special light sticks he was always asking about. He always carried light sticks around after he got buried alive in that cave. The ones like this are hard to find. They stopped making them a long time ago because some fool stared at one for so long it made his eyes hurt."

He reaches into his nightstand, brings out the box and hands it to me. I remove one from the box and stick it into my pocket.

"Thank you, Brill. I'll be sure he gets them. Now, can you tell me how to find the real location of Bethany House?"

"There's nothing to tell. The easiest way is to start at the barn and head north. Either you find it or you don't. When you get lost enough times, you learn to find it. Now, you be sure he gets those light sticks."

Brill rolls over and shuts his eyes, so we head for the door.

"If you do find the hole, be mindful of the power connection," he says. "The drones just disconnected our power tap. They didn't seal the main line or even fill our access tunnel like they should have, fool robots."

Thank you, Brill.

******

Brill's granddaughter, Pauline, gives us three rooms for the night at Capon Springs, and then feeds us breakfast in the morning. Her husband, John, gives us a ride in an ancient electric bus part of the way to our starting point. We run from there.

"The barn Brill mentioned has to be the barn that the survivors of Bethany House hid in and named 'The Manger'," I say.

"The barn owned by the Ralph's," Austin agrees. "Do you think they're still alive?"

"I don't know," I say. "They'd be over one hundred."

When we arrive, we see a young woman riding a horse around a large pasture. She rides over to us.

"Hello," she says.

"Hi. Our parents were friends of Bill and Wendy. Does either of them still live here? I ask.

160

"Bill died four years ago, but Wendy is still here," she says. "I help her out around the house and bring her what she needs. My name is Katie."

"Do you think we could speak with her?"

"I'm sure she'd love some company."

She dismounts and walks the horse all the way to the front door.

"Wendy? Some friends are here to see you," she says, then mounts the horse and returns to the pasture.

We find Wendy sitting on a soft, old chair, listening to a novel. One look tells us all that she's now blind – there's only so much that technology can do when you're over a century old.

"Hello?" she says. "Please, come in."

"Hello, Wendy," I say. "My name is Jocie. I'm here with my brother Austin and our friend, Zera."

"Jocie? That name was very popular for girls about twenty years ago. The name Austin - that's a lot less common, and I think you're the first Zera I've ever met. Are your parents with you, Jocie? I would so love to have a visit from Cephas and Martha."

"How did you know who we are?" Austin asks.

"Your father, of course. He said you'd visit."

"Then you know why we're here?" I ask.

"Of course not, dear. Cephas loves a mystery too much to ever spoil how it's going to end. He just said that I should feed you and let you sleep in the barn for a night, like he did."

"We need to visit Bethany House," I say. "Can you tell us how to find it?"

"I did go there one time when it was first being built, to deliver water," she says. "It was about a one hour walk and it was at the top of a hill."

"Anything else?" I ask.

"We had to crawl into some blackberry bushes, because we heard a drone overhead, but it turned out to be a maintenance drone inspecting hatches."

"Hatches?"

"There were access hatches to the big power lines. Brill and Austin thought it was funny that they got access to power without ever breaking open a hatch; so the drones would fly over and think everything was normal."

Find the hatches, and you find Bethany House.

"Wendy? Will you use your com to show us a satellite picture of your house?"

When the screen displays the picture, I zoom out and trace a line straight north with my eyes.

"Look at this area of the picture," I say. "A square kilometer has been altered."

"It looks normal to me," Zera says.

"That's the problem," I say. "Because it's computer-generated, it has a pattern to it. Someone altered the picture, because the Bethany House hole would be visible. See how the trees are spaced? It doesn't have the randomness of nature."

"I don't see it," Austin says.

"Trust me; there's a pattern."

"Now look here," I say. "See these silver dots? They're the hatches that Wendy saw. They're spaced at regular intervals along this line, except in the altered area. Whoever altered the database to remove the crater, also accidentally removed the hatch from the picture. The real Bethany House is somewhere in that kilometer."

It's early; so despite Wendy's insistence that we should take some time in the barn where our parents stayed, we set off in search of Bethany House. The terrain is rough, with some steep, wooded hills, sprinkled with an occasional collection of boulders that look like they were dropped randomly by a giant hand.

"Wendy said she walked to it from her house in an hour when she was sixty years old, so we must be getting close," Zera says.

"Very close," I say. "Look."

Ahead of us is an old cabinet. The door has fallen off and spilled its contents onto the ground: heavy fighting sticks and sets of reactive padding.

There are no signs of trails, as the forest has reclaimed them all. We know the house sat atop a high point, so we head uphill.

"There it is," Austin says.

On top of the hill is a stand of trees that is younger than those surrounding it. If there was once a lawn here, it too has been reclaimed. Inside the stand, we can see the edge of a large hole. Austin keeps walking.

"Stop!" I say. "Someone went to a lot of trouble to erase this spot from public databases. Maybe they did even more."

We stand for a long time, as I carefully scan the trees.

"There are proximity sensors in the trees. They're probably linked to cameras," I say.

"Can we jam them?" Zera asks.

I look to Austin.

"If we do, we wouldn't get our pictures taken, but whoever placed them would be immediately tipped off that we're here," he says.

"All the houses in the Four network had escape tunnels," Zera says. "Let's see if we can find one. Maybe we can access the hole from the inside."

We search for thirty minutes, without success, until I notice a fallen tree that has been torn apart by some large claws.

"An old escape tunnel would make a pretty nice cave for a bear, wouldn't it?" I say.

I start looking for bear scat. What I find is, thankfully, old and it leads us to a tunnel entrance hidden between a boulder and a tree.

"Do you think anyone is at home?" I ask.

"Not at this time of year …" Austin says, '…but a stunner, set on the highest setting wouldn't be a bad idea, just the same."

Zera volunteers to go first, and we follow after a muffled "all clear." The tunnel is mostly clear until we reach a bent metal ladder that leads up. The chamber above is full of debris.

"Check this out," Austin says, and I shine my light on the wall near the ladder.

"It's the initials of all the members of Four who visited," I say.

"There's Dad," he says.

"And Mom," I say, shining my light on a different section.

"They loved this place," Zera says.

"Should we add our initials?" Austin asks.

"We'd need some serious power tools to clear that debris," Zera says, when we're done carving our initials in the dirt.

"And a way to power them," Austin adds.

Power?

"That's it," I say. "Brill said to mind the power connection because the drones hadn't done a proper job. We can break into one of the hatches and get in through the tunnel they dug to steal power. We'll go under all of the proximity sensors in the trees and nobody will know we're here."

The hatch system is easy to find, because the drones keep the area clear of trees as part of their regular maintenance.

"The hatch has an ultrasonic lock on it," Austin says. "The drones just transmit the right frequency combination and the lock will open."

"Can you hack into it?" I ask.

"I doubt it. It could be a single frequency, or dozens, played in a particular order. There's no way to know."

"What if we shoot it?" Zera asks.

"The locking pin would freeze in place," Austin replies.

"Can we trick it?" I ask.

"What do you mean?"

"Well, we're in the middle of nowhere, breaking into a place where nobody would normally want to go," I say. "Security could be very low, just a simple combination of tones that would never be produced accidentally in nature."

"We could program a com to emit ultrasonic tones, starting just outside the range of human hearing, and stepping up at say 10 hertz at a time," Austin says. "It would be like singing a messed up set of scales to get every possible combination of notes."

He pulls a small computer out of his bag and starts setting it up. It only takes him couple of minutes.

"Even using a computer, this could take a while to find the combination," he says.

Half an hour later, we hear the bolt click open.

"It was just a three-tone combination, each tone about one hundred hertz apart," Austin says.

Zera is smiling at us.

"What?" I ask.

"Mom always told me to be nice to the nerds."

"I'm sending the combination to your coms," Austin says. "Let me go in first and make sure it also works from the inside."

He opens the hatch.

"What's that smell? I ask.

"Ozone," Austin replies. "The electrical lines are superconductors, but there's still some static when you're moving that much power."

He climbs down the ladder and closes the hatch. We hear it lock, and then unlock, and he opens the hatch.

"Good," he says. "I wouldn't want to get stuck down here."

We all climb down. The lines are at least thirty meters below ground level, and the closer we get to the bottom, the more I feel like there are ants crawling over my skin. The tunnel must have been dug by a massive drone that was also spraying some sort of insulating plastic on the walls as it went. The electrical line itself is at least a half meter in diameter.

"Everything looks insulated, but don't touch anything," Austin says.

We have a narrow space where we can walk beside the line, but we don't have to go far. Just twenty meters down the line, we find the hole where Four broke through. The power line they used is still there, as is a fried drone that presumably got the job of detaching it. The hole in the casing of the main line has been sprayed with the same plastic that coats the walls.

"A Band-Aid," Austin says.

"A what?" Zera asks.

"It's an expression grandpa James used. Before liquid skin was created, people would cover small wounds with a sticky piece of cotton and let them scab over."

"Gross!"

"True, but it worked. Anyway, the name became synonymous with a temporary patch."

I'm the smallest, so I volunteer to wiggle through the hole, and into Bethany House. The tunnel is only a half meter in diameter, but I'm so happy to be away from the static and ozone smell that I don't mind having to crawl. It's also good that I don't mind small spaces, because after one hundred meters, I see pinpricks of light that are still another one hundred meters away.

My knees are scraped and bruised by the time I reach the lights, where I find that a layer of broken rock has blocked the tunnel. I try pushing at the largest rock, but I can't budge it.

"Jocie?" I hear Austin call from back up the tunnel, and realize that he's crawled in behind me.

"There's a rock that's too heavy for me to move, blocking the end," I say.

"Let me try," he says.

"How will you get past me?"

"Lay flat and I'll crawl over."

I've always thought Austin has bony knees and elbows, but as he crawls over, I realize just how bony they really are.

"Sorry," he says, to my many groans of pain.

He struggles with the rock for several minutes, before he also gives up.

"There's just no leverage," he says. "If I could push with my feet, I bet I could move it, but there's no way I can turn around in here."

"Finally," I say.

"Finally, what?"

"There's finally a time when being short is exactly what's needed. It's going to be tight, but I'm just small enough that I can turn around."

I'm just small enough? That's what Dad said...

What's going on?" Zera asks from up the tunnel.

"Not you, too," I say. "We're already kind of jammed up in here."

Austin crawls backwards, and gets to feel what it's like to have someone crawl over him while he lays on solid rock. When he's out of my way, I start the process of turning myself feet first towards the rock. When I'm halfway there, I get stuck. I try to reverse the process, but I can't go that way either.

"Austin, I need some help. I'm stuck."

He can't help it, he starts to laugh.

"So much for being just small enough," he says. "I would have thought that someone as good at puzzles as you are would have seen that you're too big to fit in that spot."

I shift my left foot a few centimeters to the right.

Just big enough to fit inside a puzzle! That bar isn't just a piece of a time machine; it's also a piece of a puzzle.

"You seemed to know what would fit where, when you were driving the tube car," Austin says.

I'm able to grab my left foot with my right hand and rotate it past my right leg.

But who created the puzzle? It can't be Dad.

"You thought making me and Zera scream was really funny. I could see it on your face."

I slide my right leg forward as far as I can, which shifts my weight and allows me to lower my head slightly.

It has to be me. I create the puzzle.

"It's just a puzzle, Jocie. Figure it out," Austin says.

With my head lower, I can rotate my shoulders.

How am I going to tell Austin? It will crush him.

"Or do you need help from your baby brother?"

My shoulder blade pops free, though not without the loss of some skin, and I fall on my belly with my face towards Austin.

"I do need help from my baby brother," I say. "I need you to do that one special thing you've been waiting your whole life to do.

But it's not what you think it is.

CHAPTER FOURTEEN

The night before Dad and Austin were to take their first big ride on the composite bicycles they'd made, I spent the evening sulking in my room. Dad had taken my suggestion and was using the composite to make new rock climbing equipment for us, but I was still jealous that Dad and Austin were going to be spending the entire day together on their ride.

I heard Dad and Austin enter Dad's office below me; so I slowly opened the grate to listen to them.

"Why do you want ride, using old paper maps?" Austin asked. "Our coms will tell us all the turns to make and anything else we would need to know."

"Family tradition," Dad replied. "It started when I wasn't much older than you are now. You've heard that when I worked for The Corps, the only way for me to break the code created by the Christians was to read the Bible, right? Well, I realized right away that I needed a mode of transportation that didn't have cameras and scanners; so I bought a bicycle from an antique shop and fixed it up. I knew I'd be tracked through my com - so I learned how to read paper maps."

"There must have been some old electric bikes that you could have bought. Why did you go with just pedal power?"

"Looking back at it now, I think God had a hand in that decision," Dad said. "There's just something about exercise and athletics that feels godly, if you ask me."

"Really?" Austin asked.

"Of course. Athletics are all about challenging yourself and finding an inner strength that you didn't know you had. Our Lord lives inside us through the Holy Spirit; so what better way to feel His presence, than by reaching inward for strength?"

Austin paused for a minute; then asked exactly the question I was thinking.

"You were an atheist when you first started cycling. Why would cycling have felt godly to you back then?"

"It didn't at the start, but now I think it was the first, small step towards God – and all it took was complete exhaustion, and two days in bed to recover."

"It sounds like there's a story in there," Austin said.

Dad said nothing for a while, presumably he was deciding whether or not to tell the story.

"Locating old bibles anonymously was very difficult," Dad began. "Anything you did with a com would be tracked, so I had no choice but to research in old paper libraries and talk to people. I heard a rumor about an elderly lady in rural Maine, who was said to have an old family bible, but when I contacted her, she was too scared to meet with me at her house. She

173

suggested that we meet in a place called "Oh my god" corner on a particular road in two hours, and warned me not to be late."

"How could any place have had God's name in it back then?" Austin asked. "All religious references had been banned."

"It couldn't - at least as far as any map was concerned," Dad replied. "All I had was the name of a road, and no clue as to where to stop to find this lady."

"What did you do?"

"I rode - hard. I thought the more ground I covered, the better chance I had in finding the right spot before she left. It turned out, the road was mostly uphill, and there was wind and rain in my face the entire time. I learned a valuable lesson about mercy.

"Mercy?" Austin asked.

"Hills, wind, and rain have no mercy, and neither does time," Dad replied. "I climbed kilometer after merciless kilometer, watching the seconds tick away on my chance at getting that bible. It was beyond exhausting. It was also the first time that a new idea popped into my atheistic head. After the first hour, the thought occurred to me that muscles and sinew and bones weren't even turning the cranks anymore. It felt like the work was being done by something much deeper ... something beyond my physical body."

Dad paused, and it sounded like Austin had been holding his breath during the story, as he inhaled deeply.

"I know what scientists would say," Dad continued. "They'd say the pain caused my body to release endorphins and that I found what was known as runners' high - but that's not what it felt like to me. To me, it felt like God created hills and wind and time as a way to remind us that the only true source of mercy is Him; so that when we reach the end of ourselves, amid all that mercilessness we'll finally find that He was waiting inside us the entire time … waiting for us to finally look inward for Him."

"What happened next?" Austin asked.

"I found the strength to keep pushing forward, until I turned a corner and hit a spot where the trees disappear and you're looking out across the Carrabassett Valley. A non-believer might miss it, but anyone with even the tiniest connection to the Holy Spirit can't help but say "Oh my god" when they look out across the wonder of His creation. I hit the brakes and just stood there in the rain."

Dad went silent. He has a remarkable capacity for reliving the emotions of an experience, and I'm sure he was reliving that moment as he stood in the rain. Austin shifted his weight in his chair, and Dad continued with the story.

"A few minutes later, a woman came out of the woods. She said: 'This bible has been in my family for eight generations. I don't want to give it to you. I just know that I need to.'"

"I only said one word to her: 'Why?'"

"She said: 'I've been watching you on the public cameras along the road. I'm old enough to remember sports, and I saw something today that I haven't seen in a very long time. Your legs were done thirty kilometers ago. By all rights, you should have fallen off that bike, unable to move another centimeter up the hill - but I was watching your eyes, and I could see something burning inside of you that just would not give up. You need this book, young man. You need to understand what's burning inside of you.'"

"She disappeared back into the trees and I never saw her again, in person."

Austin said nothing at first, but I desperately want him to ask Dad the next, obvious question. After that experience, how could Dad use the bible he'd obtained to break the Christian code and kill so many?"

"What do you mean, you never saw her again *in person?*" Austin asked.

"After I used her bible to break the last Christian code, I saw her picture in the case files. The Corps picked her up, along with most of her relatives. Without intending to, I had used her family bible to end her family. I recorded their deaths in the bible, and buried it at 'Oh my god' corner as a reminder that I, as much as anyone, need God's mercy."

"Dad?" Austin asked. "You can solve any puzzle that anyone can put in front of you. Why couldn't you see that God was working on your heart through that experience?"

"I don't know," Dad said. "What I do know is that, even after that ride and what the lady said to me, I was still in a place of darkness. I think perhaps God knew that I couldn't come out of the darkness all at once, because seeing His light all at once would have been too bright for me."

******

I turn myself over and brace myself against the tunnel walls. Then, using the strength of my legs, I push the rock out of the way and listen to it crash to the bottom of the pit.

I ease myself over the edge and find that we're about thirty meters below the surface; so the bottom of the pit is another thirty meters or so down. It's not a sheer drop, and I know that I can climb down from here, but Austin and Zera probably shouldn't try it.

There's a ledge big enough for me to sit on just ten meters away, and I climb to it. Austin's head pokes out of the old tunnel.

"Now what?" he asks.

"Now, we think," I say.

I look up at the edge of the teardrop-shaped hole. We're not far from the pointed end. Around the perimeter, at about the same height of the ledge where I'm sitting, I can see where each of the three escape tunnels used to be.

If Albert shaped the explosion to protect something, it should be close to the pointed end.

"What's she doing?" I hear Zera's muffled voice ask.

Bethany House was collapsed into some old mine tunnels. How did he get down into them to place his explosives? An air shaft?

"Thinking," Austin replies.

No, it must have been an elevator shaft, which connected to various side shafts. The time travel arena must be hidden in a side shaft.

I look to the bottom of the pit. I can see what looks like a rusted metal cable, attached to some twisted metal that must have once been a small elevator.

They were so wasteful back then. They could have recycled all of that metal.

Next to the elevator cage, there's a large slab of old concrete, sitting at a slight angle.

"Ouch! What are you doing?" Austin asks.

Albert used the elevator shaft as the point of the tear drop. So where is the side shaft?

Zera's head appears. She crawled over Austin and is now lying on his back.

He needed to hide the side shaft too, so that no federal drones would find it when they investigated the explosions. How did he fill the side shaft?

"The air was getting thick back there," Zera says.

This is Albert. He would have used an explosion to cover up the side shaft. What signs would an explosion leave behind?

I scan the rocks for burn marks, and find none. Most of the wall face is solid dirt, but one spot looks like loose sand and rubble.

Bingo.

It's only thirty meters along the wall and another ten meters down from my ledge; so I start climbing to the spot.

"Where are you going?" Austin asks.

"To find a time machine."

"Should we come too?" Austin asks.

"Speak for yourself," Zera says. "I'm pretty comfy right here."

"Stay there," I say. "I only have a theory."

I reach the spot and start to dig. It goes quickly because the rocks are all hand-sized and smaller; and because I don't have to worry about where to put material, it all falls to the bottom of the pit. After just a half a meter, my hand pokes through into empty space. Soon I have a space big enough to wiggle through.

There's enough light coming in through the hole that I can see I'm inside a tunnel that was dug by machines, rather than the hand-dug tunnels built by Four to create Bethany House. Unfortunately, the light doesn't show me much beyond about ten meters; so I don't dare explore very far. I turn to wiggle back through the hole and retrieve the flashlight I left in my pack, when I remember the old light stick that I got from Brill.

Dad would be proud.

I retrieve it from my pocket and snap it to start the chemicals mixing. It gives off a faint purple light.

Brill said these things were banned because people burned their eyes. It's so faint you'd have to stare at it for hours.

Once my eyes have adapted, even the faint light is enough to let me walk around slowly, but safely. I don't have to wander very far, because the tunnel is only about twenty meters long. Along the walls, I can see the remains of wooden shelves that once held emergency supplies of canned food and water. The wood rotted away long ago, and most of the contents are now in a jumble on the floor, except for a few dozen cans that are still neatly stacked.

Near the end of the tunnel, I can see a pile of composite metal pieces in a heap.

Look away. You MUST NOT look at them.

As I turn, the little bit of sunlight behind me goes dark. Austin is standing in front of the hole as he digs it bigger for himself. When he gets inside, he snaps on a flashlight, blinding me.

"How did you get over here?" I ask.

"I may not be at your level, but I did learn a few things about rock climbing from Dad. Besides, I was digging through your pack and found your rope and some pitons; so I installed a quick safety rope for Zera."

The sunlight is again blocked, as Zera joins us.

"Well?" she asks.

"The arena is back there," I say. "Go look for yourself."

"Albert's blast must have really shaken this place," Austin says, when he reaches the pile. "This is definitely our composite, but the cage has been reduced to pieces."

He comes back with a piece in his hands. I look away.

"Dad and I used some specialized equipment to weld the bicycle frames," he says. "Jocie, I don't know if I can fix this."

"You don't have to fix it, Austin. It was never welded together."

"Then how …"

"It's a puzzle, Austin. The cage is a very complex, three-dimensional puzzle."

******

We return to Wendy's house feeling somewhat dejected. Wendy has one extra bed in the house, and I offer it to Zera, while Austin and I spread hay on the barn floor. Austin thought we should sleep in the hidden basement as a "family tradition," but Wendy convinced him that it's too stuffy and full of mice.

When I roll over for the tenth time, Austin speaks.

"It's a long list, isn't it?" he asks.

"List?"

"The list forming in your head of all the things that we need to do. We get it from Mom. I have one, too."

"Tell me your list," I say.

"Well, we can salvage enough electrical and computer cables from the ruins of Bethany House to power and control a time machine; so at least that's not an issue. We'll need several computers to run the whole thing, but since it was last done on twenty-year-old computers, I guess we can find some old ones somewhere."

Technical problems. Dad said members of Four always obsessed over technical problems.

"Software will be an issue," Austin continues. "None of us have the skill to write the necessary software from scratch; so we'll need to recruit someone for that…"

Dad says whenever technical problems come up, the first thing to do is to clear your mind through prayer.

"The time travel arena would be the next step. How on earth are we going to get the materials we need? Carbon fiber cloth, iron, and aluminum are all pretty easy, but where will we get titanium, chromium, molybdenum, and vanadium?"

Lord, I need help … and I'm not talking about finding vanadium.

"I went through the tools here in the barn and found a narrow-spectrum parabolic fiber laser that Bill must have used for cutting metal. I can adjust the beam to melt everything …"

Lord, you've even made time itself into a beautiful, perfect puzzle. Thank you for showing me how some of the pieces fit together.

"Zera's right about the crystals, too. Where are we going to find more of those?"

It's going to crush him.

"Still, it will all be worth it," Austin says. "I can't wait to travel through time."

Thank you, too, Lord, for the strength for what I have to do now.

"Austin?" I say. "I have a different list of things in my head, compared to yours. My list has just three things on it."

"Okay, what are they?"

"Pray, think, act on what I've been called upon to do."

"What you've been called upon to do? You've been called to help me."

"We've always thought that, because we were allowed to think it. When Mr. Albert saw your initials on that piece of the arena, that's what he thought. As he told people, and the rumors spread, everyone believed it - even Mom."

"But not Dad," Austin says.

"That's right. Dad suspected the first time he saw that piece."

"Suspected what?"

I turn on my flashlight and retrieve the hook-shaped piece from Austin's pack. I stand it on its end.

"This is the piece of the puzzle that held it all together. When Albert pulled it out, the puzzle fell apart. It's also the tallest point in the cage. Squish yourself down so you can sit inside a cage this small."

He squats, he sits cross-legged, he curls up in a ball ... but no matter what he tries, he's too tall to fit under the hook. I thought he'd get mad, or that maybe he'd even cry, but instead he looks ... lost.

His entire life was built around somehow following Dad's footsteps. I have to give him a new purpose.

"Austin?" I say.

"He knew all along?" Austin asks. "Why didn't he tell us? Why didn't he prepare us?"

"Nobody understands the need to let a timeline play out naturally more than Dad, but he did prepare us in the ways that he could, Austin. He taught you how to make the materials we're going to need. He taught me how to climb out of a hole. In his own way, he taught us both how to fight … but more than any of those things, he taught us how to love each other, and to work together as a team."

Austin looks up at me from the floor.

"I need you, baby brother," I say. "More than any other time in my life, I need you. I need your brains; I need your strength; and most of all … I need your love."

He stands and hugs me, with his head on top of mine.

"You'll always have that, shorty."

We lie back down in the hay.

"I never really thought about what it must be like to be Mom," Austin says. "I mean, Dad has all these things in his head, and he never tells her what's going to happen. How do either of them live with it?"

"Faith, I suppose," I reply.

"When Mom and Dad were hiding in the hole under this barn, do you suppose Dad already knew he'd someday be captured and tortured?" Austin asks. "Did he somehow know that he'd survive it? Or did he just know that God would be with him - no matter what came?"

"I like to think it was the latter," I say. "I like to think that when everything around him was dark, Dad could already see a guiding light."

"In his case, it was probably a guiding light stick," Austin says, with a chuckle.

"Great idea," I say. "This barn really is a part of our family history. Let's celebrate the connection to Mom and Dad with a light stick."

I find the box in my pack, remove a stick, and bend it.

"The chemicals must have decayed over time," Austin says. "It barely throws any light."

I look around the barn.

Of course.

"It's throwing a ton of light," I say, and snap another. "We just can't see it."

Somebody burned their eyes because these light sticks give off ultra violet light.

I walk to the barn wall, where I can see something glowing.

"There's something written on this wall that reacts to UV light," I say.

I hold the light stick higher and follow along, one letter at a time.

"The puzzle points the way," I read aloud.

"Jocie?" Austin says. "It's not just the wall that's glowing. Look up."

Above my head, there are glowing spots in the roof joists.

"Give me one of the light sticks. I think I can reach them from the hayloft," Austin says, and begins to climb a ladder someone created by nailing boards to the wall studs.

"What does it say?" I ask.

"No words," he says. "It just speaks for itself."

"What do you mean?"

"The rest are made out of wood, but this joist is metal."

"So?"

"According to the markings, it's made out of titanium, chromium, molybdenum, and vanadium - in the exact ratios that I need to make the composite. Did Dad place it here for us?"

I climb up next to him and look at the metal. Where the materials are stamped, I find a date.

"This joist has been here since the barn was built, almost two hundred years ago," I say.

"Two hundred years? Who built a joist like this two hundred years ago?"

I did.

CHAPTER FIFTEEN

"Daddy? Can I leave the house today?"

I was sixteen at the time. Mom and Dad had left the house several times, but Austin and I were under house arrest.

"I hope so," he replied. "Somebody has hacked the government computers and has been tracking our family's movements. Mom has almost finished writing the code she needs to shut it down."

"Why is it okay for the government to track us, but not someone else?"

"It's not ..." he said, "... but the government has been tracking us for two hundred years; so people just put up with it. Luckily, we're pretty good at fooling the government. Besides, there's a big difference between a government that's tracking everyone in the country and someone who is specifically tracking just our family."

"Ready for another test walk?" Mom asked. "Jocie, Dad and I are going to walk around the block, clockwise. I need you and

Austin to wait for five minutes, and then follow us. Look at cameras and up into the sky, if you hear drones."

Austin and I walked slowly, enjoying the fresh air. There were eight visible cameras along the route and five that were hidden, plus a high level drone. When we got back, Mom and Dad were at a screen.

"Our faces have been recorded too many times," Mom said. "The system is still fifty percent sure it was us and thirty percent sure it was Austin."

"What about me?" I asked.

"There isn't enough sample size of your features to make the match; so I was able to erase you from the system."

The "success" made me mad, as I once again felt second rate, but Dad smiled.

"Perfect," he said.

******

"Let me get this straight," Zera says, over the breakfast table the next morning. "One of the two-hundred-year-old roof joists just *happens* to have the right mixture of metals to make the arena we need?"

"Arenas," Austin corrects. "I need to make two."

"And it was never the boy wonder who was going. It was always Jocie," Zera says.

"That's right," I say.

"And your father has known about all of this for years, but instead of writing some of it down, he wrote 'The puzzle leads the way' in invisible ink on a barn wall?"

She looks at me and Austin, and we shrug.

"Your family is seriously messed up."

"According to Uncle Cameron, your mom is quite the piece of work …" I say, "… and you haven't told us anything about your dad."

"*You* don't want to hear about him," Zera says.

"I'm sorry," I say.

"Yeah, me too," she replies.

We finish breakfast in silence and head for the barn. A replacement joist is already sitting in the barn, and Austin starts rigging a lift drone to help us get it into place before we remove the one made of metal. While he works, Zera turns on a screen she found in one of the stalls and watches the news.

"Jocie! Come watch this," she calls. Austin follows me.

When we get there, Zera orders the news piece to replay from the beginning.

"Tyrone Bauer, CEO of Chi-One Corporation, announced a recent attack on a facility owned by the space and satellite division of his company," the announcer says. "Surveillance video shows a group of assailants, dressed in black, cutting the fence of the remote Australian facility and engaging in a gun battle that left eight security guards stunned before a larger force arrived to repel the attack."

"That's my Mom!" Zera says, and points at the security footage. "I'd know her anywhere."

In the footage, Zip can be seen shooting a security guard.

He had no clue she was there. She could have disabled him silently, but she gave away her position on purpose.

"Computer, give us the live satellite footage of this facility on the same time index as the attack we just saw," I say.

"Hey!" Zera says. "You'll miss the part where Mom takes out two guards at once."

The satellite footage appears on the screen, zoomed to the point where we can see a team of eight people cutting the fence.

"Zoom out to show the entire facility and one hundred meters outside the fence," I say.

When Zip shoots the guard, we watch as multiple security teams from all over the facility run to repulse the attack. Then two people in black emerge from the bush on the opposite side of the facility, cut the fence, and break into the building.

Zip's team keeps the guards pinned down for over five minutes. She had superior cover and clearly better marksmen, but never advanced when she had obvious opportunities. When the two who entered on the opposite side exit the building, Zip's team withdraws.

"Computer, maximum zoom on the two people who entered the building on the north side," I say.

"That's Aunt Cindi and Uncle Cameron," Austin says.

"Why are they attacking known Christians?" Zera asks.

"Computer, what's made at this facility?" I ask.

"Unknown," the computer replies.

Unknown? Since when is anything unknown to the government?

"Computer, zoom in on the loading dock," I say.

There are pallets of long metal rods, each about five meters long. In all, there are several metric tons of metal sitting on the dock.

"Computer, show us the loading dock at nine o'clock the next morning."

The metal rods are still there.

"Computer, given the reflective qualities of the metal bars visible in the image, what metals are they most likely to be?"

"Titanium, chromium, molybdenum, vanadium."

******

"Do you think Dad is mad at me for giving Five-X the composite formula?" Austin asks, as he rigs the last pulley.

The lift drone wasn't strong enough to get the old wooden joist off the ground; so Austin and Zera are going to assist it with ropes, while I wait up in the rafters to swing it into position.

"Whatever Tyrone and Five-X are doing, I doubt that you made Dad's efforts to stop it any easier," I reply, "but you know Dad. He doesn't stay mad at anyone. He just moves on and tries to figure out what's going to happen next."

"They could make thousands of shielded drones with our material," he says. "It would give them a big advantage over the Temple Guard."

The drone starts to lift, and Austin and Zera add their efforts with the ropes and pulleys.

"The Chi-One company has a separate division for drones," I say. "That facility is part of their space and satellite division. What uses would the composite have in space?"

"Plenty," Austin says, between grunts as he lifts. "It would make a great heat shield, for one."

"Why would they need a heat shield?" I ask.

"Space is cold, but there's no atmosphere to block the sun's energy; so things in space will heat up."

"Hold science class later," Zera says. "He doesn't lift as hard when he's talking."

Although the drone sounds strained to its limit, the joist reaches the correct height, and I swing it into place, and secure it temporarily. Austin reprogrammed a smaller drone that was originally designed to maintain the fences around the horse pasture to finish the job, and it now zips around with nails and screws. When it's done, it will cut up the metal joist, while the bigger lift drone eases the pieces to the floor.

The lifting was hard work, and Zera removes her jacket, revealing the tattoo on her upper arm again - a cross with black lines coming out of it.

Of course. Why didn't I see it before?

"Your father was a cult hunter," I say. "That's what your tattoo means, doesn't it? He was a cult hunter who became a Christian - just like Daniel."

"Why didn't you tell us?" Austin asks.

"It's just easier to pretend to be one of The Washed," Zera says.

"You *are* one of The Washed," I reply.

"No, I'm not. Not really. It may be recessive, but I carry 'The Mark of the Beast' gene."

"That doesn't matter to us; you know that, right?" I ask.

"You say that, Jocie, but the faces and the noises you make, whenever you see the dark lines on someone's face, make me think you feel otherwise. You immediately judge those black lines whenever you see them."

"I don't mean to sound like I'm judging. It's just whenever I see someone who was a cult hunter, I think of what happened to Dad inside the mountain."

"Your father was a cult hunter too, Jocie. I'm told that Cephas is still credited with the longest kill list in The Corps. Do you judge him on that?"

"No."

"Of course not. You judge your father on what's in his heart. Allow me to do the same for mine."

******

Austin and Zera spend the rest of the day transforming the barn into a mini production facility, while I start making drawings.

"What are you doing?" Austin asks.

"Designing an arena cage for you to build."

"*You* create the puzzle? I figured it was Dad."

"Dad's not here; so unless you want the job, it must be me."

"That's why you wouldn't look at the pieces that are under Bethany House," he says. "You were afraid if you saw them before you create them, you'd cause a paradox."

I can't help myself. I laugh out loud.

"Zera's right," I say. "Our family is messed up. I'm sure other families talk about time paradoxes for fun, but how many do you know that actually worry about creating one?"

"Nobody loves messed up people more than God," Austin replies.

"Good … because here's another product of a messed up, Paulson brain."

I hand him a drawing of a long, flat piece of metal with cuts out of it.

"Can you create this with the composite?" I ask.

"You need the precision on the cuts to be down to the millimeter?" he asks.

"If this is going to be a Paulson family time travel device, it might as well be one that only we can put back together."

******

While Austin fiddles with the equipment in the barn, I find Zera.

"Care for a run in the hills with me?" I ask.

"I'm not into running, like you guys are."

"What if I said you should bring a stun gun with you?"

"I'd say that's my kind of a run," she replies.

We tell Austin and Wendy not to expect us back until dark, and then set off. The easiest way to our destination would be to run along the hover bus line, but I don't want to risk being seen. Instead, we take to the woods and use various game trails.

"Where are we going?" Zera asks, when we reach the edge of the Cacapon River.

I start to wade across and she follows.

"All houses in the Four network had back-up locations. The back-up for Bethany House was an abandoned place called Timber Ridge Camp, which is just through those trees. I'm hoping we'll find some old computers there that we can use to control the time machine."

We're just twenty meters into the woods, when something catches my eye. I tap Zera on the shoulder and we both instinctively get low. Forty meters in front of us, someone is standing silently behind a tree.

"Is it a trap?" Zera whispers.

"They're wearing awfully bright colors for someone setting a trap," I say.

Without warning, the person yells, "Ready or not, here I come!" and starts stalking in the other direction.

"It's nice of them to warn us," Zera says.

"It's not a trap," I say. "It's an ancient children's game called 'Hide and Seek.'"

"I thought you said this place is abandoned."

We hear a scream, followed by giggling and running. None of them are coming our way; so we move off to the right until we can see a broad lawn and some buildings. There seem to be kids everywhere. Most of them are playing games, but one group of older kids is reading from bibles as they're taught a lesson by an adult.

"It's a Christian summer camp," I say.

"My summer camp involved obstacle courses and target practice," Zera says.

"Have you noticed anything about the kids?" I ask.

"Just that they're all happy."

"Look at their faces," I say.

"Some are washed, and some are marked," she concludes.

"And it doesn't make any difference to them; so, if nothing else, at least this place isn't part of Five-X."

"That's great, but it doesn't tell us where to look for an old Four back-up house."

I look around. Every building I can see has been perfectly restored on the outside but with indications of modernization. There's no way a building could have been gutted, without finding a hidden entrance.

"It will be an old building that hasn't been restored," I say. "The closer it is to the woods and the river, the better."

We continue to walk around the perimeter, until we find an old shack that's locked with an ancient padlock. It has a window on each side, but they've been covered with paint so we can't see what's inside. We're about to slip back into the woods, when we hear a voice from behind us.

"Shouldn't you girls be in a bible study right now?" the woman's voice asks.

We turn around.

"Yes, ma'am," I say. "We're sorry."

She smiles.

"No harm done. Off you go."

Zera and I sit with the group of older kids who are on the lawn listening to an older man as he reads from the bible. He acknowledges our arrival, but continues to teach.

"You have been permitted to understand the secrets of the Kingdom of Heaven, but others have not. To those who are open to my teaching, more understanding will be given, and they will have an abundance of knowledge. But to those who are not listening, even what they have will be taken away from them. That is why I tell these stories, because people see what I do, but they don't really hear, and they don't understand."

He pauses for effect.

"Cephas Paulson was hidden in a bush when our Lord Jesus spoke those words to His disciples, but then the Lord turned and looked directly at Cephas, and said: 'But blessed are your eyes, because they see; and your ears, because they hear. I assure you, many prophets and godly people have longed to see and hear what you have seen and heard, but they could not.'"

He looks around at the faces in front of him.

"In all the years since he came back to this time, Cephas has never said a word about it - other than that it happened. Why not?"

None of the kids volunteer to answer the question.

"Come on," the man coaxes. "The Lord Himself told Cephas Paulson that his eyes and ears are blessed! Why hasn't he claimed the honor that is due to him? Why is Cephas Paulson not standing in the pulpit of all pulpits so we can adore him?"

The group remains silent.

"Because it wasn't a personal blessing," I say.

The group turns to look, and a broad smile crosses the man's face.

"What do you mean?" he asks.

"The Lord may have been looking Cephas in the eyes at the time, but Cephas knew that the blessing is meant for everyone who believes in Jesus. All of our eyes and ears are blessed, because we've all opened our hearts to Him," I say.

"Hallelujah!" the man says. "The Lord may have chosen to meet Cephas when He was here on earth, but He's chosen to love all of us the same. Cephas has *never* claimed to have favor with God, and he has *never* claimed that The Washed or anyone else has favor with God. I ask you all to walk with the Lord with that same spirit of humility. Look at your brothers and sisters in Christ the way Christ sees them. Their sins are washed with His blood, and they are flawless."

I don't know what this place is, but it sounds and feels like home.

CHAPTER SIXTEEN

One of the best things about playing "The mirror game," and giving the glory to God for all that you see, is that you might catch a glimpse of yourself the way He sees you: "flawless." The danger is that we're human beings, and we see flaws. I've never much liked my freckles, or the shape of my nose, but those aren't particularly dangerous thoughts. The dangerous thoughts come when you spend time staring into your own eyes.

"When I was your age, I avoided looking into my eyes," Dad said, standing in the doorway.

I hadn't heard him come up the stairs and it startled me when he spoke.

"I'm glad you find it easier than I did," he continued.

"Why did you avoid your eyes?" I asked.

"Fear, mostly. I first started looking in the mirror each morning to convince myself that I was nothing more than a collection of cells. Of course, that all changed when I met Jesus."

"What do you see when you look into your eyes now?" I asked.

"A collection of cells."

My head involuntarily moved back a centimeter.

"It's still just a body, Jocie," he said. "I'll leave looking at souls in the hands of the one who created them."

"Do you ever feel afraid when you look into your eyes now?" I asked.

"A little," he said. "When you become a Christian, you have to accept the fact that the Holy Spirit dwells within you. At the same time, I know I'm as sinful as any man. So even though I know that I'm forgiven, looking into my eyes reminds me that the Holy Spirit knows my every thought. I guess I'm just afraid that I'll disappoint Him."

"You offered yourself as a sacrifice in His name," I said. "If *you're* afraid of disappointing Him, what chance do the rest of us have?"

"The Lord doesn't keep score, Jocie. In fact, it's often those who have done great works for Him who have ended up losing sight of their humility. King David comes to mind."

I sat and thought for a moment. I'd never thought of humility as being an issue for me, given how Austin was treated as a superstar in the Christian community. I glanced at the mirror and the first thing that caught my eye was my skin. The fact that it was free of the scars and sores of The Marked reminded me that I was not humble in my judgment of them.

"Cultivate humility, Jocie," Dad said. "The day may come when humility is what truly marks us as children of God."

******

The bible study class is dismissed.

"Young ladies, may I speak to you for a moment?"

He waits for the rest of the group to leave.

"Everyone is welcome here, and we have a substantial financial endowment fund to feed whoever comes our way, but we still do require everyone to make a reservation so we can plan for meals and beds," he says.

"We weren't planning on staying for a meal," I say. "We're staying nearby for a few days and just walked in. We were about to go."

"Please don't go. We always plan for a few extra meals, and I'd love to hear more about you and your knowledge of the bible. You're the first student all summer to understand what I was saying with respect to Cephas and humility."

"I guess we could stay a little while longer," I say.

"My name is Graham," he says, and extends his hand.

"I'm Jocelyn, and this is Zera," I say. "We'd heard that this place was abandoned. I guess we heard wrong."

"It was abandoned, until it was purchased about fifteen years ago and fully restored by the camp director, William McLeod. Now, every summer he opens this wonderful place so that children who love the Lord can have a week of play and prayer."

"William McLeod?" I ask. "The cousin of Martha McLeod Paulson?"

"You know both the bible *and* modern Christian history," Graham says. "Yes, our William is the former member of Four, and relative of the Paulsons."

If tube stations were being watched, someone could easily be watching my cousin.

I change course and head for the nearest building with a porch, out of the sight of high level drones.

"The museum is closed right now," Graham says. "The younger kids would never leave if we didn't lock the doors."

"Museum?" Zera asks. "What kind of museum?"

"It's a Four museum," he says.

Zera and I exchange a look.

"Is there any way we could have just a short look around?" I ask.

"I'd love to give you a tour, but William is the only one who can open the door."

An old brass bell starts to ring.

"It's time for dinner," Graham says. "William will be there. You can ask him yourself, if you like. The only rules we have for meals are that you thank the Lord for the food and don't wear a com to the table."

He points the way to the dining hall; then strides off.

"Everyone's at dinner. Let's just break in," Zera says.

"It may look like an ancient building …" I say, "…but William was part of Four. It will have excellent security."

I take a computer pad out of my pack.

"On the other hand, I'm half McLeod," I say, and set to work.

"There are motion sensors on every door and window," I say, after a minute. "I can disable them, but there's nothing I can do about the fact that the door still has its original metal lock that requires voice command from William."

"We could kick it in," she replies.

I have a memory of Dad from when I was seven years old. He told me that not all problems have technological solutions. I look at the building. The cosmetic features were all updated when William restored the place, but he kept the original centuries-old frame, including the original door and doorframe.

The doorframe has shrunk and warped, there's nearly a half centimeter gap.

The siding is carbon fiber, which is just over a millimeter thick. There is a small piece above the door that is loose.

"Boost me up," I say to Zera.

With a few hard pulls, the piece comes off. I slide the piece of siding into the gap and push down hard when I reach the lock. The latch slides back and the door swings open.

"I'm going to have to remember that," Zera says.

We let ourselves in and close the door behind us.

The first room of the museum is set up to look like a typical bedroom in a Four safe house. The walls are covered with fake dirt and there are informational screens describing how the rooms were dug by hand. The next room is a replica of the Bethany House command center, which I find creepy because there are holograms of the people who used to live there, including my parents.

A hologram of Mom is sitting at a workstation, when a Dad hologram enters. I expect to see her smile, but she and all of the other holograms look angry that Dad is even in the room. He starts asking her questions and she takes out a knife, and looks like she's going to throw it at him.

"This is crazy," I say. "This couldn't have really happened!"

Dad puts his arms out into the shape of a cross, and says he would rather die as a Christian than become whatever Mom is.

"Can you believe this garbage?" I ask.

The scene ends when a woman, who can only be Amelia, yells "I forgive you!" and begs for Dad's life.

Zera puts her hand on my shoulder.

"Jocie?" she says. "It happened, and it wasn't the first or the last time your dad was threatened by Four. When my mom was leader of the Four council, she sentenced your dad to death."

I stand there, trying to wrap my brain around watching Mom hold Dad at knifepoint.

"I think I know how you feel," Zera says. "There's no hologram of it, but I've seen the pictures of the cult hunter massacre my mom lead at McIntosh."

"Forget it," I say. "What's important is that I think these old computers are actually functional. We're going to need to borrow some of them."

The next room is just as creepy for me as the Bethany command center. It's a replica of the arena cave where Dad, and two other people, became the first human time travelers. There's a metal arena and a ball-like structure above it that must represent the time machine.

Off to one side, in a separate exhibit, is a tiny metal cage with a small package wrapped in brown paper under it and a tiny version of the time machine above it. The cage and the machine don't look like replicas. You can see where the time machine was scratched and dented, then pulled back into its original shape. The small cage, on the other hand, looks pristine.

We hear the lock being turned at the main entrance, so Zera and I hide behind the replica of the time machine controls.

One set of feet walks slowly through the other rooms, then stops in the doorway of the area where we're hiding.

"You should have come to dinner," a man's voice says. "You're missing some excellent fried chicken. You also missed that there are motion sensors in the ceiling that run on an independent system."

Zera uses hand signals to indicate we should attack from two directions, but I shake my head, then stand up. Zera follows.

"This is the most popular room in the museum," he says from the shadows across the room. "Kids stand in line for hours to take their turn in the cage and pretend to travel through time. Let me show you."

He uses him com to activate the simulation. The lights dim and the lasers on the time machine replica put on a show, as they map the exact location of the cage. Then the machine starts to hum, like it's drawing massive amounts of power, followed by a flash of light that's much brighter than I expected, and all goes dark.

"You're now alone, in a dark cave, over two thousand years in the past," a recorded voice says. "Do you have faith enough to find your way out?"

When the lights return to normal, the man has used the simulation as a distraction to move from the shadows and is standing with a stun gun pointed at us.

"That's pretty sloppy work, considering who your parents are," my cousin William says, and lowers the gun.

Zera and I both bring our hands up from where they were hidden behind the exhibit to reveal our own guns.

"If you're here to interview for jobs as camp counselors, you're hired," he says.

"Maybe next summer," I say, and he smiles.

"I suppose you have a hundred questions," he says.

"I do, but you're better off if I don't ask them."

I start to wander around the room.

These computers are running the original time machine software that was stolen in Israel, and the exhibit of the tiny arena cage and the small time machine aren't replicas. They're the real deal. If Four stole a time machine as big as the replica in the ceiling, but only used enough of the components to build that little thing in the corner ... where are the rest of the components?

When I reach the small cage in the corner, I notice for the first time that there's a piece of white paper sitting on top of the replica of the package that Dad sent with Grandpa's name on it. William starts to show Zera around the control room, so I slip the paper out of the cage and into my pocket.

I follow them into the control room simulation and a different hologram program begins. This time it's a scene of Bethany House shutting down as they realize the Four Network is under attack.

"This is a very detailed replica," I say. "Who built it?"

"It was a team effort," William replies. "Most of the Bethany House staff had a hand in it, including your parents."

"What parts did they work on?"

"Your mom did a lot of the programming. Your Dad, of course, filled in many of the finer details."

"Which work station did Dad use?" I ask.

"He was best known for taking over Amelia's station, when everyone thought she was dead from the plague," William says, and points.

When I sit at the station, the hologram program cuts out, and a new one begins.

"What is this?" William asks. "It's not part of the museum exhibit."

A hologram of Dad stands in front of us, holding a baby. Various members of my family walk in and out of the scene, talking to Dad and to each other.

"I remember that day…" Williams says, "…but it didn't happen at Bethany House. This is the day you were christened in Ogallala. That's you he's holding, Jocie."

Holograms of William, Albert, and Uncle James are talking to each other, when Dad walks to them. He looks Albert in the eyes and whispers something, which makes Albert smile, but not another word passes between them. Dad walks away and the program ends.

"Do you remember what Dad said to Albert?" I ask.

"I didn't know he said anything."

I sit at the station and the hologram starts again from the beginning. This time I stand in the same spot as the Albert hologram. When he reaches that spot, there's no mistaking the two words Dad spoke to Albert.

"The tombstone."

CHAPTER SEVENTEEN

"Why the upset look?" Dad asked me. "It's a beautiful day, and we're at the park together."

I was four years old, and Dad and I were playing at the "old-fashioned" park that had real grass and rose bushes.

"In a couple of minutes, that man is going to tell that woman that he doesn't like her anymore, and she's going to be sad," I said.

"Are you sure? They're holding hands."

"I'm sure," I said. "He doesn't even want to hold her hand, but she took his hand and now he doesn't know what to do."

The man shook his hand loose, and the couple sat on a bench.

"See how he won't look at her and how his hands are fidgeting?" I said.

The man turned to the woman and said something.

"That could mean a lot of things," Daddy said.

The woman slapped the man across the face.

"She acted mad, but she's mostly sad," I said. "She's going to be okay in a couple of days, though."

"How do you know that?" Dad asked.

"The way she walks."

I jumped onto the ancient slide and slid to the bottom.

"Daddy? Sometimes it's not fun to know things before they happen. What do you do when you know something sad is going to happen?"

Daddy looked up at the mountains and got a serious look on his face.

"I've never worried much about the things I know are going to happen," he said. "I worry most when I don't know what's going to happen."

"That's silly," I said. "You always know what's going to happen."

Daddy got that look of bottomless sadness.

"How I wish that was true," he said.

******

We talk with William for the next hour, while Zera and I devour fried chicken. After Bethany House was destroyed, William and Albert came to Timber Ridge Camp to establish a new Four safe house, and William fell in love with the place. Mom and Dad secretly gave him the money to buy and restore it, then to run it as a church camp. I'm disappointed to learn that neither Mom nor Dad have ever visited publicly to advertise the place. I suppose Dad knew he'd one day need to disappear and that all of his old friends and relatives would be watched; so he couldn't draw attention to the place.

When we get back to Wendy's barn, Austin first eats the fried chicken we bring, and then proudly shows us that he's finished ten of the pieces needed for the new arena cages.

"I've also been watching the news as things heat and cool," he says. "I think we over-estimated Tyrone Bauer and his people. The aerospace division of Chi-One botched a rocket launch this morning."

He brings a replay onto the screen for us. The launch looks flawless off the pad. Austin skips ahead to about the seventh minute after liftoff, where the thrust ends and the whole thing starts to be pulled back into the atmosphere.

"They didn't calculate the required thrust correctly," Austin says. "Honestly, how could they mess up something so simple? The math is over two hundred years old."

"What happened next?" I ask.

"It took several hours, but it fell. It made a nice explosion, too."

He calls up more video. The vehicle is already glowing, when an explosion separates it into multiple parts, which then glow individually. The biggest piece is less than six kilometers from the surface when it explodes again.

"At least they waited until they were over the ocean to take care of that last piece," Austin says. "It was big enough to do some damage if it had come down over land."

"Can you tell if any of the pieces were made from your composite?" I ask.

"Probably just the payload, which was the last big piece," he answers. "It wasn't really burning up like the others, which must be why they equipped it with a secondary explosive."

"Is there any way to know what it was?"

"The news said it was a communications satellite."

Why do I doubt that?

Austin finishes the pieces he's working on, then turns in for the night. Zera offers him the bed in the house and I realize that I'm not going to get a turn on the bed, since leaving Austin and Zera in the barn by themselves would not be appropriate.

We lie on the hay for a long time, before Zera speaks.

"Are we heading back to Ogallala?" she asks.

"Why would you think that?"

"We can't build a time machine without the missing components. I was thinking that maybe your dad buried them at your grandparents' tombstone - the one that he cracked in half."

"How do you know about that?" I ask.

"Really?" she asks. "It's been in books, documentaries, and a movie about your parents and Four. Everyone knows about it."

"Oh. Did they find a cute baby to play me in the movie?" I ask.

"Sorry. The movie ends before you're born."

"If everyone knows about it, then it's not the tombstone we need to find," I say.

We return to silence.

"Zera? Everyone seems to know more about my own father than I do. I understand now why he wanted to shield me and Austin from the spotlight, but to me, he's just my dad."

"You want me to tell you things about your own dad?" she asks.

"No, I want to hear about your father," I reply. "You're right about how I react when I see the black lines of a former cult hunter. I guess I just want to understand who they are, so that maybe I can learn to open my heart to them more easily."

"Jocie, you're not the first and you won't be the last of The Washed to judge someone based on the black lines on their face. I've had to face that simple truth for most of my life. There were even times when I wished I had the black lines, rather than being washed."

"Really? Why?"

"Just to show my dad how much I loved him, and to make things easier for him."

"Easier? How so?"

"When you're a former cult hunter, everyone knows it just by looking at your face. Just being out in public with Mom would draw stares and judgment from people on the street."

"But your father had left The Corps and accepted Christ as his savior," I say. "People who really knew him must have seen that."

Zera takes a long time to respond.

"When I was five, our family visited a church full of washed people," Zera says. "Do you know what one of the accepting, Christ-loving elders of the church asked my dad, right in front of me? He asked my dad if he raped my mother just so he could have a washed child."

"I'm so sorry," I say.

"So was that man, once Mom was through with him. She left little doubt about her ability to defend herself against any would-be rapist. The funny thing is, I never thought of Dad as the one with more scars. That was always Mom. I think that's why they were so good for each other: Dad had more scars on the outside, and Mom had more on the inside."

"I assume you're talking about the attacks your mom led," I say.

"Yeah, she killed a lot of cult hunters, and Dad was almost one of them. He was at McIntosh. Everyone knows that Mom was so weak from dehydration that she needed I.V. fluids, but nobody remembers that the Four team that went in to save her got caught. My dad had been watching your dad inside the mountain and disobeyed orders, when he found out the Four team was on a humanitarian mission. He helped the Four team get Mom out, then visited her in the hospital to make sure she was okay, and the next thing you know, they were in love."

"I bet he had a lot of questions for your mom about faith and Jesus," I say.

"Questions, yes, but faith was always in his heart. If anything, I think Mom learned more from him. She learned how to truly forgive and to let go of all the anger she was carrying."

"How did he die?" I ask.

"Response to the Mark of the Beast varies. He had a particularly strong reaction that affected his lungs, and eventually it killed him."

"Thanks for telling me about him," I say. "You and your mom must miss him very much."

"We'll see him again, someday."

******

The next day, I leave Austin and Zera working on the puzzle pieces, and sit with Wendy.

"Wendy? Do you know anyone named Hannah?" I ask.

"Just your grandmother."

"That's the only Hannah I can think of, too," I say. "But I don't think she's the Hannah I need to find."

Even though she's blind, Wendy still tilts her head as if she can see me to indicate that she's confused by my statement. I take the piece of paper that was under the brown package out of my pocket and read it again.

"I think Dad left this piece of paper where he knew I'd find it," I say. "It says 'Hannah holds the key.' It must have said something more than that, because the writing goes right up to a ripped edge. Dad didn't write it, it's not in his handwriting, so I'm not sure who I should be looking for."

"When it comes to your father dear, I've noticed that it's best to just put the information into the back of your head and wait. When the time comes, his note will make sense."

When the time comes... I still don't even know what time I need to travel to... I wonder if Wendy may know something without even realizing it.

"What do you know about the mine that Bethany House was built over?" I ask.

"It's very old. Nobody even realized that there was coal in this region; but in the mid 2020's world politics and terrorism got so bad that the West had no choice but to stop funding it by no longer buying oil from the Middle East. The United States began looking for new energy sources, and found coal in all sorts of unexpected places."

"Do you know when the mine opened?" I ask.

"It opened in 2028, but it wasn't open for long. The Final Holy War broke out in 2036. With nearly four billion people dead, worldwide energy consumption went way down; so the mine was closed sometime in 2039.

So Dad needs me to travel to sometime after 2039, when the mine is closed. But when?

I think for a long time, and Wendy is content to sit in silence - until something occurs to me.

"When Four started building Bethany House, they didn't know the mine was there. Why not?"

"People had forgotten about it. It had been buried for nearly two hundred years."

"Buried? What do you mean? None of the tunnels were filled in."

"Of course they didn't fill it in; that would be too much work. They just covered the main shaft with a concrete slab."

The concrete slab that now sits in the bottom of the hole.

"That's how my family came to live in this part of the country," Wendy says. "My great-grandfather was a concrete man. He went all over the country covering old mines to keep people safe. He did so many that he got the nickname 'The Undertaker.'"

"Why would they call him that?" I ask.

"Well, the work he did was called 'laying the mine to rest,' so after a while, the concrete slab came to be known as the tombstone."

******

"Okay - so now the three of us are going to move a multi-ton hunk of concrete?" Zera asks, as we run to the site of Bethany House. "Do you plan to part the Red Sea, too?"

"I'm definitely hoping for a little divine help, but I'm betting it comes in the form of divine inspiration," I reply.

"That seems to be something your family has in excess."

"Maybe some of us, but this time I'm hoping it was Albert who was inspired," I say. "He's the one who dropped that slab when he blew up Bethany House. Even if I can't see it, I'm sure he created a way to get under it."

Zera stops and sits on a rock.

"Are you tired?" I ask.

"I'm not tired of running …" she says. "… but I'm tired of secrets. I may be the goddaughter of Cephas Paulson, but I don't have to put up with Paulson family secrets the way the rest of the family does. I want to know why you're mad."

"Mad? I'm not mad."

"Jocie, I'm Zip's daughter. I know anger when I see it. Now spill it."

I sit on a rock opposite from her.

"I'm not Cephas Paulson," I say. "I'm Jocie Paulson."

"Yeah, the red ponytail pretty much gave that away. What's your point?"

"The point is, Dad would already know exactly what to do next. He'd already know how to get under the slab; he'd know exactly what year and day to go back to and what to do when he got there. Don't you see? I'm barely figuring things out as I go along."

"Oh," Zera says. "I guess that could be a problem ... but what are you mad about?"

I stare at her.

"Really?"

"Jocie, if you're so sure that your dad has everything figured out, why haven't you considered that he wanted you to barely figure things out as you go along? Maybe that's the timing he anticipated all along?"

"I have considered it," I say, and sigh. "I guess that's what I'm mad about. I'm mad that assuming I'm slow was always part of the equation for him."

"Ha! I got you," she says. "If assuming you're slow was always a part of the equation, then assuming you'd eventually figure it all out was also part of the equation. He knows that you're the only person on earth - other than himself - who can actually solve one of his crazy puzzles. Having Cephas Paulson place that much faith in me would make me smile for the rest of my life."

"Then start smiling," I say. "It's not just me. He's placed his faith in all three of us."

******

We return to the side tunnel where the arena cave was hidden, and I sit on a ledge, looking down at the "tombstone."

"Why didn't Albert just hide the extra time machine pieces in this one tunnel?" Zera asks. "Why risk crushing them by hiding it under tons of concrete?"

He wouldn't.

I crawl into the tunnel and turn on my flashlight. Zera follows.

"What are you doing?" she asks.

I pick up one of the cans that are stacked neatly against the wall, and find it's much lighter than expected.

Dad would have seen it right away. Actually, Dad did see it right away.

The seal of the can was cut with a hand laser and then set back into place, so it pops off easily. Inside is a carefully packed piece of electronics.

"Canned time machine," I say.

We find dozens and dozens of components, all perfectly preserved. If the plan to seal the tunnel hadn't worked, a Federal drone would have found nothing but piles of ancient cans and scrap metal.

"I don't believe it," Zera says. "Your dad got this one wrong. Albert didn't hide anything under The Tombstone."

"That's right," I say. "The tombstone was never Albert's hiding spot."

It was mine all along.

CHAPTER EIGHTEEN

A year ago, when I was seventeen, my grandfather died. Everyone knew about Dad's life, but in many ways, my grandfather's life had been just as big an adventure. James Paulson had been one of the earliest members of Four; had helped to build both Bethany House and Gethsemane House, and then spent a decade keeping Four's biggest secret, as he and my grandmother carried vaccine to Christians around the globe.

After the funeral, we all gathered at Aunt Kimberley's house. As friends and family came and went, I spent the time with my cousins, but never took my eyes off Dad. He slipped away and out the door; so I followed him, and caught him sitting on a park bench two blocks away.

"It was a little crowded in there," I said, as I sat beside him.

"Actually, I thought it was a little lonely," he replied.

I put my head onto his shoulder.

"You miss grandpa."

"Even when you know it's coming, you're never really ready," he said.

"I think everyone was surprised and disappointed that you didn't give a eulogy."

"I didn't know what to say to everyone," he replied.

"I believe you," I said. "But even if you didn't know what to say to everyone else, you still composed a eulogy in your head, a tribute to grandpa for your own ears. Will you tell it to me?"

Dad thought for a few moments, and then cleared his throat.

"They say the world shrinks a little, the day your father dies. Our father's strong arms are the first to lift us high in the air when we're just babies. They lift us high above their heads and we feel like we're so high up, that we can see more of the world. Then, when they think we're ready, they'll toss us into the air. It's like a father has an instinct to show his children more of the world than they can see for themselves, so higher and higher they'll toss us, to expand our worlds; but no matter how high we go, we're never afraid. We know with the same certainty that the sun will rise tomorrow, that those strong hands are going to be there to catch us. So today, knowing those strong hands have left this earth, I could let my world feel a bit smaller; but I'm not going to allow that to happen to myself or to his memory. Instead, I'd rather that his passing lift me and expand my world one last time; so I'll lift my eyes and my heart to the place where our Father has lifted him, knowing that those strong hands have caught him."

"Dad?" I said. "I noticed that you didn't cry at the funeral."

It occurred to me that I'd never seen Dad cry, ever.

"Maybe crying a little would be a good thing," I suggested.

He rested his head on top of mine.

"Jocie, with all the things I've done in my life - some of them good, and some of them bad - I'm afraid of crying."

How could Dad be afraid of crying? He's the man who was tortured nearly to death in the mountain and stood strong in Christ's name. He shouldn't be afraid of anything, anymore.

"Afraid?" I asked.

"Afraid that once I start, I'll never be able to stop."

******

I send Zera back to the barn to get Austin; then secure a rope and throw the loose end into the pit. Soon I'm standing on The Tombstone. On one corner of the concrete, I find a line of letters. These are the initials of the people who poured the concrete to lay the mine to rest. One of them also wrote "and the Angel." I look at the remains of the elevator that was used to raise and lower the miners and their equipment.

The elevator wasn't at the bottom of the shaft when The Tombstone fell. Why not?

I look at the smashed elevator and realize that it is actually two cages. There was a smaller cage underneath the main cage. It was probably a place to carry equipment.

There must have been a hole in the floor for the lower cage to drop into so the miners would be level with the floor as they got on and off. Anything in the hole would be protected when the Tombstone fell.

I jump off the massive slab and see that it's resting on a couple of boulders. I don't need to move The Tombstone; I just need to clear enough room to wiggle under it. A long, straight piece of metal is lying between the boulders, which I use to lever out the smaller rocks, while I clear the sand and gravel with my hands. After an hour, I find the edge of the hole. I reach in and feel something made of metal, which I can just squeeze through the opening. It turns out to be a metal lockbox. When I dust it off, I find the name "Paulson" written on it, in my handwriting, along with a message.

I'm not sure how long I sit, staring at the box ,before I hear Austin emerge from the electrical tunnel above me.

"Jocie? What are you doing down there?" Austin asks.

Zera emerges next.

"She's been under The Tombstone," Zera says. "What did you find?"

"Pandora's box," I say.

"Why do you say that? What's in it?" Austin asks.

"I don't know. That's why we can't open it."

"You make as much sense as your father," Zera says. "Come up here and explain it to us."

I climb up the rope and meet them on a ledge.

"Here's what I know," I say. "I'm going back to the year 2039, but I don't know why. When I'm there, I'll place that box in the bottom of the mine."

"Then why can't we open it?" Zera asks.

"Paradox," I say. "What if it's a letter saying goodbye, because I'm stuck back in time? Whether it's good news or bad, anything in that box could affect the decisions we all make."

"Why would you send it, if not to open it?" Austin asks.

"It's for you to open, after I'm gone," I say. "That's what I wrote on it."

******

For the next week, Austin is the star of the show. He leaves me to the busywork of tending the oven as the composite puzzle pieces are heated and cooled, while he builds a time machine from the pieces found in the cans. William closes part of the museum display and helps us move the computers from Timber Ridge Camp to the ruins of Bethany House.

It's Zera's night on the bed inside Wendy's house, and I'm lying on the hay, when Austin finally asks the question I've been waiting for him to ask.

"Jocie? This has been a great adventure, but the adventure will be over without some large crystals of tellurium 120. Where are we going to get them? I've read stories about this one formation under a deep rock gold mine near Cripple Creek. The miners had broken through into a natural cave on their way to a gold vein, but left them alone. They sat there for decades, but when the government came to take them for The Traveler's Initiative, the crystals had disappeared. Maybe we can find out what happened to them and…"

I raise my hand to stop him. He's read everything there is to read about time travel and he'll go on all night.

"Have you ever heard Dad say that the first piece of a puzzle is as important as the last? The crystals were actually the first piece to be put into place. I've known about them nearly my entire life. I just didn't know what they were, until you realized that the shepherd's hook was part of a time machine."

I remove a small leather pouch from an outer pocket on my pack and dump the contents into my hand. I pick out all the worthless diamonds, rubies and emeralds, and put them back in the pouch.

"These are the last eight minable crystals on earth," I say. "Dad had them all along."

"Eight?" Austin says. "I know you're small, but it took twenty-six crystals to transport Mom and Dad. How am I supposed to transport you with just eight?"

"I'm small and I'm only going back two hundred years rather than two thousand."

"I don't care if you lose ten pounds and I send you into last week. This is a matter of physics," he says.

I have no way to respond.

"Jocie? Is the reason none of us can look in that box because eight crystals is only enough for a one-way trip?"

"I don't know."

"Then I'm going to open the box …" he says. "… and if it says you're stuck two hundred years in the past, then I'm not going to send you. I'd rather face a paradox."

"Don't face a paradox, Austin. Face a puzzle. Ask questions. Ask what limits the crystals, and then figure out a way to overcome that limitation."

"Physics, Jocie. The limitation is physics, and there's no magic combination of puzzle pieces that's going to change it."

"I know," I say. "But we also know that there was an arena that you built sitting in that cave, and a box with my handwriting on it under The Tombstone. It's going to happen, Austin. The best we can do now is to make it happen in a way that's consistent with what we know."

"You mean create a new solution to the puzzle," he says.

"We are Paulson's," I reply.

******

The next day, Austin and Zera carry much of the time machine to the cave, leaving me with the tedious job of heating and cooling the composite pieces of the arena cage. After two hours, I'm thoroughly bored with the job and find myself singing to pass the time. I like singing, but I rarely do it when others are around because I know I'm not very good. I'm singing the classic "He'll Find You," when I hear Zera giggling behind me. She and Austin snuck into the barn and have been listening. I stop singing and feel my face turning many shades of red.

"Don't stop," Zera says. "Austin and I will sing harmony."

She starts the song again from the beginning, and I join in. Zera's range is much higher than mine, so I have a hard time staying on key. Austin joins in at his much lower range, and I become completely lost. Halfway through the song, Austin drops out. I expect him to laugh at me, but instead, I find him staring into space. Zera and I stop singing.

"Austin?" Zera says. "You know that look Jocie gets on her face, just before she solves a puzzle? You have it too."

"Harmony!" Austin says.

Zera and I exchange a confused look.

"The tellurium crystals," Austin says. "All crystals have a resonance frequency. For the most part, two crystals of the same material have the same frequency when subjected to the same energy, but there is some variability, due to imperfections in the lattice. The people who made the first time machine probably ignored the variance. They let the crystals sing out of harmony."

"The crystals sing?" Zera asks.

Austin finally stops staring into space.

"Let me show you," he says.

One of the barn stalls is an old workshop where Austin has set up some equipment. He takes one of the eight remaining crystals out of a protective case and carefully places it inside a chamber taken from the original time machine.

"We can apply a small amount of energy without hurting it," he says, then uses his com to activate the device.

"The crystal is resonating far outside the range of our hearing, but we can use the computer to give us an audible signal," he says.

We hear a low-pitched hum.

"Now - listen to this," he says, and places a second crystal in another chamber.

"It sounds exactly the same," I say.

"That's why nobody sings duets with you," he says. "You can't hear the difference in the crystals, just like you can't hear your own voice."

"They sound the same to me, too," Zera says.

Austin repeats the process with each of the eight crystals, until all eight are humming.

"It sounds like white noise," Zera says.

"Exactly!" Austin says. "It has a randomness to it, caused by the variations and imperfections in the crystals. The power output has a matching randomness, too."

He points to a screen where power output is displayed in the form of a bell curve.

"If I'm right, getting the crystals to resonate in harmony will increase the power output."

He starts to adjust the resonance of each crystal, using miniscule changes to the power flow. It's clear that he can hear each individual crystal and is bringing them together. Even I can hear the sound moving from white noise to a single perfect note.

"Look at the power output!" Zera says.

What was a broad bell curve is now a single, perfect spike on the monitor.

"We've increased the power output by ten times," Austin says. "I think it will be enough ... but you could still lose a pound or two ... just to be safe."

******

Transporting the necessary equipment to the ruins of Bethany House takes a few days, but I'm glad to have a little more time. When Dad travelled the first time, it was done with great fanfare. When he and Mom travelled, they were sent off with a gunfight and an explosion. My turn feels like a disappointment in comparison.

"Do you have everything you need?" Austin asks, as we walk with the last load.

I have what looks like a bundle of sticks on my back - the pieces that I'll assemble into two time travel arenas.

"A little more courage would be nice," I reply.

"I have a going away gift that might help in that department."

He reaches into his pack and takes out what looks like a thick cylinder of his composite, less than half a meter long, and hands it to me.

"Hold it horizontally and push both buttons at the same time," he says.

When I do it, the cylinder telescopes out and locks. It's now about a meter-and-a-half long, exactly the size of a standard sparring stick.

"Won't the chip in it fry during transport?" I ask.

"There are no chips. It's just springs. I made two. I was thinking we could try them out together when you get back."

"I'd like that," I say.

"Promise me, Jocie. Promise you'll come back."

"I'll be back," I say. "There's no way I'm going to miss a chance to end your undefeated streak of sparring wins over me - especially with your own stick."

"It'll be worth it."

******

We haul everything into the old tunnel.

"I still can't believe that bundle of sticks is going to be part of a time machine," Zera says, as I set to work.

The pieces are precise. Many of them appear to be identical, but are actually different from each other by a millimeter here or there. Those millimeters are just enough to ensure that the cage only fits together in one way. Austin and Zera watch in fascination, as I slide and twist the pieces.

"You worked so hard to get that piece in," Austin says. "Why are you taking it back out?"

"It's part of the puzzle. Not many people think about going backward in order to move forward."

"As far as we know, nobody but us is ever going to see this puzzle," Zera says. "Why go to all the trouble?"

"I guess it's a Paulson thing. As we worked on this arena, I was actually thinking of an even more complex design, but we don't have time."

After fifteen minutes, I'm down to the last piece of the first arena.

"I need you to hold pressure on this piece," I say to Austin, as I place his hand on the right spot while sliding the piece shaped like a Shepherd's hook into place, then twist it to lock the entire structure together.

"Was needing a second person also part of the puzzle?" he asks.

I raise my eyebrows in response.

"Of course it was," he says.

The second arena goes together even faster. Austin isn't watching this time though, his eyes are darting to the metal box that I retrieved from beneath The Tombstone.

"The sooner I go, the sooner you can open it," I say.

******

"How bad will the blackout be?" I ask, when the arena is set up under the time machine.

"At least the Eastern seaboard; maybe most of North America," Austin replies.

"How quickly will they figure out the source of the power drain?"

Austin's face falls.

"I hadn't thought of that," he says. "When Dad went back, every day that passed for him back there corresponded to a day passing in our time. We don't have that kind of time. Once the power comes back on, the government will be here in less than an hour."

"I'm sorry," I say, and climb into the arena. "Defend the machine as long as you can."

"Zera, you push the button," Austin says. "I can't do it."

She doesn't want to do it either, but she knows it has to be done. The machine starts to hum, as it draws massive amounts of power from the Sunspot One fusion reactor that supplies electricity to the entire Western Hemisphere.

I'm just moments away from transport, when Austin runs past the control computer and dives for the old metal box.

"Austin, don't!" I yell.

There's a single piece of paper inside the box, which he reads. His jaw drops slightly and he looks at me; then this head snaps towards Zera. Whatever he planned to say to her is lost in an immense flash of light, followed by complete darkness.

CHAPTER NINETEEN

"Why hasn't it been torn down?" I asked Dad.

We were walking around Washington, D.C. like any other family of tourists, when I was fifteen. I never expected Dad to take us to the national atheism monument.

"We fought hard to ensure that everyone is free to believe however they choose to believe," he replied. "As Christians, tearing down monuments and silencing the voices of those who believe differently is not our way."

The monument was carved from many tons of granite and was commissioned by Henry Portman's grandfathers.

"Look at it closely. What do you see?" Dad asked.

The side we were looking at was divided into four sections. One was devoted to the evolution of man; another to the creations of man; the third to the laws of man; and the last to the future of man.

"It's about mankind taking credit for everything," I said.

"That's right," Dad said. "Now let's look at it from farther away."

We walked across the street.

"How does it look now?" he asked.

"Man's accomplishments are getting smaller," I replied.

We walked another block away.

"Now that we can't see man's accomplishments, what's left?" Dad asked.

I thought I'd fall to my knees when it struck me. The two top panels of the monument were smaller than the lower panels and the four quadrants were divided from each other by channels carved into the stone.

"It's a cross," I said. "The national atheism monument is actually a giant cross. How could that have happened?"

"The Lord is never hard to find," Dad said, "When your heart is open, you'll find He's often hiding in plain sight."

******

Dad loved to talk about his experience of time travelling with Mom. Seeing her thoughts and experiencing her emotions created a sense of intimacy between them that few couples will ever achieve. All these years later, I sometimes wonder if they can still hear each other's thoughts.

On the other hand, Dad has little to say about time travelling alone. He called it "the very definition of loneliness," where you have an entire lifetime to review and reflect upon the choices you've made in your life. In his case, it wasn't a happy review, as he thought about his time as The Cult Hunter.

I spend an eternity reflecting on my own life, and I find that I have very little to be sad about. I was raised by two loving parents, and was surrounded by family and friends who love the Lord. Even when I try to think about sad times, it's hard to truly feel sad. I decide to focus on the times I felt I was a disappointment to Dad by creating an image in my mind. It's a picture of me free-climbing a difficult overhang at Red Rocks Open Space for the first time. Dad's face looks proud for just a moment, then shifts to sadness. It begins to rain, and the drops on his face look like tears.

That's wrong. It didn't rain that day - but if this isn't a memory, then what is it?

I look again, and realize that the raindrops are shaped like puzzle pieces, each with a picture from my life on it. I can't help but smile with wonder as I look up at the sky and watch the puzzle-rain falling all around me.

Dad says that our lives are wonderfully complex puzzles that only the Lord fully understands.

I watch the rain hit the ground. Some of the pieces run off like rain, but others stick and start to form a larger picture. All of those moments of sadness weren't my sadness. They were Dad's. He pieced this puzzle together himself, but all he knew was that I was going to go back in time. Like me, he doesn't know if I'll ever make it back, and it makes him sad.

Even without knowing the outcome, he's willing to send me. Why?

The picture on the ground melts away, and I realize that my thoughts are affecting the drops. Maybe the answers I'm looking for are already here and I just haven't pieced them together. I focus on the question of what I'm supposed to do, or see, in 2039 A.D. To my surprise, the drops form a picture of Amelia Lake, and then the map of all the places where she took ice cores.

A toxin sample! In 2039 it won't have degraded. The purpose of the mission was hiding in plain sight the entire time.

With an original toxin sample, Amelia can cure everyone from The Mark of the Beast. There would be no more black lines; no more open wounds.

The picture changes to the Chi-One failed satellite launch.

What does that have to do with toxin samples?

My entire memory of the satellite falling back to earth and exploding replays several times.

The payload was heat shielded by Austin's composite. What was the payload?

I focus so hard on trying to solve the puzzle that all of the pictures blur. Dad once told me that he most often solved puzzles when he wasn't really trying, so I let my mind wander.

The picture on the ground goes bright. It's Dad, chained between two posts inside the mountain, with a blazing map of the world behind him. He struggles to his feet, then holds his arms out to his sides so that his silhouette forms a perfect cross over the glowing world. He looks into the camera and says: "Christ came as a light to shine in this dark world, so that all who put their trust in Him will no longer remain in the darkness."

Henry Portman comes into view and Dad says: "I believe it's now been about six minutes, Henry, and I feel fine. Are you ready to believe in miracles now?"

"How is it possible?" Henry asks. "You should be dead."

"My father never conspired to commit mass murder," Dad replies. "When he wrote 'distribute it through the water' in his notebook, he was referring to the vaccine - not the toxin. Four hid the vaccine in spring water, and has had over a decade to take it all over the world, giving it to the faithful."

"But the toxin dose I gave to you was five times what you could get through the air or water. It was enough to kill even someone who's vaccinated. We tested it."

"That's true for someone who took your 'Mark of the Beast' vaccine; but the extra bit of DNA you put in there as a family legacy makes the vaccine less efficient. Go ahead and release your toxin if you like. It's nothing more than dust."

No. It can't be… it was also in plain sight the entire time…

******

I wake up shouting "Five-X."

I feel slightly dizzy; so I leave my eyes closed.

The little girl said that all of the bad people are going to go away. When Tyrone Bauer hired Amelia, he wasn't looking for a cure. He was getting access to toxin. "Five-X" stands for the concentration of toxin they need to

241

achieve in the atmosphere in order to kill every marked person on the planet, while leaving all of The Washed alive. The remnants of Four has been at war with them all along: destroying air tankers to prevent a mass toxin release; buying time until I was old enough to go on this mission.

The pieces were in front of my face the entire time.

I open my eyes to find there's very little light here in the tunnel, with what little there is coming from the main shaft where The Tombstone will one day be poured. I leave the arena and stumble towards the light. The food shelves that have crumbled in my day are still intact and the emergency supplies are all arranged in neat lines. On the lowest shelf, I see something I'm going to need: the metal lockbox.

When I reach the edge of the shaft, I realize that the little bit of light is filtering around the edges of the elevator, which is at the top of the shaft, blocking my escape.

There's an elevator control panel on the wall. I try it, but the electricity has been shut off.

How do I get out? There's no other airshaft.

I look at the rock face opposite me. The elevator shaft is larger than I would have guessed, having only seen it after two hundred years and a demolition effort by Albert. There's a large channel cut into the rock that houses multiple cables.

They used a heavy counterweight to make the elevator more efficient. If I can disconnect the counterweight, the elevator should fall.

I bend a light stick and shake it. The glow is enough to help me search the area, but I can't find anything that would help me cut the cables - just a small hammer and a couple of wrenches.

I put them into my pack, and use the cables to climb to the bottom of the mine. Hammers and wrenches are interesting historical pieces in my time, but now I'm glad Dad made me pay attention when we visited museums. The counterweight is a large concrete block with the cables connected to it using nuts and bolts.

I get to work with the wrenches and the nuts loosen up with remarkable ease, thanks, I think, to a sticky black substance that Dad referred to as 'grease.' There's tension on the cable, so when I remove the last nut, I leap out of the way – expecting the elevator to come crashing down next to me.

Nothing happens.

I climb back up the cable, until I reach the underside of the elevator car. It's equipped with some kind of friction brake that's strong enough to hold the car in place, even without the counterweight. It's stupid, but out of frustration I transfer to the bottom of the car and hang there. With a loud squeak, the car drops by several centimeters. I start bouncing and moving the car from side to side. The car gives up more squeaks and more downward movement.

Luckily, the car wasn't at the very top of the shaft; so once I've pulled it down a half meter, I'm able to climb from the counterweight groove onto the top of the car. There are two light, metal hatches that must have closed automatically to cover the shaft when the car descended. When I push them open, I'm bathed in sunlight - but also cold air.

The area doesn't look anything like the beautiful forest I know in the area of Bethany House. There are no large trees at all; just shrubs and piles of fractured rocks. The sight is so depressing that I just want to get away; so I start walking. There's one place I know I'm going to visit, so I might as well start off there.

Within a few kilometers, I find myself in the familiar comfort of trees. After walking for nearly an hour, I find myself where I know Wendy's little house should be - but isn't. The remains of an old barn have been piled up in a large heap and the barn that I know is under construction. They laid a new floor over the old one and have raised three of the walls. The roof joists are being constructed by hand, ready to be raised once the walls are finished. I stare at the job, wondering how I'm going to accomplish what needs to be done.

"Where did you come from?" a middle-aged man asks, as he emerges from the barn.

"It's going to be a pretty barn," I say. "Do you own it?"

"I just build them …" he says. "…but in a way I feel like it's mine."

"I can see that you build things to last," I say. "I'm sure this barn will still be standing in two hundred years."

"I don't know that anything will still be standing in two hundred years, the way this world is going."

I hear a strange rumbling and crunching sound behind me, and turn to see what it is. It looks like a small version of Brill's electric bus. The crunching is made by the wheels, as they run over the ground, but it's the rumble that draws my attention. Whatever it is, it's not electric. It has a pipe on its back end that's spewing smoke.

How gross.

"There's my ride," he says.

The vehicle stops and a woman gets out.

"Where on earth did you come from?" she asks. "Dave? She's got to be freezing. Why didn't you offer her your coat?"

"I'm fine," I say. "I should go."

"Go? Where?" the woman asks, as her face softens. "You wandered here out of the city, looking for work and food, didn't you?"

I say nothing.

"You're coming home with us," she says. "We have more than we need."

"Elizabeth?" Dave says.

"Don't you argue with me, David!"

He doesn't, so I open the back door of the vehicle and get in. The woman drives much faster than a hover bus and the whole experience feels unsafe to me. Luckily, it doesn't take long to reach their house, which is on a high point overlooking ridges and valleys in each direction. When we come to a stop, Elizabeth shuts the vehicle off by removing a small bundle of metal pieces, and then opens the door to the house with a different piece from the same bundle.

The inside of the house is warm and homey. I walk around studying things, while my hosts make dinner, which is flavored

245

rice, homegrown vegetables, and a lean red meat that I know must be wild game of some sort.

When we sit down, I bow my head in thanks, and Dave and Elizabeth awkwardly follow suit.

"Where are your parents, Jocie?" Elizabeth asks.

"I don't know," I say. "They disappeared, and I'm looking for them."

It's not a lie.

"Where are you going?" Dave asks.

"I have family in Baltimore. I guess that's my next stop," I say.

"Baltimore? By yourself?" Elizabeth asks. "It's too dangerous. Whole sections of the city are under Marshall Law. People will rob you for a nickel, and it's really no place for a young woman. Girls like you get raped the day they arrive."

"Is Baltimore worse than other cities?" I ask.

"Of course it is," Dave says. "How could you not know?"

I give him an expectant look.

"For years, Baltimore has been the U.S. hub of middle eastern immigration; so now it's got the biggest concentration of the gene. The death toll and suffering from the toxin is immense. All order has been breaking down."

Then that's where I'll start the search for a toxin sample.

CHAPTER TWENTY

By the time I was sixteen, Austin and I weren't allowed to walk the streets of Colorado Springs alone, but we could go out with either Mom or Dad. Dad enjoyed walks to the park; so if Mom was busy, he would invite me or Austin. Most marked people stayed indoors, but there was a marked man named Willy, who often sat at the ancient park. Willy's scars and sores were worse than most people's, but that didn't stop him from sitting in public and talking to anyone who happened by.

"Hello, Cephas! What's the good news today?" Willy said.

"It's the same good news as yesterday and tomorrow, Willy. Christ loves you."

"Do you have a prayer for me?"

"Don't I always?"

Dad walked up to the man, placed his hands on his shoulders, and said a prayer for him. I hid behind Dad. I didn't want to look at the scars or think that Dad was touching them.

"Is this your daughter?" Willy asked, when the prayer was over. "My, what a beautiful young lady she is."

Dad thanked Willy and we continued our walk.

"Dad? Is it ever hard for you to pray for someone who calls me a beautiful young lady one minute, but might try to kidnap and sell me into slavery in the next?"

"I've never regretted kindness…" he said, "… no matter how it was repaid."

"Evil doesn't understand kindness…" I began.

Dad's eyes flickered to the mountain.

"I know a thing or two about evil, Jocie. I've felt the lash of evil on my back…"

His eyes went to the ground.

"… and I've held the whip in my hand. I'll choose to receive the lashes over delivering them every time."

He looked me in the eye.

"The Marked are not the enemy, Jocie. Indifference to their suffering is the enemy."

******

Dave and Elizabeth's guest bed is soft and warm, and I find myself drifting off immediately. It's dark when I wake up and the glowing clock near the bed says it's nearly midnight. I can see a light under the door; so I carefully open it and find I can hear Dave and Elizabeth talking in their room.

"There's something odd about her," Dave says. "She studies everything, like she's casing the place to rob us."

"I don't know about robbing us, but I noticed it too," Elizabeth says. "She watched me unlocking the door as if she's never seen a set of keys before. It was the same way when I lit the burners on the stove and used the mixer to mash potatoes."

I hear something downstairs, but Dave and Elizabeth don't seem to notice it. I cross the room and look out the window, to see two strange vehicles with Maryland plates parked at the end of the driveway. There's a crash in the kitchen.

"What is she doing?" Dave asks, and I hear him get out of bed.

By the time he crosses the hall, I've opened the door. His eyes go wide when he realizes there's someone else in his house.

"Lock yourself in the room," he says.

I close the door, but grab the expanding fighting stick Austin built for me, then open the window. There's a porch roof under the window that I can use to reach a tree to get to the ground. By the time I get there, I can hear shouting inside. Dave has some sort of hunting rifle, but either he couldn't bring himself to shoot someone, or he realized there are many robbers in the house and he'd quickly be overwhelmed regardless.

There's just one man outside, standing guard. He looks like he's barely older than Austin. He doesn't even appear to be armed.

"We don't want food!" one of the men inside yells. "We know you have money."

"I don't have cash," Dave yells. "Mine was all confiscated by the government, just like everyone else."

"Yeah, but you're a builder," the man says. "You must have metals. Metals we can trade."

"I build with wood."

"Take him outside. I need room to swing."

Seven men, none of them much older than me, wrestle Dave out through the door. I don't see any guns, but they all have weapons, like baseball bats, lengths of pipe, and knives. They force him onto his knees on the lawn. I feel like they should all have black lines across their faces.

They're all looking to a tall but thin man for what to do next.

He's the leader, but he doesn't really have control of them.

"Life sure is an interesting series of choices," I say from the dark, then step forward so they can all see me. "You choose to jump in a car; you choose to drive all the way here from Maryland; you choose to rob and beat an honest man."

"Where did you come from?" the leader asks, with a sneer on his face.

I've seen a sneer like that one before.

"I've been getting that a lot lately ..." I say, "...but we're not talking about my choices right now. I think you boys need to choose to leave - now."

The largest of the group kicks Dave in the back, sending him to the ground.

"Leave? The party has just started!" the largest one says. "We drove all the way out here just to throw J.W. here a party."

He nods to the leader, who is apparently known as J.W.

"Now that you're here, we're going to have a special party … just for you. Go get her boys."

They look to J.W. for his approval. He doesn't appear to like this new plan, but I watch as he resigns himself to it, and nods his head.

Five of the group drop their weapons and start walking towards me. The expanding weapon that Austin made for me is in my hand. When the bravest one is at the right distance, my weapon springs to full size and I hit him in the side of the head.

"Party time, boys" I say.

******

The rest try to scramble back for their weapons, but two of them never make it before I trip them up, which causes J.W. to laugh. Dave tries to use the confusion to roll away, but J.W. pushes him back to the ground, and then puts his foot on the back of Dave's neck. The first guy I hit is still dazed, but the remaining five surround me while the leader watches.

"Last chance, boys," I say.

Their attacks are awkward, wild swings, without any thought about follow-through or pattern or coordination amongst themselves. The big guy has a baseball bat, and the rest of his friends have to keep diving out the way to avoid it, allowing me to hit them when they're defenseless. I haven't done real damage to any of them; I'm just trying to give them enough bruises to reconsider their plan. Eventually, one of them catches a backswing from the bat in the face, and I'm down to just four opponents.

"That bat is dangerous," I say. "Just not to me."

He takes another swing and I block the bat downward, allowing my staff to rake his knuckles, so he drops it. When he tries to pick it up, I kick him in the face. He backs away, holding his bloody nose.

"Stop fooling around, you guys," J.W. says.

"Why don't you give it a shot?" a guy with a short metal pipe says. "She's just too fast."

"Put that thing down or I'll stand on his neck," J.W. says to me, and increases his weight on Dave.

I stop moving and stare at him.

"I wouldn't do that," I say.

"Why?"

"Because the only one here who's been fooling around - is me."

Within ten seconds, the remaining three attackers are all on the ground. It was one fluid attack. One perfect solution of anticipation and movement to solve the puzzle.

"Take your foot off his neck ..." I say, "... or prepare to lose some teeth."

From the look on his face, it's already a done deal.

I hear one of the guys behind me getting up and grabbing the baseball bat. I hear his weight shift and the beginning of his swing. It's aimed for my head. It makes a slight swish in the air, and smile starts to form on the leader's face.

Puzzle pieces. Wonderful puzzle pieces. Thank you, Dad, for not training me. Solving the puzzle for myself is wonderful.

I duck and spin, and the bat passes over me while I jab the man in the gut. As he doubles over, I come down on the bat, breaking it near the handle; then spin again and turn a full round-house swing loose on the leader's jaw. His neck turns a little too far for my comfort before he's spun to the ground.

The rest take off running for their trucks. Their leader must be the only one with the metal sticks needed to start one of them, because they all jump into the other one and take off.

Dave stands.

"Help me carry him into the house," I say.

"Why? The police should be here soon. Let them carry him to jail."

"Fill out a police report ..." I say, "... but please leave me out of it. I'd rather not talk to the police. They'd ask too many questions that I can't answer."

I dig through the young man's pockets and find the ring of metal sticks, which I throw to Dave, and ask him to hide the vehicle that brought this young man here. We carry the young man to the basement, which is apparently called a "recreation room" and lay him on a couch. Upstairs, the doorbell rings.

"I'd ask if you can handle any trouble out of this guy ..." Dave says, "...but it would be a stupid question."

I listen to the muffled voices of Dave, Elizabeth, and a policewoman for fifteen minutes before the young man on the couch begins to stir. He sits up and his eyes go wide at the sight of me; so I clamp my hand over his mouth and whisper that the police are upstairs. He's confused, but has an instinct for being quiet when he hears the word "police." Even so, he spits part of a tooth and some blood into his hand.

After another half hour, the policewoman leaves, and Dave and Elizabeth join us.

"She's gone," Dave says. "Now, do you mind telling me why she didn't take this guy with her?"

"I told you. Too many questions," I answer.

"Then how about answering some of my questions?" Dave says. "Like, how is that while my face was in the dirt, seven guys ended up getting their clocks cleaned?"

"I can answer that one," Elizabeth says. "I was watching from an upstairs window. Jocie mopped the floor with them. She's like a perfect ballerina - but with a stick."

"Tell me about it," says our young captive, rubbing his jaw.

"I told you that life is an interesting series of choices," I say, then turn to Dave. "Do you have more of the meat dish you served for dinner?"

"It sounds like you had enough for one day."

"It's for him. His stomach has been growling since he got here."

"He broke into my house, dragged me outside, stood on my neck, and now you want me to feed him?"

This young man is not my enemy. Indifference to his life is my enemy.

"He looks like what he really needs is for someone to show him kindness," I reply. "I suspect it's not very common in his life."

Ten minutes later, he's eating like a hungry dog.

"You can sleep down here," I say. "You can't start your truck, so don't try to leave. We'll talk in the morning."

"He'll run ..." Dave says. "...or attack us in our sleep."

I turn to J.W.

"You can attack us in our sleep, if you want. Just keep in mind that I tend to wake up violently."

******

The next morning, I find the young man sitting at the table, speaking with Elizabeth as he eats a stack of pancakes and scrambled eggs.

"Jocie, come join us," she says. "J.W. here has been telling me about himself. He's a war orphan, just like you."

"He can tell me all about it while he gives me a ride into Baltimore," I say. "Is Dave still here?"

"He's in the garage, getting together the tools and supplies he needs for the day."

When I reach the garage, I notice Dave looks like he hasn't slept.

"Dave? I need something from you, and it's going to sound strange."

"Strange is pretty relative, for a girl who appears out of the woods and beats the tar out of a group of armed men. What do you need?"

"Were they right last night when they said that, as a builder, you can get your hands on metals?"

"Sure, but I don't work in metals, and funds are pretty tight."

"Don't worry about the money. I'll take care of that. How much would you need to make one of those barn trusses out of metal instead of wood?"

"I know a guy in Winchester who could make a steel truss for a few hundred."

"What about other metals?" I ask. "Could he get his hands on metals like chromium, titanium and vanadium?"

"That would be a lot more expensive."

I take the pouch of gemstones from my pocket and empty it into my hands.

"Are those real?" he asks.

I hand him the two biggest diamonds.

"Get a price," I say.

CHAPTER TWENTY-ONE

Dad taught his class at the university until the day before he disappeared. He would often invite me, Mom, and Austin to attend the lectures. I think he particularly enjoyed it when Mom would go, because if none of the students were up to it, she'd raise her hand and challenge him to defend whatever he said. It's not that she disagreed with the points he was making; it was just the weird way my parents flirt.

Last year, Dad asked me to attend one lecture in particular.

"We talk a lot about the events that led up to the Final Holy War. We talk about the bombs, and the blame, but from there we tend to skip straight to the long-term repercussions, and the ways in which the war was secretly used to shape society," Dad said. "We spend very little time talking about the immense suffering. It's easier to just cite the statistic that over three billion were killed, than it is to dig into even one of their stories and try to understand what it was like."

The class stayed silent.

"What year did the bombs fall?" Dad asked.

His board lit up with students eager to answer the question, but Dad didn't call on anyone.

"You all know that the answer is 2036; so try this question: In what year did the killing end?"

Nobody was eager to take a stab at it.

"The last known death attributed to toxin poisoning was in 2047, over eleven years after the bombs fell. Granted, most deaths happened in the first five years, but for some, the suffering lasted for eleven years. Who can tell me why?"

Dad called on a young man named Eugene.

"The genetic damage was cumulative," Eugene said. "Each particle that entered your body did a miniscule amount of damage; so if your exposure came slowly, so did death."

"Exactly. For some, it was a long, slow march, filled with daily agony as they felt their body slowly fail. Who can tell me about the societal reaction of those who didn't have the target gene? What did the world do to help those poor, suffering souls?"

Dad looked directly at me; so I answered.

"They turned their backs," I said.

"Yes," Dad replied. "People with the gene couldn't find jobs. Why hire someone who's going to die soon? Without work, they couldn't feed themselves, and soon they had nowhere left to turn except into government-run areas - called Dead Zones - where they could at least eat while they waited to die. The Dead Zones developed their own culture - a culture of death."

******

I insist that J.W. come to work with Dave and me and do some labor to repent for his behavior. He's a hard worker and a quick study. I leave them for a while and run to the old mine. The brakes have continued to slip on the old elevator, and it's ten meters farther down the shaft than when I left it. While I was gone, a crew started bringing equipment and supplies to pour concrete.

I look at the cement-pumping machine the crew left. The controls depend on electronics; so I use my knife to cut a couple of primary connections. They'll need a whole new control board to make it functional again.

That might buy me a week. If I don't get back here before they pour The Tombstone, this really will be a one-way trip.

When I get back to the barn building site, Dave looks relieved to see me.

"Jocie, there are bears in this part of the country," he says.

"I told him to worry for the bears … not you," J.W. adds, then smiles to show his broken tooth.

"Are they just coming out of hibernation?" I ask

"It's June. They've been out of hibernation for months," Dave says.

"June? Is it always this cold here in June?" I ask.

"It didn't used to be," J.W. says, "It's amazing what a couple of dozen nukes exploding on the other side of the world will do."

Of course. The Final Holy War was just a few years ago.

I must get a blank look on my face, because Dave is about to say something, but J.W. interrupts.

"We're done for the day," he says. "Dave said we could have dinner with him and Elizabeth before we head off for Baltimore."

Elizabeth feeds us something called a "chicken pot pie" and a green vegetable I've never seen before, that she simply refers to as "greens."

They walk us to J.W.'s truck, which is still parked behind the house.

Elizabeth looks worried.

"I hope you're worried for my safety, and not Jocie's," J.W. says.

"It's such a dangerous place," she replies.

"It's not an easy life, but this area can always use hard-working young people like you two," Dave says, and hands me a piece of paper with his name and number on it. "Call me any time, day or night."

He turns to J.W.

"J.W., you listen to Jocie. Maybe she can help you get your head on straight."

There's a moment of awkward silence.

"We're not going far without the keys," J.W. says.

"I gave them to Jocie," Dave replies.

"Keys?" I ask.

Oh! The metal sticks.

I dig them out of my pack and hand them to J.W. Soon we're hurling down the road at what feels like an unsafe speed. Hover buses and tube cars don't have the randomness of human drivers. Every time something catches his eye, I feel a slight turn of the wheel, followed by a correction to get back on course.

We say nothing to each other for at least thirty minutes, when J.W. breaks the silence.

"Jocie? Where are you going after Baltimore?" he asks.

"Home," I reply.

"Where is that?"

"The more I see of the world, J.W., the more I think that 'home' isn't a place. It's more like a state of mind. My parents are 'home' anywhere that they're together, and they rarely leave each other's side. My friend, Zera is 'home' anywhere that she's having fun, even if she and I were back to back in a fight for our lives. My brother, Austin…"

J.W. drives off the road, and I realize that he was looking at me, rather than where he's driving.

"Sorry," he says.

"Why were you staring at me?" I ask.

"Dave said you just appeared out of the woods. You don't seem to be afraid of anything or anyone, and yet you seem to have forgotten that the earth is in a mild nuclear winter and don't know what car keys are. You beat up seven good street fighters like it's a game, and then insist on feeding me rather than sending me to jail. Wherever you're from, I want to go there."

"You didn't let me finish. The people I'm talking about, J.W., they carry 'home' inside of themselves. We call it the Holy Spirit."

"It figures," he says. "If there's anyone on the planet that can't catch a break, it's me."

"If you were going to ask to travel with me, then you're right; but I'd be happy to tell you about the Lord. Maybe you could find home inside yourself, too."

"Where do your relatives in Baltimore live?" he asks.

"I don't know."

"Well, you'd better figure something out. You can't come into The Zone with me.

"What's The Zone?"

"It's short for 'The Dead Zone.' There's one in most cities. It's where everyone with the gene goes to die. It's full of angry people who already hated each other anyway."

"I don't understand," I say.

"The toxin affects anyone with the gene and the damage is cumulative. People who were near the bombs were dead in days. The rest of us are waiting for the wind to bring enough of it to our doorstep to finish us off. The toxin doesn't care if you're Muslim or Jewish or Christian. The target gene is ancient and has had thousands of years to spread around the world. The different religions represented in The Zone already blame each other for this mess; so for some of us, it's better to die fighting than to wait for the toxin. There are murders in the street every day."

"You have the target gene," I say.

"Worse. I have a mutation of the gene. According to the doctors, my death will be much slower and more painful than average."

"You look fine," I say.

He rolls up his sleeve to reveal an open wound. There are scars where others broke out, but have healed.

"The pain on my skin isn't that bad," he says. "It's the feeling that something is eating away at my insides that I hate. Every time I take a breath or a bite of food, I wonder if I'm taking in another particle that drifted in as if it has my name on it."

"Maybe you won't die," I say. "I've heard there are some survivors."

"Urban legends," he says. "People in The Zone whisper about things like that all the time. People even come to the edge of The Zone to sell things they say are miracle cures, but it's all snake oil."

"You don't seem like the 'wait-around-to-die' type," I say.

"You're right. I don't want to go like that. I have a plan."

I reach out and touch his arm, and close my eyes.

"Lord, I ask you to bring healing to J.W. I know that there is no toxin that's beyond Your power …"

He pulls his arm away before I can finish.

"Save it, Jocie. I've met Christians. There used to be one called "Father Zeke" who ran a mission on the edge of The Zone. He was always walking around and telling anyone who'd listen about Jesus. I didn't see anyone cured by his prayers."

"I understand," I say. "May I start again?"

I touch his arm again, without waiting for a reply.

"Lord, this is your child, J.W., who you've known since before he was even born. He's most likely going to die a miserable, painful death very soon. I pray instead that you'll give him a peaceful death. Bring to your child a death where all he feels is Your love inside him. Teach him where home is."

"Am I supposed to say 'thank you' for that?" he asks. "Is that really the best your God can do? A peaceful death?"

"You can thank me, or not," I say. "I wasn't talking to you."

"Keep talking to Him. If He's not too busy, see what He can do about this."

We reach a high point in the road, where I can see much of the city in front of me. It looks grimy. The exit we're passing has a sign that says "Local traffic only" and there's a police car parked across the road to ensure the sign is obeyed.

"We can't go into that area?" I ask.

"If you have I.D. that says you live there, you can. My I.D. says I have the gene. The only place I can go in the city is The Zone."

"What if you don't have any I.D.?" I ask.

He looks over at me.

"Is that why you refused to talk with the police in Virginia? I guess you're coming into The Zone with me, then. We'll need to cover your hair. There aren't many redheads in The Zone."

He reaches behind my seat and brings out a hat with a triangle that must represent a prism, because a light ray enters one side and is split into colors on the other. I look at the back.

"Was she your girlfriend?" I ask.

"What? Who?"

"The girl who gave you this hat. Her name is on the back: Pink Floyd."

He doesn't answer, but the look on his face tells me that I've asked another stupid question.

We switch from one highway to another and pass dozens of exits that are all being watched by police cars, until we reach a bumpy dirt ramp where J.W. turns off. It's not like the other exits. This one looks like it was built in a hurry. It doesn't even have a street name, there's just a large sign that features a human skull and the words "The Zone" in black paint. There is no police car here and I have the feeling that none would come if called.

******

We don't enter a neighborhood with quiet streets and trees. Instead, we're in some sort of an industrial park with warehouses. In the first block, I'm struck by the amount of trash that's blowing around. In the next block, there are burned-out buildings. By the fifth block, I've seen more burned cars than I care to count.

"You said there's a place like this in most cities?" I ask.

"Most aren't quite like this. We're on a big peninsula that juts out into the river. It makes it pretty easy to keep everyone with the gene contained. I imagine that once we're all dead, they'll just bulldoze it all and try to forget we were here."

"Where do the people live?"

"Here's a row of gene apartments now," he says.

"Those are just big metal boxes."

"That's right. This used to be a port and those used to be shipping containers. Now we live in them."

"Did you all come here voluntarily?"

"Nobody with the gene can find a job, and the government makes it free to live here; so it's a pretty easy choice - once you run out of money. They provide food, water, electricity, and pain killers, and then let the toxin do its work."

"They must send doctors," I say.

"They send coroners."

We reach another row of gene apartments and J.W. pulls in.

"Home sweet home," he says.

He knocks on one of the metal doors.

"Mrs. Haddad? How are you doing?" he calls, and we hear a weak 'come in.'

A woman, who I judge to be about fifty, is lying on a filthy mat on the floor. She's covered with sores and her eyes are glassy from pain.

"Do you need a pill?" J.W. asks.

"It won't help. It's almost time. Then the pain will end. I can't find my cloth, J.W., can you see my cloth?"

J.W. reaches down and picks up a piece of cloth the size of a handkerchief that's fallen off the mat, and places it into her hand.

"She needs a doctor," I say.

"Is someone with you, J.W.?" Mrs. Haddad asks, and I realize that the toxin has made her blind.

"I'm a friend," I say.

I kneel down beside her and take her hand, which is extremely warm. I close my eyes and bow my head. She reaches up and touches my face, and realizes that I'm praying.

"You are Christian?" Mrs. Haddad asks. "I am Christian too. You have been sent to pray for me."

"That's right. I'll pray over you, until you're home."

CHAPTER TWENTY-TWO

"Jenny and her family moved away today," I said to Dad. "She was the last of my Christian friends to leave."

Dad knew exactly what I was talking about. Each of the five friends who had been attacked at the party that Dad kept me away from when I was thirteen had left the area in search of a community where The Washed could feel safe.

"I've never asked you about that night ..." I continued, "but now I'd like to know some things."

"You want to know why I didn't warn the other families of your plan to go to that party."

"That would be a good start," I said.

"I've regretted that decision for over four years, Jocie. If I had known..."

"Didn't you? Isn't that why you stopped me from going to the party?" I asked. "You had everything else about that night figured out. Didn't you put the pieces together and know they'd be attacked?"

He stared at me for a long while.

"I've been accused of being a monster, Jocie, and given the things I did for The Corps when I was your age, I deserve it … but I don't remember any accusation ever hurting as much as this. How could you think that I would consciously decide to let your friends be assaulted?"

"You consciously decided to let yourself be beaten and almost killed inside the mountain," I said. "Maybe in your head, my friends were just another necessary sacrifice in some greater plan."

"Bad things sometimes happen to good people, Jocie."

"Don't give me the answer you'd give an eight-year-old," I snapped. "Just tell me if you knew what was going to happen, and let them go to the party anyway."

"I gave up on making my own plans long ago, Jocie," he said. "If I thought for a moment that my plans were better or wiser, then I'd…"

He trailed off into that well-known expression of bottomless sadness. Usually when he did that, I'd feel sad, too, but this time was different. For the first time in my life, I looked into my father's eyes, and instead of wanting to know all of the secrets running around in his head, I was afraid that he might tell them to me.

******

J.W. leaves with a grunt, and I hear the door to the next apartment in the line open. I pray and read the bible for the next hour, until I hear a car drive up and someone shout "J.W."

271

For twenty minutes, I have to listen to J.W. as he lies to his gang friends about what happened after they left. He weaves a tale in which he woke up, and then escaped by beating me in hand-to-hand combat, followed by a long chase by the police. All the while, Mrs. Haddad is moaning louder and louder in pain, while I continue to hold her hand and pray.

"Hey, J.W., is the lady next door almost dead?" one of the gang asks. "Does she have any good stuff?"

"Leave her alone," J.W. replies.

"C'mon, man. She don't need it no more."

The door begins to creak open.

"I said, leave her alone," J.W. repeats.

"I'll just see how close she is."

A head peeks in the door. I've taken off the hat and don't try to hide my face.

"We will not mark the passing of this good woman with the breaking of a commandment - Thou shalt not steal. Not while I'm here," I say.

"J.W.? What is *she* doing here?"

The door opens farther, and the rest of the gang poke their heads in.

"You're going to pay, little girl!" the big guy says.

"We will also not mark the passing of this good woman with violence," I say, then return to praying.

Mrs. Haddad is beginning to shake and lets out a loud groan from the pain. The cloth that J.W. found for her is still in her hand, and she stuffs part of it into her mouth, which muffles her cries.

I run through every prayer that I've memorized, which is a lot. Her eyes open, and although they're blind, they appear to be pleading with me … begging me to somehow end her suffering. When I look deeper, I see something I didn't expect: Joy.

"My prayers are done, my sister. Let go of this world," I say, softly. "Go home."

When her shaking stops, I pray for a while, then gently close her eyes and place her hands onto her chest.

When I look up again, the gang is still outside, staring at me.

"Remove your hats and show some respect," I say

Much to my surprise - and I think theirs - they do it.

"How do you call the coroner when someone passes?" I ask.

"The red switch on the wall will turn on a light on the top of the apartment," J.W. says. "They'll see it, and come running."

I turn on the switch and exit the apartment, passing through the group.

"You've got a lot of guts to turn your back on me," the big guy says. "This time I have a metal bat, and I don't see your fancy stick anywhere."

I turn.

"I feel like I've been praying for hours, but I'm sure I have one more in me," I say, and bow my head. "Lord, these men just witnessed the passing of your child, Mrs. Haddad, into your loving arms. I pray to you: please don't wait until the end to take these men into your arms. Open their eyes and their hearts. Show them that you are with them, always, and lead them onto the path of everlasting life."

"Are you done?" the one with the bat asks.

I turn and start to walk down the row, looking ofr an empty apartment where I can sleep.

The one with the bat follows me and I hear the rest follow him at a distance.

"Don't you turn your back on me, little girl!"

His steps are awkward. The streetlight casts a shadow telling me that the bat is already above his head, ready to come down. Apparently he doesn't want a repeat of me ducking under one of his wild swings. I continue to watch the shadow as he closes the gap.

"Let it go, Jake," J.W. says. "Let me tell you what really happened after you guys ran out on me."

Jake gets closer, and I watch the shadow of the bat go up an inch.

"C'mon, Jake. We were robbing that dude. She was just doing the right thing."

As Jake swings the bat down at the top of my head, I sidestep. The ringing of the bat on the ground alone must hurt his hands terribly, but I kick his wrist to make him release it, just the same. It's easy to catch his ear and force him to his knees.

"Don't pinch my ear!" he says. "My grandmother would do that, and I hated it."

"Clearly, you all need someone to minister to you," I announce. "Everyone be back here tomorrow at ten o'clock for morning services."

They all look to J.W.

"You heard her," he says, "It looks like we have a minister."

******

I sleep soundly in the abandoned apartment, until the sun wakes me through the skylight, which also serves as a fire escape. There's an old broom in the corner, which I decide the former resident didn't know how to operate, based on the amount of dust and dirt in the place. I open the door wide and give the place a thorough cleaning.

There are two broken chairs, next to a small wooden table, so I set them up neatly and spread an old blanket over the table to act as a tablecloth. Outside, I pick some small, purple wildflowers and arrange them in an old bottle as a center piece. I beat the sleeping mat until the dust coming out of it subsides, and then toss it on top of the apartment - hoping the sun will disinfect it.

When everything is as tidy as I can make it, I walk down the row of containers until I reach J.W.'s apartment. The door is ajar; so I knock lightly and look inside.

J.W. is sitting at a table, wearing a pair of magnification goggles. In front of him is some sort of air purification system that he's studying under magnification. Every now and again, he sprays the filter with a liquid, and then continues the inspection.

"Got you," he says, as he carefully picks something off the filter.

"Thought you could get into my lungs unnoticed, did you? Well, you and two of your little friends didn't make it today, did you?"

He uncaps a vial of a yellow liquid and drops whatever he picked off the filter into it. He takes the vial to a small bookshelf and places it inside a hollow book.

I ease my head out of the door and knock harder.

"Just a minute," he says.

When he opens the door, the filtration unit is back to work, purifying the air.

"Hello, neighbor," I say.

"Shouldn't you be writing a sermon?"

"Jesus never wrote sermons. He just spoke from His heart," I reply.

"Good. I never much liked sermons."

I look at the apartment where Mrs. Haddad lived. The red light is off.

"They came for her ten minutes after you went into that abandoned apartment," J.W. says. "I'm surprised you didn't hear the arguing and come out."

"Arguing?"

"Two coroner vans saw the red light at about the same time. Their monthly bonus is based on the number of bodies they collect, so they were fighting over Mrs. Haddad."

"They're lucky I fell asleep. How could anyone be so ghoulish? She was a human being who died a horrible death. Her remains deserved honor and respect."

"Can I give you some advice, Jocie? I know you only knew Mrs. Haddad for a couple of hours, but it's not smart to get close to people here in The Zone. I left last night, as she died, because I couldn't watch it again. I've seen it too many times."

"Are you going to do the same thing, as each of your friends die?" I ask. "You'd let them die alone? And what about you? Do you want to die alone?"

"I'd rather die alone than make a friend watch. Luckily, I have a better plan."

As he says it, Jake's truck drives up. Every member of the group showed up. Some put on clean clothes, and did their best to wash the grime off their hands and faces. I appreciate the effort. This is the first time I've seen them in daylight and I realize that they are all showing signs of toxin exposure. They all bear open wounds from the cumulative genetic damage.

Like Mrs. Haddad, I see that they all have pieces of cloth. Some are tied around their heads or their arms, and some are just sticking out of pockets.

We all walk to my new apartment and I ask them to sit on the ground outside the door. Behind them, I see two girls emerge from an apartment. They say something into the door and many more heads emerge. They, too, all have the same pieces of cloth somewhere on their bodies.

"How many of you are Christian?" I ask.

Three hands go up, one of which is J.W.'s.

"How many of you are Jewish?"

Two hands go up. Once again, one of them is J.W.'s"

"What about Muslim?"

Two hands.

"What about no religion?"

The last two hands.

"I can't pretend to know much about the Jewish or Islamic faiths," I say. "I will say that I'm glad to see that so many different types of believers have chosen to be friends. Maybe it's because of the one thing you all have in common: death. You all carry the gene. The fact that you're here tells me that you all have something else in common, too. You all have love and hope inside you. As a Christian, I call that love and hope 'the Holy Spirit.' I'm not going to promise that the Holy Spirit will save any of your lives here on earth, but I hope you'll all consider that the Holy Spirit can do something much greater. He can save your soul."

As I've been speaking, a dozen young men have been walking up the street towards us. The girls all scurry back into the apartment.

They're led by a big man who has a cloth tied around his neck, and many more toxin wounds than the rest. Although it's a cool morning, he's sweating heavily. He probably has only days left to live.

"I wouldn't have believed it, if I hadn't seen it for myself," the big guys says. "The Masonville guys are begging God to save them."

The members of my little congregation jump to their feet and reach for weapons.

"Get lost, Slash," J.W. says.

"Why don't you join us?" I say. "The Lord has enough love for all of you, too."

'Slash' spits on the ground.

"That's what I think of your Lord," he says.

"I can understand why you think the world is full of nothing but hate," I say. "You came here for a fight. What if I told you that His love is stronger than your hate, even in a street fight?"

He spits on the ground again.

"Here's the deal," I say. "The strongest fighter in my group will take on the best three fighters in your group. If you win, the Masonville territory is yours, and these guys will act as your servants for a month. If Masonville wins, you come and listen to me talk every day for a week."

"Three against one?" he says. "With or without weapons?"

"You get weapons, we don't …" I reply. "… but if you drop one, it's fair game for anyone to use."

His jaw drops.

"You're going to be my servant around the clock, J.W.," Slash says.

The group backs off a few steps to decide which three of them will be fighting.

"It's going to be me, Wings, and Babe," Slash announces when they return. "I don't know who this girl is, J.W., but her mouth is going to put you into a world of pain."

"I'm not fighting," J.W. says. "She is."

Slash watches me, as I walk past my "congregation." There are several light posts and a small boulder, but otherwise the area is clear. The three of them walk towards me, shoulder-to-shoulder.

Dad once asked why the world seemed to be constantly putting weapons into his hands. I'm starting to understand what he was talking about.

As I assess their weapons, their nicknames make perfect sense to me. Slash is holding a short knife; Wings has a half-meter section of chain that he's spinning like the blades on a drone; and Babe is holding a wooden bat.

Babe decides to step up first.

"Hit a homerun for us, Babe," one of the guys in the gallery yells.

"Did you go to church as a child, Babe?" I ask.

"My parents took me sometimes," he says, then takes a few practice swings.

"I don't know what sort of church you went to …" I say, "…but my Lord is the prince of peace. So, I'm pretty sure attacking me with a bat wasn't part of their teachings."

"Religion is dead," he says. "It committed suicide when it decided to drop bombs. Islam and Judaism are dead. Christianity is dead. We're all dead."

"My Lord is very much alive," I say. "He will protect me from your bat."

He runs forward and takes a hard swing at my head, which I duck under.

"Don't hurt me," I shriek in a little girl voice, then run.

The rival gang all starts to laugh. J.W.'s group stands with their mouths open, but J.W. is smiling.

I reach the closest light post, with Babe on my heels, and use it to swing around and kick him in the chest with both feet. He staggers back, but doesn't fall. The laughing and jaw-dropping switches groups.

"God loves you, Babe," I say, as I kick his wrist to make him drop the bat.

His eyes go to his bat.

"Leave the bat, Babe. You think it's your source of power, but it's not. You think it gave you your name, but it didn't. The Lord protected me from that bat. If you want true power, let it go and join Him."

He lunges for the bat, but I kick it away from him and watch him fall into the dust. I pick up the bat and toss it to J.W.

"I need my bat!"

"It's mine now," I say. "You can have it back, when you're ready to write your real name on it - the name that God gave to you. Now go sit down."

In the background, the girls are appearing again.

Wings decides to step up next. He swings the chain over his head, where it makes an impressive whirring sound, but will force his attacks to be slow and choppy to ensure he doesn't hit himself in the head in the process.

"The Lord loves you, Wings," I say. "He wants you to know Him."

The spinning of his chain slowed by a few revolutions per minute when I spoke.

He advances and takes a few exploratory swings at me. It's easy to jump back. With each attack, the chain loses most of its momentum, causing a lag as he gets it back up to full speed.

"You went to church as a child," I say. "You remember singing the songs. You remember how happy and peaceful you felt. Swinging that chain doesn't make you feel peaceful."

I begin to slowly sing an ancient song that Mom taught me called "Jesus Loves Me." It should be well-known here in 2039.

"Jesus loves me, this I know …"

As I sing, I back towards the light post on my left. He's sees what I'm doing, and smiles. He knows his chain will be less effective if I put the post between us, so he runs to beat me to it. To run, he stops spinning the chain over his head and spins it vertically on his right side. He realizes to late that my move was a fake, made to open his left side up to attack just as I reach "They are weak, but He is strong" and connect a kick to his left knee.

"Yes, Jesus loves me!" I sing at the top of my lungs.

He starts the chain spinning over his head again, and has it up to full speed as I finish the refrain and start the next verse as I back towards the boulder.

"Jesus loves me, this I know …"

I jump onto the boulder as he makes his next attack, and then use the height advantage to jump over the chain. He was so sure the chain would connect that he's thrown off balance. He has no choice but to release the chain or it will come around and hit him in the back.

"Taking children on His knee…" I sing, as I plant my knee into his stomach and then into his face as he doubles over.

Using a knee at that line in the song was a touch obvious, but gets a good laugh out of the Masonville guys.

I casually pick up the chain and start spinning it over my head. Wings runs to the light post as I return to the refrain. I spin the chain as fast as I can and hit the post, breaking the chain in half.

"This is nothing, Wings. The Lord can break the chains that are binding your soul. Now, go sit with Babe."

I turn to face Slash.

"You can't get into my head with your religion talk," he says. "I never went to church."

"Me either," I say. "It's never been a question of walking into a box with a cross on top of it. It's a question of what's in your heart."

He points his knife at me and takes a fighting stance, but it looks half-hearted.

"Have you looked in a mirror, Slash? You're sweating, and you have a lot of open sores. Don't spend your last days filled with anger."

"Yeah … me and three million other Americans, and a billion others around the world. We're all angry. Who wouldn't be?"

Even after three years, they still don't understand how bad it's going to get. Twelve million Americans, and over three billion worldwide, are going to die from the toxin before it's over.

"Anyone would be angry," I say. "It's easy to be angry when we have no control. What we have a hard time understanding is that we've never been in control."

He takes a weak swing at me with the knife.

I could disarm him. I could hit him three times before he felt the first one.

"You should save your breath, Ginger. I've seen people like you come into The Zone before and preach about love and forgiveness. What do you know about us? What do you know about what it's like to be dying, when you're standing there with your perfect skin?"

"I know a lot more than you think, Slash."

I leave my fighting stance and roll up my sleeve, revealing a small, open wound.

"I have the gene."

I wish it was another synthetic scar, oozing polymer, but it's very real.

CHAPTER TWENTY-THREE

"Does anybody know what this is?" Dad asked his class, as he carefully unfolded an old piece of cloth.

Even I didn't know the answer, despite everything Dad had taught me about religious history.

"I'll give you a hint," Dad said. "This cloth is nearly two hundred years old. It comes from the time of the Final Holy War."

There were still no volunteers.

"Pieces of cloth like this were carried by those who had the target gene. In some cases, they were issued by local governments, but mostly they were an invention of the toxin victims themselves. Carrying one was just part of the culture of living in a Dead Zone. What do you think it was for?"

A woman from Montana guessed that they were used to signal for help, and a man in the live audience guessed that they were used to carry painkillers.

"This was known as a 'screaming cloth,'" Dad said. "No painkillers were sufficient to dull the pain; there was no help coming to end the suffering. The culture of the Dead Zones was to at least be considerate enough to stuff one of these in your mouth so that those around you wouldn't have to listen, as you screamed your way towards death."

******

With my congregation doubled, we talk for several hours. Given the mix of faiths, I do my best to let them come to me with questions about Jesus, rather than overwhelming them. Dad always said it never works to be "a spiritual dump truck" where you try to bury someone in scripture. He knows that the Lord won't be hurried, and will open a person's heart at the pace *He* chooses.

Mostly we discuss plans to make The Zone a better place. We agree to make sure that everyone gets the food and water they need when they become too sick to get it for themselves, and that nobody will be left to die alone. Best of all, we agree to pray for each other.

The girls have been watching the entire time, but when I wave for them to join us, they disappear again.

"We need to talk," J.W. says, after the meeting breaks up.

"How about if we go for a walk? I've been standing for hours."

I speak before he gets the chance.

"The girls across the street are pretty skittish. How could we get them to join us?" I ask.

"Forget it," he says. "They're all too afraid of being raped. People come to The Zone to die, not start a family."

"Then I should go to them …"

"They're even more afraid of you," he cuts me off. "In the early days of The Zone, there were girls who were captured by the gangs and forced to act as bait for the others. They'd never trust you."

We walk silently for a while.

"None of that is what we need to talk about," J.W. says.

He reaches down and takes my hand, but I gently shake loose.

"That's not really appropriate," I say.

"I only need to hold it for a few seconds," he says, and takes it again.

We stop and he turns me to face him, with a huge smile on his face.

"Since you appeared out of the woods, everyone has been asking, 'who are you?' but it turns out that wasn't the right question. We should have asked 'what are you?'"

His grip tightens and he twists my arm around. The smile leaves his face and is replaced by anger.

"Look at your arm, Jocie. That wound is gone and there's not even a scar. I watched it heal! There's a small one on your face, and it's already starting to heal."

I look at my arm. The skin is smooth and perfect.

I have the gene that releases the toxin, but I also have the vaccine from the future.

J.W. releases my arm.

But the toxins are different. The vaccine must not work perfectly on the original version.

"Are you going to say something?" J.W. asks.

Something else is going on … but what?

He grabs me by the shoulders and looks at my face.

"Now the one on your face is almost gone. It's like your body eats toxin for breakfast. What are you, Jocie? Are you immune? Are you some sort of genetic freak?"

That's it. My genes slow the toxin down, but my body is creating an antivenin, just like Amelia predicted.

The scowl on his face reminds me of Austin. He has the same enthusiasm and unjustified confidence. One day, it will be replaced by patience and the confidence formed by experience.

"I've been looking for you, and only just now realized that I had found you," I say. "As for whether I'm immune, the short answer is 'yes'."

"What's the long answer?"

"We both have a mutant gene," I say. "It slows our exposure and allows our bodies a chance to fight back."

"I don't heal before people's eyes."

"Maybe not, but your body is fighting back. The mutation is giving you a chance to heal the genetic damage."

"I don't feel like I'm healing, Jocie. Things are worse every day."

"It's the wind," I say. "Over the winter, the area was getting more wind out of the north. Now, it's getting more out of the west, which is bringing in more toxin. Everyone in this area with the gene is going to feel it. A lot will be lost before the wind pattern changes again."

"Can we get out of its path?" he asks.

"It'll be circling the earth for a decade. You can go live in a bubble, or you can face it head-on."

"Head-on?"

"Keep breathing it in," I say. "It won't be easy or pleasant. It's going to hurt, and there will be scars."

A young man that everyone calls "Abbi" spots us and comes running.

"Jocie, Mrs. Turani sent me. They need a minister."

J.W. nods that I should go, but the look on his face tells me that this conversation is not over.

Abbi leads me through a maze of container apartments. I see three different black coroner vans cruising the streets. They're black like vultures, and they circle like vultures, waiting for people to die so they can swoop in on the remains.

When we reach the metal box occupied by the Turani family, Mr. Turani is on the floor, surrounded by his wife and four children. His clothes are drenched with sweat and his face is a mass of open sores. The rest of the family appear to be just days behind reaching the same state.

"How much painkiller have you given him?" I ask.

"Any more, and would kill him," Mrs. Turani says.

She looks at me intently.

"Yes, I've thought of ending it that way, but Allah does not permit it," she answers the unasked question.

"I know very little about your faith or customs," I say.

"I know, young lady, but all are talking about what you did last night and this morning. Many are saying that God is with you. Will you just sit with us?"

"Of course."

******

It's nearly dusk, when I walk back to my new home. Mr. Turani's death was violent. He writhed in pain for hours, while we all took turns holding him down. He didn't have the strength or control to place the piece of cloth in his own mouth, so his family did it for him. His oldest son will be next, then Mrs. Turani. I vow that their younger sons will not die alone.

I hear someone step out from behind a tree after I pass it, and begin to follow me, but I keep walking. He speeds up and slows down as I do.

"I'm almost home Slash; so if there's something on your mind, you should probably say it."

I turn around. He looks awful.

"It's not safe to walk around in The Zone by yourself, Jocie. If you had any sense, you'd be afraid."

"If I was alone, I would be afraid," I say.

He looks around.

"What I mean is, I'm never alone," I say. "The Lord is with me."

He looks at the ground.

"Two days ago, I never would have come here by myself," he says. "I know I'm in Masonville turf, but when you say things like that, you make this place feel … safe."

I sit on the curb, but say nothing. He sits beside me.

He needs to talk.

"I'm supposed to be a leader, you know?" he says. "I'm not supposed to be afraid of anything, but …"

"You're afraid of death," I say, and he nods.

"I've seen it plenty of times; I know that I don't have long," he says. "I've had a fever for days and I'm covered with sores.

There are sores on the inside too, on all of my organs. I know it's going to hurt, but I'm not afraid of the pain. I'm afraid of what comes next."

"I thought you didn't believe," I say.

"How am I supposed to believe in a God who would allow this?" he asks. "You say He loves me. Well, I say He has a funny way of showing it."

"We're all going to die …" I say, "… but I assure you: whether you get one year on earth or one hundred, it doesn't change how much He loves you. Paul said it well in Romans: 'And I am convinced that nothing can ever separate us from God's love. Neither death nor life, neither angels nor demons, neither our fears for today nor our worries about tomorrow - not even the powers of hell can separate us from God's love.'"

As we've been speaking, the sun has set. Although my back is to him, I know that J.W. is quietly walking toward us.

"I should go," Slash says, looking over my shoulder.

"You're in the wrong section of town," J.W. says, from behind me.

Slash jumps to his feet.

"Things are dangerous around here after dark," J.W. continues. "A guy like you could get hurt."

J.W.'s voice has changed.

Slash looks back and forth, searching for the rest of J.W.'s gang.

"So, you'd better come to my place," J.W. says. "I've been saving up some chocolate bars for a special occasion. I think we should talk."

Looking at me, J.W. throws me some sort of protein bar.

"Mrs. Henderson needs you," he says. "It won't be long."

J.W. and Slash take turns checking in through the night, as I sit with Mrs. Henderson. Her sores are so bad that she bleeds through her clothes, so J.W. and Slash bring blankets. I pray almost endlessly, and eventually fall asleep sitting up, mid-prayer. I awaken to find that J.W. has taken my place, with Slash nearby, reading a bible.

"It's over," J.W. says, then reaches up and flips on the red light.

******

The next two days go like that. Over and over, I'm called to every section of The Zone to pray for people who are near the end. It always ends with a cloth in the mouth, a red light, and vultures in black vans.

I find myself cursing the wind that's been blowing since I arrived here, and wondering how many particles of toxin are kicked up, whenever I see dust in the air. Twice more, I catch J.W. cleaning his air filter and carefully picking toxin off it, as if he's trying to clean up the atmosphere, one particle at a time.

His efforts don't seem to be working. The number of sores on his face and arms have increased dramatically and he's sweating constantly. Even so, it's clear that his body is fighting back. The sores on his skin are smaller than anyone else's and begin to close up after a few days, though they leave raised scars after they heal.

Slash is not so fortunate. His trip to find me was his last. Since then, he hasn't left his apartment. Yesterday, the sores in his throat and digestive tract reached the point where he stopped eating. Today I heard he's refusing water; so I'm going to check on him. There are lookouts on the edge of his territory, but I pass them, unchallenged. I can walk anywhere in The Zone, and runners who are looking for me can cross the invisible gang lines, as if just saying my name puts them under my protection.

"It looks like both me and J.W. are about done," Slash says, without getting up.

His eyes are glassy from the high dose of painkiller he's taken.

It's his deathbed, and he knows it.

"We both talked to our guys," he continues. "Everyone agrees that we're done with gangs and turfs. We want to be one congregation. I think all of the other gangs will follow. Actually, I think they'll follow you."

"Not me," I say. "They need to follow the Lord."

"Jocie? Do you think Jesus sent you here? That's what I think."

"He sent us all here, Slash. He sent us here to love and comfort each other until we're in His arms again."

"Will you do me a favor?" Slash asks. "When it's close to the end, will you send the guys away? I don't want my friends to see me like that."

My dear friend ... Dad's prayer suddenly makes sense.

"Have you ever thought about why you like your friends, Slash? One reason is that you like who you are when you're with them. My dad taught me to begin prayers by saying 'My dear friend.' I do it now, too, because I want Him close. I want to be the Jocie who can only exist when Jesus is near. Please let the guys be here for you."

"Okay."

Slash closes his eyes.

"Jocie? Will you read me the part in the bible where Jesus tells the thief on the cross that he's going to heaven?"

I spend the next four hours reading the bible and praying over Slash, as he's gripped with a pain that the drugs can't relieve. Guys from his gang come to help me hold him down. When the time seems near, I get close to his ear and whisper to him.

"You can stop fighting, Slash. You've won. It's time to go home."

The thrashing slows and he lies so still, that I think he's passed, when his eyes open.

"It's so beautiful," is the last thing he says.

I leave the gang inside the shipping container apartment so they can say goodbye to their leader in private, and walk into the darkness to cry a little. The only problem is, I don't feel like crying. Before I know it, I've taken the extending fighting stick from where it hangs on my belt and start attacking a tree with it. I spin and weave and strike so fast that the world feels like a blur.

Yes, make the world a blur, so I don't have to look at it anymore.

I stop when I'm unexpectedly bathed in red light. Someone flipped the switch to signal the coroners to come and pick up Slash.

I'll never look at a red light the same way again.

The door is slightly open, with Babe's head sticking out. He's been watching my tantrum.

"Jocie? Are you okay?"

"No, Babe, I'm not okay. I want to smash things. I want to start with that red light and every other red light in The Zone. Then I want to travel to the next zone in the next city and smash those lights, too. I want to go to every city in the world and smash every red light so I never have to look at another one for the rest of my life."

"Not you, Jocie!" he says. "Not now. I can handle it from anyone else … but not from you."

"What?"

The door opens wider, as more members of the gang look out to see what's happening.

"You can't lose it on us, Jocie. You're the only thing keeping us all going. You're the only one who can bring peace to this place. You're the only one who…"

"Stop it!" I cut him off. "Just stop talking to me!"

I begin to pace back and forth.

"Has every second I've spent here been wasted?" I ask. "Have none of you paid any attention?"

I receive blank stares.

"I'm not the only one to do anything!" I yell. "I am the weakest person on the entire earth. I have nothing special. I am nobody!"

More and more apartment doors are opening, and people are coming out to listen.

"Look at me! I'm short and skinny. Is this the body of someone who can beat up seven gang members at once? Do I look like I have the strength to pray for hours on end, while holding down a man who's thrashing in pain?"

My voice drops to a whisper, but the growing crowd is so quiet that they can all hear me.

"Do you think it's by the strength of my own will that I can watch someone die, and minutes later, move on to the next person who needs prayers? If that's what you think, then my time here really has been wasted."

The faces around me are mostly looking at the ground.

"I thought something was happening here. I thought you knew that when two or more are gathered in His name, He would be here with us. I thought you were ready to be a part of something more than yourselves. I thought you were ready to find out where true strength comes from."

Nobody says a word, and I walk towards the edge of the crowd, away from that horrible red glow.

"Stay here and die alone," I say. "I'm done with all of you."

"Timothy!" a familiar voice yells.

I stop and turn to face Babe.

"What did you say?" I ask.

"My real name is Timothy. I'm ready to write the name He gave to me on that old bat, and use it to protect the weak in His name."

"My name is Luke…" Wings says, "… and I stand with Timothy."

One by one, the former gang members come to me and tell me their real names.

"Do you know what your name means in Greek, Timothy?" I ask.

He shakes his head.

"It means 'Honoring God.'"

CHAPTER TWENTY-FOUR

When I was seven years old, our entire family went on a summer vacation at a wonderful old hotel on a lake in Maine. All of my aunts, uncles, and cousins were there, as well as lots of other children. The kids would play all day, but Mom and Dad and most of the other adults spent the whole day inside a big room in the hotel, talking.

On the second day, I wanted to show Mom and Dad a cross that I had woven out of the long grass that grew near the lake; so I snuck away from the other kids, and into the hotel. The door to the big room was closed, but I could hear people arguing on the other side. They were talking about how there were not enough washed samples to give to everyone who wanted to have a baby. They couldn't seem to agree on what to do about it.

One man, with a mean voice, wanted to stop giving any samples at all because he wanted to keep The Washed pure. Other voices wanted the opposite, to increase the samples so there'd be as many washed children as possible. Everyone seemed most concerned about the safety of their children, and how kidnapping of The Washed was on the rise.

That evening, I went for a walk with Mom and Dad while Austin played with our cousins inside the hotel. We heard some shouting on the other side of a big hedge, and Mom and Dad stopped to see what was happening.

Soon we could hear what sounded like someone being beaten up. They didn't want to leave me by myself; so we all crawled under the hedge at a spot where it didn't quite reach the ground.

Five men were standing around a man who was on the ground, moaning. They were taking turns kicking him and calling him names because he was marked.

"Stay right here," Dad said to me.

"That's enough," Dad said, to the men.

One man kept kicking, and Dad kicked him in the back of the knee, which sent him sprawling. He sprung back up and the five washed men assessed their situation. They seemed to know what I already knew: that the five of them were no match for Mom and Dad. Three more washed men came running along the hedge. From the look on everyone's face, I knew that Mom and Dad's odds were not improving. Nobody was watching me, so I slowly slipped a com into my ear and whispered "call Aunt Cindi."

"What's happening here?" one of the newcomers asked.

It was the man with the mean voice that I'd heard earlier.

"We caught this guy spying on washed children through the hedge," the man Dad had knocked down said. "The animal was probably planning to grab one of them."

"Now do you understand what I've been trying to tell you, Cephas?" the mean-voiced man asked. "The Washed are vastly outnumbered. Even here, we're being stalked. How long will it be before we're all hunted down and used like breeding stock? Where will it end, if we don't do something?"

"We found your guys kicking a helpless man, Tyrone. Where will that end?"

Daddy knows something.

"It's not your concern, Cephas. We'll take our prisoner now."

Mom and Dad shifted to fighting positions.

"You would fight your own kind to protect this marked animal?"

"You and I are not of the same kind, Tyrone."

Uncle Cameron and Aunt Cindi burst through the bushes. Uncle Cameron started laughing when he saw the eight men.

"Jocie called us," he said. "We thought you were in danger."

He turned to Tyrone.

"Next time, bring at least ten more."

We helped the marked man to a hover bus and watched until it was gone.

"Daddy? Were they right that the marked man was here to take children?"

"I don't know."

"What if he was? We helped him to escape."

"Maybe so, but Jesus didn't teach us to only protect the weak and helpless people we like."

******

We're praying in a large circle, when a young member of a gang from the south end of The Zone runs up. He looks scared to be here.

"I don't want trouble," he says. "I'm looking for Jocie."

A member of the circle named Christopher jumps up and runs to his apartment. He returns a minute later with food and water for the young man.

"There's no trouble here, friend," Christopher says. "Rest and pray with us."

The young man turns to me.

"Jocie? It's Mrs. Wilkes. She's asking for you. It won't be long."

"Jocie's tired," Timothy says, and stands. "I've got this one."

He takes a step away from the circle, then looks back at Slash's body. I turned off the red light; so it still hasn't been collected.

"Slash traded some food for an old bible," Timothy says. "He was reading it day and night. Do you think he'd mind if I took it with me to pray with Mrs. Wilkes?"

"I think he'd be proud," I say.

******

Over the next two days, I have one or more prayer partners with me wherever I go, taking my place when I need rest. Someone starts a list of the people who are showing the worst toxin symptoms and organizes "prayer patrols" to ensure that nobody will suffer or die alone.

I'm nearing my apartment to get a few hours of rest, when I notice that one of the girls who watched me on my first day here is sitting outside of it. I approach slowly.

"Hello," I say. "I'm Jocie."

I sit in the dirt with her.

"Everyone in The Zone knows who you are," she replies. "My name is Hannah."

So this is Hannah. The note from the tiny time machine said that Hannah is the key. I wonder why I need her.

"Hannah is also my grandmother's name," I say. "It means merciful."

Her eyes finally meet mine, and I see that they're the same icy blue color as mine. As I look deeper, I can't help but smile, because it's clear that she's not beaten down and broken like everyone else I've met in The Zone. She's definitely full of life.

"You're not afraid of me," I say.

"I was at first. We moved here because J.W.'s gang was the best of the bunch. He wouldn't let them go wild and rape anyone. When we saw you, we thought he'd changed his mind. Guys sometimes change when they're close to the end, like he is. Then we saw what you did to Slash, Wings, and Babe, and we knew that nobody was controlling you."

I look her over carefully.

"You don't have the gene, Hannah. Why do you live here?"

She's startled by my observation and looks around to be sure nobody heard me.

"Nobody knows. I came here with my family and they all died, but I was adopted. I don't have any other family, so where would I go?"

"Somewhere happier?"

She's silent for a long time.

"I heard about what happened when Slash died," she says. "I heard about what you did and said. The other girls and I have been talking, and we want to help you too. We want to be a part of it."

"We go everywhere in The Zone," I say. "What about the rape gangs?"

"Timothy's bat took care of that," J.W. says, from the front of his apartment.

He looks awful, but Hannah blushes slightly as he approaches.

"This morning, he was in Stonehouse turf on a prayer patrol, when he caught five of their guys who had cornered a girl. He told them that the girl was under the Lord's protection and then he stared them down."

"I heard that he gave them a choice of facing his bat or facing Jocie," Hannah says, and giggles.

"Choose the bat," J.W. whispers, and Hannah giggles again.

Now it's J.W. who's blushing slightly.

"I really need to get some sleep …" I say, "…but you two keep on talking."

When I wake up, several hours later, I find them sitting in J.W.'s apartment, with the door wide open, still talking.

"It's J.W.'s turn to rest," Hannah says, when she sees me.

"Good idea," I say. "Let's go talk to the other girls who live in your apartment."

We close the doors as J.W. lies down. Hannah lets out a long sigh.

"Why do so many good people need to die?" she asks. "He's the kindest person I've met here in The Zone. I think you're right, Jocie. I think I should leave."

I notice a large black coroner's van parked near the apartment where Hannah lives with at least a dozen other girls.

"What are they doing here?" she asks. "Nobody in our group is even close to death, and the red light isn't on."

The coroners are three young men. Two are pounding on the door and another has climbed onto the roof.

"Open up for a safety inspection," the oldest-looking one is yelling at the door.

"Since when do you do anything other than pick up bodies," Hannah asks.

"Since we said so," he replies. "But now that you two are here, we're going to do a safety inspection in the van, instead."

"These two don't look sick at all," the one on the roof says, as he starts to climb down. "I could see us coming back here for a lot of safety inspections."

Apartment doors are opening and people are looking out.

"Yeah, we have a new therapy right here in the van," the shortest one says.

"The only thing that's going to happen in that van is that you're going to drive away in it," I say. "You try anything more than that with me or any of the girls in this apartment, and they'll be sending a coroner for you."

"Apartments?" he asks. "Stop acting so high and mighty and call them what they are - coffins."

"High and mighty? You think asking for normal human decency and respect makes me high and mighty?"

I should hang my head in shame. He's treating me like I've treated The Marked in my own time.

"Humans? You people are barely that anymore … but if you want to feel human for a few hours, how about if we take you two back to my place for a while. You'd need a shower to get the stink of this place off before I'd let you sit on the furniture though."

They all laugh.

"C'mon, Ralph," the one who was on the roof, says. "Let's stuff these two into the van and go somewhere quiet."

Most of the neighborhood is now watching and listening. They've clearly see coroners force "safety inspections" on the women of the zone before.

"You're supposed to be here to help us," I say.

"Help you?" Ralph asks. "There is no helping you. You're all dead; so you might as well have a little fun with us before you go. Now get in the van."

He takes a step towards me.

"I wouldn't do that," Hannah says, and Ralph laughs.

"This isn't your first time attacking women in The Zone," I say. "But it may be your last."

In what seems like just ten seconds later, all three are on the ground. There are two bloody noses, a sore jaw, bruised abdomens and maybe a cracked rib. There is also applause from the residents of The Zone.

"Answer one question, and the bruising stops," I say. "Has anyone ever survived the toxin?"

"I've heard rumors about a case in England and another somewhere in Asia," Ralph says, "but I think people say it just to give hope to the hopeless. You're getting more toxin with every breath. It'll get you all, eventually."

"Mark my words," I say. "There will be a survivor, and it's going to happen right here in the Baltimore Zone."

A murmur goes through the crowd.

"It'll take a miracle," Ralph says.

"Yes," I say with a smile. "Yes, it will."

******

"Why did you do it?" J.W. asks me, that evening. "Spreading false hope is even worse than having no hope at all."

He's so weak; he can barely sit up in a chair.

"I did it because I believe in miracles," I say. "There will be a survivor in The Zone. He's going to suffer greatly, but his survival will bring hope to this place and all the other zones."

"You mean me, don't you?"

"Of course I mean you. I've been watching your symptoms and they definitely progress slower than anyone else's. All the scars you have are proof of just how much toxin you've inhaled, yet here you are - still alive."

"All that proves is that I'm going to have a slower death, just like the doctors said I would."

"Then maybe it's time for you to believe in miracles."

"It's impossible, Jocie."

"Impossible? You mean impossible, like parting the Red Sea? Or impossible, like bringing Lazarus back to life? Is that the sort of impossible you're talking about?"

Hannah knocks on the door, then sticks her head in.

"J.W. should be sleeping," she says.

As I close the door behind me, I see J.W. reach for the hollowed-out book that contains vials of toxin and the magnifying glasses that will allow him to pick more off his air filter.

"I'm glad you're here, Jocie," Hannah says. "I don't want to go through watching him die all by myself."

"Do you believe in love at first sight, Hannah?"

She seems startled by the change of subject.

"Why would you ask that?"

"My family has a long-standing habit of experiencing love at first sight, even if they don't always recognize it until later. My parents actually beat each other up and Mom twice held Dad at knifepoint before they both came to the realization that they had been in love all along."

"That's not an easy way to start a relationship," she replies.

"Maybe not, but now they'll stand back-to-back with knives pointing outward, ready to face anything. They've proven that they would sacrifice anything, including their lives, for each other."

"Do you remember when I said I'm not afraid of you?" she asks. "I'm getting ready to take it back."

I stop walking and face her.

"I'm going to ask you to do something that I have no right to ask, and it's going to take the sort of commitment to a person that I just described, because I think you fell in love with J.W. at first sight - and I think he did the same."

"You want me to be there all the way through watching him die."

"No. It's going to be much harder than that. You're going to be there all the way through watching him live. With your help, J.W. will be the miracle of The Zone.

The look on her face instantly brightens.

"I'll do it! Anything you say, I'll do!"

"Hannah, I need you to understand something that I've only recently come to understand. It's hard to explain, but here goes. My parents were once forced to watch a man as he was being tortured to death. They were powerless to stop it, just like we're going to be powerless to stop what happens to J.W. There was a point during the torture where Dad said he wanted to end it himself, where he would have thought of it as an act of supreme mercy and love to drive a knife through the man's heart and end the torture."

"If you're suggesting I'll be tempted to kill J.W.…."

"No, I'm suggesting that the only thing J.W. will find more painful than the toxin will be watching you being tortured by the experience. I think he'll be tempted to drive a knife through his own heart, just to end *your* suffering."

"So you want me to plaster a smile on my face?"

"He'd see through that, and even if I thought you could pull it off, I wouldn't ask you to do that. There's nothing wrong with suffering together. As long as he can always see that fire of grace and hope in your eyes, he'll keep fighting along with you."

We walk in silence for a while.

"Jocie? The man your parents watched being tortured … did he live?"

"He did more than just live. Much, much more."

CHAPTER TWENTY-FIVE

"Dad? Have you ever thought about how easy you and Mom have it, compared to the rest of us?" I asked.

We were sitting on top of a rock we had just climbed, praying, and eating snacks.

"Easy? How so?"

"You travelled through time and met Jesus. You were there at Gethsemane, and the crucifixion, and you saw Him resurrected in Galilee. He touched you on the neck, and He spoke directly to you. How could life not be easy after that?"

Dad stared at the horizon for a long time.

"If anything, Jocie, Jesus' time here on earth should demonstrate how hard we all have it, just as life here was hard for Him."

"Jesus is the son of God; how was life here hard for Him?" I asked.

"When Jesus was here, He didn't call himself the son of God," Dad replied. "His favorite title for himself was 'the son of man,' because He was a man. It was the only way."

"The only way? What do you mean?" I asked.

"If Jesus was God on earth, just pretending to be a man, then His experience here - and His teachings - can't be a model for us to follow. It would be too far beyond our abilities and understanding," Dad said. "That's why Jesus had to choose a genuine humanity. He had to draw His power from the Father, just like the rest of us, to show us that men can model our lives after His."

I didn't know how to reply; so Dad turned back to my original question.

"Could it be, that meeting Jesus actually made things more difficult for Mom and myself?" he asked.

"How so?"

"Maybe we miss Him more, compared to the rest of you. Every day, maybe we wish He was here ... or we were there."

"Do you wish you had spent more time with Him?" I asked.

"Of course ... but His message to me was too strong to be disobeyed."

"You mean when He told you to return to your people?"

"That was a specific message to me, but it's always been the larger message of His life that I've found more moving. I think about His choice of timing in when He visited earth. In so many respects, He came at a time when all hope seemed lost for humanity - and He restored hope. Then I think about our own choices, and how, when we follow Christ, our actions can bring hope when all hope seems lost - even if it's for just one person.

"That's why you did what you did inside the mountain," I said. "You were trying to bring hope back during a time of hopelessness."

"What *I* did inside the mountain?" Dad replied. "*I* didn't do anything inside the mountain."

He thought for a long while, as he bit into and chewed an apple. I'd seen Dad do this many times. He'd nibble at the core well beyond where anyone else would have thrown it aside, until there was little more than a stem and some seeds remaining.

"I've heard people talk about the mountain," I said, when he had finished the apple. "They say you never gave up; that you stood there and took the beating and that you never quit."

"Those people completely missed the point," Dad replied. "They saw a man continue to get up after each beating and they saw strength; but the truth is that what happened inside the mountain was all about weakness."

I tilted my head to the side in confusion, so he continued.

"There wasn't much left by the time Henry was done with me, Jocie. I was beaten, whipped, starved, and dehydrated. I could see exactly how weak I really am, and I owned every bit of that weakness. That's when I truly understood."

"Understood what?"

"That you can never really own your Christianity, until you learn to own your weaknesses and hand them over to the Lord."

******

I assign Hannah to permanent prayer patrol with J.W., and then get back to work praying for anyone in The Zone who needs me. I'm praying for a former member of the Stonehouse gang, when a girl named Lisa knocks, accompanied by a young man named Patrick.

"J.W.'s not doing well," Lisa says. "Hannah really wants you to come. We'll take over here."

When I arrive, I can see that Hannah is barely containing her fear of the worst. J.W. is curled up in a ball and his clothes are soaked with sweat.

"He's in a lot of pain," Hannah says.

"Armpits and neck?" I ask.

She nods.

"It's in his lymph nodes," I say.

"The worst part is the stomach pain," J.W. says.

"It tells me that you have open sores in the digestive tract," I say.

"It tells me that I'll be dead in two days."

I turn his head to face mine and stare into his eyes.

"No way. It's not going to happen. Not in two days. Not in two years, or two decades."

He stares into my eyes.

"You and Hannah have the exact same eyes," he says. "Any man who would waste a second staring at any part of either of you, other than your eyes, is a fool. Your eyes alone tell me that you both have faith, and confidence, and strength. You could be sisters."

I hear Hannah shift her weight from one foot to the other. The idea of J.W. staring into my eyes is making her uncomfortable.

"Except ... your eyes have one thing that Hannah's don't have. When I look at your eyes, beneath all of that strength, there's an unbearable sadness that makes me want to look away. Here you are, surrounded by death, and yet I'd swear there's something even heavier weighing on your heart. Part of me hopes I never find out what in the world it is."

When Mom and Dad fought at Aunt Kimberley's house, Dad said the burden is now mine to bear. He's right. Understanding even part of what's going to happen - before it happens - is a lot to bear.

"J.W., don't be like that." Hannah says. "Jocie's the strongest, most faithful person I've ever met."

Yet, even when Dad could see that the solution to a puzzle was horrible, he still had faith that it was part of God's plan. Even when he thought he might die in the process.

I break off the stare with J.W.

I could never do what Dad did in the mountain. I would have run away and hidden.

"Thanks, Hannah…" I say. "…but J.W. is right."

I leave the apartment and wander the streets.

"They're wrong about me," I say to a tree. "I'm not strong or faithful; and the only reason I can fake being confident is because it's easy to be confident, when you can anticipate what's going to happen next. It's easy to pray, when you already know whether the person you're praying over is going to live or die. The truly faithful are those who can pray without knowing the results ahead of time - and place their trust fully in the Lord's hands."

Dad has it easy. He watched the crucifixion and then saw Jesus risen; so he has no doubts.

I hear footsteps behind me.

"You should be in bed, J.W.," I say, without turning around.

"Saying I'm sorry seemed more important than waiting around to die."

"You don't have to apologize for being right," I say.

He sits down hard, and leans against a tree with a groan, so I turn around.

"I think I know what's bothering you," he says. "Guilt. You feel guilty because you're going to survive, when so many others are going to die. It's like being the only survivor of a plane crash; you spend your time wondering 'why me?'"

"Yes," I say. "Why me? Why am I the one who's here? It should be my father, or my mother, or even my brother, Austin. They're all stronger than I am."

"I think you may have just named your greatest strength, Jocie. Humility. Everything you do, you announce that you're too weak to do it on your own and that your only strength comes from the Lord. He has a long-standing habit of demonstrating His strength through that sort of humility."

He begins to cough and I see droplets of blood on his hand.

"Right now, I hope your arms are strong," he says, and sticks out his hand. "I'm not going to be able to stand back up without your help."

Together, we get him to his feet, and I let him lean on me as we walk back to his apartment. We stop several times for coughing fits, which seem to be producing more blood each time.

"Jocie? What do you think about Hannah?"

"I think when you survive this, you should marry her," I reply.

"She'd need to survive, too. Isn't one miracle in The Zone enough to ask?"

"Have you ever seen a mark on her?" I ask.

He thinks for a long while.

"She doesn't have the gene," he concludes. "Why would she stay here?"

"I suggest you ask her … and it looks like you're going to get the opportunity right now."

Hannah is walking towards us, looking mad.

"I told you that I would find Jocie for you!" she says. "You should be in bed."

"And you should be living somewhere else," he says. "The Zone is for people with the gene."

Hannah shoots me an angry look.

"He figured it out on his own," I say.

I leave them inside the apartment. I could easily find a dozen other people to pray for, but I choose to pray for them.

******

Hannah and I agree to switch off looking after J.W. every six hours, though she's usually back after just four. His fever intensifies, but the coughing subsides. Unfortunately, the coughing is replaced by vomiting anything he eats, along with more blood.

"Jocie," he says, during one of my shifts. "I want you to send Hannah away. I don't want her to see this."

"She won't go," I say.

"Then make her! Beat her with that stick if you have to."

"It wouldn't be enough," I say. "When it comes to loving you, she's the one with God's strength behind her."

His eyes wander to the hollowed-out book on his shelf, then he closes them and falls asleep.

Of course.

I pray for the next two hours and can practically feel his fever increasing. Hannah joins me, and places her hand on his forehead.

"He's burning up," she says. "Should we put more blankets on him?"

Before I can answer, J.W. bolts upright, his eyes looking like a wild man's. He grabs my arm.

"You! You're the cure. You eat toxin; so you're the cure. Why are you letting us all die, when you're the cure?"

"J.W., wake up," Hannah says. "The fever is making you hallucinate. People don't eat toxin."

"It's not the fever," he says. "Jocie eats toxin. I've seen it. You ask her and she'll tell you. She can cure us all, but she won't. That's what makes her sad all the time."

He turns my arm.

"Look at her arm, Hannah. Remember the day she showed us that she has the gene? There's not a mark on her."

"I'm upsetting him," I say. "I should go."

I remove my arm from J.W.'s grip, but before I can leave, Hannah reaches out and runs her finger over the spot where I had a lesion. She stares at me, with a hurt look.

"It's hard to explain," I say.

"I don't want an explanation. I just want to know if he's right. Are you somehow the cure? Can you stop the deaths of millions of people?"

"No, I can't," I say.

Not in this century.

"I'm just an aberration. I'm immune. J.W. has partial immunity, which is why he has a shot at living."

"Then let's get him covered back up. Mom always said the best cure for a flu is a warm bed."

I stare at her for a few moments.

This isn't the flu, it's a toxin.

"J.W., where are the sticks that start your truck?"

"Sticks?"

"The little metal things. What are they called?"

They both look bewildered as I search for the word I need.

"Keys!" I yell. "Where are the keys?"

He points to the small bureau where he keeps his clothes, and I lunge for it.

"Get all the blankets off," I say to Hannah. "I don't care how much he shivers. Cool him off as much as you can."

I run outside and start pounding on the metal doors.

"Help! I need help!"

Jason, a young man from J.W.'s gang, comes out to see what's happening.

"Do you know how to drive?" I ask.

"Sure."

I toss him the keys.

"Take me to Jake's apartment."

When we arrive, Jake is sitting in front with two other guys.

"Jake, we need some guys and your truck," I say.

"Where are we going?"

"We need two teams. One team is going out to find something that holds water and is big enough for a man to lay down in. An old bathtub would be perfect. The other team is going to get ice."

"There's no ice anywhere in The Zone, Jocie," he replies.

"Then I guess we're leaving The Zone."

******

Jake and three others go to find some sort of tub, while I take Jason and a man named Larry in search of ice. We head west until we've left the old industrial district behind and are seeing the signs of suburbia.

"Who would have a large amount of ice?" I ask.

"Restaurants," Jason says.

"Grocery stores," Larry suggests.

"We have no money, and no way to carry it," I say.

"And no way to get into the right section of town," Jason adds. "These exits all have private security that'll stop us."

"Take the next exit," I say. "There's a hospital. They usually have ice machines on every floor."

As Jason predicted, there's a security car at the bottom of the exit, checking each vehicle as it comes down the ramp. There's only one guard, a young but severely obese man sitting in the running vehicle.

"Go in fast and stop hard. Tell him I don't have the gene and you found me injured in The Zone. Beg him to be allowed to go to the hospital," I say, then slump over in the seat.

Jason plays it well, screeching to a stop. I hear the guard get out of the vehicle and walk over.

"The license plate reader says this truck is from The Zone. Turn it around and go back," the guard says.

"We need to get to the hospital," Jason says.

"They can't help you. Go die in The Zone where you belong."

"It's not for us. This girl is clean. She wandered into The Zone and a gang jumped her."

"Animals," the guard says.

There's a pause in the conversation.

"I know what you're thinking," Jason says. "It wasn't us that jumped her. We're doing the right thing for a girl who was attacked, and you still see us as pieces of trash. What are you afraid of? You afraid that we'll die in one of your nice clean gutters where decent folks might have to look at us and be reminded of what the world is really like?"

"It's not my problem, Zoner. I've got orders. Move her to my car and I'll call someone to get her."

Jason gets out and walks around the truck. I hear the guard move back, as if being within a foot of Jason will somehow contaminate him. He opens the passenger-side door and bends down to pick me up.

"Jump him?" he whispers to me.

"No. Put me into his car, then distract him."

He lifts me easily.

"How does someone who's so light hit so hard?" he asks softly, but I don't answer.

He gently places me in the back seat of the security car, which is covered with food wrappers and drink containers.

"We're going to sit here until we know she's safe," Jason says.

"What's that supposed to mean?" the guard asks.

The guard is following Jason back to the truck, so I jump into the front seat.

"It means I'm not leaving a helpless girl alone with you."

I've been watching. All I should need to do is move the handle from "P" to "D" and then push on the pedal on the right. It can't be as hard as driving a tube car manually.

"How dare you question my integrity? I could get the police over here and have both of you arrested and your truck towed away. Get out of my sight, you Zoner filth.

It turns out that you don't push the pedal on the right all the way to the floor. The car shoots forward with a squealing sound and over a curb, then over some bushes, before I find the other pedal and make it stop. On the next try, I only push the pedal half way, which isn't quite so violent, but does destroy some more bushes. The hospital sign has an arrow pointing to the right; so I turn the wheel hard, which produces a different sort of squealing sound.

I look in the mirror and see the obese guard running down the street after me. Then I see J.W.'s truck race past him, but I almost hit a street sign when I take my eyes off the road.

Who would've thought driving a tube car would be easy in comparison?

Once we're out of sight of the security guard, I pull the car to the side of the road and move the handle back to "P." Jason pulls up and I jump back into the truck.

"Smooth," Larry says, from the back seat.

"It was either beat up his car, or beat up him," I say. "Besides, I thought I did pretty well for my first try. Now let's get to the hospital before he calls someone to chase us."

"You see how it is for anyone from The Zone," Jason says. "They don't care. They just want us to go away. I bet the hospital will be even worse. The medical community can't help, and they don't want to be reminded of their failure."

"Do they not have enough beds? Why did they give up trying to keep people comfortable, at least when the end is near?"

"They did at first, before they understood what was happening and how many people were going to be hit; but when the first big insurance company declared bankruptcy, that was it. The government called it an act of war and exempted them from paying for care. For most people, the money ran out quickly."

"Why aren't the churches sending people into The Zone?" I ask.

"They're not allowed," Jason says. "The government ordered a bogus quarantine and never lifted it. People donate stuff, but the government brings it in for them."

So the people never see for themselves what it's like in there.

"There's the hospital," Jason says. "What now?"

"Drive around to the back and find the loading docks. All hospitals have kitchens. Maybe they'll have something we can use to transport ice."

On the edge of the dock, I see a pile of empty plastic buckets bearing labels for various foods that they used to contain. We each grab two buckets and walk in through an open door. There's no sign of an ice machine; so we wander until we find ourselves in an open room with people in chairs, where we're quickly spotted by the staff. A nurse at the desk runs for a doctor and we're soon confronted by a young woman in a perfectly white coat with "Beverly H., M.D." embroidered on it in pink.

"Get out of my E.R.," she says.

"We don't want trouble. We just want ice," I say. "Our friend back in The Zone has a high fever from the toxin, and we need to cool him off."

"It won't help, and it might kill him," she replies. "There are faster ways to put him out of his misery."

"The ice, please."

"Security!" she yells.

A large man in a dark uniform walks towards us.

"The idea that you're wrong would never occur to you, would it?" I ask the doctor.

"The toxin quickly binds to DNA when it enters the body," she says. "Cooling someone off won't stop it."

"We don't want to stop it, just slow it down," I reply.

"Show them out," she instructs the guard.

"In a month or so, a young man named J.W. is going to walk into this room. He's going to tell you that ice saved him from the toxin. Then he's going to tell you that you're an idiot."

"Out!" she yells.

"We know the way," I say to the guard.

I lead the way and the others follow closely. We're almost to the loading dock, when the guard instructs me to take a left. It isn't the way we came, but I do it anyway. Twenty meters down the hall, I find myself in front of an ice machine.

"The toxin got my best friend from the army just a month after the bombs were dropped," the guard says. "If you want ice, you come to this machine."

CHAPTER TWENTY-SIX

"Dad? Why don't you ever talk about what happened to you inside the mountain?"

We were rock climbing again, side-by-side.

"Talking about it won't change what happened, Jocie. It won't make me feel any differently about what happened. It won't help me to …"

"Maybe it would help me," I cut him off. "I've never seen what the rest of the world has seen. So if you won't let me see it, then maybe hearing about it from you is the next best thing."

He said nothing for a while.

"They were truly rotten days …" he said, "… rotten enough at the time to make me wonder, at first, if my faith was being tested by the Lord."

"You wondered," I said. "Did you reach a conclusion?"

"Yes. It was when the guards were whipping me. I knew in my heart that the Lord would never test faith in that way, and that it was definitely the evil and brokenness of man at work. That's not to say the Lord wasn't at work in the room though. I definitely felt my faith growing with every lash. I came to realize that even a truly rotten day was still a gift from the Lord; so I lived through those rotten days the way He commanded us, by doing my best to love those around me more than I loved myself."

"You were loving the people who were beating you?" I asked.

"There is no better way to spend a truly rotten day."

******

When we get back to The Zone, Jake's team is pacing back and forth, waiting for us. They found an abandoned house on the edge of The Zone and ripped an aluminum bathtub out of the wall so quickly that the plumbing is still hanging from it. Hannah rearranged J.W.'s apartment to accommodate the new feature, and the team carried the tub right in.

"Put him into the tub," I say.

His friends all jump on my orders.

"Now, get a tarp or something waterproof so the ice isn't in direct contact with his skin; then start dumping the buckets."

"How soon will we know if the cold is helping?" Hannah asks.

"We'll see a drop in his body temperature fairly quickly, but we won't know if the cold is working on the toxin for some time. We want him to go to the edge of hypothermia, about thirty-seven degrees Celsius, but we'll need to warm him back up periodically too.

"Thirty-seven degrees Celsius?" she asks. "What is that in Fahrenheit?"

"I have no idea," I say. "I never learned Fahrenheit. Luckily, I picked this up as I walked past a cart in the hospital."

I hold out a digital thermometer that you just stick in the patient's ear.

"It looks like thirty-seven is about ninety-five Fahrenheit. We'll check his temperature every quarter hour and rotate him out of the ice if he dips below ninety-five. Once he warms back up to ninety-seven, we'll ice him back down."

She reaches out and puts her hand on his forehead.

"He's still hot, but I think it's already working," she says.

Jake starts to swing the apartment doors closed.

"Leave them open," I say. "We want everyone to see that this isn't some sort of scam; that he really did survive the toxin."

People start to gather at the doors.

"Jocie?" Larry asks. "How is freezing him going to help him survive?"

"Fever is our body's way of fighting a natural infection. Most viruses and bacteria function best at normal body temperatures, and are slowed down by the extra heat. The toxin is similar in a way, because it's not very heat stable; so it breaks down faster when you have a fever."

"Isn't breaking the toxin down a good thing?" Hannah asks.

"Not always," I say. "With this toxin, by the time you break it down, it's too late; the genetic damage is done. We need to slow the process down so the body has a chance to recognize the entire molecule, and create antibodies that will bind it up before it can enter cells and cause damage. It's similar to how antivenin is created for snake bites."

I look over the people who have gathered. They believe there may be a scientific argument for cooling J.W. off, but I don't think any of them believe he'll actually survive.

"In the meantime," I say, "let's pray."

The crowd dwindles over the next two hours, but I keep up my vigil of reading J.W.'s temperature and either adding or removing ice. Even Hannah leaves to take a rest, so I'm alone and deep in prayer when J.W. speaks.

"Jocie? Is that you?"

"Yes, J.W. It's me."

"You're all blurry."

"You had a very high fever and now we're cooling you with ice to slow down the toxin. Either one could be messing with your vision, but it should only be temporary."

"Is the book with the red cover still in the bookcase?" he asks.

"Yes. Do you want me to read it to you?"

"No. I just feel better knowing that it's still there. Jocie? Have you ever wondered what it would be like to meet Jesus?"

"We'll all meet Him, one day."

"No. Not in heaven. Have you ever wondered what it would be like if you could meet Him in the flesh, here on earth?"

"You mean inventing a time machine and going back to the crucifixion? What a crazy idea," I say.

"So you have thought about it."

"I used to think about it a lot, but I don't anymore," I say. "Since I came to The Zone, I don't need to see Him in the flesh in order to see Him all around this place. I never would have dreamed that a place like this one is where I'd feel the strongest connection to Him."

"I know exactly what you mean," he says. "I just look at people who are caring for, or loving others, and I know He's there with them. I just wish…"

I give him an expectant look to continue, and then realize he can't see me well enough.

"What do you wish, J.W.?"

"I just wish I would have had enough faith to stop being the person who watches and to start being the person who cares for others. Like you, Jocie."

We sit in silence for a long while.

"You give me too much credit," I say. "I don't have nearly as much faith as you think I do."

"I doubt that."

"You asked me a hypothetical question about meeting Jesus," I say. "Now let me ask you one. What do you think it would be like to know about the future before it happens? Even if it was just a glimpse? If you had an idea, ahead of time, who had a shot at living through the toxin and who was certainly going to die, would praying for them still be a demonstration of faith? Or would it just be saying comforting words while you wait for a known outcome to occur?"

J.W. has slipped back into unconsciousness without hearing the question, but I look up to find Hannah has been listening.

"Jesus knew everything that was going to happen to Him before it happened," Hannah says. "Are you suggesting He lacked faith?"

"I never thought of it that way," I reply.

"That's how you win fights, isn't it?" she asks. "You use visual cues to predict the next move."

I give her a respectful nod.

"It's more than just fighting, though," she says. "You see other things, too. You see a million little things; and where everyone else sees chaos, for you, things come together …"

"Like a puzzle," we say together.

"Why would you interpret a gift like that as a lack of faith?" she asks. "You're doing exactly what you were called to do. Think of first Peter: 'God has given each of you a gift from his great variety of spiritual gifts. Use them well to serve each other.'"

I don't answer.

"Let me put it another way," Hannah says. "With all that's going on in the world, maybe all of the angels are busy. Maybe none were available to watch over the Baltimore Zone, so God sent you instead. Maybe I'll start calling you 'Angel.'"

"Let's just stick with 'Jocie'," I say. "When I was little, my father would sometimes call me 'Angel' and I…"

I stare into space without finishing the thought.

Did Dad solve this entire puzzle years ago? Was he sprinkling my life with clues to help me?

"Jocie?" Hannah asks. "What's wrong?"

"Go ahead. Call me Angel if you like."

******

I'm asleep when Hannah knocks on my door.

"Jocie? We've run out of ice and J.W.'s temperature is spiking. The guys have tried three times to get more, but they've doubled the security at all the ramps near The Zone."

I instruct Jake to drive his truck to the same ramp we used before. The obese security guard is there, as is his car - with a few good dents in the front - along with two other cars and similarly obese guards. We stop one hundred meters before the checkpoint, and I walk down the center of the road with my arms stretched out to show that I'm not a threat. Jake crawls along behind me in his truck.

"You shouldn't have come back. You're going to jail!" the obese guard says.

He reaches for his radio, and the other guards stand to block my path.

"No. I'm going to the hospital to get ice that will save a man's life. You're going to let us pass."

I continue to walk slowly towards them.

"You're going to let us pass, because it's the right thing to do, and because you want to play a role in saving a life," I continue. "Look at my arms. They're outstretched, just like our Lord's arms were outstretched on the cross."

He raises the radio, but doesn't speak into it.

"I'm going to stay here with you while my friends get the ice," I say.

The guards look hypnotized. I wave Jake and the others through, and then walk straight to the obese guard whose car I stole, and wrap him in a hug.

"I'm sorry about your car," I say.

"It's just a car," he says. "I'm sorry for the way I acted."

"Why do you do it?" he asks. "You obviously don't have the gene. Why hang out with the Zoners?"

I spend the next twenty minutes talking with the guards about the unending love of God, when Jake pulls up again.

"I'm the Angel of The Zone," I say. "Thank you."

I kiss them each on the cheek, then climb into the truck.

"I thought for sure you were going to beat all three of them up," Jake says. "How did you get them to just stand there? Are you a hypnotist too?"

"I told you. I have no power of my own. That was God's work."

"You really are 'The Angel of The Zone.'"

******

When we get back, J.W. has lost his sight completely, but he can hear the ice rattling in the buckets as we walk.

"I was just feeling warm again," he says. "Not another cool down. Please."

His voice is weak.

"Look at his face," Jake says, as he walks in with two ice buckets.

"What about my face?"

"Your face is covered with small sores," I say. "I imagine your entire body is covered."

I signal Jake, and he dumps the first ice bucket on top of J.W.

"I've never seen the toxin do this before," I say. "We should take it as a good sign."

As Jake and I leave to get more buckets from the truck, he catches my arm.

"Thanks for trying to keep his spirits up, but that looks worse than anything I've ever seen," Jake says. "He's never going to make it through the night."

"I wasn't just trying to boost his spirits. I meant it," I say. "I think he's survived to a stage that's never been seen before. I think his body is building a resistance. The biggest problem we have now is that those sores are all going to burst open at once. He's going to lose a lot of blood. If the blood loss is enough to lower his blood pressure, we're going to need a lot of ice to compensate, and maybe an I.V. to replace the fluids. Can you get more ice?"

Jake thinks for a moment, looks at his truck, then smiles.

"Count on it."

******

The sores start opening and bleeding two hours later. I can tell that the scarring will be horrible, but then, I already knew that. Hannah and I do our best to cover the wounds and stop the bleeding, but coagulation isn't the problem; the sheer number of open sores is. As quickly as old sores stop bleeding, new ones open. Soon, J.W.'s clothes are soaked in blood.

"Jocie, we're out of ice. I'm going to look for Jake," Hannah says.

She's barely out the door, when J.W. speaks.

"Every square inch of my skin hurts," he says, through clenched teeth.

"All of the sores have opened up," I say.

339

"Is Hannah doing okay?" he asks.

"She's as solid as a rock. In fact, I think you two should have children, and when you have a boy, you should name him Peter, which means 'rock.'"

He starts to laugh, but winces from the extra pain caused by the movement.

"Jocie, you're the only person who could be sitting in The Death Zone and find a way to talk about bringing a new life into the world. You're like an endless well of hope in a place that's better off without it."

"Better off without hope? How could any place be better off without hope?"

"You can't crush something that you no longer have," he says. "I've been here long enough to see that it's the roller coaster of building up hope and then having it crushed that kills people. The people who have no hope left actually live longer."

"And what about you, J.W.? Have you lost all hope?"

"I don't know. I know that I want to scream; and I want to cry; and I want to hit things. Dying seems like such a simple solution. We shouldn't have to die like this. It's inhuman. At least death would make me human again. Do you know why we went to Virginia the night we met you, Jocie? The boys convinced me to go out and rob people so we'd have something we could trade for alcohol to throw a party. We all knew I was next to die, and they wanted to have one night together where we could feel normal again. You know what's funny, though? Nothing about it felt normal. I didn't want to rob anyone. I didn't even want to go, but something made me do it. So we weren't there to rob. We were there to meet you. It was God's plan all along."

"Part of it was God's plan…" I say, "… but you choosing to stand on a man's neck wasn't from Him. That was all you."

"You can't judge me, Jocie! You don't know what it's like to feel your insides rotting away a little more with every breath. You can feel a breeze on your face and just enjoy the moment without wondering how many particles of toxin just entered you. What hope do you think you'd have left if you were the one lying in an old bathtub, covered with blood?"

"Look at me, J.W."

"I'm blind."

I get close and gently nudge his chin so we're face to face.

"You don't need your eyes. They're an impediment. Now look at me. You're in a pool of blood while I, as you say, eat toxin for breakfast, but we are exactly the same. Our days on earth are not our own. The Lord didn't give either of us this day on earth for ourselves. He gave each of us another day because somebody else needed us. My day here is probably because you need me. Your day here is because you're meant to love someone on this day more than you love yourself, just like the Lord commanded you. I know you're in pain. I know you're lying in a stinking pool of your own blood. You're having a rotten day, but get busy living this rotten day the way you were meant to live it. Give up on your part of today's plan, and live solely for His plan."

We hear laughing outside, so I look up.

"Jake's back with more ice," I say. "A lot more ice."

"Hey, Angel …" Jake says, "… is this enough ice for you?"

I watch as part of the gang unloads an ice machine, while the others string garden hoses from the community spigot and lay out a variety of plumbing tools and fittings to jury rig the whole thing together.

"Did you steal all of that?" I ask.

"We didn't have to. We just requested it in your name, and the hospital let us borrow it."

"My name?" I ask.

He steps aside so I can see the side of his truck. A feathery wing has been painted on the side, above the words: "The Angel of The Zone."

CHAPTER TWENTY-SEVEN

When I was fifteen, Dad went on a prayer tour of the east coast. I wanted to go with him because the tour included Philadelphia and I wanted to see Independence Hall, but he said not this time. On his return, he met us at Aunt Cindi's house, where he sometimes sent all of us when he was away. I gave him a long hug, like I always did when he had been away, and then asked him if he had a good trip.

"I've had better," he said.

He was smiling, but his eyes and nearly imperceptible facial movements told me that he was upset. All through dinner, the adults laughed and traded funny stories, but even as he laughed, Dad kept stealing glances at me that conveyed the usual, bottomless sadness.

I was asleep on the extra bed in my Cousin Gwen's room, when I was awakened in the middle of the night by the sound of someone outside doing combat training. I expected to see Uncle Cameron, but it was Dad. He had arranged a dozen or so practice dummies in a rough circle and was pounding them at an unbelievable pace with a fighting stick.

Uncle Cameron and Aunt Cindi were standing in the shadows, watching. I think even they may have been afraid to go near the whizzing stick.

After ten minutes, the dummies started to break apart, which I didn't think was possible. Heads and arms were flying off, but Dad didn't slow down. He was winding up for a particularly vicious hit when, out of the shadows, a stick blocked the attack and held it. It was Mom.

Dad was shaking with anger, and for a moment I thought he might hit her too, but instead he dropped the stick and fell to his knees, panting. Cindi and Cameron walked back into the house.

"You're going to tell me what it is this time, Cephas …" Mom said "… or so help me, we're going to repeat the fight where each hit results in a question being answered."

"I found it," Dad said. "It was in Baltimore."

Mom hit her knees beside Dad.

"You're sure?"

"There was news footage of her in the local archives. They called her "The Angel of the Zone."

******

"Fine," I say, as I look at the faces around me. "Call me Angel. All I ask is that you make it all or nothing. No more calling me 'Jocie,' okay?"

"Whatever you say, Angel," Jake replies.

"Now, what do you mean you asked for an ice machine in my name? Who did you ask?"

"We painted up the truck with the wings and all, and the highway guards just waived us through with smiles on their faces. Then, as we were driving to the hospital, I noticed people were pointing and waving, so I pulled over and asked them what was going on. It turns out that the guard you stole the car from is a journalism student at night. He did some digging around and wrote a story about the conditions in The Zone and how you've organized the gangs to pray and care for others instead of fighting. It got picked up on the web, so when we told an ER doc why we needed ice, he handed over the whole machine."

I leave them discussing how to plumb the machine and return to J.W.'s apartment.

"Could you hear all of that?" I ask.

"Yes, Angel," J.W. replies.

"I'm not an angel."

"You look like one to me."

"You're still blind," I say.

"My eyes were an impediment."

******

J.W. seems better; so I take a prayer patrol and end up sitting with a Jewish man for several hours. He asks about the ice treatment, but I tell him that nothing has been proven - yet. I can tell just by looking at him that he doesn't have the same mutation as J.W.

When I get back, J.W. has stopped bleeding from his sores, but Hannah looks worried.

"His temperature won't come down," she says.

"This is it," J.W. says. "One way or the other, your experiment is almost over."

"How's the pain?" I ask.

"I think I've gone beyond the concept of pain. I think the nerves have been fired so many times that they're stuck in the 'on' position."

I look at the bottle of pain killers that sits on his shelf. It's nearly empty. He's already had more than he should.

"Anything else?" I ask.

"I can see a little again. It's mostly movement and outlines, but it's something."

"I'll take that as a good sign," I say.

"Hannah?" J.W. says. "Can I have a few minutes with Jocie?"

She looks hurt, but she leaves.

"I'm not going to make it, Jocie," he says. "But even if I do, there's something I want you to have. In my top drawer, under the socks, is a woman's scarf. It belonged to my mother."

I retrieve it. It's a modest pattern of white with blue stripes.

"It's beautiful. Why do you want me to have it?"

"I'm not sure. It's been on my mind for days and I just can't shake the feeling that you should have it. If it was anyone else, I'd be giving them a screaming cloth, but since you don't need one, I know you're the right person. Mom wouldn't have liked having it used in that way."

"Thanks."

"I don't need eyes to know that something is bothering you," he says. "Do I look that bad? Are you counting the minutes I have left?"

"You do look horrible…" I reply, "…but I'm thinking about the man I was praying with before I came back here. He asked about the ice baths, and I realized that I could already tell that it won't work for him. It makes it hard for me to spread hope."

"Is that it? I'm lying here in pain, in a tub of ice. The least you could do is deliver a good soul-baring. You might as well, since dead men tell no tales. Why don't you tell me about your family? I bet you have some good skeletons in your closet."

"Your minute with Jocie is up," Hannah says, as she re-enters. "I'd like to hear about Jocie's family, too."

"There's nothing to tell," I say.

"That statement alone tells me it's one heck of a story," J.W. says.

"It's their story to tell, not mine."

"Give us something," Hannah says. "Tell me, what's the first word that comes to mind to describe your mother?"

I think for a moment.

"Fierce. Everything about her is fierce."

"She sounds more like a mother lion," Hannah says.

"Why do I have the feeling I'd rather face the lion?" J.W. says.

"I didn't appreciate it when I was younger," I say. "No kid appreciates a mom who cleans their room or reviews their homework in a fierce sort of way, but when I think about her now - the way she fights, the detailed way she plans things, the way she loves my dad and her family - I've really come to admire that fierceness."

"What about your dad?" J.W. asks. "What's one word to describe him?"

I shake my head.

"I know every detail there is to know about my dad. Part of me thinks I understand him better than anyone ... even my mother. Then there are times when I swear that I've never met him before. He's like looking at a complex geometric pattern. Just when you think you've discovered how the pattern works, you realize that you were only looking at one small piece and that there are patterns within patterns, extending outward farther than you imagined."

"I may be blind, but I can feel that sadness is back in your eyes," J.W. says.

"It's just one of the patterns of my family," I say.

I see Timothy running our way.

"Angel! There are some people looking for you, and you're not going to believe it."

I see a group of people walking and talking to one of the prayer patrols. They have cameras and microphones.

"They found me on a patrol," Timothy says. "The reporter says that the world has been shut out of what's happening in The Zone for long enough, and she's going to show them what's really going on in here."

The reporter is a petite blonde woman with brilliant white teeth. She walks into the apartment uninvited, followed by the camera crew. They take shots of everything, including J.W., so I throw a blanket over him.

"My name is Rita. Are you the one they call "The Angel of The Zone?" she asks me.

"There are hundreds of angels in The Zone," I say. "You've already met a number of them."

"Yes, I have. They all say you're The Angel."

Her attention switches to J.W.

"How much time does he have left?" she asks.

"The rest of his life."

She looks up, and we scrutinize each other.

"I think what you're looking for is a private interview," I say.

Blowing up interviews with the press is another family pattern.

"I'm glad I did a little digging," she says, as we sit down in my apartment and motions for the cameraman to start rolling. "Everyone said this would be just another story about a little old lady praying for people in The Zone. Imagine my surprise when I found out that The Angel is a young, red-headed fireball. Then I get here and start hearing stories about you beating up three guys who tried to rape you. I knew I'd have to get this interview."

"There were seven."

"What?"

"I beat up seven guys the first time; then a group of three. Then three coroners who prey upon the girls who are still healthy."

"They say you have the gene," Rita says.

"That's right."

"You have remarkable skin for a girl who claims to have the gene."

So that's it...

"I exfoliate daily and stay out of the sun."

Rita smiles.

"We could waste an entire afternoon doing this sort of posturing," Rita says.

"I didn't want to mention it. It seemed like your journalistic style."

"Why are you *really* here?" she asks.

I smile at Hannah, who is standing in my doorway.

"The way things are in the world right now, all of the real angels are busy," I say. "So the Lord sent me instead. I pray with people when they're near the end. Why is that such a mystery to you?"

Rita leans across the table, as if to intimidate me.

"You're a scam artist," she says. "You can't be making money in The Zone; nobody here has any. I think you're looking for your fifteen minutes of fame so you can get a book deal or something. Care to take a little challenge that will prove it?"

"I'd love to."

"I brought a skin test that will tell if you have the gene or not," she says. "It's just a little pinprick. If you have the gene, we'll know soon enough."

When I roll up my sleeve, she knows I'm not simply calling her bluff, but she takes a small test kit from her pocket, shakes it, and removes the cap. I can see a small needle on the cap.

"Hold out your arm," she says, and aims for my wrist.

"Higher up on my arm, please," I say. "It'll make a better view for the folks at home."

She presses the cap against my arm and I feel a slight prick of the needle.

"We'll know if you're telling the truth in about three minutes," she says. "If you have the gene, you'll get a reaction on that spot."

"I won't make you wait," I say.

I nod to the spot where the needle pricked me. It's raised a large, red bump. I rotate my arm slightly so the camera can see it from a few angles, then roll my sleeve back down. By the one minute mark, my body will have neutralized the test and started to heal the spot. In five minutes, there will be no trace.

Now I lean in close to her.

"If you want the real story of what's happening in the Baltimore Zone, you'll have it in less than forty-eight hours. Leave a camera in the apartment of the man in the bathtub."

"The world has seen enough footage of people dying."

"He's going to live. He's going to be the first, and you're going to document it and show it to the world."

She looks unsure.

"If I'm wrong, you throw away the footage," I say. "If I'm right, you collect every prize for journalism you can name."

Her eyes say it all.

Gotcha.

******

The news team sets up a camera in the corner of J.W.'s apartment. They wanted it in a different corner, but I insisted on its current location so I could more easily sit with my back to it. The less footage of me for a historian to see in my time, the better.

"They're still just a bunch of peeping Toms, if you ask me," J.W. says, while looking into the camera. "Why would I want my last day on earth recorded like this?"

"Why did Jesus wait so long before He resurrected Lazarus?" I ask.

I get a blank look.

"Documenting with a camera makes a more effective demonstration," I add.

"I'm sorry, Jocie, but you're wrong. I'm not going to make it. Something has changed. I feel different. I wouldn't have thought it possible, but the pain has even increased. It's as if I'm on fire inside."

"On a scale of ten, put a number on the pain," I say.

"Eight out of ten."

"As my Mom would say, that's only a B-minus," I reply.

"Your family is seriously messed up."

You don't know the half of it.

He shutters a little, then grimaces.

"Can I change my answer to nine out of ten?" he asks.

"What if I told you that you're going to reach eleven?"

He looks to the red book on the shelf.

"Aw, now you've gone and ruined the surprise," he replies. "Will you go get Hannah?"

"Are you looking for more sympathy that I'm giving out?"

"Something like that."

Christopher happens to be in sight, so I ask him to sit with J.W. for a while; then I head for the apartment with all the girls. Hannah is there, praying alongside a girl named Catherine who I've seen on many prayer patrols. The girl on the bed only has a few hours to live.

"Hannah? J.W. wants you. How about if we switch?"

I take a moment with her, when she steps outside.

"Do you remember our conversation about how J.W. would rather die than watch you suffer along with him?" I ask. "That point is coming soon. When it comes, be strong in the Lord, and give him reason to live."

I pray aloud for the young woman in front of me, but in my mind I'm praying for both J.W., and Hannah as well. The young woman can't speak, but I'm told that her name is Abasi and that she's a Coptic Christian who emigrated from Egypt three years before the war. Egypt was hit with seven different Israeli bombs filled with toxin, and the concentration was so high that most people with the gene died in a matter of days. I wonder if Abasi would have been better off had she stayed in Egypt and died quickly.

When I take breaks from praying aloud, I can sometimes hear J.W. across the street in his big metal coffin. It's clear that he's in agony, and I wonder if he, too, would have been better off with a quick death rather than what he's going through. Unfortunately for both Abasi and J.W., they can't run away from the plan that God has for them.

I can also hear Hannah, as she tries to comfort J.W., and realize that her emotions are strained to the breaking point.

Lisa and Patrick come to relieve me. I've hardly slept in two days, but I stop by J.W.'s apartment for a minute. The ice machine is chugging away just outside the doors, so I fill a bucket, then step in through the open doors.

"No more ice," J.W. says. "It's making the pain worse."

"He's melting it like a hot wood stove, anyway," Hannah says.

"Where's the pain now?" I ask.

"Ten-and-a-half," he replies.

I dump the entire bucket onto him, causing first him, and then Hannah, to shriek.

"It's time, Jocie," J.W. says. "I tried it your way and I can't do it anymore. This was never my plan. Hand me the red book from the shelf."

"Get it yourself," I say.

"Jocie!" Hannah says. "Why are you being so mean?"

She reaches for the book.

"The book is hollow," I say. "J.W. has collected toxin particles from his air filter. If he drinks even one of those vials, no amount of ice - or prayer - will save him."

She withdraws her hand from the bookshelf.

"Get it yourself," Hannah says.

He tries to lift himself out of the tub, but the effort is too much.

355

"Hand me the book, Hannah," J.W. says. "I can't take anymore. Help me."

"I need to sleep," I say, and turn to leave. "I'll be back in a couple of hours."

"Take the book with you," Hannah says.

I turn back towards them.

"Removing temptation isn't the same thing as resisting and overcoming temptation. Leave it on the shelf."

CHAPTER TWENTY-EIGHT

"Happy Easter!" I said to my grandmother.

We were all gathering at great Aunt Kimberley's house. There were so many of us that there were tables set up in the living room, kitchen, and dining room. Aunt Cindi's old farmhouse would have fit us all better, but nobody dared ask great Aunt Kimberley to break the tradition of gathering here.

"That's a pretty necklace, Grandma," I said. "Where did you get it?"

The necklace was a large tear-drop shaped ruby, hanging on a delicate gold chain.

"It was given to me by my mother," she said. "It's been passed down by the women of our family for generations. Someday, I'll give it to you - but I think I'd like to enjoy it for a little while longer."

"How long has our family had it?" I asked.

"It first belonged to your great, great, great, great, great ..." she paused for a moment as she thought and counted, then added, "great-grandmother. As I've heard the story, she was a very rich woman who lived through the Final Holy War. Over the years, she gave all of her money away to the poor, until the only thing left was this necklace. She gave it to her daughter and asked that it always stay in the family, and so it has."

"It looks just like one that Daddy gave to me," I said, then closed my lips tight and looked around.

It was too late. I saw Dad's head shift down and to the right by several millimeters.

"I shouldn't have said that, Grandma," I whispered. "The jewels Daddy gave me are part of a family secret."

She got down close and whispered back.

"I'm very good at keeping family secrets. Want to know another one?"

I nodded my head.

"This ruby was given a name all of those years ago. It's called 'The Angel Tear Ruby.'"

******

I wake up a few hours later to find that the coroner team I knocked down is taking Abasi away. She was young, and pretty, and the men aren't above making disrespectful comments about her looks.

"When it's your turn, we'll have a really special ride to the morgue planned for you," one of them says, when he sees me. "Too bad you won't enjoy it as much as we will."

I want to make him feel something he won't soon forget, but I decide to turn the other cheek and walk away. I'm halfway to J.W.'s apartment when they decide to provoke me a little more.

"We should hang out here for a while. That guy will be dead in a couple of hours, and it would save us a trip."

The biggest of the three runs after me, but I can hear that he's going to give me a wide berth, so I don't react. Through the open door to J.W.'s apartment, I see the camera change position so that it's on me and the coroner. Someone is watching to see what happens next.

If the reporter is watching, she needs a show. She needs to understand what life is like in The Zone.

The coroner runs to the ice machine and scoops a bunch into a soft drink cup that had one last sip in the bottom. He tips the cup up to finish the drink, and then dumps the ice on the ground.

"I'm glad this ice machine got the chance to be useful today," he says.

When I say nothing, he turns around and starts to scoop the ice directly onto the ground.

"You're going to need some of that ice for your aching head, if you don't walk away," I say.

He stops and faces me.

"We all know what the ice is for. You're wasting your time, and perfectly good ice. The doctors tried and they can't save you people."

"I know they tried," I say. "They tried everything they could think of to do, and I appreciate that. The problem is that they stopped trying. You all stopped trying. You stopped trying to counteract the toxin. You stopped trying to give kindness and caring. You stopped trying to treat your fellow man with human dignity and respect. The only thing you're good at trying - is trying to forget."

I hear the camera zoom in on me.

"So maybe this is all just a waste of time and J.W. will die. Maybe he'll melt into history, just like that ice you threw on the ground has melted, but at least I will have tried. I won't have just thrown him onto the ground. I will have done everything that I can do to save him. More importantly, I will have given him the decency and respect he deserves through his last breath, and beyond."

The coroner stares at his feet.

"But then, what if we're all watching a miracle as it unfolds?" I continue. "What if J.W. survives? What if he's the only person with the gene in the entire world to survive? Even saving just one man will have made it all worth it. And what will it have cost the world? A little bit of ice? A little bit of time and compassion? From where I stand, that's a pretty good trade."

"I hope you save him," the coroner says, meekly.

I walk over and put my hand on his shoulder.

"I didn't say all of those things as part of saving J.W.," I say. "I said them as part of saving you."

******

Hannah asks me to go for a walk and, once we're out of sight of both J.W. and the camera, she speaks.

"His eyesight is nearly back," she says. "He's barely talking to me, and he won't stop glancing at that hollow book. The worst part is, neither can I. I don't want him to die, but if he's going to die anyway, maybe it's better for him to die quickly."

"Is it so hard to believe in miracles?" I ask.

"Here, in The Zone, I guess it is," she replies.

We've been walking down the row of container apartments and have arrived in front of mine; so I open the door and grab my backpack.

"There's something I want you to have," I say. "Always keep it safe, and keep it a secret."

I hand her the little bag filled with gemstones that travelled through time once before. They're virtually worthless in my time, but will make Hannah a very wealthy woman here. She pours them into her hand.

"Are these real?" she asks. "They'd be worth a fortune."

"Never think of them as your own," I say. "These gems are real, but they belong to Christ. Everything you own belongs to Him, and you've been chosen to steward that wealth in His name. Use them as He would use them."

She doesn't know what to say.

"The big ruby shaped like a teardrop has always been my favorite," I say. "It matched one that my grandmother wore as a necklace."

"Then you keep it," Hannah says.

I close her hand around them and shake my head; so she drops them all back into the bag.

She doesn't have any time to ask more questions. Jake is running towards the open doors of J.W.'s apartment, so we run, too. When we catch him, we find him helping J.W. to his feet. J.W. managed to climb out of the ice bath, but fell as he reached for the red book.

"No more," he says. "End this."

I look at him. Even covered with half-healed sores and scars, he looks pale blue. I imagine how Job must have looked after enduring the devil's torments.

"Put him on his bed," I say. "We can take away the ice bath."

We cover him with blankets, and as he falls asleep, as I hear the camera turn to watch his bed.

"Now what?" Hannah asks.

"Now, we pray."

I take one of his hands, and Hannah takes the other, and we pray. I'm aware of others gathering outside, but I don't stop. After a half an hour, I ask for water. When I look up to receive it, there are people as far as I can see outside the door - all on their knees. Behind them are new crews. Hannah quietly explains that the camera above me has been broadcasting us live on the Internet.

******

An hour later, J.W. wakes up in a sweat.

"Eleven," he says.

Maybe so, but he's turned a corner ... whether he realizes it or not.

"The cold gave you enough time to build an immune response..." I say, "... but forget about toxins and antibodies and biochemistry. There's one thing you need to focus on right now, and one thing only. Do you believe in miracles?"

"Miracles?"

"Yes. Do you believe that some power that you can't comprehend could be at work to save your life? Do you believe that there really is an angel in The Zone?"

"I'm looking at her."

"Not me. A real angel."

"I think maybe angels come in many forms. Some of them have wings and harps. Some of them carry fancy fighting sticks and break teeth with it. In the end, if they manage to touch people's hearts, what does it matter?"

The camera in the corner zooms again.

"Jocie? How did you know what I was planning to do with that toxin?"

"An angel told me."

I stand up and retrieve the book, then open it, revealing an empty space.

"I took it a week ago," I say.

"I thought removing temptation wasn't the same as overcoming it," Hannah says, from the doorway.

"I took the toxin. The temptation was still sitting on the shelf."

J.W. smiles, but it fades from his face and his head droops, as he loses consciousness. I slap him lightly and say his name, but he doesn't wake up. Soon, he begins to shake.

"Jocie, do something!"

"It's not up to us anymore," I say.

He shakes for an hour before regaining consciousness, screaming.

"The pain is at twelve out of ten," he says, between gasps.

He looks at his screaming cloth, which is on his bedpost, but he can't reach it. I pick it up and first look at it, and then the camera.

"This is part of the problem," I say.

Standing in the doorway, I address the crowd and the cameras.

"It's not a cloth to ease our suffering. It's a gag. We are all the children of God, and we will not be silenced any longer!

Whether we live or die, let God hear us, as we cry out to Him for mercy!"

I rip the cloth in two. Soon, members of the crowd are doing the same.

I lean down.

"I can't call you J.W. anymore," I say. "It's time for you to use the name that God gave to you, Jordan."

Hannah sits up.

"He's never told anyone here his real name ... not even me. How do you know it?" she asks.

"An angel whispered that into my ear, too."

Jordan is my grandfather six times over. His name means 'to flow down' - and like the River Jordan, his mutated gene flowed down to me. Once it combined with the vaccine, it made me more than just immune. It made me the cure.

Over the next hour, Jordan's shaking increases to the point where Hannah and I are virtually sitting on him to protect ourselves from his thrashing limbs. His cries of agony truly become cries seeking the mercy of God. He screams "I love you Lord" so many times that the crowd eventually joins him.

He owns his faith down to every last fiber of his being.

When he goes still and lets out a deep sigh, the shock of the sudden calm travels through the crowd like a wave.

Tears roll down Hannah's face.

I lean down and whisper into his ear: "I believe in miracles."

Then I reach up, and flip on the red light.

CHAPTER TWENTY-NINE

"I don't know how you did it, Martha," Dad said to Mom.

It was two days after my eighteenth birthday, and I was listening through the old heating grate again.

"How I did what?"

"After you got me out of the mountain, how did you sit at my bedside - not knowing if I'd live or die - without going crazy? How did you deal with knowing that there was nothing you could do to help me?"

Mom sighed.

"It's soon, isn't it?" she asked.

"You know it is."

"I remember watching the strain growing on you eighteen years ago, Cephas, as you put pieces together and concluded that you would sacrifice yourself to Henry. You fought God's plan then, and you're fighting it again now."

"I wish I was sacrificing myself this time, too. This time I feel more like Abraham, being told to sacrifice Isaac."

******

I sit for a minute with my hand on Jordan's arm, while Hannah does the same, sobbing. After a couple of minutes, her head jerks up abruptly. She looks at Jordan's hand, and then at me. I smile, then stand and walk outside, watched by every eye as I climb to the top of the container.

"I know you're all waiting for me to say something. Maybe you want to hear an apology for raising false hopes. Maybe you want to hear a word of thanks - to our Lord for bringing us all together in prayer. If you're looking for a long speech, you're going to be disappointed, because I have only two words…"

In one fluid motion, I take the fighting stick from my back, extend it, and smash the red light that sits atop Jordan's apartment.

"He's alive!" I yell.

It takes a moment for the meaning to sink in; then the crowd rushes forward. I can see them reaching in - needing to touch Jordan, just like Thomas needed to touch the scars on Jesus' hands and side. Timothy and Jake take charge in order to keep J.W. from being trampled.

By the time the crowd thinks to turn its attention to me, I've slipped away into the darkness.

I hear them chanting "Angel," but I don't stop.

News trucks rush past me, and when I do look back, the area of Jordan's apartment is so lit up, it seems like a hundred brilliant angels are looking over the crowd.

"Be happy, great-grandfather and great-grandmother six times over," I say.

I walk for miles. When I reach a residential district, I can see people through windows, glued to large screens on their walls, watching the scene that I just left.

A girl of about ten comes out of a house, waves over her shoulder to someone inside, and jumps on her bicycle. She's smiling from ear to ear as she approaches.

"You sure look happy," I say.

She points at the house she was visiting.

"That's my friend Janie's house. She has the gene, but now that someone has lived, maybe she'll live too."

"She might not," I say.

"I know, but now there's hope."

"Do you happen to have one of those things people use to call each other?" I ask.

"A phone? Everyone has a phone."

"Not me."

She reaches into her pocket, and hands me a pink phone with yellow daisies.

I look at it, but there's no way to input the number I want to call.

"Just say the numbers," she says, with a roll of her eyes.

"Hello? Dave?" I say, when the connection is made. "Do you mind taking a drive into Baltimore?"

******

"You've barely said a word since we picked you up, and we're almost home," Elizabeth says, from the front seat. "Did you not find your family?"

"I found the one I was looking for. He's nice," I say.

"Did he tell you where you can find your parents?" she asks.

"No, but I know where I can find my brother, so I'm going to him as soon as possible."

"That's wonderful news!" she says. "Do you need us to take you anywhere? An airport maybe?"

"No, he's not very far away."

Dave looks at his watch.

"I'm going to be late," Dave says. "Jocie? Do you mind a quick side trip to the barn? It's almost finished and I need to meet the buyer there. Besides, I want you to see the metal truss you asked me to build. It came out perfect. From the barn floor, nobody would even notice it."

Dad will.

"I passed it off to the owner as a safety reinforcement," he says. "Now that it's installed, would you mind telling me the real reason why you bought a stranger a complicated, unnecessary roof truss?"

"I'm sorry," I say.

"That reminds me," Dave says. "Those diamonds were worth a lot more than the metal for the truss. I couldn't get cash, of course, but here's a card with the balance."

He reaches for his back pocket.

"Keep it …" I say. "… as a tip."

There's a new and expensive-looking car waiting, as we drive onto the lot with the barn. The back bumper has a small plastic fish stuck to it. I wait in the car while Dave and Elizabeth get out and greet a man and a woman. They talk for a while, until their conversation is interrupted by a boom that echoes off the surrounding hills.

"What was that?" the man asks Dave.

"They're closing up an old mine," Dave replies. "There were a couple of good explosions yesterday, too."

The Tombstone.

I jump out of the car.

"Dave and Elizabeth, I have to go. Thank you for everything … and God bless you."

"You're the Angel!" the woman says.

Dave and Elizabeth look at each other, and then at me.

"You cured that man in Baltimore. Millions of people with the gene are looking for you. Planes and boats filled with people are heading to Baltimore as we speak."

I pause to reflect on that for a moment.

"I'm needed more somewhere else."

"Is that it?" Dave asks. "You appeared out of nowhere; now you're going to just disappear without a trace?"

I hug first him, and then Elizabeth.

"There's a trace," I say. "In Baltimore, I left behind hope. Let's keep everything else that I left behind our secret, okay?"

I nod to the barn and the metals hidden in the truss; then, without another word, I quickly melt into the woods.

I only walk for twenty meters before I break into a run, and don't let up until I approach the future site of Bethany House. I'm at the tree line, looking at the ugly piles of mine waste, when there's another loud boom - followed by laughter. Four men are standing behind a clear plastic shield, watching dust billow out of the mine shaft. The supports for the elevator and other equipment have been removed; so the shaft is now literally just a hole in the ground.

"We have plenty of leftover charges. Let's do one more," the youngest-looking of the men says.

"Yeah, a really big one," another agrees.

"Enough fun. We've got concrete to pour," the oldest one says. "Besides, it's lunchtime and I don't want any more dust in the air that might get on my food. Sally packed me some of her beer can chicken, and I want to enjoy it."

The group moves to two white pick-up trucks. They're parked with a view of the shaft; so there's no way I can climb down without being seen. When one of the trucks starts, I hope they'll all drive away, but instead I hear the radio come on.

Since I don't want to hurt them, I'll need to distract them somehow. The cement pumping machine that I sabotaged is out of their line of sight and a new control system has been attached to it. I turn on the display and find that it has no software security. Although the equipment is brand new - to me - it's an ancient computer language, and I'm able to break into the source code and rewrite what I need.

When I'm done, I circle around some piles of mine waste until I'm a hundred meters behind the trucks. I have to walk back and forth several times before one of them notices the movement in a side mirror. The oldest man gets out of the truck and the rest follow. I smile, and walk into some thick brush.

"That looked just like the girl from Baltimore ... the one they're calling an angel."

"Angel? Come back," one of them shouts, but I'm already running silently. I hear at least two of them crashing through the bushes, shouting for me.

I make it to my pre-planned vantage point and am crouched in some brush, when I hear the diesel engine of the cement pumper roar to life by itself, due to the new coding I entered. There's more crashing through the bushes as they all run back to see who turned on the machine. I slip over the edge of the old mine shaft unseen, as they argue about angels and ghosts.

With the sun high in the sky, light isn't an issue, but the going is slow. When the crew removed all of the support structures for the elevator, the steel cables that I could have used to climb down quickly, fell to the bottom of the shaft. At least the side channel that the counterweight used to run up and down in is small enough that I can climb down it like a chimney.

When I reach the side channel where the time travel arena is located, I stop just long enough to pop and shake a bunch of light sticks. I throw several to the bottom, along with the metal lock box, which hits with a clatter.

The going from there seems agonizingly slow, as I have less and less natural light. When I reach the bottom, I see that the elevator must have slowly descended the entire shaft on its own after I disconnected the counterweight. It's sitting neatly with its bottom cage fitting down into the hole in the floor.

I need that hole! It's the only safe place to leave myself a message that won't be crushed when Albert drops the tombstone in two hundred years. I had wondered why the elevator wasn't at the bottom of the shaft - it's because I moved it!

I push against the heavy metal elevator, but it won't budge.

Out of the corner of my eye, I see a long, straight piece of metal and realize that it's the same metal bar that I'll use in the future to dig my way under the fallen tombstone. There are plenty of rocks to use as a fulcrum, so I put one into position and try to lever the elevator cage up enough to tip it over. Arm strength isn't enough, so I'm soon jumping on the end of the bar. The elevator starts to rock back and forth. Finally, with one big jump, the entire cage tips over and out of the way.

I look at the cheap plastic watch on my wrist that was given to me by a dying man in The Zone. I estimate the time that it will take for me to climb back up, and write a note to Austin, detailing the exact date and time that I'll be sitting inside the time travel arena. I give myself an extra ten minutes of leeway, just to be sure. Then I scratch the note to myself on the outside and place the box into the safety of the hole.

Does the fact that I saw the note before I scratched it make this a paradox? I hate thinking about time travel…

"Do you guys see a light down there?" a voice from far above says.

I look up and see a head peeking over the edge, so I throw rocks over the light sticks.

"It's just a reflection; get back to work on the forms."

All the way up on my return climb, I get showered with pebbles and dust as the men above work near the edge of the hole. They talk about seeing the "Angel," and are clearly spooked by the experience. It's not until one of them says "Okay, last one," that I allow my focus to shift from the rock wall I'm climbing to the men above.

"It's going to be a big one!" the youngest one says.

I look up to see something descending towards me on a wire and know it's an explosive. They've put a plank across the shaft to lower the charge down the center. I reach as far as I can, while hanging on with just one hand, but there's no way I can reach the wire and disable it. The chimney I'm using to climb faster is on the wall opposite from the opening to the arena cave. It's an easy horizontal climb around to the opening, so if I can get there fast enough, I can break the food shelves and use the wood to pull the wire into the opening. Unfortunately, I have no way of knowing how long it will be before they set off the charge.

I've never taken so many climbing risks in my life, but then, I've never needed to climb this fast before, either. I don't test hand holds, or estimate reach, or plan the next move. I just climb on instinct. When I reach a point opposite the opening, I hear a long blast on a siren. I don't know if that means I have thirty seconds, or just ten, before the detonation, but it's clear that I don't have time to climb around or break shelves apart. My only choice is to hurl myself across the shaft, catch the wire in mid-air, and land in the opening.

There's a second long blast on the siren. I hope that means there will be three sirens in all.

I find a good hand hold, set my feet, say a prayer, and launch myself. I know it happens in a fraction of a second, but it feels like I'm hanging forever, as I twist one hundred and eighty degrees in mid-air. My hands completely miss the wire, but it gets caught in my armpit and swings with me, as I land in a heap in the opening.

The third, and I presume final, siren blast begins as I haul the explosives back out of the pit. I have no way to cut the wires, so I have to somehow pull the detonator out of the charge. As the siren blast ends, I grab the device and just yank on the wires as hard as I can. One wire comes completely free, which is good enough; so I toss it over the edge again. My watch says I have ten minutes before transport.

Plenty of time.

I reach the back of the cave and stop in my tracks. The arena is a pile of individual sticks. The arena was designed to be a puzzle. It wasn't designed to stand the concussive force of idiots playing with explosives.

I have ten minutes to assemble a puzzle - in the dark - that took me fifteen minutes to solve under ideal conditions. And it takes two people to do the final step.

I snap and shake all the remaining light sticks as a single bundle, then throw them into the air to scatter them around the area.

There can be no trial and error. Each piece selection has to be perfect on the first try.

I have the first dozen pieces in place, when I hear a scraping sound behind me. The men above are pulling the explosives out of the mine shaft. I just hope they're not planning on a second attempt.

I reach the point where I have to remove pieces. I'm one-third done. I sneak a peek at the watch. I have just over seven minutes left before transport.

At this pace, I'll only have seconds to spare.

More and more pieces slide and twist into place. I silently curse myself, as I choose a wrong piece. Behind me, I hear a bumping sound and know that the explosive is being lowered into the mine shaft for another try. I have no time to disarm it again, and even if I did, the puzzle will fall apart if I let go now. I glance up and see that they're not lowering it as far this time. It's stopped descending, right in front of the opening.

The first siren sounds as I reach for the last piece. The one shaped like a shepherd's hook.

Please ... I need a shepherd to look over me right now.

Without the pressure of a helping hand, the hook refuses to slide into place. I try to reach down and hold while pushing down in the middle, but there's not enough leverage. I designed it to be pushed from the top and twisted, while someone holds the bottom. My arms just aren't long enough to do both.

The second siren sounds above me.

Tie it in place.

I don't have time to untie a shoelace and I don't have any other string. My backpack is sitting open inside the arena, and I catch a glimpse of blue and white.

The scarf!

I make just a single overhand knot and pull it as tight as I can. From above, I make a desperate push and twist, and almost cry when the hook slides into place. I dive under and untie the scarf, then look at the watch, before I take it off and throw it out of the arena. I'd rather not have it fry on my wrist during transport.

Thirty seconds. Austin, please don't be late.

The third siren blast begins.

If they hit the detonator at the end of the siren, transport will be ten seconds too late.

The siren continues on for longer than the earlier two.

Five, four, three...

The siren stops ... and then so does the world.

******

What thoughts would most people have, if they were stuck for a lifetime between clicks on the second hand of a clock? It doesn't seem like there are any more puzzles for me to solve. I just need to get back and get the toxin sample to Amelia Lake, so she can create an antivenin and save the world from an attack by Five-X. How hard could that be, given all that's happened so far?

My thoughts start to drift to Dad. It would have been nice to repeat his mission, and meet Christ face-to-face and see Him risen, rather than going on a mission where death felt so final. The images in my brain shift to those who died in front of me in their horrible metal apartments made from shipping containers. I study their faces in my mind until I've pictured every detail. I listen to their screams of pain, and their pleas for mercy. When I get to Jordan, looking at me wild-eyed and saying "You're the cure," I can't take anymore.

I was the cure for all of those people. My body had everything they needed to save billions of lives, and all I could do was save Jordan. Maybe my mission was even worse than watching a crucifixion. Maybe the choices I had to make were just as hard as the ones Dad had to make. Maybe they were even harder.

I find myself again standing on a rock with Dad in a rain of puzzle pieces. I'll never think of that day as one where Dad was disappointed in me again. He was sad because he didn't know if I'd survive the mission he knew I was destined to undertake.

Or did he?

Dad knew there was something significant under The Tombstone. Could he have dug it out before me and opened the box? Finding the same straight piece of metal, exactly when and where I needed to be - twice - was pretty convenient. Was it there the second time because I used it to tip the elevator? Or did Dad also use it, and leave it there for me?

If Dad knew I was going to return, then what was making him sad?

The puzzle piece rain continues to fall and, without realizing it, I begin to cry. I look up and find that Dad is crying too. Our teardrops join the rain, and fall as puzzle pieces. I watch as the drops form a puzzle on the ground. There are missing pieces, which are being filled in as we cry.

Why must the puzzles of my life be filled in with tears?

The picture is of Christ, hanging on a cross, with Dad standing nearby, crying … with joy. The picture suddenly shifts to Dad being tortured between two posts inside the mountain. This time it's Jesus who is standing nearby, crying with joy.

The strength of Dad's faith has nothing to do with the fact that he met Jesus face-to face. The strength comes from their relationship.

The section of the picture showing Dad blurs, but Jesus remains clear. He's still crying, but I can't see who he's crying for anymore. Whoever it is, Jesus wants a deeper relationship with them. Then I catch a glimpse of red hair.

It's me. Jesus is crying because He wants a deeper relationship with me.

CHAPTER THIRTY

"Daddy … of all the things you've done, do you think Jesus is most proud of how you stood for Him inside the mountain?"

I asked him that a week before Mom and Dad disappeared.

"Most proud?" he asked, and smiled. "I know I too often describe the world in terms of puzzle pieces, but I like to think that Jesus would look at my life like a puzzle. I hope that standing up and forming a cross for Jesus, when by all rights I should have been dead, is no more than another piece in the puzzle to Him."

"It's a pretty important piece," I said.

"It's a unique piece, but it took every piece around it in order for that piece to fit into place."

"Maybe I asked the wrong question," I said. "Maybe I should have asked if *you* think of it as the proudest moment of your life."

"It doesn't change my answer," he said. "There were countless other moments that led up to that moment, each one building upon the other - each of which has the same thread running through it - making the moment by moment choice to live my life in relationship with the Lord. From that perspective, each one of those moments is just as special as any other."

I stared at him intently, not knowing if I should ask the question on my mind.

"When you stood up, did you think it was going to be for the last time?" I asked.

"It didn't matter. If there was one thing that was perfectly clear at that point, it was that my life is not my own. It belongs to Him. I had surrendered.

******

I wake up to the sound of stunner fire and Austin yelling.

"Jocie! We can really use some help!"

Zera is at the mouth of the side tunnel, shooting at something. Austin is at the time machine, stuffing critical components into his backpack.

"I thought you'd pull me back immediately. How long was I gone?"

"A crystal fried when we sent you and put the rest out of harmony. It took me almost an hour to get them all aligned again."

Under a hail of stunner fire, Zera jumps back into the cave. She gets pelted with flying sand, but isn't hit.

"Can you do that thing, where you're the only person in the world who can shoot down a drone?" she asks. "There are three patrolling out there."

Just inside the cave entrance, there's a broken drone on the floor. It's been smashed almost to bits, probably with a chunk of metal from the broken food shelves.

"They won't make the mistake of coming in again …" Zera says, "… but we're pretty much trapped here unless you can shoot them down."

I look at the drone wreckage.

"It's made of Austin's composite," I say. "I take it that Five-X was first to find us and it didn't take them long to arm their drones?"

"Yeah, but why are they shooting at us? The drone's cameras have gotten plenty of footage of our faces. They know exactly who's in this cave."

"Five-X is the enemy," I say. "They've been at war with the remnants of Four for years."

"They're both Christian groups," Zera says. "Why are they fighting?"

"Do you remember what Henry Portman said inside the mountain, when Dad survived the toxin? He said the dose was five times the normal amount and that it was enough to kill someone who'd been vaccinated with his Mark of the Beast vaccine. Five-X plans to drop enough toxin to kill all of The Marked, without harming The Washed."

"The heat-shielded rocket payload," Austin says. "I gave them the perfect delivery system."

"You brought back a sample of the original toxin," Zera says. "You have what Amelia needs to produce a cure, and Five-X is here to make sure it never reaches her."

"We need to go," I say.

I walk back to the arena cage, pull out the key piece, and kick it until it falls into a bundle of sticks. Then I start to weave them back together in the shape of a solid rectangle.

"You're making a stunner shield," Austin says. "Was it designed that way all along?"

I snap one of the pieces in half to make it work better where I need it.

"No."

While I finish the shield, Zera and Austin dig the hole bigger on the inside, leaving just enough dirt that we can quickly break through with the shield in front of us, rather than crawling.

"Are you ready?" Austin asks.

"Only two fit behind the shield," I say. "They've only seen you two. If you go, they might think it was just you and send in a drone to check out the cave. I'll take it by surprise and help even the odds."

Austin doesn't want to leave me behind.

"It's a good plan," Zera says.

I extend my fighting stick.

"Stay as flat against the wall as you can …" I say, "… and be ready for a pounding."

As soon as they break through, the stunner shots start beating against the shield. For a moment, I think they may retreat, but they keep moving along the ledge. The number of shots eventually slackens and the drones buzz around, looking for an angle. Zera keeps them at bay by occasionally returning fire, until I hear one of them break off and approach the tunnel entrance.

The drone is just barely narrow enough to fit through the entrance, so it enters at minimum speed, scraping its sides a little as it comes. I stand to the side and wait, trying to ignore the fact that my brother and friend desperately need my help. Its front camera stays focused ahead; so it never sees me, as I first break the camera and then land a crushing blow dead center. Its new composite armor keeps me from smashing it on the first try, and it tries to back up, but my second blow removes one of its rotors. Normally it could fly with as little as two, but wedged in as it is, it careens to one side, allowing me to finish it off. I have to crawl over it to get a view of what's happening.

Austin and Zera have reached the big ledge under the electrical tunnel, but can't go any further. From the stiffness of their movements, it looks like they've both been grazed with stunner fire.

I shoot down one of the remaining drones on my first try. Distracted as it was, it never saw the crossfire coming. The last drone compensates quickly, positioning itself so one camera is on me and the other is on Zera and Austin. Zera continues to shoot wildly from behind the shield, causing the drone to weave back and forth.

"Zera, calm down," I yell. "Shoot a burst of three, slightly to the left of its center."

"I can't get my head out long enough to see where center is!"

"Take a single shot," I say, and she does.

The drone easily evades and returns fire.

"A few degrees to your right," I say.

The drone again evades.

"Adjust that amount to the right again and shoot three times, moving to the right between shots."

On her third shot, I also fire and hit the drone dead center. My next shot disables its gun, but doesn't knock it down, so it buzzes out of range and stays there.

"Into the electrical tunnel," I say, and quickly follow them.

The shield doesn't fit, so they abandon it. When I catch up, they've barely crawled anywhere. They have too many numb spots from being stunned.

"It's not far to the top of the pit …" I say, "… and it hardly matters if we trip some motion sensors now. Let's climb out and take our chances in the woods."

"I agree," Zera says. "They'd probably be waiting for us as we come out through the hatch anyway."

When we re-emerge from the tunnel, the drone has flown off. I can hear it through the woods, hovering over the electrical hatch. I help Austin and Zera as much as I can, but the climb is painfully slow. When we get to the top, Austin and Zera try to run, but are too stiff from stunner hits to go very fast. I spot a half dozen motion sensors hidden in the trees, so it's not long before the drone is hovering above us, marking our progress.

I look at Zera and Austin. They've both been through a ringer, and yet, they'd both follow me to their last breath, and I them. I think about the message in the puzzle pieces. Being a Christian is all about relationships - loving others more than yourself.

"You have to go, Jocie," Zera says. "You have to get the toxin to Amelia so she can create a cure for the Mark of the Beast."

It's too late for that. The drone I damaged has been joined by others. They're just the 'dogs;' the hunters have already surrounded us.

"Wait here and rest," I say. "I'll take a look ahead."

A minute later, I find myself sitting in the middle of a blackberry patch.

This is the spot Dad described. This is where he realized the cure was in the water. Of all places, how did I end up here, if not to show me what to do next? I have to surrender.

"I'm sorry," I say aloud. "I'm sorry Dad. I'm sorry Mom, and Austin and Zera, and everyone else. I never believed that when a moment like this came, that I'd be strong enough to do what is asked of me. I guess I was wrong."

The final piece in the puzzle is clear. I know what I have to do; so I do it.

******

When I get back, Austin and Zera aren't ready to run, but they try anyway, for me.

"I can't run anymore," Zera says. "Jocie, you have to go without us."

There's a large clearing in front of us.

"It's okay," I say. "We're done running. We've been running our entire lives, and now it's time to make a stand."

Six drones converge above.

"Perfect," I say. "We have their full attention."

From the other side of the clearing, a half dozen armed men emerge. We walk to the center of the clearing, and they surround us. I put my stun gun down, at which point Tyrone Bauer emerges.

"I might have known it would be Paulsons," he says. "Who else would use a time machine to cause me trouble?"

Austin drops to the ground, unable even to stand.

I know the feeling, but I have to stand a little longer.

"You used me," Austin says. "It makes me sick that I taught you how to make a material that will destroy the world."

"I didn't use you, boy," Bauer replies. "God used you, and not to destroy the world, but to give it new life. The world will be born again, cleansed of the beast."

He looks at me.

"If I had only known the time machine still existed, it would have saved me years of research, and a few billion dollars to just go back and collect an original toxin sample."

Zera is next to sit. I feel as if I can barely keep my eyes open, but I continue to stand through sheer willpower.

Like Dad.

"Would you like to hand it over peacefully? Or will I need to have you searched?"

I drop my backpack. It feels good to have the weight off my shoulders.

"Don't give it to him, Jocie," Austin says.

Zera lunges for my stun gun, but it's shot twice before she can reach it, throwing up dirt and numbing her hand further.

"Jocie, you have to fight them," Zera says.

"I'll fight them to my dying breath," I say. "With every cell in my body."

One of the men rips through our packs, and comes away with the blue and white scarf. He carefully hands it to Bauer, who unwraps the vial of toxin.

"How much toxin is this?" he asks.

"Just the right amount to hold your attention," I say, as a stunner blast sends the man on Bauer's left to the ground.

The man to his right is next.

"I'd put your guns down," I say. "Dad never misses."

"Cephas is the least of your problems," Mom says, from behind Bauer. "You have two very angry mothers to contend with first."

Mom and Zip step out of the woods.

"Martha and Cephas? This is quite the family reunion," Bauer replies.

As Zip disarms the remaining men, Dad - with half of my family - emerges from the woods, out of breath from running, but still ready to fight.

"You have a bit of a problem, don't you think?" Bauer asks. "Come any closer and I'll smash this vial of toxin on the ground. It is what all this trouble is about, isn't it? Your last chance at creating a cure?"

He looks at me.

"You don't like that idea, do you? Your cheeks are flushed at the very thought of it. Still, you are a Paulson; so I bet you're calculating whether or not you can catch the vial, when your lovely mother stuns me in the back. I've done the calculation too - and I think you can."

He holds the vial over a rock … and drops it; so I lunge forward to catch it. Under other circumstances, I probably could have done it, but I'm so tired that I hit the ground and watch helplessly as it smashes. I get back to my knees.

"I'd always heard that you're a disappointment to your parents," Bauer says.

He looks at Mom and Dad.

"The Mark of the Beast ends here," he says. "All will be cleansed."

My eyes blur, as he says it, and his voice sounds far away. The next thing I know, I'm on the ground again, with Dad kneeling beside me. All of Bauer's men are on the ground too, but they didn't get there voluntarily.

"Daddy," I say. "This is going to be a really rotten day."

"Is it a time travel side effect?" Mom asks.

"No," Dad says. "There were two vials of toxin. She drank the other one."

Austin kneels beside me, too.

"Dad, look at her face," he says. "She's getting black lines, just like the Cult Hunters."

"I'm sorry, Daddy," I whisper. "It was the only way. You can use my blood to make the antivenin. I'm the cure now."

"I know, Angel," he says.

"Daddy? Before I die, you need to know…"

He places a finger across my lips, says "Shhhh," and then looks at Mom.

"Not today, Angel. Definitely not today."

"I'm sorry it came to this," Bauer says. "We'll need every Christian we can get in the new world we're going to build. You were definitely right about one thing though, young lady; the contents of that vial were just enough to create a wonderful distraction. Soon, you'll get a chance to see firsthand that I'm right."

He turns back to Dad.

"It's over, Cephas," he says. "The Temple Guard managed to ground or secure every air tanker on the planet, and their attacks made quite a dent in our plan to deliver toxin through air detonation of rockets … but it wasn't enough. They didn't find all of my facilities. As we've been speaking, dozens of rockets have been launched around the world, each with a multi-ton payload filled with toxin. Go ahead and pull it up on a screen. I'd love to watch your face."

"It's never over Tyrone, and it wasn't the Temple Guard who has been thwarting you. It was Four. We grounded your air tankers. Four is not going away. We're going to watch you and fight you. Luckily, we're also going to love you, and pray for you, until you understand that being a Christian includes loving everyone - Washed and Marked. Someday, maybe you'll finally understand that we're all marked in one way or another."

Aunt Cindi comes into view.

"The transport is three minutes out, but it can't land here. We need to move to the large clearing two kilometers to the east."

Dad lifts me, and begins to walk away.

"Cephas, I do hope you appreciate your place in history," Bauer says. "You made all of this possible."

Dad spins around, and somehow manages to draw a stun pistol and aim it at Bauer without dropping me. He's so angry that I can feel him shaking, as he fights the temptation to shoot … until a calm comes over him, and he holsters it again.

"History …" Dad says, as he turns away again. "… the Paulson family will always take its chances with history."

"What should we do with him?" Uncle Cameron asks.

"Let him go."

"Daddy …" I say, weakly, "…the rockets…"

"Don't worry about the rockets," he says. "The only thing that matters is you."

Austin walks behind us and uses a tablet to watch the news.

"Dad? Bauer wasn't lying," Austin says. "Chi-One Corporation launched heavy lift rockets from sites all over the world. It's the same as the test flight. They're designed to achieve a sub-orbital height; then they're coming down and exploding a few kilometers above the ground."

"Composite," I manage to say.

"Yeah," Austin agrees. "They're all bright balls as they descend. They're surviving re-entry because I gave them the composite."

The whole world seems to shake from a rumbling above us, and there's a bright flash that I can see through closed eyelids.

"That one is heading straight for Washington, D.C.," Austin says. "Jocie told me not to trust them ... but I didn't listen."

I focus all of my energy into speaking, but instead of words, a loud groan comes out. We're getting close to the transport and soon nobody will be able to hear me over the engines; so I try again. I manage to say the word "hot."

"I understand," Dad says.

No, you don't. For the first time in my life, I'm the one who has more pieces to the puzzle.

CHAPTER THIRTY-ONE

"Dad ... I've been thinking about our conversation, when I asked if standing up for Jesus is the proudest moment of your life."

It was on the last day I saw Mom and Dad, before they disappeared.

"I take it you have more questions."

"It's more of a thought than a question," I said. "I'm just wondering if maybe there's a special place reserved for you in Heaven."

"I certainly hope not," he replied. "In fact, I hope that what I did inside the mountain is considered commonplace in Heaven - just another act of faith and sacrifice among countless others."

"You don't think there should be any special reward waiting for you?" I asked.

"There is one thing I'd like," he said. "The next time I see Jesus, there are two words I'd love to hear Him say to me."

"Just two words? What are they?"

"Well done."

******

I dream that I'm lying in an old bathtub, and that Jordan and Hannah are dumping bucket after bucket of ice on top of me.

"Scream," Jordan says.

"It doesn't hurt that badly," I reply.

"You can scream now, or save it for the next time you look in a mirror."

"Jordan! Be nice!" Hannah says. "Jocie looks good with black lines."

Hannah holds up a mirror. My face is covered with the same black lines that mark old members of The Corps. They also run down my arms and legs.

I try to view them as ugly, but I can't, because I know that Jesus wouldn't see them that way. Things like skin, scars, and deformities don't mean anything, when you can see what's inside a person's heart.

I think about the fact that I invented "living scars" to hide the fact that I'm washed from the world, and laugh. To Jesus, we're all covered with the living scars of our sins.

"This is barbaric," I hear a voice say, and realize that it's from outside of the dream. I focus on it until I've pushed the dream aside and am sure that I'm awake.

"Just keep the cryo-pads at thirty-seven degrees Celsius," I hear Dad's voice say. "Her body is breaking down the toxin at an amazing rate, but she took a massive load. The cold will buy her the time she needs to fight the toxin naturally."

"How could you possibly know that?"

"I know that because I read, doctor. The method was first invented in Baltimore over two hundred years ago, after the Final Holy War. It's called 'The Angel Protocol.'"

I try to speak, but I can't because there are tubes down my throat. I'm able to open my eyes just a sliver and can see Dad sitting beside me. He takes my hand and touches it to his face. What I can see of them, my arm and hand are covered with black lines.

Mom and Aunt Cindi enter the room, and Mom takes my other hand.

"Doctor?" Dad says. "Do you think we could have some family time?"

"I've sent data and samples to every Four house around the world; so there's no way for Five-X to contain the antivenin," Cindi says, once the doctor leaves. "It also means I don't need Martha acting like my personal bodyguard anymore."

She looks at Mom.

"You were always there when I needed a bodyguard," Mom says.

"Actually, I'm beginning to think that I was Jocie's bodyguard when you were pregnant with her," Cindi says. "Now I know why."

"Is it going to work?" Dad asks.

"Perfectly," Cindi replies. "We could have made an antivenin using the toxin sample, but it might have taken months. Jocie's unique combination of natural genes, vaccination, and exposure to both the original and modern toxin, created a powerful antivenin within minutes of her drinking the toxin."

Aunt Cindi looks down at me as if she's going to cry.

"Jocie really was the cure," Cindi says. "She's just like you, Cephas. She was willing to sacrifice herself. I just hope the sacrifice wasn't in vain."

"When will the antivenin be ready for distribution?" Mom asks.

"We've already shown that we can reproduce it and scale it up. We'll save a lot of people, but we don't have years like we did with vaccine distribution. There's a toxin cloud circling the globe, and there's just no way to get ahead of it."

Dad sighs.

"What are the casualty numbers?" he asks. "I haven't dared to ask."

"So far, just over a million worldwide are showing the initial signs of toxin poisoning, but there are only a few thousand reported deaths - mostly among people who were already showing sensitivity and extensive prior genetic damage."

"Only a million worldwide? There should be a billion by now. How can that be?"

Dad? Why can't you see it? The puzzle pieces are right in front of you.

The sedatives that they gave me for the pain must have a paralytic effect. I try to squeeze first Mom's hand, and then Dad's, but I can't make my muscles work.

"All we can figure is that since it was air detonated, the toxin is taking longer to reach the ground than it did during the Final Holy War," Mom says. "It might buy us a few days, but our casualty projections are still in the billions in the next week alone. Unfortunately, panic is already setting in. The urban centers closest to the detonations are reporting rushes out of the cities before quarantines are put into place. Once people realize that the toxin is global and there's nowhere to hide, there's going to be worldwide chaos."

"Sooner or later, someone is going to realize Bauer's involvement. When that happens, the backlash against The Washed could quickly get violent," Cindi says. "We should quietly warn everyone to be ready to hide."

"It's too late for that," Dad says.

He uses his com to turn on the large screen on the wall. It doesn't take long before a pre-recorded announcement from Tyrone Bauer comes onto the screen.

"The days in which The Washed will hide are almost over," he says. "The earth will be cleansed, and a new era of Christianity will begin."

Dad mutes the sound.

"He explained everything. He couldn't resist the urge to gloat."

"We should get out of here," Aunt Cindi says. "We can take Jocie to a safe house and care for her there."

Dad silently stares at me.

"No," Dad says. "We can't just hide anymore. Our daughter risked everything to save billions of people. She understands the value of spreading hope in a hopeless situation. We owe it to her to do everything we can."

Thanks Dad, but I've got this.

I try again to focus on my hand and make it move, but instead, I slip back into sleep.

The next time I awaken, I'm able to open my eyes a little wider. Mom and Dad haven't left my side, and the newscast has been left running. Global panic has already set in, and the screen is filled with scenes of chaos and destruction, but Dad is ignoring it and staring at me. I'm still unable to give him any indication that I'm awake.

"Who is this woman?" Dad asks.

"Cephas?" Mom says from somewhere behind him.

"This woman," he repeats. "She took away my baby girl."

He continues to stare at me.

"I wish I could have travelled through time with her," Dad says. "I wish for just one second she could have heard and seen my thoughts, so she could see herself through my eyes.

I'd show her her own birth, so she could feel how I felt at that moment, and countless moments since that day."

"I've shared your thoughts and emotions, Cephas," Mom says. "I think that moment could be overwhelming.

"Overwhelming," Dad whispers to me. "There's no better word. I never expected just how overwhelming it would be, to be your father. From the moment you were born, I've been working on the puzzle. I had lots of ideas about what I wanted you to become, but instead of giving me what I thought I wanted, the Lord gave me something much better. He gave me you."

Uncle Cameron comes to the door.

"It's time," he says.

Dad kisses me on the forehead, just like he did countless times when tucking me into bed at night.

"It's time for the world to meet the next Paulson," he says. "You've been a ray of hope once before, Jocie. Let's see if the Angel of the Zone can do it again."

When Mom and Dad leave, Uncle Cameron takes up guard duty outside the door. He's not as ferocious as Mom, or as skilled as Dad, but I'd still take him as my guard over a hundred armed policemen. He only stands there for a few minutes before he looks at his watch, and then comes into the room and sits in the chair next to my bed.

There's a picture of Dad on the screen, and the newscaster is trying to fill time as he waits for something to happen.

"We're about to go live to Winchester, Virginia for a surprise interview with Cephas and Martha Paulson. The Paulsons fueled weeks of speculation, when their whereabouts were unknown to even the government, and have promised to shed light on various world events."

The screen switches to a live shot of Dad. I can see Mom, Aunt Cindi, Austin, and Zera in the background. Dad must have hand-picked the reporter. She's wearing a modest but classic dress that leaves a small silver cross visible on a necklace. Her clear skin indicates that she's Washed.

"Cephas, I'd love to feel like I'm digging to the bottom of a story, but the truth is that all anyone seems to know is that the horror of The Final Holy War is back … and this time it was brought down upon us by Christians. In just a few days, we've seen power outages, rockets crashing back to earth, and worldwide panic as people start to get sick. So how about if I just give you the floor?"

Dad looks so sad.

I force my eyes open a little wider. Uncle Cameron notices and blocks my view for a moment as he stares into my eyes, and then leaves the room.

"Thanks, Dana," Dad says. "I've given a couple of pretty big speeches and interviews in my life, but I must admit that this one is giving me more pain than I felt when I was inside the mountain."

He takes a deep breath.

"The unity of the Christian movement didn't last long after I was rescued. We all worked together to restore the First Amendment and religious freedom, but in other ways, division was with us from the start. As the problems caused by the Mark of the Beast vaccine became apparent, and Washed Christians were driven into hiding for our own protection, those divisions became even more pronounced. I guess you could say that as the Mark of the Beast was eating into The Marked, there was also something eating into many of The Washed."

Uncle Cameron comes back into my room, followed by a doctor, who shines a light in my eyes.

"From among a few of The Washed, a new Christian organization called Five-X was born, and with it came a new Holy War. You see, the name Five-X refers to the toxin dose needed to kill all of The Marked without affecting The Washed. The organization 'Four' was reactivated, and we've been fighting Five-X from the shadows for over a decade."

"She couldn't possibly be conscious," the doctor tells Uncle Cameron. "The eyelids opening must be a muscle spasm."

The doctor leaves.

"You now know that the leader of Five-X is Tyrone Bauer, CEO of Chi-One Corporation. I'm sorry to report that everything he said in his message is true."

Uncle Cameron snorts at the screen, but he's been watching me.

"Did you know that both your Aunt Cindi and your mom had kids without taking any pain killers?" he asks me. "They tell me that you're in more pain than you could possibly bear, but they don't know the women of our family like I do."

"We estimate that the rockets from Chi-One Corporation have dropped approximately five hundred and twenty metric tons of toxin over major population centers worldwide," Dad says. "That is a concentration high enough to slowly kill anyone who took the government vaccine eighteen years ago, and their descendants. The full effects should be felt soon, as the toxin drifts to the ground."

Uncle Cameron looks at me, and then at the line of fluids being dripped into me. He stands and I hear beeping, as he adjusts the machine.

"Your parents always have something to say, and I'm betting that you do, too. I know you can handle cutting the pain killers by half."

Thank you, Uncle Cameron ... but you need to do one more thing. You need to shut off the cold.

"And I'm tired of looking at blue lips," he says. "Let's warm you up."

"A lot of people are going to die, but I want you to know that there's still hope," Dad says. "Scientists from Four have long speculated that it would be possible to create an antivenin against the toxin, much like those that are created for snake bites. I wouldn't reverse the mark of the beast vaccine, but it would prevent the toxin from doing additional damage. Unfortunately, creating the antivenin required a sample of the original toxin from the Final Holy War was required, and none existed."

A wave of pain shoots through me.

"The two brief power outages that darkened the eastern seaboard were the result of time travel, to get the necessary sample. The trip was a success, and the antivenin is being produced. We just need time."

Austin stands and walks up behind Dad.

"The trip wasn't a complete success," Austin says. "My sister, Jocie, is the one who travelled back two hundred years to the time of The Final Holy War. She got the toxin sample, but when she got back to this time we were attacked by Five-X. The only way to save the sample and make the antivenin was for her to drink it. She's upstairs in this hospital, right now, fighting for her life."

"Austin, I don't think…" Dad says, before Austin cuts him off.

"I know Jocie's life seems like a small thing when we're talking about the entire world, but my sister is the world to me."

Thanks, little brother.

"Don't disappoint him, Jocie," Uncle Cameron says, beside me. "You're as tough as a McCleod and as smart as a Paulson. You can beat this thing."

"She willingly sacrificed herself for the Marked. The very people who have hunted us, and kidnapped us, and used us as breeding stock," Austin continues, then turns to Dad. "Dad, you once said that if you had to die, you wanted to die as a

Christian. I think the world needed to hear that if Jocie dies, she'll have done just that. She humbly placed her life into the hands of the Lord and put the lives of her neighbors above her own."

Austin walks away from the microphone. I see Zera put an approving hand on his shoulder and they walk out of the shot together.

I'm not dead yet, but I now understand the concept of pain being an eleven out of ten. Something else makes sense too — I understand what Dad meant when he spoke about how reaching the end of your physical endurance makes you finally look inward for strength. I've never felt closer to the Holy Spirit than I do right now.

A nurse enters the room.

"Her heart rate has increased," she says, looking at the equipment.

The paralytic effect of the pain killers is wearing off, so I'm also starting to shake.

"Everything is going to stay just like it is," Uncle Cameron says and puts himself between the nurse and the equipment.

The nurse hurries out of the room.

"I think the world should see Jocie," Dana says, in the interview. "Could we send a camera crew to her room?"

Dad looks at Mom, and then nods. As the screen goes to a commercial, Uncle Cameron taps his com and starts directing security personnel.

Austin and Zera arrive first and stand together at the foot of my bed.

They make a cute couple.

"Aunt Cindi estimates she took at least twenty times the usual lethal dose," Austin says. "How is she still alive?"

"She's a Paulson," Zera replies. "Your Dad was on the edge of death inside the mountain, and yet he stood there - standing tall with his arms wide. I'd expect no less from Jocie."

The camera crew - along with Mom, Dad, and Dana - crowds into the room, forcing Austin and Zera to stand aside. My shaking is worsening and the nurse has returned with a doctor, presumably to freeze and drug me again. I focus all of my energy into my right hand, calming it.

"What's going on here?" the doctor asks. "Why was the treatment changed?"

Dad puts his hand on the doctor's shoulder.

"It's not about the treatment anymore, doctor. It's no longer in our hands."

My hand, Austin. Look at my hand!

Dad sits next to me and takes my right hand. I pull it away. I'm able to open my eyes more and stare at Austin. Dad tries to take my hand again. I pull it away a second time and continue to stare at Austin.

"It's me!" Austin says. "She wants me! We developed a finger motion code for communicating silently."

Hallelujah!

Austin pushes his way through the people and takes my right hand. I focus my energy into using our hand code.

Austin looks at Dad.

"It doesn't make any sense. She's saying '2501c.'"

"What do you think that means?" Dana asks.

Whoever Dana is, she's getting the interview of a lifetime.

That was stupid.

I switch messages.

"She switched it around," Austin reports. "Now she's saying 1c 250.'"

Come on Dad! The pieces are all right there. Put it together.

Dad looks at the doctor.

"I want that tube out of her," Dad says. "Get it out right now."

"It would kill her," the doctor says. "I examined her two hours ago and her lungs were filled with cysts."

"Examine her again."

The doctor walks over and scans my chest with a device. She looks at the screen, and then scans me again.

"That's impossible," the doctor says as she scans me a third time. "Her lungs are almost completely healed."

"Look at her face," Austin says. "The black lines are fading."

"She eats toxin for breakfast," Dad whispers to himself.

With a simple order from the doctor's com, the breathing tube starts to withdraw from my throat by itself. When it's out, everyone seems to lean a little closer. I try to speak normally, but my first attempt comes out sounding like a hiss.

Dad leans in closer, so I can whisper.

He leans down, and I say something into his ear that makes him sit up. Dad looks at me, with his mouth open.

"God has given me some tough puzzles to solve, Jocie," he says, to me, "but you are truly the most difficult and most wonderful of them all."

For the first time in my life, I see tears starting to well up in Dad's eyes.

"We're not all puzzle solvers," Mom says. "Can you let the rest of us in on what's happening?"

"Bauer used the composite formula that the kids left at the safe house before they escaped," Dad says. "Jocie changed the annealing process to a single heating step of two hundred and fifty degrees."

"What does that mean?" Cindi asks.

"It means the payloads would have been better heat shielded if Bauer had covered them with peanut brittle. Jocie cooked his entire stockpile of toxin. That's why so few people are getting sick."

"Cephas?" Dana interrupts. "Are you saying that the threat has passed?"

Dad won't stop staring at me. He doesn't care about the cameras, or the fact that the world is watching. A tear rolls down his cheek.

"I'm saying that one person - with great faith - can change the world."

I try to smile, but I can feel it fading from my face as my head rolls to the side and I lose consciousness.

CHAPTER THIRTY-TWO

"Do you remember the first time you climbed this rock face?" Dad asked.

I was seventeen - and had once bragged that I could make the climb with my eyes closed.

"I remember the first time I was successful," I replied. "It was on my eighth attempt."

And I remembered how disappointed you looked on the first seven attempts.

"What changed on the eighth attempt?" Dad asked. "Did the rock face shift? Did new cracks open up and new handholds form?"

"Of course not. It took the earlier attempts to understand how to climb the face."

"And how about now?" he asked. "Is it still a difficult climb?"

"Not really."

"So, you know this rock face?" he asked.

I gave him my best seventeen-year-old "Where are you going with this" look. He smiled. We were past the point where I needed to use words to get a point across.

"I went to a prayer meeting in Carlsbad, New Mexico last week," Dad said. "There was a young Marked man there who was praying aloud, and his prayers made Jesus sound far away - like the only place Jesus exists is up in the sky. There was more than that though; his prayers sounded like he was worried about bothering Jesus - as if his troubles were the sort of thing that Jesus wouldn't care about."

I decided to climb with my eyes closed, to see if I could actually do it.

"As the young man went on praying, it became clear that no matter what he had in his life, it would never be good enough for him. He berated himself for not doing enough service in Christ's name. He apologized for not spending enough time in worship. He worried that his very thoughts betrayed him and labeled him as a disappointment in Jesus' eyes."

I slid my hands and feet from one hold to another. I really did know the rock with my eyes closed.

"The worst part of all was that he seemed to think that the perception he held of himself must also be the way that Jesus perceives him - not good enough. He had allowed his own brokenness to shape his perception of Jesus."

I came to the most difficult part of the climb. I'd need to reach out and grab a distant handhold and swing over so that my feet could land on a small ledge. There was no way to half do it or turn back, once the reach began. It required full commitment.

"So what changed on your eighth attempt at this climb, Jocie?" Dad asked. "You said there were no new cracks or handholds."

"I was wondering when you'd get back to the original question," I replied.

I made the swing with my eyes closed and landed on the ledge; then opened my eyes and smiled at Dad.

"Jesus is the rock face, Jocie," Dad said. "Your perception of the rock face was always based on *your* limitations - not His. Jesus hasn't changed, and He never will.

For once, Dad looked proud of me.

******

"I hate to sound like a little kid, but are we there yet?" I ask.

Dad has me wearing a blindfold, as we ride somewhere in a private tube car.

"My first trip after I got out of the hospital was very special; so I thought I should do the same for you," Dad replies. "Besides, I bet you can narrow down the possibilities, if you think about it."

He says it as the car comes to a stop and the door opens.

"That was a short ride ... so we're still somewhere on the east coast, probably no more than one hundred and fifty kilometers from Winchester, Virginia."

"Your family is weird, the way they do things like that," Zera says.

"Don't look at me," Austin says. "It's just the two of them."

Dad let me pick my own security detail for this trip, and I chose Mom, Dad, Austin, and Zera.

"If you think that's weird, you probably don't want to think about how I'd know that you two are holding hands."

I hear their hands quickly come apart and Mom laughs.

"Don't worry, Zera. If you hang out with Paulsons for long enough, you get used to it," Mom says.

"Okay, smarty pants. Where are we?" Austin asks.

In my mind, I draw a one hundred and fifty kilometer circle around Winchester. Part of the circle is in the ocean; so I start to the south and follow the circle clockwise. Although I wouldn't mind going to a beach, this trip is presumably to somewhere with more sentimental meaning for our family. Nothing near the circle stands out in the south or west, but when I reach a point to the north and east, I inhale audibly.

"You can take off the blindfold," Dad says. "She knows."

The sign on the station wall says "Welcome to Baltimore."

"We're going to the Baltimore Death Zone?" I ask. "It would be over two hundred years old. It must have all been plowed under ages ago."

"Most of it was," Dad says. "But there's something there I want you to see."

We take a private car from the station to the peninsula where the Zone used to stand. What had been an industrial district

415

full of old shipping containers is now a beautiful riverfront community, complete with a peaceful, tree-lined river walk.

"You'd never suspect what happened here," I say.

"Then tell us," Dad says. "Or better yet, tell them."

A line of people has gathered along the walking path. Their backs are to us, as they quietly wait their turn to see whatever Dad has brought me here to see. Dad must have anticipated a crowd today because my hand-picked security detail is not alone. I catch sight of numerous family members, and other members of Four, among the crowd. We're waiting along with everyone else, when I hear Uncle Cameron's voice yell from somewhere in front of me.

"Look everyone! Jocie Paulson is here! Let her through," he says.

As a hush falls over the crowd, it slowly parts until I can see what the main attraction is. This is the site of the national Final Holy War memorial, and the centerpiece is an old shipping container with a bronze statue on top, depicting a girl with angel wings who is just about to smash the red light with a stick.

There's even a news crew recording my visit.

"Welcome to Angel Park, Jocie," Dad says.

I understand, now, why Dad walked so slowly across the stage when he visited the site of his torture inside the mountain. My feet feel like stones as I slowly walk to the old container. Inside is a recreation of the old bathtub - complete with a statue of Jordan, covered in sores and under a pile of ice.

There's a statue representing me, too. It's ripping a screaming cloth in half.

It's not until I turn to walk away from the container - and the memories it represents - that I realize the crowd has been waiting for me to speak.

"Everything you've heard on the news is true," I begin. "I was there. I was in the Baltimore Death Zone. I was there to hear the screaming, and to watch the pain, and the death of The Final Holy War. I want you all to understand what it was like, but there are no words I can say that would ever describe it."

There's a marked girl who looks to be about eight years old standing at the front of the crowd. She has bright eyes and a cheerful smile that reminds me of the girl I met outside Baltimore the night J.W. was cured. Like the girl two hundred years earlier, the one standing in front of me is lit up with hope.

"You don't need to describe it, Angel," she says. "What you did for us tells us how bad it must have been. It must have been so bad that you'd do anything to not see it again -even drinking toxin."

"They called me 'Angel' when I was in the Zone, but I don't want to be called that here. I'm not an angel. I'm just..."

My voice trails off, as I look at Dad. I've always focused on the sadness in his eyes, and today is no different. He's sad because I'm sad; but I realize that there's something else that's always been there - hidden under the sadness.

Hope. It's the light that burned inside him on that bike ride to 'oh my god corner' and digging himself out of the cave and when he was tortured inside the mountain. Nothing could put out the fire of hope. It's who he is ... and it's who I am.

"Daddy," I say, as if he and I were the only two here. "I understand, now."

Dad smiles and many in the crowd turn towards him.

"The crucifixion; your time in the mountain; my time in Zone. Jesus was there. He was there to take something horrible and ugly, and turn it into something beautiful."

"Look around you, Jocie." Dad says. Then finish the sentence you started."

I scan the faces in the crowd and everywhere I look, I see the same thing, hope. When I look up at Dad, there's not a trace of sadness anywhere in his eyes.

"I'm not an angel," I say. "I'm just an ordinary person who stood next to Jesus, when He took something horrible and turned it into something beautiful."

I then realize who is standing beside Dad, with a hand on Dad's shoulder.

"Daniel?" I say.

The black lines are gone from Daniel's face. Just a few black dots remain, looking like nothing more than dark freckles. I walk to him and reach out with my hand to touch them.

"Dot, dot, dot," I say, as tears roll down his cheeks.

"I was the first in line when Cindi and Amelia asked for volunteers," Daniel says. "With your antivenin in me, they were able to reverse the genetic damage from Henry's vaccine. It's going to take a lot of testing, but the hope is that the mark of the beast will be gone forever. Just think, if this works then there's going to be a little bit of you running through the veins of most of humanity - but I think we'd be better off if we could all share a little of what runs through your soul."

******

The next two hours are spent among the people of Angel Park: praying, answering questions, and generally sharing the collective joy of being together. Eventually, Mom decides that I'm physically and emotionally exhausted, and announces that I need to rest. I take Dad's hand and pull him aside so we can enjoy the river walk together. When I take his hand, I feel that his wedding band is back where it belongs, and I give it a curious look.

"Another family secret," he says.

There's a question on my mind, but Dad speaks first.

"I learned something from you today, Jocie," he says. "I've avoided it for all of these years, but I think I should visit the mountain on the next anniversary of my time there."

"What changed your mind?"

"I watched you at the container today. The memories were painful for you, and you were sad as you remembered the suffering and the death; but I sensed that you pushed them aside and focused on what kept you going through the experience: faith and hope. Then I wondered to myself if

419

Christ would want to visit Golgotha - the next time He walks on the earth - and remember what happened to Him there. I think He would. I think He'd push the memory of the suffering aside and focus on the joy that His suffering brought about."

We walk in silence for a while again, before I ask my question.

"Dad? If you had to do it all again, would you have told me what was going to happen, or prepared me for it?"

"In what way were you not prepared?"

He's right. Knowing what was ahead wouldn't have prepared me. He prepared me best by just being with me, and being my dad.

"The truth is, Jocie, you're the one who spent the last eighteen years preparing me."

"Preparing you? For what?" I ask.

"To get a glimpse of how I imagine Jesus sees you, and for the joy I imagine Jesus must feel, as He watches all of us solve an entire universe worth of the puzzles that He created."

EPILOGUE

I hear Austin walk to the base of the tree and begin climbing. I know it's him without opening my eyes. For someone with such a confident gait when he walks, his climbing is cautious. He's not quite scared, but not quite comfortable, either. He's also probably very tired.

"I assume you won," I say.

"Yes, but it was much closer than we thought it would be. Uncle Cameron and Aunt Cindi were on my tail until the last big climb."

For the first time ever, our generation has been allowed to participate in the competition between the old houses of Four. This year, each house was allowed to choose an event; so we stacked the deck a bit by choosing a bicycle race, which Austin was sure to win.

"Who came in second?" I ask.

"Uncle Cameron beat Aunt Cindi by about a bike length. That means we face him and Gethsemane House in the final event."

Reaching the finals wasn't easy. The older generation didn't make it easy on our team, which is made up of me, Austin, Zera, and all of my younger cousins. When word got out that I could shoot down a drone with evasion software, no house was willing to pick an event involving stun guns. We came in third in Uncle Cameron's newly-designed obstacle course, but only because Cousin Alice has an incredible ability to balance on a moving log. Mount Carmel House added something that was foreign to everyone: archery. Austin and I already have plans to create a more flexible composite for making our own bows. The only event remaining is the traditional finale: combat with fighting sticks.

"It still makes no sense to me," Austin says. "How did you learn fight moves by sitting up here and watching, as everyone else trained?"

"Moves? Moves are just single pieces in a puzzle. I was up here to get perspective on the entire puzzle at once. The moves are nothing more than pushing the pieces into place."

Austin is quiet for a minute.

"You know, Jocie ... I think I always knew that I wasn't the special one. Growing up, everyone gave me all the attention - but somehow I knew it was you."

"I don't see it that way," I reply. "I didn't build a time machine or figure out how to align the crystals to boost the power. If anything, we were always meant to be a special team: Paulsons to the end."

"Speaking of the end, it looks like everyone is gathering for the final round," Austin says. "You don't get to watch from up here this time. Are you sure you want to stick to the plan we discussed? It's never been done before."

"That's why it'll work."

When we arrive at the combat area, Uncle Cameron turns to Mom and Dad.

"I bet you two wish you were participating this year, instead of letting Bethany House's winning streak die. I taught combat to every one of these kids, except for Jocie. Gethsemane House will soon be back on top."

"I do believe there's a final event to determine which house is on top this year," Dad says.

Uncle Cameron turns to me, as Austin, Zera, and the rest of our generation stand up behind me, while the members of Gethsemane stand behind him.

"Gethsemane is ready to take on … hey, what is the name of your house, anyway? Since you're all kids, maybe we should call you the 'Play House'? Or maybe the 'Tree House'?"

"We haven't agreed upon a house name," I say.

"Then I guess we'll call you the Play House. So, Play House, I guess it's time to find out just how much of our knowledge has flowed down to your generation."

"That's it!" I say. "We select the name Jordan House. Jordan means to 'flow down.'"

There are smiles of approval all around.

"Jordan House," I say to the team. "... as we discussed."

The younger generation standing behind me take seats, leaving me alone in the center of the ring. Just the slightest smile forms on Dad's lips, but his eyes dance as he sees the puzzle unfolding in his mind.

"I think you must not have read the rules, Jocie," Uncle Cameron says. "This is a house-on-house competition. We can bring all eight of our members against you.

Now the slightest smile forms on my lips, as I push the buttons and extend my composite fighting stick to full length.

"I read the rules. Go ahead, Gethsemane. Bring the house."

******

Hours later, Jordan House is still celebrating its victory over the "grown-ups" when I notice Mom, Aunt Cindi, and Amelia sitting together under a tree with computer pads. It doesn't take any special powers of observation to see the concerned looks on their faces.

"I'd hoped to let you enjoy today's victory for a while longer, but I can see from the look on your face that we've been caught," Mom says. "You may as well hear the news firsthand from the experts."

"It's good to see you, Jocie," Amelia says.

"You said that like we're meeting at a funeral."

"I guess I did - and I suppose we are in a way. There's no easy way to say this, so I'll just say it. The antivenin is losing its effectiveness. The dose we have to give people to protect them from the toxin is jumping at a rate of one percent per month. It won't be long before the effective dose is too large for a human body to process. It's like getting bitten by a snake every day - eventually it's just too much."

"I don't understand," I say. "Just a few months ago everyone said it was a miracle.

"It was. It saved several million lives of the people with the highest exposure after the Five-X toxin drop."

"But we cooked the Five-X toxin," I say. "There shouldn't be that much in the atmosphere and whatever did survive should be degrading."

"We don't understand it," Aunt Cindi says. "The only thing that's clear is that the antivenin isn't a long term solution anymore."

I look at the sky.

In the months since I drank toxin to create antivenin, billions of people were "unvaccinated" to remove the genetic junk that resulted from Mark of the Beast vaccine. Nobody is walking around with open wounds, or bruises anymore because the antivenin promised to protect them until the last of the toxin in the atmosphere had degraded. There are no more "washed" or "marked."

"We can't go back," I say.

"I'm sorry, Jocie," Mom says. "There's no choice. Everyone who took Henry's vaccine will have to take it again if they want to live. I'm afraid the Mark of the Beast is here to stay."

SNEAK PEEK AT "THE ANGEL PROTOCOL"

PROLOGUE

Washington D.C. 2225 A.D.

I watch the jury enter the courtroom. Some have smiles on their faces, some look at the floor. The verdict was never in doubt, and by watching their faces I know what's written on the piece of paper in the foreman's hand as surely as if I'd been sitting in the room as it was written. I glance at Dad, he knows, too.

The foreman holds the paper up for the bailiff to take to the judge and their eyes meet. Both have painful looking scars on their faces and anger in their eyes. Every member of the jury except for one is marked. The single washed member is staring at me. She wants to cry, but is holding it back.

The judge glances at the paper and hands it back to the bailiff, who returns it to the foreman.

"Have you reached a verdict?" the judge asks.

"We have, your honor. On the count of conspiracy to commit mass murder, we find the defendant, Jocelyn Kimberly Paulson, guilty."

I'm now officially a war criminal.

There are eight uniformed officers and twelve wearing plain clothes in the courtroom, they all move their hands toward their stun guns as the verdict is read. The room is also full of former members of Four. They won't try to rescue me though. They could easily disarm every officer in the courtroom, but there's a veritable army waiting outside should they try it.

"Does the defendant wish to make a statement prior to sentencing?"

There are cameras in the courtroom, my statement will be to a worldwide audience.

"I speak to the faithful, both marked and washed. I know that you see no justice in what has happened here today, just a handy scapegoat for misplaced anger. I ask that you all stand firm in your faith and know that the Lord has a purpose in all things. Don't meet anger with anger. Now is the time to love and pray for your enemy as if they were your brother. Good things will come from this, I promise."

I look to the judge.

"Under any other circumstances I would be restricted in sentencing you, but recent changes in the law have opened up the options available to me. Therefore, I will say the words that no judge in this country has uttered for well over a century -

Jocelyn Kimberly Paulson, for crimes committed against humanity, you are hereby sentenced to death."

I have been sentenced to death, but not in the way that you think...

I look at Dad and smile.

Even he doesn't know.

CONNECT WITH THE AUTHOR

As you can see from the "Sneak Peak," there will be at least one more book, called "The Angel Protocol." At this point in time I don't have a clear vision for a book after that, but you never know...

I find the prospect of writing some "Puzzle Master Prequels" interesting though, so we can all see how the world came to be such a mess by Cephas' time.

I'm still here and listening if you want to ask questions or just want to say hello. My email address is (puzzlemasterbook@gmail.com).

ABOUT THE AUTHOR

T.J. McKenna lives in Colorado with his wife, three kids and a belligerent rabbit. He feels the *Puzzle Master* trilogy is a natural step following his non-fiction work: *The Constitution at Your Dinner Table* - because like the Constitution - The Bible is a book that was meant to be read and enjoyed by everyone. It's his sincere hope that through fiction his readers will be encouraged to pick up and read God's Word.